NB

G

D0383589

IMMORTALITY IN A KISS

Ever so slowly he lowered his mouth, seeing her luminous eyes widen in surprise, then flood with fierce emotion. Thick lashes fluttered down, concealing summer-sky blue. Her lips parted, sought his, eager, a tiny cry rising in her throat. And the knowledge that she wanted this kiss as much as he did humbled him, enflamed him.

She tasted of the nectar of the wildflowers she'd wandered in. She offered herself up with the generosity of the mother goddess who had once given life to all Ireland. Her hair burned warm red, with the immortal fire of bardsong, her courage and strength as humbling as that of Deirdre of the Sorrows, who had risked everything for the love of heroic Naosi.

Why was it that the mere thought of that ancient tale filled his own chest with such sadness and anguish, like a wound still raw?

A shiver of surprise rippled through him. He remembered . . . remembered that story. Love . . . that greatest of all beauties, the most lethal weapon of destruction, the bronze blaze that could cleave comrades in arms, brothers in spirit, into factions of enemies.

Had he ever tasted love before? Was danger an aphrodisiac? Or was there something else at work here? Fallon's own unique brand of magic. . . .

PRAISE FOR KIMBERLY CATES
AND HER BELOVED ROMANCES

MORNING SONG

"Kimberly Cates delivers a finely crafted story, capturing the flavor of the period. . . . Her handling of the characters, independent, young Hannah Gray, her nephew Pip, and hero Austen Dante, will pull readers in deeper and deeper until the satisfying end."

—Thea Brady, Compuserve Romance Reviews

STEALING HEAVEN

"Kimberly Cates has the talent to pull you into a story on the first page and keep you there. . . . *Stealing Heaven* is a finely crafted tale . . . a tale you won't soon forget. It can stand proud beside Ms. Cates' other excellent romances."

—*Rendezvous*

"Stunning in its emotional impact, glowing with the luminous beauty of the love between a man and a woman . . . *Stealing Heaven* is another dazzling masterpiece from a truly gifted author."

—Kathe Robin, *Romantic Times*

"[A] beautifully poignant tale. Kimberly Cates can always be counted on for a choice reading occasion, and this time is no exception."

—Harriet Klausner, *Affaire de Coeur*

"A powerful and enduring tale filled with the magic and lore of Ireland. . . . This idyllic romance will capture readers' hearts."

—Elizabeth Hogue, *Gothic Journal*

PRAISE FOR KIMBERLY CATES

THE RAIDER'S DAUGHTER

"A wonderful and neatly blended mixture of romance and suspense. . . . Kimberly Cates always provides her readers with a treasure, but in this work, she displays new profound literary depths."

—Harriet Klausner, *Affaire de Coeur*

"A special book for readers looking for an out-of-the-ordinary adventure. You will long remember the tenderness, passion, and excitement of this well-written sequel."

—*Rendezvous*

"Spunky Lucy and tormented, sexy Valcour's thrilling adventures, dangerous escapades and sensual encounters engulf the reader in a riveting tale. . . . Another stunning achievement from a master of the genre."

—Kathe Robin, *Romantic Times*

THE RAIDER'S BRIDE

"Kimberly Cates takes the reader to new emotional heights. . . . *The Raider's Bride* is more than just an enthralling reading experience; it's a gateway to a world of mystery, intrigue, and historical insights."

—Harriet Klausner, *Affaire de Coeur*

"High adventure, suspense, and sensuality make *The Raider's Bride* a story you must read."

—*Romantic Times*

"Original . . . endearing characters. . . ."

—*Publishers Weekly*

Books by Kimberly Cates

Restless Is the Wind
To Catch a Flame
The Raider's Daughter
The Raider's Bride
Crown of Dreams
Stealing Heaven
Gather the Stars
Angel's Fall
Morning Song
Magic

Published by POCKET BOOKS

For orders other than by individual consumers, Pocket Books grants a discount on the purchase of **10 or more** copies of single titles for special markets or premium use. For further details, please write to the Vice-President of Special Markets, Pocket Books, 1633 Broadway, New York, NY 10019-6785, 8th Floor.

For information on how individual consumers can place orders, please write to Mail Order Department, Simon & Schuster Inc., 200 Old Tappan Road, Old Tappan, NJ 07675.

KIMBERLY CATES

MAGIC

POCKET BOOKS

New York   London   Toronto   Sydney   Tokyo   Singapore

The sale of this book without its cover is unauthorized. If you purchased this book without a cover, you should be aware that it was reported to the publisher as "unsold and destroyed." Neither the author nor the publisher has received payment for the sale of this "stripped book."

This book is a work of fiction. Names, characters, places and incidents are products of the author's imagination or are used fictitiously. Any resemblance to actual events or locales or persons, living or dead, is entirely coincidental.

An *Original* Publication of POCKET BOOKS

POCKET BOOKS, a division of Simon & Schuster Inc.
1230 Avenue of the Americas, New York, NY 10020

Copyright © 1998 by Kim Ostrom Bush

All rights reserved, including the right to reproduce this book or portions thereof in any form whatsoever. For information address Pocket Books, 1230 Avenue of the Americas, New York, NY 10020

ISBN: 0-671-01494-3

First Pocket Books printing April 1998

10 9 8 7 6 5 4 3 2 1

POCKET and colophon are registered trademarks of Simon & Schuster Inc.

Front cover illustration by Fredericka Ribes;
tip-in illustration by Steven Assel

Printed in the U.S.A.

MAGIC

PROLOGUE

Mary Fallon Delaney dragged her slippered feet as she trudged down the hallway, her stomach tighter than the knot in her crisply ironed hair ribbon, her fingers crumpling handfuls of the snowy-clean muslin gown old Nurse had laced her into minutes before. Her face still stung from a ruthless scrubbing, her scalp tingling from the raking of the hairbrush through the red curls the wild Irish winds had made a mad tangle.

But she would have let Nurse scrub the skin right off her nose and not made a peep as long as she didn't have to go into *The Room*.

Fallon hated The Room.

Shadow monsters stretched their bodies in the corners, scritch-scratch-scritching to sharpen their claws. Even when she was tucked up in her own bed, clear across Misthaven House, Fallon could feel how hungry they were. They laughed at her. Dared her to come inside where the air was too thick to breathe.

She was afraid.

Not that she'd ever admit it. She was six and a half years old, after all. Not a baby. And she never cried anymore. Not even when the tears poked against her

1

eyelids trying to come out. But it got harder and harder to keep them locked up inside.

Maybe that was why Papa stayed away from Misthaven House now. He heard the monsters, too. But he was lucky. Nobody could make him go into The Room. Nobody, Fallon thought, wistful.

Fallon chewed at her bottom lip. Only Nurse's gnarled hand against her back kept her moving forward. Fallon could almost remember Nurse laughing, her eyelids so crinkly only sparkles of blue peeped out as they'd played hoodman blind, just like Nurse and Mama had played when Mama was a little girl.

But Nurse had caved in on herself, just like everyone else at Misthaven House, too sad and solemn to bother about Fallon anymore. She'd heard servants whisper that Nurse let Fallon run wild. She liked to be wild. Except when she was sad or afraid. Then she liked to climb up on someone's lap and pretend she was tired. But nobody's lap had time to hold her anymore. Not Nurse or Papa or Mama or even her big brother, Hugh, so she'd just quit asking.

Fallon's eyes widened, and she fought the urge to turn and run. The door loomed ahead, like a dark mouth trying to swallow her. Fallon dug her slippered heels into the roses on the carpet, her chin jutting out at a belligerent angle. "I don't want to go in there," she insisted. "It smells all sicky and makes my nose itch."

"Selfish girl!" Nurse looked as if she'd like to slap her, and Nurse's slaps had gotten harder and harder, maybe 'cause she'd been practicing lots more lately.

"With all the sufferin' in the world, you could surely spare a bit o' your precious time! Not another word, now, or you'll be sorry, I swear you will!"

Fallon's cheeks stung with shame as Nurse thrust her into the chamber.

"Don't scold her, Nurse." The voice was like music that drifted from the music-room harp when Fallon sneaked in and plucked it. Soft and pretty and gentle. But the voice only made Fallon's stomach hurt worse. Fallon dug her fingers into her skirts so tight, her hands shook. Maybe Nurse could make her come to The Room,

2

but she couldn't make Fallon look up. Couldn't make her see . . .

"Don't upset yourself, treasure. This is not a fit place for a little girl, is it, Fallon-my-love?"

Nothing except the understanding in that voice could have made Fallon raise her eyes to the woman lying in the big bed.

"You shouldn't be trapped in a sick room, little one," the woman said. But eyes blue as her own gobbled Fallon up, as if she were a plate of sweets someone was about to snatch away.

Fallon nibbled on her lower lip, staring at the woman beneath the coverlets. She wore Mama's favorite nightgown with the lace lilies on the collar. The heathery blue bed shawl Nurse had knitted on long, wicked-looking needles draped about her shoulders. But she didn't look like Mama any more.

The fire that always seemed to burn in Mama's hair had grown cold, and someone had pinched great hollows around her eyes. Worst of all, whenever Fallon dared to hug her, she wasn't soft anymore, or warm. Bones poked into her wherever she touched. And Mama was cold and so thin she made Fallon think of the china lady from the drawing room. She'd sneaked her out to take treeclimbing with her one day when she'd been lonely and broken one arm right off her. Maybe Mama would break, too?

Stinging things nipped at Fallon's eyelids. She could almost remember what it had been like at Misthaven before the coughing had come, and the fine handkerchiefs Mama loved, edged with lace like frost on a windowpane, had come away from her lips stained with blood. Before Nurse started clucking and crooning over Mama as if Mama were six years old instead of Fallon. Before Papa had ridden off on his horse pretending Mama wasn't sick and Fallon wasn't frightened, and Hugh didn't even exist.

On those long-ago days Mama had taken Fallon everywhere with her—whenever she went to the snug white cottages, her arms laden with baskets of food and clothes, sewing needles, writing things and books and

3

medicines. Even little as Fallon had been, she'd known Mama was something special to the people in those cottages. Something that made angels shine in people's eyes. She belonged to them, somehow, like the standing stones on Finnegan's Hill, or the cliffs on the shore. She wondered who put angels in the people's eyes now.

A frail hand reached up, twisting one of Fallon's curls around a finger. The red strands were so bright against the thin white skin that it seemed they should burn it. Fallon tried not to pull away, expecting the bitter scent of medicine to sting her nose. But a baby pink rose tucked in the bosom of mama's nightgown covered the smell a little.

Hugh.

Fallon winced. She wished *she'd* thought to bring mama a flower. No one had to make Hugh come here. He just did it all on his own. He'd even tried to coax her to come with him sometimes. But she shook her head and ran off into the fields and stayed until long past dark.

She'd never told him why. The truth was too big, pressing on her chest until she couldn't breathe. She was afraid. Afraid that someday they'd make her give Mama a kiss, and Mama's cheek would crumble like the curl of ash she'd touched once at Potter Dan's when the fire on the hearth had gotten cold.

But tonight something was different from all those other times. There was a peacefulness about Mama's face, a softness. A shine in her eyes, almost as if . . . as if she were getting better. Fallon's heart lurched with hope.

"Fallon, do you remember when I first was sick?" Mama asked. "You'd come and sit beside me in the garden, and I'd tell you stories."

Fallon shrugged. But she did remember. Remembered so hard it hurt inside. Then Mama had only been tired and a little pale. She'd filled Mama's lap with flowers and filled up her imagination with Mama's stories of mischievous fairies and bold heroes that rode in chariots.

Cuchulain, half god, half man, the bravest of Irish heroes. Finn MacCool, who had led his bold army, the Fianna, into a glory so bright its blaze still shone in the

Irish mists. And always, the Tuatha de Dannan shone like bright gold threads woven through the tapestry of tales. The *sidhe,* magical folk of the other world who made their home in the hills and the trees, the seas and the cliffs, more a part of Ireland than the very earth beneath Fallon's feet.

Fairies who soured milk and stole babies from their cradles and danced their way through the soles of six pairs of slippers in just one night. Her mother's words echoed through Fallon's memory. *Remember, treasure. Save up the legends like the pretty pebbles you find.* Mama had spun out the stories time and again, as if she were stitching them into Fallon's mind, the way she embroidered silks of blue and red and green on bits of tapestry.

"Do you remember your favorite tale, love?" Mama's voice drew Fallon back from a whirl of fairies dancing in star-shine gowns. "Ciaran of the Mist." How *could* she forget, with his castle perched high on a sea cliff, near enough that she could walk there on a fine morning? *Caislean ag Dahmsa Ceo,* The Castle of the Dancing Mist. Even its name breathed magic.

From the time she could first remember, Fallon had loved how the castle's walls and crumbling towers seemed to almost bend over the ledge, loved peering through arched window eyes down at the fingers of water scrabbling at the cliffs.

In the years since Mama had gotten sick, Fallon had run away to the castle often, making believe the towers were her very own.

"Do you remember what happened to Ciaran?" Mama asked.

Fallon nodded. "The fairies took Ciaran away," Fallon said.

Everyone in Ireland was afraid of the fairies taking someone away. 'Specially naughty children. But even though Nurse had threatened her again and again, the fairies had never come for Fallon, no matter how wicked she'd been.

Now Nurse said the saints were going to take Mama away because Mama was so good. It made Fallon's head ache, trying to sort it all out. But she thought it *must* be better to be bad and go where everyone lived forever and danced until their slippers wore through instead of being good and going to a place like church, quiet and cold, with painted faces always turned up to heaven.

"I remember the stories, Mama," Fallon admitted. "You used to feed me cherries till my mouth got all red 'cause that's what the fairies used to 'chant Ciaran away." If Fallon closed her eyes really tight, she could see what the garden had looked like, flowers spilling about as if someone had broken a rainbow and scattered the pieces all over the ground.

She could remember the sun sparkling in the blue glass bowl Mama held on her lap, and the cherries glowing so red they seemed magic. Maybe they *were* magic, because just thinking about them made The Room get blurry all around Fallon, until the medicine bottles melted away, and all she could see was Mama's eyes, the way they used to be—warm and bright and full of fairy dreams.

A little bubble of excitement pressed in Fallon's throat, and she burst out, "Tell me the story again, Mama."

"Wicked, thoughtless girl!" Nurse grabbed her by the arm so tight it pinched. "Can you not see my angel is worn to a thread?" Mama was Nurse's angel. Nobody ever called Fallon that. But before Nurse could pinch harder, Mama raised her head off the pillow.

"Nurse, please. Leave us alone. My daughter wishes me to tell her a story."

"I'm sorry, Mama." Fallon stuffed her hands behind her back as if Nurse had caught her trying to snatch a tart off the Queen's plate. "You don't have to tell me Ciaran. You need to rest."

Mama's lips curved in a way so close to Mama's smile a hook seemed to tear inside Fallon's chest. "I'm going to have plenty of time to rest, soon, treasure. I'd much rather tell you a story, unless . . ." She hesitated, and looked as if *unless* would make her very sad. "Unless you want to leave. I'd not keep you inside if you're thirsty for the sunshine."

Fallon glanced at the window where a slice of clear blue sky peeked in. But suddenly, she didn't want to be outside so very much. She looked at Mama. "I'd like to stay."

Mama's eyes got all glisteny, like with tears, but she smiled even wider and patted the space next to her. Fallon started to bounce up on the feather tick, then stopped, casting a nervous glance at Nurse. But even though Nurse's lips were pursed so hard all the wrinkles showed, she didn't say anything at all. She only grabbed up some crumpled cloths and half-filled glasses and slipped out of the room.

Glad she was gone, Fallon edged onto the bed as if it were made of spider's webs, careful not to so much as brush against her mother. But Mama reached across the space that separated them, urging her closer, her hand stroking back a lock of flyaway hair that tickled Fallon's forehead.

It felt so strange to have someone touch her softly now, or to want her to stay close by, instead of shooing her off somewhere. Fallon stretched up to try to hold on to the brush of Mama's fingers as long as she could.

"Once, long ago," Mama began, "when the standing stones were new, the magic in Erin was so strong that the hills grew more heroes than flowers. Heroes proved their valor in battle, and upon the hurling fields. The crack of ash-wood hurling sticks into the hard leather ball sounded like battle drums as teams of men fought to slam the sphere through the goals at opposite ends of the field. Men warred against each other, dodging, leaping, swinging with all the passion and power inside them, as if they were the old druid gods locked in combat for the mist green isle St. Patrick and his angels had stolen away.

"Now, little did the heroes know that other games were being played beyond the veil of the mist at the very same time. For the fairy kings did battle upon the hurling fields with far more fury than even the warriors at the royal seats of Tara or Emain Macha. The fairies, who are ever-watching, loved to peer from their hiding places, to laugh at mortal men, and jeer at their clumsy efforts, until one day . . ."

Mama paused, waiting as she always had for Fallon's delighted shiver, and the words Fallon had always said.

"He came out of the mist." Fallon could picture it as clearly as her own snub nose in the nursery mirror— mist, glittery as bits of angel wings, fluttering over the green hilltops, billowing into the valleys, snagging on the twisted tree roots, and the earth that cradled them, the wind carrying the news to the sea, *he comes . . . he comes.*

And then, a man striding out onto the hurling field, white teeth flashing in the smile of one who could never even imagine being beaten in any contest one could name.

"Ciaran strode out of the mist," Mama continued. "And every man on the field fell silent. Never had they seen such a man before. Even the cunning fairy king, Jarlath's, face couldn't have looked more regal. Draped in great loops of heathery wool and creamy linen, Ciaran towered above the other warriors, lean and hard-bodied as a wolfhound run wild in the forests. His shoulders were nigh as wide as the hurling stick strapped to his back, his arms powerful from sword play and spear casting. Yet despite his fierceness, there was a sensitivity glowing within him, for Ciaran carried the soul of a bard within his warrior body.

"He was brave as Cuchulain. Wise as Finn MacCool. And the greatest hurler ever to breathe. Yet within him beat the most noble of hearts. He believed the true measure of a man was a triumph of the spirit, defending those weaker, caring for the aged, the young, the helpless. He wanted nothing but to love Ireland and guard his people. Who could have guessed that his greatest battle wouldn't be with the high king's foes, but rather with the Fairy King?"

Fallon closed her eyes tight with imagining. The Room spun away.

'Tis said Cuchulain's courage was never matched, nor the wisdom of Finn MacCool. But Ciaran MacCailte, Son of the Mist, surrendered nothing less than his heart to those who needed the strength of his body.

Scarce two cycles of the moon had passed before he became champion of the High King at Emain Macha.

MAGIC

Boldest of warriors, finest hurler ever to take the field in a contest, Ciaran's greatest battle would not be with enemies of his king, but rather, two more subtle foes. Jarlath, king of the fairies, and his own loneliness. For people wish to keep heroes high above them, to shimmer and never be touched.

Now, beyond the mist of enchantment, the fairy folk played at hurling with even more passion than men did. Once Jarlath saw Ciaran's skill, he had to have the hero as his own champion upon the fairy fields.

One morning, as Ciaran wandered the sea cliffs alone, Jarlath appeared in all his mystic glory. "Come to my kingdom. Be my champion. You shall live for eternity," proclaimed Jarlath. Ciaran refused. He knew every man should have only so many days to love and laugh, or he might forget what a miracle life is.

Jarlath waved his hand. Enchanted weapons glittered in the air, magnificent as Cuchulain's spear, the Gae Bulga, and Finn MacCool's sword, Son of the Wind. "Come with me and I promise you will become a legend. People will sing your praises in bardsong for a thousand years." Still Ciaran refused. He would earn that honor with his own strength or not at all.

Scarce believing his own ears, Jarlath made one final offer. "Be a prince in my land, take my most beautiful daughter as your wife, possess riches beyond the imaginings of your mortal mind."

But Ciaran wanted none of the fairy king's gifts. He knew that if he accepted anything from the fairy king, he would be his slave. Besides, he wanted a wife who came to him with nothing but the passion in her heart, and the only riches he craved were nets full of salmon and fields of red deer to fill the cooking pots of those who were hungry.

"I shall take you, then," Jarlath threatened, but Ciaran only laughed.

"You can steal me away to the land of the fairies, but you cannot force me to play. I vow to you, I will die before I step onto the hurling field."

In a fit of rage, Jarlath vanished. He offered rewards to any fairy who could bring Ciaran to Tir na nOg, and through the winter Ciaran was plagued with fairy tricks, but he was too wise to be bewitched. He showed no weakness until one day, walking in a grove of trees near the cliffs, he glanced up. Dangling above his head were cherries, green and sour. He sighed, his fingers reaching up to touch the fruit with longing.

Little did the hero know a kelpie watched him from the shadows. When next he returned to the grove, the cherries had ripened into the most glorious fruit he had ever seen. He filled his tunic with them, ate of their sweetness until his mouth was stained red and his eyes drooped into sleep.

He awoke in the land of the fairies. Furious, Ciaran claimed he would never touch a hurling stick, but the fairy king set forth a challenge. If Ciaran could beat Ronan, his champion, in one game, he could return to the people he loved.

The battle waged three days and three nights, brutal enough to break twenty men. But the fairy king had tricked Ciaran again. Ronan was a shape-shifter. He changed into showers of gold and soaring hawks, monsters with claws sharp enough to cleave a man in two.

Despite the wicked enchantments, Ciaran scored three times. Still, Ronan won. Despairing, Ciaran cared not that the fairies chanted his name to honor his courage. He had lost everything he loved. Moved by his bravery, Jarlath offered him one boon. If Ciaran played as his champion, he could return once every three hundred years—for each of the three goals he'd scored—to the people he loved. He could not change the course of their history, but he could help them in their direst need.

Ciaran accepted. Jarlath unfastened the jeweled brooch that held his cloak. He summoned up the winds, and they carried the brooch to the sea cliffs Ciaran had wandered. There a girl found it, and Ciaran whispered the legend to her fairy-kissed heart, putting into her hands the power to summon Ciaran of the Mist.

Quiet fell for a heartbeat, and Fallon opened her eyes, astonished to find that it was Mama's voice story-spinning, that medicine bottles and sickness still crowded round her. But she didn't mind The Room so much. Shimmery shadows seemed to dance on the walls.

The cunning fairy king draped in robes of purple mist. Ronan, the shape-shifter, deliciously fierce and frightening. And Ciaran of the Mist, bold and strong and alone, missing the world he'd left behind just as Fallon missed days in the garden with Mama, a bowl of cherries on her lap.

Mama's thin hand curved over hers, squeezing ever so gently, as if she understood the sad places in Ciaran's heart and in Fallon's own.

"The girl Ciaran entrusted with his magic gave life to all our family, Fallon. Generation after generation, Ciaran of the Mist's brooch has been passed from mother to daughter. Generation after generation, the legend of Ciaran has burned brighter.

"And now . . ." Mama paused a moment, trailing her fingertips down Fallon's cheek. Fallon suddenly became aware of just how fragile those fingertips were. The land of Tir na nOg shivered and wavered like candle flame, rainbows and shape-shifters, fairy kings and heroes flickering, then sputtering out, leaving only the four walls of the room, and Mama's face, her eyes pleading.

"Do you believe in magic, Fallon-my-heart?"

Fallon nibbled at her lip, uncertain. She wanted to believe. Oh, how she wanted to. If you believed in magic, anything could happen. If you believed in magic, Mama could even get well. "Sometimes. I–I think I believe," Fallon breathed.

Slowly, mama drew something from beneath her pillow—a handkerchief, wrapped around something else. She placed the bundle in Fallon's hand.

It was heavy, hard. Fallon folded back the corners of cloth. A gasp caught in her throat, and she forgot all about medicine smells and shadow creatures and any other jewels she'd ever seen.

Pillowed on the square of cloth was a gold circle with just a little piece missing at the bottom. It was bigger than Mama's palm. A long pin, with a blue stone at the top, pierced through the open space in the circle's center. Red stones glittered on the gold. It felt warm, and Fallon could feel the specialness of it seeping through the cloth into her hand.

She wanted to trace her finger around the sparkling jewels, but did magic go away when little girls' hands touched it? She didn't let even her littlest finger smudge the shine, just in case.

"Fallon, can you guess what this is?"

She hardly dared think, hardly dared hope. It's *his,* her heart whispered, magic and mist seeming to swirl in her blood. *It's his . . .*

"This is the pin the fairy king gave to Ciaran of the Mist. Every generation, it's given to the girl with the most fairy-kissed heart. My grandmother entrusted it to me. Now, my little one, I'm giving it to you."

Fallon could hardly breathe. "But Mama, Nurse wouldn't let me keep it. She doesn't b'lieve in jewels for little girls."

"I don't care what Nurse believes, Fallon. It's what *you* believe that matters." Mama said, tightly. "As long as you have this you'll never have to be afraid, sweetheart. Ciaran will always be there to protect you, even when I can't . . ." Mama's voice cracked a little, the sadness slipping through.

The shadow creatures in the corners woke up again, pressing against Fallon's chest. Something stuck in the back of her throat, bitter as green cherries. "You don't have to take care of me, Mama. Not until you get better."

Better. The word welled up in Fallon, full of hope. Ciaran could come back when someone needed him. He could fix anything. She could call him back, and he could fix Mama, too. The thought was almost too big, too wonderful to hold.

"Mama, how do I make it work?" she pleaded, her heart pounding. "How do I make the magic? Tell me—"

"At the feast of Beltane, go to the castle of mist, to the hearth Ciaran is said to have carved with one blow of his sword. It's there that the fires of legend, the fires of hope are still kept alive. Place the pin in the center of the hearth, and wait until the light of the full moon strikes the jewels. The glow will dance, writhe skyward, set ablaze by magic fire. Then, call him, Fallon. With your heart, with your soul, with all the courage inside you. Can you remember that, my little one?"

"Yes, Mama." It was only three days until Beltane, Fallon thought. Three days until she could make magic.

Mama was trembling all over. "You're so . . . so very young, Fallon, my heart. So small to understand . . ." She caught Fallon's hand, held it tight. "You must remember, this is a sacred trust. Just because you have the power to call Ciaran doesn't mean you should. Only once in three hundred years can Ciaran step out of the mist. If you call him, it must be for something important, something so large, so vital, that no mortal can manage."

No mortal could make Mama well, Fallon thought fiercely. The doctors had tried and tried.

"You can't call Ciaran back to mend a broken fence, or tie the tongue of some cruel little girl into knots. You can't summon him for the thousands of things we all have to endure."

Fallon imagined summoning Ciaran, sending him charging down on the mean-spirited Alberdale twins. She would have liked to see those girls bristling with big, long javelins. But Mama was looking at her so pleadingly, and so very sick.

Fallon let the image go. "I won't call him, Mama. Not unless things are terrible bad. I promise." But what could be more terrible than Mama being so sick?

Relief settled over her mother's face, a breath rattling in her chest. "I know that I can . . . can trust you. That you'll make me so proud—even in heaven. Fallon, I'm . . . so very tired, all of a sudden," Mama said in barely a whisper. "You will come back to me tomorrow, won't you, little one?"

Fallon tightened her hold on the brooch. "Yes, Mama. I'll come." And suddenly she wanted to. The Room couldn't scare her anymore, not now that she had Ciaran's pin. She'd come see Mama like Hugh did, every day, and bring her flowers and Mama's stories would chase the shadows away until Ciaran came and made her well again.

She couldn't remember ever being so happy as she gave her Mama a kiss on the cheek, then climbed down from the bed.

She sneaked past Nurse, and out into the sunshine,

running through banks of flowers over the hills, clutching the precious secret inside her.

She would take the brooch where it would be safe, to the castle where the sea crashed and the mist whispered inside her. She would tuck it in the secret place she'd found, behind a loosened stone. She shivered with delight and waited. Three days. Only three days before the magic could come.

Sunlight pried open Fallon's eyelids with sharp fingers the next morning. She burrowed her face into her pillow, waiting for Nurse to start scolding. It was late, and Nurse was bound to be cross.

But then Fallon remembered. Her lips curled in a sleepy grin. She didn't care if Nurse was cross. She was going to see Mama this morning.

She struggled up out of the tangle of coverlets, then stilled, her forehead crumpling in confusion. Someone else was sitting in Nurse's chair by the fireplace.

Hugh. He was hunched over, his thin face all blotchy beneath a mop of sandy-blond hair, his eyes so red it scared Fallon. But she stiffened her backbone like Ciaran had when he faced the fairy king. Soon she wouldn't have to be afraid ever again.

"I have to go see Mama," Fallon told Hugh as she climbed out of bed. "She promised to tell me more stories today."

Hugh's eyes got so bright it almost looked as if he were crying. Hugh never cried. Fallon's chest hurt. His mouth twisted, all tight, as if he were trying to hold something in.

"Fallon—" Hugh's voice broke over the words. "Mama's dead."

Fallon heard a scream deep inside her, where no one else could ever hear it. *No, no, no* . . . Mama was going to get better. Beltane was coming with its magic fire, and Fallon was going to bring her the first spring flowers and Ciaran was going to make Mama well.

But heaven with its angels and saints had stolen Mama away to where fairy-magic could never touch her. And all Fallon had left were the stories Mama had told.

CHAPTER

1

It was time.

Once every year, Fallon drew the mystic golden circle from its hiding place within the stone walls and cradled it in her hands while the spring winds of Beltane sang to her alone. But never once did she dare the magic of the ancient brooch.

Sixteen full moons had sailed on sixteen more Beltanes, each spinning its own special magic. But this time . . . this night was different. Fallon felt it, sensed it.

Druid-trees breathed warning, standing stones reached out in long fingers, awakening unquiet spirits that clung to every shadow, every hollow, every glen. Billows of shimmering mist swirled up past Fallon's knees, and branches caught at her skirts as she made her way up the path that ran perilously close to the cliffs.

Closer . . . She could hear the ghosts of drowned sailors calling from the Soul Cages beneath the crashing sea, luring her nearer the crumbling ledge that plunged to the jagged rocks below. *Just one misstep and you will be ours . . .*

But she only clutched the folds of her blue velvet cloak more tightly about her, retracing steps she'd taken a

thousand times in the years since her mother had died—
the twisted, dangerous path that led to her castle in the
sky.

How many times as a lonely child had she tried to
outrun the sting of her grief, bathe it in an elixir of magic
and legends and possibilities. She'd fought so very hard
to believe the tales she had hoarded in her imagination,
the myths devoured in countless books. Even when the
march of time and her own reason waged war against it.
Even when she'd begun to doubt just a little.

It was well past time she leave off childish dreaming,
her brother Hugh would say. She was in danger from
other hazards on the road to the castle—thieves, wan-
derers, once farmers, thrown off their lands by landlords
attempting to squeeze the last drop of wealth from their
holdings. English patrols, meant to drive the centuries-
old talk of Irish rebellion into the shadows.

Or, failing that, Hugh would predict, she'd face the
pain of her own disillusionment.

No, Hugh would never understand why she had come.

Her eyes turned to where the ghostly battlements of
the castle pierced through the unearthly haze, straining
toward the full moon that sailed forever beyond its
grasp.

At Caislean ag Dahmsa Ceo she'd never felt alone.

The earth trembled with the pagan rhythm of Beltane,
the veil between the other world and the world of
mortals thinning for this night of Bright Fire. She could
almost see the shadowy apparitions of unquiet spirits,
almost understand the language whispered between the
druid-trees. And she was certain that if her mother's
ghost was wandering anywhere on earth, it would be
here, among the battered stone walls of the Castle of the
Dancing Mist.

Fallon swallowed hard. The outermost wall of the
abandoned castle rose up in front of her. Every year,
she'd made this pilgrimage, every year she'd listened,
waited, tried to hold the wispy edges of ages-old enchantment. But tonight was different somehow; the air too
thick for her lungs, the floor unstable beneath her feet.

She couldn't rid herself of the feeling that she was

being watched. By whom? The ancient spirits? The stones themselves? Was the castle waiting for her? Waiting for the summons that had been passed from generation to generation? Were the window spaces' all-knowing, all-seeing eyes fixed upon her? Or was there something else? Something far more sinister that had dared come out into the night?

No. She was being absurd. She shook away the odd sensations. She'd come here every Beltane, hadn't she? She'd taken out the magic brooch and sat on the flat stone at the edge of the cliff until dawn streaked the sky.

Every girl in Glenceo came to that stone at some time in her life, anticipation singing in her veins as she waited for the stone to conjure up dreams of the man who would be her true love.

The Lady Stone . . . one more piece of Ciaran's enchantment. A place to stir up dreams of love, and hope, bright ribbons leading to a man's embrace.

Not that Fallon had ever hoped for such a future, such a dream. She was wed to her legends, her stories. Every dream she'd ever had while seated on that enchanted stone was of Ciaran, walking out of the mist.

She stretched out her hand and pressed her palm against the rough surface of the wall, making her way by touch until she reached the hiding place she'd found so many years ago. With the tips of her fingers, she loosened the stone and drew it out. Heart hammering, she eased her fingers into the dark space revealed.

Her fingers collided with something hard, and she gathered the handkerchief-wrapped bundle into her palm.

She froze at a sound out of synch with the night, the crunch of a boot sole nearby. Did the *sidhe* make such solid sounds when they moved? Her fingers clenched over the pin, and she turned, scarcely able to breathe. She wouldn't have been surprised to see the pagan son of the sun, Lugh himself, or Mannan Mac Lir, god of the sea, rising up from the waves. But nothing, no one could have chilled her more certainly than the figure silhouetted against the stone.

Redmayne.

Light from the full moon struck him like the shaft of an arrow, eerily illuminating the blood-red of his regimentals, shadow accenting the sharp planes of his face. And his eyes—even despite the mist and the darkness, they glowed as if they held some dark sorcery of their own.

She'd seen the man for barely a heartbeat when he'd come around to introduce himself to the neighboring gentry. But she'd never forget how terrifyingly civil the captain had been as he left no doubt what would happen to any of the landlords weak-hearted enough to give aid to those he'd come to destroy.

It was rumored Lionel Redmayne could peel the skin from his enemies' faces, pry out their darkest secrets with no torture-weapon but his eyes. Eyes that seemed to draw in every flaw, every sin, every weakness in the human soul, and take a jaded pleasure in them.

What in God's name was the man doing *here? Now?*

Was it possible he'd known she was coming here tonight? Was it possible he knew *why* and planned to . . . to what? Arrest her? Fallon yanked herself back from the edge of panic. Calling centuries-old heroes back from the land of the fairies wasn't a hanging offense in Ireland. At least not yet.

"What have we here?" he asked in a voice so low Fallon had to strain to hear it.

Fallon groped desperately for that elusive, invisible mask other people donned so easily to hide their emotions.

Those inscrutable eyes raked Fallon slowly from the top of her head to the mud-spattered hem of her cloak. "Miss Delaney of Misthaven. So we meet again."

Ruthlessness rippled from him in thick waves, an odd sort of omniscience all the more terrifying because of the icy, emotionless calm draped about Redmayne like some dark mantle. He was Satan surveying bumbling mortals with diabolical patience, certain they would sin.

Was it possible he *had* come searching for her? The possibility was too terrifying to even consider. Fallon gripped the pin so hard it pierced her skin, but she didn't feel the pain, didn't feel anything except the primal need to escape that probing gaze. She couldn't let him know how afraid she was, and yet, she longed to slice into that insufferable arrogance. What better way than to pretend she didn't remember him.

"Do I know you, sir?" she asked in her loftiest tone.

A chuckle of disbelief rose from his chest, a kind of admiration curling his smile. "We met at your brother's house a week ago. Captain Lionel Redmayne, your obedient servant." He sketched her a bow that reminded her of sleek panthers lunging ever so gracefully to tear out a victim's throat.

"I'm surprised your brother has allowed you such freedom in a time of unrest. Hasn't he warned you that the night is full of dangers?"

"I'm not afraid."

Fearsomely sensual lips widened in a smile that thrust slivers of ice beneath Fallon's skin. She could hardly breathe.

"Would you be afraid if I told you I was searching for a band of smugglers? Desperate men who might enjoy having the sister of one of the landowners in their power?"

Was *that* what Redmayne was doing here at the castle? Had the captain traced the smugglers so close to their secret lair?

It took all her strength of will not to glance in the direction of the secret entrance to the tunnels that wound beneath the castle.

For generations, the labyrinth had given shelter to those in need. Priests had sought shelter there when they were hunted down like rabid dogs, and scholars had struggled down beneath the castle, reading forbidden books in the time when English law forbade any Catholic to learn to read.

It was a haven for rebellion, where time after time men had sharpened rusty swords and horded questionable ammunition, readying themselves to throw off the yoke of English rule. It was there the tattered remnants of defeated rebel armies had staggered, to tend their wounds before fleeing to France. And there, in the dark tunnels beneath Caislean ag Dahmsa Ceo, that their sons and their sons' sons had drawn out the battered weapons, brushed off the dust and taken up the battle again.

Five years had passed since the last rising, and the scars were still visible in the land—the hollow-eyed grief of mothers who had watered Irish soil with the blood of their children, the whipping trees where the lash had fallen again and again, on innocent and guilty alike, and always the crushing poverty, the stranglehold on any trade that might leave Irish shores.

Was it possible that anyone might be in the souterrains tonight? Fallon wondered, dread tightening her throat. No. It was Beltane tonight. Most likely everyone was at the celebrations, the tunnels empty.

But would anyone be truly safe in these glens until Lionel Redmayne was far away?

"If you'll excuse me, I'll be on my way." She started to stride past but, with a deceptively negligent shift of booted legs, Redmayne blocked her way.

"I must repeat my warning. Even now I am searching for a most elusive fellow—not some bumbling crofter thrashing about with his grandfather's rusted musket, but an adversary far more subtle. He is as insubstantial as your precious Irish mist. No one sees his face, and yet he leaves his mark everywhere. Known rebels about to be taken up by the soldiers disappear, never to be seen again. Families whose men have died on the gallows, or who have fled like the base cowards they are, suddenly produce their rent money just before the landlord is about to evict them. From Dingle to Galway, people whisper of him, but no one, not even under the most persuasive torture, has ever given him a name except Silver Hand—a ridiculous sobriquet."

Fallon had heard of the mysterious force that had done so much good the past five years. But the people of Glenceo were as ignorant of his identity as the English. She'd tried, herself, to discover who he was and had failed, just as everyone else had. The only ones to see Silver Hand had been his own men, and they were as elusive as their master.

"I understand this person has kept the garrison chasing its tail for an embarrassing length of time."

"Indeed. I intend to change that. You see, he has made a fatal mistake. Killed my predecessor, a general's nephew. You, of course, would offer any help you could give? You might have seen something, someone—"

"You are the only person I've met tonight."

"Little wonder, considering the weather. I'm certain you understand my curiosity, Miss Delaney, finding a lady such as yourself out on such an unpleasant evening. Exactly where are you bound for? Are you an angel of mercy braving the coming storm? Have you succumbed to a pressing need to deliver calf's foot jelly at this late hour?"

Even through the haze of darkness she could feel the probing of those unnerving eyes.

"No, you couldn't be on a mission of mercy," Redmayne answered his own question. "You're carrying no basket. Besides, who would live here on the cliffs except, of course, spirits of the dead, and legends that should have faded away generations ago?"

She feared he'd see the pounding of her heart beneath the bluebell muslin of her walking dress. "I often walk at night," Fallon said. "And the castle is beautiful in the mist. It's quiet here. A place where one can be alone, think. Or is thinking against the law now, Captain?"

"That depends." His voice felt like fingers trying to pry into her mind. "During my visits with your neighbors, they've mentioned that you have some rather unsavory acquaintances among the peasantry. A folly that can be very dangerous, Miss Delaney."

Fallon swallowed hard, images flashing behind her eyes. Uilleann pipes filling the night air with haunting refrains, sweet Irish tenors blending, weaving ballad after ballad filled with heartache and hope that never died. Hushed whispers that were already rising among the young men like the wind, *fight again . . . die again . . . this time, perhaps, the sacrifice will be enough.* Freedom.

Dangerous? Perhaps. But only with these simple crofters did she feel truly alive.

It was obvious the man wasn't going to let her leave until she gave him some reason for her outing tonight.

Best to stick as close to the truth as possible to keep from stumbling. "I happen to love storms. The power of them, the wildness. I often go to the cliffs to watch them."

"And your brother allows it? A guardian should take better care of his ward."

"My brother has more pressing concerns."

"A pity. A young woman of your kind has need of guidance. Women are so easily moved by romantic tales and such nonsense, they can easily be led astray."

He shoved himself away from the wall, pacing the stone floors, running his fingertips over the walls as if searching for some weakness in the structure—or for the loosened brick that had hidden Fallon's treasure.

"I was told that torchlight often flickers here, late at night, have you ever seen that?"

Fallon shook her head.

His teeth flashed, white, in a feral smile. "I fear I'm never able to resist solving a puzzle, Miss Delaney. And this place puzzles me exceedingly."

"It's a castle ruin, just like so many others."

"This is no ordinary castle, or so the simple folk say. It's supposed to be the lair some sort of ghost, spirit—a hero who is doomed to return generation after generation to perform epic feats. Abominable waste of energy, in my opinion. If he fixed things right the first time, he wouldn't have to keep returning to do the job again. But then, you know all about this Ciaran of the Mist person, don't you, Miss Delaney, despite the ignorance you feign? The legend is linked somehow with your family."

He was watching carefully for the slightest shift in her features. Fallon swallowed hard. "You don't strike me as the type of man who believes in fairy tales, Captain Redmayne."

She surprised a laugh from him. "No, I am not. I expected a nest of smugglers, or rebels or gypsies at the very least—not a wayward young woman, or a mythical hero. But I *do* believe in learning everything I can about my adversary, Miss Delaney."

God in heaven, Redmayne *did* know or at least suspect that the smugglers were linked to Caislean ag Dahmsa

Ceo. He must. What could she possibly do to distract him, turn him away?

"You aren't likely to learn anything of value here, Captain Redmayne. The castle has been abandoned for almost two hundred years."

"You disappoint me, Miss Delaney. I had begun to hope you were a lady of some intuition and subtlety. From the moment we English set foot on Irish soil, this island has been nothing but a hornet's nest of trouble. Even now, I can feel the hum of rebellion, just beneath the surface, waiting to break free. I think it is time we put an end to this countless round of revolution and destruction."

"Then pack up your soldiers and go back to England."

"And let your good friends the French sail in? Set up camp such a short way from English beaches? I think not. No. I'm afraid I must take another tack. A more permanent one."

"After six hundred years, you believe you have the answer?"

He met her gaze with such calm, such certainty, it chilled her to the bone. "Astonishingly enough, I do. Men think countries can be subdued with pistols and swords, but that's not true. Bloodshed only crowns more martyrs to feed the fires of rebellion later on. If you want to destroy your enemy once and for all, you must look into his soul. Every man—or woman—every people has a weakness, some fatal flaw. Apply the right pressure to that vulnerable point and they shatter."

Cold sweat crawled down Fallon's spine, her fingers trembling where they clutched the brooch. Ireland had faced formidable adversaries before, ruthless ones whose horrible deeds still echoed, like screams in the wind. But even devil Cromwell who had swept through Ireland in the 1600s like the horsemen of the Apocalypse could not have been more dangerous, more cunning than the man who stood before her now.

"One can reassemble broken pistols, smuggle more ammunition ashore. One can even grow more sturdy sons to take up their fathers' place in battle. But if you burrow into a people's soul and destroy the very essence of who they are, then they'll no longer have the will to fight back. Rebellion will be at an end, not just for a decade, but forever." Redmayne's theory was hellishly clever. Terrifyingly true.

His voice dropped low. "You wonder what I'm doing here tonight, Miss Delaney? Searching for the soul of the Irish. And I think—" His fingers ran over weather-pitted walls. "—I have found it."

"I can't imagine what you mean."

"The trouble with Ireland, Miss Delaney, is this absurd clinging to past glories. Tales of high kings and heroes that have been dead for centuries. Every urchin who can lisp can recite three hours of tales about such nonsense. The people behave as if those feats happened yesterday at the site of their own pigsty. It's time they faced the truth—that natural order placed them where they are. They need to stare into the mirror and see what they are—dirt-scraping, illiterate beggars, the offal on the boot soles of those who now rule, tolerated only because one cannot find an expedient way of scraping them off."

"You English were still painting your faces blue when the Irish held all the learning of the world in their hands!"

"Ah, yes. I had forgotten. That is your overriding flaw, isn't it, Miss Delaney? You are tainted by Irish blood. A high enough crime, in the eyes of many. Of course, according to the local gentry with their ties to England, your unforgivable sin is that you take pride in it."

Her chin jutted up. "I could not care less what that pack of greedy, pompous fools think of me!"

"Perhaps not. But it's obvious you do care about this island, the people here. This . . . place." His gaze swept the castle, as if it held every secret in her heart. "This entire country is littered with standing stones, ancient dolmens, tombs of warriors long dead. Castles, like this one, towering over their meager little cottages, whispering to them of past greatness. A greatness they believe they can achieve again, if they only have the courage to reach out, take it."

He understood them, Fallon knew with a sick clenching in her stomach. Understood these people she loved, this land of mist and magic and dreams no sword could cut down. To be understood so completely by such a dangerous enemy was more terrifying than she had ever imagined.

But the Irish had clung to their past with astonishing tenacity, through the most horrendous trials imaginable. One lone Englishman couldn't destroy what they'd built over a thousand years. "You cannot obliterate a people's history, Captain."

"Perhaps not. But I wonder how many of your precious Irish would recall the ancient stories without constant reminders?"

"Reminders?"

"What would happen, Miss Delaney, if there were not a ring of standing stones in their pasture, or a dolmen halfway up their hill? If fairy rings and castles steeped in legend were no more?"

She froze, staring into the chasm of that possibility, one more hellish than any she could have imagined. Ireland without the ancient stones carved with pagan symbols, Ireland without the whispering of ages past. It would become a place hollow-eyed with hopelessness. God in heaven, don't let her betray that to this man with his fiendish gift for peering into the soul.

She tossed her hair and gave a scornful laugh that sounded brittle even to her own ears. "You should send a missive to the king regarding this brilliant plan, Captain Redmayne. Considering the massive debt left from the war in the Americas, I'm certain His Majesty would be overjoyed to pay an army while they tumble piles of rock God knows where. I only wish I could be present when you explain your *strategy* to your superior. Is there a military ceremony for being stripped of one's rank?"

He was smiling, even white teeth flashing in the moonlight. The sick knot tightened in Fallon's gut.

"It's been most illuminating speaking with you tonight, Miss Delaney. I look forward to furthering our acquaintance. You'll forgive me if I confess that I can't recall when I've been this intrigued by a lady."

The words unnerved her, and she could almost feel him reaching out to her with his razor-sharp intellect, trying to untangle the tightest secrets in her breast. Her hand trembled, the brooch she held suddenly seeming like a ridiculous bauble to fend off such a man.

He sketched her a bow, then turned and walked back out into the night. Fallon shifted to peer out the empty eye of a window, watching as he mounted his horse, guided it into the mist. She listened, long after horse and rider disappeared, tracing the fading sound of hoofbeats, straining to hear them over the thundering of her heart and the crash of the sea.

But was he really gone?

God above, what was she going to do? The castle, the standing stones ripped from the earth? It would be like tearing out Ireland's very soul. But what could she do to stop him? It would take a miracle. A miracle . . .

The edges of gold bit into her hand, the wicked-looking pin thrusting through the brooch and drawing blood. She stared down at it, as if she had never seen it before.

Had the old ones who watched over Ireland made certain she learned of Redmayne's diabolical plan tonight? On Beltane, the one night of all Ciaran could be summoned from the mist?

He can appear only once every three hundred years . . . her mother's warning echoed through her. *When things are most desperate.*

But what could be more desperate than this threat, hovering over Glenceo? And once Redmayne's plan worked, once the English high command saw the effect it had, wouldn't the destruction spread throughout the whole island, raging through it, sucking the life from it, the way consumption had drained the life from her mother?

Madness. Was she stepping into madness? Or reaching out for a miracle? Even now, she wasn't certain which.

She only knew one thing.

She had to find a way to stop Redmayne before it was too late. Ireland needed Ciaran. Desperately.

And what if she bumbled? Made a mistake? So many

years had passed since her mother had spun out the instructions for summoning the hero from the mist. What if Fallon had forgotten something vital? Worse still, what if the tale of Ciaran was nothing but pretty words, a mother's attempt to soothe her grieving child, to make her feel safe?

The thought twisted in Fallon, spilling hurt in its wake, and understanding. But the ancient brooch felt heavy. Real. If only the legend had as much substance. Soon, soon she would know for certain.

Did she dare even attempt to summon Ciaran now? The thought of Redmayne's inscrutable eyes watching from the shadows as she performed the rite made her cheeks burn. If she failed he'd be so amused.

No. She had to do this as quickly as she could. Surely a legend could dispatch one English captain.

Fallon hurried to the stone hearth and lay the brooch upon fire-blackened stone. She cast a desperate glance toward the windows. What had Mama said? That the light of the full moon would strike the jewels? But it was so misty, the silvery light a darting, uncertain thing. What if it never touched the jewels at all?

This was crazed. And yet, they needed Ciaran more than ever now, to battle an adversary like Redmayne.

Mama had said to call Ciaran with her heart, her soul. She settled for her lungs. "Blast it, Ciaran, wherever you are, we need you! Please, for God's sake—" But they'd been pagan when Ciaran walked Ireland. Had she committed some sort of blasphemy?

"Please . . . Mama said you'd come." Tears stung her eyes, the mist swirling, mocking, darting about in feathery wisps, obscuring the moonlight. She wished she could reach up, bend the rays with her hands.

"I don't know what else to do," she choked out. "Please, Ciaran, we need . . . *I* need . . . This is hopeless! Hopeless!" She caught up a broken piece of stone and hurled it at the brooch, the pin skittering to one side. At that moment, a piercing ray sizzled down, burying itself in one of the jewels.

Fallon couldn't breathe. She stared, half afraid, half hopeful, disbelieving, yet believing with all her heart.

She stared at the golden circle until her eyes burned and blurred and her head ached. Was it her imagination, or did light sparkle, fragment, swell within the stone? Was it some trick born of her desperation, or the mist itself? The brooch burst into countless fragments of light—red and green, blue and gold, leaping like a hungry flame up the beam of moonlight. Even if Redmayne hadn't doubled back to the castle, what were the chances that this odd light might bring him riding? If it was real . . .

The fire in the jewel soared, raged, half blinding her. A gust of wind buffeted Fallon as if to punish her for her lack of faith. She stumbled back, half expecting Ciaran to emerge from the pin like Athena bursting from the head of Zeus.

Then, in a heartbeat the wind stilled, the brooch dulled, emptied of all its magic.

Fallon sank down, drained, tears searing her eyes, disillusionment battering at her. Had she truly believed in the legend? She'd wanted it to be real, needed it so badly. A hollow ache swelled in her chest. What had she done? She'd been a fool. A fool. How could she have failed to realize how much she would risk by testing the brooch's power? Now she understood, but it was too late to change anything, she thought, sick at heart. A world that could summon Ciaran from the mist was a far brighter place than the world she stood in now.

"Hugh was right. It was only a story, something to drive back the chill, or the hopelessness. I was a fool ever to believe it was true."

She stilled, the sound of a footstep making her cheeks burn, her hands tremble. Oh, God, it must be Redmayne. If he had seen what foolishness she'd been about, she'd never recover from the humiliation.

She pushed to her feet, swiping away her tears and squaring her shoulders as she turned.

Damned if she'd let him see her heartbroken.

"Come out, Captain Redmayne," she ordered. "Show yourself."

No one. Nothing. Fingers of unease trailed down her

nape. Silence stretched out to what seemed an eternity, and she felt like a doe facing the barrel of a huntsman's musket.

Redmayne would have come striding from the shadows by now, wearing that insufferable sneer. If it wasn't the Englishman, then who could it be?

She swallowed hard, remembering the captain's warning about gypsies and thieves, and the mysterious smuggler he'd been seeking. No. She was being ridiculous. It was probably no more than a lost sheep, or a red deer foraging in the night. Then why did the quiet tighten about her throat like a hangman's noose?

For the first time in Fallon's life, she hated the mist that obscured the castle walls, the cliffs, the trees, and whoever or whatever lay hidden among them. But she'd always masked fear with belligerence. Squaring her shoulders, she called out.

"I dare you to step from the shadows! Or are you too much of a coward?"

She caught a faint rustling, the stealthy sound of movement, the crunch of stone. Breathless, Fallon wheeled in the direction of the sounds just as a dark shadow tore from its veiling of mist.

A man took shape, as if sculpted from raw night by the hands of the coming storm. But the figure that stumbled toward her had none of the dangerous elegance or hard polish of Captain Lionel Redmayne.

He staggered to a halt, half hidden by a mass of gray stone, bracing himself against it. Dark hair tangled about a face almost terrifying in its savage beauty, a square jaw, high cheekbones all shadows and planes. Moonlight silhouetted thickly muscled arms and a magnificent breadth of masculine chest. Something sharp and lethal glinted in one strong, square hand—a dagger?

Fallon reeled. God above, could it be Ciaran? Who else would plunge out of the mist, looking so—so primitive?

By the snakes of St. Patrick, *she'd done it!*

It was Ciaran.

She'd imagined this moment a hundred times, pictured the warrior of the mist, but nothing had prepared her for the reality of the man who stood before her, draped in midnight shadows.

This was no gallant warrior, flinging his cloak over puddles so she could cross, battling her enemies like Galahad from the Arthurian legends of old. This was a man of raw animal power, fearsome intensity, not some languishing knight ready to surrender his soul to kiss the hem of her gown.

She could sense something feral in those burning eyes, a wild creature balancing on the thinnest sheen of ice, expecting to crash through at any moment.

She should say something! She *would* say something, just as soon as she was able to breathe again. But it was a surprisingly difficult task when confronted with such a daunting specimen of masculinity. Would it be rude to pinch him to make certain he was real flesh and blood?

Her throat squeezed shut as eyes of searing green met hers. No. Better not poke him unless she wanted to feel that dagger blade pressed against her throat.

St. Patrick and the angels, what had she done? She'd called back an Irish Galahad, and gotten Dailraid the Destroyer. What if he decided that bashing and thrashing was such great fun, after three hundred years, that he refused to go back where he belonged once she was through with him? This whole night was turning into a disaster! She had to take control of this situation somehow.

She forced words past the knot in her throat. "I can . . . can hardly believe you're really here! I was so afraid you wouldn't come. But things were getting so desperate, and you'd promised."

He was staring at her strangely, angry, wary, searching her eyes almost desperately. Something dark darted across his features. Could it be fear? No. Impossible.

"Do you know why you're here? I mean, is that included in the magic? Or do I need to explain—"

"Magic?" he echoed. The first sound of his voice shivered through her as if she were a harp string he'd touched, the richness of his voice tempered with a slight rasp, as if it hadn't been used in a very long time.

"You—" His mouth hardened in accusation. "You cast a spell on me?"

Fallon took a step backward, beneath the force of those fierce eyes. "No! I mean, yes. But it wasn't malicious. I . . . I didn't trick you, like the fairies did."

"Fairies?" his face grew even grimmer.

"This is proper magic," she tried to reassure him. "The only way to get you here. But I . . . I don't know exactly what . . . what to do with you now that I've—"

She was blathering like an idiot. Blast, she had to keep her wits about her. After all, just because Redmayne hadn't made a second appearance yet, didn't mean he wasn't on his way back up the cliffs. Trouble was, once she'd gotten the infernal warrior of the mist *here*, she'd expected *him* to explain the rules to *her*. It seemed that hurtling through the centuries and crashing through the gates of Tir na nOg must be more of a shock than she'd realized. She tried to stem the quiver of panic that worked through her. It was no wonder the man was sensitive about spell-casting, considering his past. The last thing she needed was to anger him.

"About the magic. Naturally, I wouldn't have bothered you if it wasn't truly important. If you'd just let me explain—" She made a move toward him, and he leapt away from the stone, light as a cat on his feet.

Whatever explanation had been in Fallon's mind vanished.

Moonlight filtered down, washing him—all of him— in a waterfall of silver. She only glanced at him a moment, but the image seared itself into her memory forever.

Shoulders gleamed like freshly cast bronze, droplets of silver light snagging on a hair-roughened chest before they trailed down a flat belly to long, hard-muscled legs. And there, framed by narrow hips, a dark nest clung between his thighs, outlining . . .

A squeak of disbelief erupted from Fallon's chest, fire spilling into her cheeks as the realization struck her.

Ciaran of the Mist loomed before her, naked except for the dagger in his hand.

∽≈≋

She knew him.

The fact slammed against the inside of his skull with the force of a battle hammer. He didn't dare fall, must keep alert, ready. A warrior's senses throbbed through him as he fought to hide the cold stone of fear weighing his belly and to still the tremor in his hand.

The whole world writhed in mist, strange, unearthly shapes looming above him, below him, grasping at him with cold fingers. An even thicker, more terrifying haze filled his brain—confusion, bewilderment, emptiness.

No matter how desperately he groped, nothing was there but a thundering pain in his temple that made his stomach churn, a brutal chill that lanced through his veins with the battering of the wind. He couldn't catch a shred of image, of memory. Lost. He was lost, somehow. But he'd never known a man could be so lost he couldn't even find himself. Even his body felt strange, unfamiliar, as if it didn't quite fit. As if it belonged to someone else.

But who? He struggled against the choking sensation of panic that swelled into his throat.

The only thing real in his world was the woman, with her rippling flame-colored hair a banner against the backdrop of stone. As unearthly as the place itself, she seemed to shimmer in the veil of mist, her heart-shaped face painted with lantern light, skin creamy as a babe's, chin determined, tip-tilted eyes brimming with fairy tales, lips full and ripe, parted in astonishment, awe. Unspeakably strong, terrifyingly vulnerable, she seemed to have cast a net woven of moonbeams across his senses.

Even so, the *knowing* in her raked across his wire-taut nerves. Did she suspect the truth? That he was suffering a blow worse than death. A kind of death of the very soul?

He was no one. Nothing. A creature lost within his own haze-filled mind.

Who am I? Help me. The scream echoed through him, silenced by a hard core of pride not even panic could banish. Fear filled his mouth, unfamiliar enough to taste bitter. He loathed himself instinctively for feeling it.

With all the effort he could muster, he crushed the horror welling inside him, his voice rusty and unfamiliar as he forced out the words.

"Where . . . where am I?" Sweat soaked him despite the chill.

Blast, she'd been staring at him so hard she'd all but bored holes through him, but suddenly her gaze flitted around like a berserk moth, up above his head, to the side, anyplace it didn't touch him. "I . . . I . . . can't—"

"It's a simple enough question!" he roared. "Where am I? What happened to me? An accident? Accursed thieves? Damn you, tell me—"

"I can't! I can't even think with you . . . you standing there—"

"Would you prefer me flat on my face? It would be easy enough to arrange!" he snapped as the earth heaved again. He reached out, bracing himself against rough stone with the palm of one hand.

He'd obviously wrenched at her temper. "At least then I wouldn't see quite so much of you! Maybe you're accustomed to . . . to running about like that in Tir na nOg, but these days we prefer more . . . more covering." She yanked off her cloak, revealing a willowy form garbed in delicate blue muslin, a white sash caught beneath lush breasts. She thrust the cloak toward him, embarrassment emanating from her in red waves.

"What are you babbling about?" He started to snap, then glanced down. Bare flesh gleamed in the moonlight. Naked. He was standing here naked! His face flamed. "My clothes! Where the blazes are my clothes?"

"You came this way. It might have been nice if someone had warned me! Although, I imagine Mama didn't think the information appropriate fare for a six-year-old."

His gaze slashed up to the woman, his skull splitting with pain as he lunged for the cloak, struggled to put it around him. But his fingers felt clumsy as oxen hooves. The garment swirled around him, still warm from her body. But it couldn't stave off the hideous sense of being vulnerable, helpless, imprisoned inside himself.

"Answer me, now! Where am I?"

She blinked, bewildered, as if he were a particularly dull child. "We're at your castle."

"Mine?" His gaze slashed about, trying to pierce the mist, grasp some wisp of familiarity, some shred of his lost self. But even his eyes betrayed him, his vision blurred, distorted, useless. But even still, he could see the jagged rubble. "Falling down. Must not care for refurbishing."

"It's just . . . very old, and—"

"Damn the castle." His hand swept up to rake back the hair tangling across his face, but his fingers collided with something sticky, wet. A gash in his temple. The woman noticed it at the same moment.

"You're hurt!" she gasped. "The stone! When I threw it, I must have injured you."

Blast, why did it hurt so much to glare? "You did this to me?"

"I didn't mean to . . . I was just so . . . I thought it was all a lie—the stories I'd believed for so long."

"You're not making any sense. You know who I am."

"Of course I do. I summoned you."

"Summoned me? Why? Who am I?"

He could sense the leap of her pulse, the nervous

thundering of her heart. "You mean you don't know who you are?"

"Answer the question!"

"You are Ciaran MacCailte."

Ciaran. A name. *His* name, the woman claimed. Why didn't it mean anything to him? "Ciaran." He echoed, testing its syllables like a blind man seeking with the tips of his fingers, striving to recognize the lines of a familiar face. But it was still as strange, as unreal as the mist swirling around him.

"I can't remember," the admission tore from him, his voice cracking. "Why can't I remember?"

The woman's voice gentled. "All that hurtling through time and space must've been more difficult than I realized. Must've left you in shock."

"Through time?"

"From the land of the fairies."

"Fairies?"

"That's where you've been, ever since they cast their spell on you. But you won the right to return every three hundred years when things were bleakest. You—"

"Stop! Damnation!" He pressed one hand to his splitting skull. "My head hurts enough without you mocking me. I—" the words died, a sick sensation knotting in his stomach. "You mean . . . you're serious. She's serious!" He rolled his eyes skyward to whatever fates were perched on the storm clouds, roaring with laughter at his plight. Wasn't it bad enough he'd been bashed in the head, that his memory was gone? He had to be found by a woman who had lost her mind. Mad Irish. The label flickered through his consciousness. He'd heard the term a hundred times somewhere he couldn't recall, never entirely appreciated the truth of it until now.

"You're Ciaran of the Mist," the woman insisted, her chin jutting out at a stubborn angle. "Come to right great wrongs, to fulfill the promise of your legend."

My legend? What the—?" He couldn't help but reach out with one hand, brace himself against some stone abutment. He took a staggering step, as if he could outpace the haze choking his mind. If he could clear it for but a heartbeat, he could make sense of this whole mess, grasp it somehow.

"Listen, woman—whoever you are."

"Mary Fallon Delaney. Fallon of Misthaven House. My mama gave me the cloak brooch to summon you, her grandmother had it before her."

Perfect. She'd been spawned by an entire family of lunatics. "Miss Delaney, I might not have a clue who I am, but I know damned well I'm not this figment of your imagination. No legend. No fairies."

"You are Ciaran. You just can't remember yet. I'm certain it will all come to you after you get some rest. If you'll just come with me to Misthaven . . ."

He grimaced, and it hurt like hell. He could rest until the millennium, and he'd never remember any land of the fairies. He knew he wasn't that insane, whoever he was. But what was he going to do until he *did* regain his memory?

He could hardly go traipsing door-to-door, his hips swathed in a woman's cloak, demanding to know if anyone recognized him. But the sooner he got away from this lunatic woman the better.

"Take me to the nearest authorities. There must be a local magistrate? A garrison of soldiers?"

"No! You can't possibly go there!"

Hope flickered inside him. "Someone might have reported me missing."

"I doubt they have files reaching back a thousand years." She said it so gently he wanted to shake her until her teeth rattled.

"Damn it, this isn't some sort of game of make-believe! And I'm not going to let you pretend otherwise. I'm a man, not some kind of myth. I'm flesh and blood, and I'm going to find out who the devil I am the quickest way possible."

"I know you're confused. Upset. Who wouldn't be, considering what you've been through. I never guessed how difficult it must be for you, plunging into a different place and time."

"I didn't plunge anywhere, except off my feet or into

somebody's fist! Blast it, I'm going to the authorities whether you help me or not!"

Fear echoed through her voice. "Don't you understand? It would be too dangerous. Why, minutes before you appeared, the new commander of the garrison at Galway was here at the castle, poking around."

"Thank God." Finally he was making progress. The prospect of coming face-to-face with someone still possessed of their senses was more wonderful than he could have imagined. "Take me to this commander."

"You can't mean that! I couldn't possibly—it's far too dangerous. Even if he didn't believe you were Ciaran—"

"No fear of that. I'm not about to tell him this ridiculous story you've come up with. He'd think me a lunatic."

"No. He'd think you were something far more dangerous. Don't you even wonder what he was doing here? He warned me to beware of thieves prowling around this area. Ireland is filled with desperate men shoved off their land, shattered in the wake of the last rebellion. And then, of course, there is the main reason Redmayne has been transferred here. He's searching for some mysterious leader of a ring of smugglers who have been making the Crown's soldiers look like fools for some time now."

He squirmed inwardly, dark possibilities spilling out before him. "You're being ridiculous. I'm no rebel! No thief!" he cried. Yet why did he feel this creeping sensation of danger at her words, this prickling of instincts even the blow to his head hadn't dulled? What did he really know about himself? Only that something had driven him out into the night, to this remote place with its unearthly shadows. Was there the slimmest chance he might be the fugitive this Redmayne sought?

"Please, Ciaran, think! Redmayne won't recognize you, won't be able to give you back your identity. But that won't matter! Considering all the unrest, Redmayne will think it safer to keep you behind bars rather than leave you to run about the countryside. Is that what you want?"

Cold claws tightened about his chest, and he couldn't breathe as a flash of memory washed over him. Walls imprisoning him, his hands bloody as he pounded against the locked door. Quickly as the fleeting image had come, it was gone. All that remained was the sensation of panic. Terror. Helplessness. Icy sweat broke out all over his body. No. He couldn't risk being imprisoned. Didn't dare.

She clutched at his arm, her fingers trembling. And he was stunned at the sizzle of recognition that seemed to race through him at her touch. "You have to come with me to Misthaven. I beg you."

He tugged away from her, breaking the disturbing contact, and snarled an oath. If there was even the slimmest chance he was one of the fugitives this Redmayne sought, he'd be putting his neck in a noose if he went to the garrison. For all he knew, this Redmayne could be an enemy he should remember. The man had been here just before he'd stumbled out of the mist. What if the gash on his head was a souvenir of Redmayne's regard?

He concentrated, probed into the dark reaches of his memory, trying to catch hold of the reason that the very name Redmayne slid like a blade's edge across his nerves. Or was it merely this woman's odd delusions that were unnerving him?

After all was said and done, what choice did he have except to go with her? He was at this mad woman's mercy.

Only until I can discover who I am, he assured himself. *Until I can make some other arrangements. Until I can find the self I lost somehow in this infernal mist.*

Maybe the woman—Fallon, wasn't that her name?— maybe Fallon was right. If he just had some time to rest, to plow through the morass inside his head, he might find some fragment of the man he was, and his memory would return. It *would.* It must.

What if you never remember? a voice inside him jeered. *What if you've lost your very soul forever?*

No, he couldn't think that. Wouldn't. He would remember, somehow. Resolve settled, heavy in his gut. Something to hold on to in a world gone mad.

He gripped the ancient dagger, the only thing that felt

familiar, *right,* in his hand. This was the only clue to his identity that his attackers had left him.

He would unlock its secret, find himself again. And when he did . . .

He turned to Fallon. "I'll go with you because I have no other choice. I have to find out who I am, who did this to me. Someone left me here on these cliffs, naked, alone, my head bashed in. Maybe they left me to die. I intend to find them before they return to finish what they started. And when I do . . ." He touched his fingers to the gash in his temple. "I'll make certain they'll pay for what they've done."

Relief stole across Fallon's animated features. "Thank God. You won't regret it. I promise you, I'll prove I'm right about—"

"Stop. You can take me home with you. I'll even let you call me Ciaran for the time being. I'll call myself Ciaran. Why the blazes not? I don't have any other name." His eyes narrowed. "But if you bludgeon me with this ridiculous story of yours for one more minute, I vow I'll take my chances with this Redmayne you hate so much."

"Fine! I won't say another word until you're settled. Now, we just need to get you down from the cliffs. I left my horse a ways down the hill. I'll just whistle and—" Her brow wrinkled. She caught her lower lip between her teeth. "Oh, no. When I left Misthaven, I wasn't thinking clearly—"

"What a surprise." Ciaran muttered.

"I rode Cuchulain."

"C—who?"

"My horse. He has a somewhat uncertain temper."

"You mean he's wild? A man killer?"

"He has an unfortunate habit of breaking people's bones whenever he gets the chance of it. He's gentle as a lamb with me, but loathes everyone else. When I left Misthaven, I didn't come here intending to call you back. Even if I had, I wouldn't have thought to bring another mount for you. I suppose I always assumed you'd come, uh, fully armed and . . . and clothed, and—"

"Don't tell me. Delivered from the mists of fairyland astride a mount of thunderbolts or some such?"

Dark red stained her cheeks, and she looked almost sheepish. He didn't want to think her beautiful. "I've never summoned back a legend before," she admitted. "Next time I'll be better prepared."

She whistled, and a massive stallion trotted out of the darkness, white coat shimmering against the night. A devil-horse, many would have called it, towering strength, raw muscle, eyes wild as bedamned. Beautiful and dangerous as the jagged cliffs below. Anyone who had allowed a woman near it must have lost their senses. But then, he'd almost forgotten the type of family he was dealing with.

"Be careful," she warned. "He's terrified of strangers. I found him wandering, lost, badly hurt, half maddened with pain. My brother Hugh wanted to put him down, but there was something—a wildness inside him, as if he were lost, desperate. He was so beautiful, I just couldn't let him be killed."

Her explanation trailed off as the beast's nostrils flared, liquid dark eyes fixing on Ciaran, doubtless contemplating the best way to crush him into dust. Ciaran marveled that anyone had ever been able to mount the animal, let alone this young woman with her delicate body and small hands. But then, the horse looked as if he had an unbalanced mind. Perhaps he and the woman were kindred spirits.

Ciaran frowned, wondering if he had had much experience with horses. Was he a decent rider? Did he know what it felt like to meld his body with a beast bred to fly like the wind?

Driven by an impulse he didn't understand, Ciaran reached out a hand, holding it toward the amazingly beautiful horse.

"Don't touch him!" Fallon cried. "He'll bite off your fingers if—"

But instead of baring his equine teeth, Cuchulain sank his velvety muzzle into the cup of Ciaran's palm. Hot breath blew out as the animal snuffled against him, accustoming himself to Ciaran's scent.

Ever so slowly, the tremors of unease shaking the

stallion smoothed out, like the calming of some inner storm. A soft whicker greeted him. Almost as if the animal knew him . . . had been waiting for him.

Ciaran leaned against one glossy shoulder, letting the warmth of the animal seep into his battered body.

"How did you do that?" Fallon marveled. "It took the head groom nearly six months before he could even open the stall door without Cuchulain snatching a bite out of him. Even I couldn't touch him for weeks after I brought him home."

"I don't know how, or why." Ciaran stroked the horse, gliding his hand into the secret, soft cove between silky mane and arched neck. Strange, but he knew only that this animal, so wary, so wounded in its proud soul, had offered him a precious fragment, a tiny piece of the puzzle that was his identity. There was something in him the stallion trusted.

"Climb on, and I'll try to mount behind you." Ciaran said.

"It's too dangerous. Cuchulain doesn't . . . I mean, it's a miracle, his even allowing you to touch him. The cliff path is so narrow, so treacherous. If he shies, we could both plunge over the edge."

He could hardly risk an accident that might result in hurling a feeble-brained girl over a cliff.

"You're right. I'll walk." But how far away was the girl's home? What were the odds his battered body could make the trek?

No. There was another way. A pulse of something like excitement worked through him, a need to test this strange fragile bond with the magnificent creature before him. Dangerous. It would be dangerous. All the more so because his own balance was so uncertain. But a part of him craved that risk, answered to it as if it were the strains of a battle drum.

Ciaran caught hold of the animal's reins, paused a moment, eyeing stirrup and saddle. Head still throbbing, he grasped the horse's mane and dragged himself up onto its back.

He heard Fallon's cry of protest through a haze of

motion and sound, the stallion's hooves striking stone as it sidestepped, a nervous whinny, Ciaran's own body scrabbling for purchase on the animal's back.

His stomach churned, his head swam as he fought for equilibrium, the stallion sidestepping, tossing its majestic head. Blast, I'm a fool, Ciaran thought scathingly. Had he thought he'd swing astride the stallion and discover he was the world's best horseman? More likely the animal would rear up and plunge down the narrow path at a dead run. But after a moment, Cuchulain calmed again. He pawed the ground once, angling his head to gaze at Ciaran with questioning dark eyes.

What the hell did he do now? How did one guide the animal? He had to see if it would take the cliff road safely. He grasped the reins, tightened his knees. With a toss of his head, the stallion started to trot down the path. Ciaran's head felt as though it were bursting, every jarring movement thrusting spikes into his brain.

"Stop! Wait—" The devil! He could end up at the bottom of the mountain, leaving the girl behind. How did you make the infernal beast stop?

"Pull back on the reins, gently!" He heard Fallon call. He braced himself, did as she directed. Miracle of miracles, the beast stopped. Ciaran didn't. The momentum flung him over the stallion's head.

So much for the idea that he was a great horseman.

The girl was beside him in an instant, helping him to his feet. "I told you not to try to ride him! He—"

"My own . . . clumsiness . . . fell off." Ciaran pressed a fist to his thundering head and struggled to catch his breath.

When he was able to straighten up, he looked into Fallon Delaney's face and managed a half-smile. "I suppose this dashes your theory that I'm a legendary hero. It seems that riding a horse would be the first requirement of a Ciaran of the Mist. I don't know the first thing about it."

"Of course you don't. It was stupid of me not to think of it, warn you, before you tried. Ciaran was no knight on a destrier. He's something older, more primitive, from a time when the first legends were stirring in the most secret, most magical places in men's souls. Ciaran of the Mist would never have ridden. Warriors of his time rode in chariots driven by charioteers. They were incredible runners, and he was the swiftest of them all. Able to outrun an entire herd of red deer, so agile he could race through the forest and not break the tiniest twig—"

The knowledge was oddly unsettling. "Fallon, I'm not this hero of yours. I may not be able to ride, but I can understand your language. Other things are strange, unfamiliar, but your clothes, the way you're dressed, is not."

She hesitated for an instant, and he thought he'd at last found a chink in her delusions, made her glimpse reality. But the light in her eyes flared again, more determined than ever. "You've come back other times, Ciaran. There's no way to understand the magic. You would have—"

"Never mind!" Ciaran dragged himself back to his feet. "Mercy. Please. I'm sorry I even brought the subject up. My head won't tolerate any more singing of his praises without bursting. As for the horse, he'll carry us down safe enough."

"H–How can you be so certain?"

"He told me." Ciaran's first stab at a joke—his head might not be whole, but it seemed his sense of humor was intact. But the woman wasn't laughing. She merely stared at him, big-eyed, believing.

Why should I be surprised? Ciaran thought wryly. It was a small leap indeed to believe a horse could talk if you were already downright certain that a nine-hundred-year-old hero could pop back from the land of the fairies and land in your lap. Without a horse, unfortunately. Or clothes. Damned inconsiderate of him.

"Since you can talk to Cuchulain, perhaps you'd like to take the reins?" she asked earnestly.

He glanced at the cliff road, stretching down, perilous, unfamiliar, with little room for error. He didn't have the slightest idea where they were going, or how to make the horse go where he wanted it to. Yet the idea of handing control over to this madwoman made sweat break out across his brow.

Still, what choice did he have but to trust her? She'd gotten herself *up* the infernal slope in one piece.

"No. I, uh, he'd rather have you steer him."

Obedient as a child, Fallon Delaney mounted her hell-born stallion and looked down at Ciaran expectantly. It was one thing clambering up on the animal's back with no obstructions in the way, but Fallon Delaney's lithe, slender legs looped around some impossible looking contraption, then both draped over one of the horse's sides.

She eased one slipper out of the stirrup, offering it to him. He wished to hell he could talk to the blasted horse. He'd ask it to kneel down, so he could climb on without dragging the girl off.

Tangled up in the folds of the blue velvet cloak, Ciaran attempted to grasp the saddle again, one arm on either side of Fallon's body. Straining, struggling, he heaved himself upward.

The cloak was dragged back, the chill wind burning his bare skin. His chest collided with the tender column of her arm, his momentum skidding that contact lower, to the flat plane of his stomach. He heard her gasp of surprise, dismay, but there was no escaping it. Flinging his leg over Cuchulain's broad barrel, Ciaran slid into place, the front of his bare body thudding into Fallon's back. His arms caught hold, hard about her slender waist, trying to anchor himself upright.

Cuchulain, objecting to such clumsiness, sidestepped, and Ciaran had no choice except to fall ignominiously on the ground, or to cup his body tight around Fallon's. His legs crushed hard against the horse's coat, the V formed by his thighs cradling the roundness of Fallon Delaney's bottom.

Whoever had beaten him hadn't bludgeoned the life out of him yet, because he felt the bulge in his groin stir at the contact with soft female flesh.

She was aware of it, too, trying to edge away from him, put some space between them. Did she feel the same dismay, the same shock of unexpected pleasure he did? No, there was an innocence about her, a newness. She was a girl on the brink of womanhood. And he was the lowest kind of scum for feeling any sexual stirring at all in these circumstances.

He sobered as a thought stole through him, cold, unwelcome. He had no idea what he'd been like with women before he'd lost his memory. For all he knew, he *was* the sort of blackguard who preyed upon young women like Mary Fallon Delaney.

"Hold the horse still," Ciaran snapped, trying to keep balanced on the beast while at the same time grabbing handfuls of the cloak to stuff between his body and the woman before him.

But Cuchulain's patience was at an end. The monster-horse struck out down the path at a teeth-jarring pace, and all Ciaran could do was clutch Fallon's waist with all his strength.

There was no more time to worry about modesty as moonlight filtered across the treacherous path. He couldn't distract Fallon by writhing around, trying to preserve her sensibilities. They wouldn't do her a damn bit of good if she was crushed on the stones below.

"We'll . . . we'll have to be careful. If Redmayne or anyone were to . . ." She scooted a fraction farther away from him, the next jar nudging them back together. "If anyone were to see you here, like this, it might be dangerous."

"Dangerous? It would be awkward as bedamned. Unless, of course, whoever we met also happened to be waiting to cast hawthorn blossoms across a legend's path."

But he braced himself, alert, trying to focus his gaze enough to pierce the billows of mist that swirled up from Cuchulain's massive hooves. It was a grim prospect, the possibility that they might run afoul of someone, especially since the most likely person to be in the area would be his attacker. Worse still, Ciaran wouldn't even recognize any enemy even if they were face-to-face.

For a brief while, he was distracted enough by the prospect not to think of the brush of those feminine curves against his body. Even Fallon seemed locked in fierce concentration. But the blessed perilousness of the path couldn't last forever. After a while, animal, woman and man settled into an even pace. The countryside swept out, deserted, quiet, as if there weren't another soul on earth.

Panic dislodged from throats, muscles that had been locked in a life-or-death grip loosened ever so slightly.

Ciaran's head still pounded like blue blazes, his muscles aching as if he'd taken the devil of a beating. That was a torture he could endure. But as the path widened into a sea of shadow-veiled Irish green, it seemed the jeering fates had another variety of torment in store.

Hair the color of flame teased his jaw, his neck, spilled down the sensitive skin of his arm. The scent of her— wild and windblown, heathery and fey and feminine— filled his senses.

Whatever it was she wore was gauzy thin as the wings of the fairies she believed in. He could feel every dip and hollow, every delicate bump of her spine searing itself into his skin. She was in his arms, so tightly, so intimately they might have been lovers—a mere wisp of muslin between them.

Did he know anything about women—the feel of them, the textures of mouth and breast and thigh? Was there a woman, even now, somewhere waiting for him?

No. The feel of her, the scent of her was unfamiliar, something longed for, yet unreachable as the moon. There was an emptiness, a hollow place, whispering of a longing unfulfilled.

Yet he was man enough to feel the ache, the urge to try to fill it.

Grinding his teeth, he yanked his thoughts away from such dangerous ground. What kind of a monster was he? He didn't know anything about Mary Fallon Delaney except that she was delusional. Unforgivably vulnerable, especially where this Ciaran of the Mist fantasy was concerned. He had real problems of his own, monumental problems to deal with: he must fight his way from the shadow land his wound had left him in.

Unable to bear the faint rubbing of their bodies

against each other for another moment, Ciaran grabbed a handful of the cloak, trying yet again to slide the velvet between his body and Fallon's.

Cuchulain stumbled, and Ciaran all but fell off, but he persevered with the fold of cloak. Maybe it would be a good thing for him to crash headfirst into a few rocks. Drive some sense back into him. At least it would shatter these thoughts, these feelings, these echoes in a body that didn't even seem his own.

He concentrated on the pain in his body, embracing it, feeding its fire, the jarring of the horse grinding hot spirals deeper into his joints, intensifying the aching, until it drove back the astonishing sensations Mary Fallon Delaney had stirred in him. He gave himself up to the red burning gratefully.

It didn't bode well for the future, Ciaran thought just before the haze engulfed him. All he could remember was the past hour. And already he had something he needed to forget.

CHAPTER

3

He was holding her. Tight. The warmth from his body seeped into hers, the rhythm of his heartbeat echoing in her own veins, the moist whisper of his breath tickling the back of her neck. With every strike of Cuchulain's hooves upon the turf, Ciaran melded closer to her, until she could feel the uncertainty in him, the bewilderment, the anger, the pain.

God in heaven, what was she going to do with him?

It had sounded so simple when Mama spun the tale in the garden, playing games with the bright, ripe cherries. Take the enchanted brooch, summon Ciaran, hand him his quest the same way Hugh handed his steward orders to build a new stable or a new fence.

It should have been as fated and lovely and magical as Arthur pulling the sword from the stone, recognizing in a blaze of glory and wonder his unique destiny.

Arthur hadn't made any trouble. He'd merely sharpened up his new trophy and embraced his fate. All the sorcerer Merlin had had to do was nod with approval as the once and future king trotted obligingly off to marry Guinevere, befriend Lancelot, send Galahad on the Grail quest.

Could her crusade have been so simple? No. Ciaran MacCailte, Son of the Mist, had the innate stubbornness of all the Irish race. Doubtless, he would have taken one look at the sword in the stone and refused to give it so much as a tug. He was already determined to be uncooperative. What would Ciaran say when she told him the reason she'd drawn him out of the mist: to save a castle that was already half-ruined, lead the glen folk to preserve a hope few had the courage to believe in anymore?

How could this man lead anyone when he didn't even believe in himself?

And what if he is someone else? a voice inside her whispered. *What if he's not Ciaran of the Mist at all?* No. That was unthinkable. Who else could he possibly be? *Anybody,* the voice mocked her. *The world is full of people wandering about. Isn't it possible one lone man could end up at the Castle of the Dancing Mist? After all, hadn't Redmayne?*

Fallon suppressed a shudder, remembering the captain's eyes, so piercing, leaving secrets nowhere to hide.

The Englishman had come to the castle searching for something, someone—perhaps the man whose arms were now around her. But why was he naked? Why did he carry the ancient dagger unless . . .

No. He *was* Ciaran. She was certain of it.

And now she was taking him to Misthaven House. Fallon chewed at her lower lip. Ever since Mama had died, Misthaven had seemed to be hushed, waiting for her return. Servants haunted the rooms like ghosts, careful not to be seen as they polished and swept. Hugh barricaded himself in his study, only striding off, a preoccupied frown on his face, riding crop in hand, when it was time to survey the lands and the countless business interests that were his only passion.

Few guests ever braved Misthaven's doors, the manor house never hosting the convivial dinner parties or musicales or balls that drove the ennui from the neighboring gentry.

But even Hugh with his single-mindedness would notice if he tripped over Ciaran in the hallway. And she doubted the servants would suddenly believe she'd taken to eating an entire rack of lamb by herself at dinnertime.

Blast, why hadn't she thought this whole escapade through before she'd trotted up to Caislean ag Dahmsa Ceo and dug the cloak pin from its hiding place with her eager hand? Why hadn't she realized that the possibilities for disaster were endless?

Because no one had ever warned her that even legends have to be fed. It had never occurred to her that she would have to make provisions for Ciaran—simple things, infinitely difficult ones such as what he would eat, the clothes he would wear, where he would sleep. Exactly where did one hide six feet four inches of angry, bewildered male?

She could hardly keep him hidden in a bandbox beneath her bed, the way she had an injured fox pup when she was eight. The man was dangerous—a powder keg ready to explode, a runaway coach hurtling down a cliff's edge.

Was she making a terrible mistake bringing him to Misthaven at all?

She forced back the doubts. So things hadn't turned out the way she'd expected. What did it matter? All the snarls she'd encountered thus far would smooth out as soon as Ciaran regained his memory. Then he would turn into the Ciaran of legend—invincible, cunning, the noblest of warriors and the bravest. She just had to muddle through until then, stave off as many disasters as possible. Imagine how contrite he'd be for causing her so much trouble.

Forgive me, my fairest lady. I shall carry the shame of my oafish behavior toward you throughout eternity.

The image of this towering, powerful man kneeling before her, head bowed, hand outstretched, started a fluttering in her breast. She'd find it in her heart to forgive him, she decided. Once he had groveled enough.

"Ciaran?" She reined in the horse, felt Ciaran start, his body stiffening against her.

"What is it? Is someone coming?"

"No. I–I just . . . we're nearing Misthaven, and I wanted to explain to you—" She paused, gathering surprisingly scattered thoughts. Apparently her wits were more affected than she'd imagined by thoughts of Ciaran on his knees.

"I'm going to have to keep you hidden for a while."

He breathed a sigh that could only be relief. "That should be easy enough. I'm not likely to hold any dinner parties. Can't remember anyone to invite."

"It's just that my brother, Hugh, is . . . very protective of his situation. He dislikes anything that interferes with his business interests, or tending his estates. That is why I think it would be best if we kept you hidden for the time being. From the servants. And, uh, from my brother."

She felt Ciaran stiffen, knew with a sinking sensation that she'd jabbed at his pride and the stubbornness that was as much a part of the man as his waves of midnight hair.

"You'd sneak me into this man's home? Have me eat his food, sleep in his bed, without telling him?"

"Hugh's bed wouldn't be near large enough for the both of you," she said with forced lightness. "I imagine you're a restless sleeper."

"This isn't a jest! I won't sneak about, stealing hospitality from a man like some sort of thief."

"It would be the safest way to handle things. Until you regain your memory you're vulnerable. Misthaven is vulnerable, too."

"All the more reason your brother should know about me, about what he's risking."

"Don't you see? That's how I'm going to protect him, by keeping him ignorant of this whole scheme. That way, no one can blame him. No one can use it as an excuse for taking Misthaven away."

"Taking it away? You could lose your estate because you offered me shelter?"

"They'd confiscate Misthaven if Hugh sneezed the wrong way. They've been trying to snatch it since the time of Cromwell."

"I don't understand. Who is trying to take it?"

"The—" Shame spilled through her, familiar, hated, inescapable as if the word "betrayer" were branded into her cheek. She saw the puzzlement reflected in Ciaran MacCailte's eyes.

What would he think, this noblest of all Celts, if he learned the truth about the Delaneys, the tainted blood that ran through her veins? How could she even begin to explain the lengths her family had stooped to in order to cling to land and wealth and some modicum of power? No. He could never be made to understand. And she couldn't bear to see the scorn, the loathing, the *pity* cross his rugged face.

"It doesn't matter why," she dismissed his question. "The point is that Hugh will be safe enough. There are more than a few hereabouts who think that I'm touched in the head. It would be easy enough for them to believe I was behind such a wild scheme, and that Hugh knew nothing about it."

"You think I would put you in danger? A woman?"

"No need to stir up your sense of chivalry. This is the least of my crimes against the Crown, I assure you. I—" Fallon choked off the words, horrified at what she'd almost confessed: a thirst for Irish freedom some would call treason.

God above, what if this man *wasn't* Ciaran? What if he was an English officer, lost? Or, what if he had a hunger for British coin? What price would such information bring from a man like Captain Lionel Redmayne?

She couldn't see Ciaran's face, but she felt the sudden tensing, the *awareness* in him.

"I won't have anyone taking risks for me," he asserted stubbornly. "I should get down off this hell-born beast, and—"

"Oh, no! I'm not about to let you go wandering off into God knows what trouble. There's probably some cosmic punishment for misplacing a legend. And I don't intend to find out what it is!"

She sucked in a steadying breath, trying to reason with him. "If I thought you'd be caught, do you think I'd be fool enough to bring you to Misthaven? I've already figured out a perfect place—a *safe* place—to keep you. A priest hole. It's a secret room where an outlawed priest could hide to tend his parish—"

Ciaran grasped her arm, hope surging into his voice. "I know what that is! Perhaps I'm a priest! The priest hunters caught up to me, and—"

Fallon couldn't stifle a bark of laughter. "You're no priest." Imagining this man taking a vow of celibacy was absurd. There was something vital in him, primitive, pagan—something that called to the untamed reaches of any woman's body and soul. Her laughter died, crushed by a tingling echo in her most secret places.

Instinctively she tightened her knees. The horse broke into a walk.

Ciaran clenched his jaw in irritation as she guided the horse along a narrow path through a wooded area. "Why the devil couldn't I be a priest?"

"Priests don't run about naked, ancient daggers clutched in their hands. Besides, we haven't had to hide priests for quite some time."

"But—"

His protest was lost as the horse skirted a copse of blooming hawthorn. The hell-born beast skittered, reared. Ciaran glimpsed a shadowy form huddled among the tangled tree roots.

Ciaran's heart jolted against his ribs as a cry rang out and the figure leaped up, taking on human form. In a panic, it darted in front of Cuchulain, its tattered clothing rippling in the wind, terrifying the horse. Instinctively, Ciaran grabbed at the reins in Fallon's hand to try to stop the horse, but he only made matters worse. The animal shied in an attempt to evade the apparition, but failed. His massive chest cracked into the figure hard, sending it sprawling.

In a heartbeat, Ciaran slid to the ground, the horse's, flashing hooves nearly catching him in the ribs. He knelt beside the shadowy form as Fallon scrambled over as well.

It was an old woman, white hair a mass of snarls in the wind, her body thin as winter-burned twigs. Hollow-eyed, she scrabbled against a tree trunk, shivering.

"Beggin' yer pardon, me lor'," the crone pleaded. "I didn't mean t' frighten yer horse, I didn't."

She looked afraid, as if he might strike her. The

realization sickened Ciaran. "I won't hurt you. Don't be afraid."

"Quiet, now. It's no matter," Fallon soothed. "Are you hurt?"

"The blasted horse all but ran her over," Ciaran snapped, unable to quell the panic in his chest. "Of course she's hurt! Lie still," he ordered gruffly. "I'm going to check for broken bones." He gathered the old woman up in his arms, steadying her, running his hands down fragile limbs. Familiar—this was familiar, this pounding anxiety, this *knowing* what was injured, what was not.

Eyes bright as ripe blackberries stared at him as if he *had* just risen out of the mist. "Just . . . just a wee bit shaken. 'Twas me own fault, not payin' attention. Me mind was jest flitterin' on other things."

"What is your name?" Fallon smoothed a lock of white hair back from a face wrinkled and sweet as a dried apple.

"I be Maeve McGinty."

"What the devil are you doing out alone, so late at night?" Ciaran said. Why did he feel this awful, crushing sense that he was responsible somehow for her fall? "Can't you see there's a storm brewing?"

"That's what Bridie would say. But take more'n a few thunderheads t' keep me at me own hearth t'night. Me girl, she's givin' birth t' her first babe, an' I wanted t' be there t' hold 'er hand."

"Your daughter sent for you on a night like this?" Ciaran growled. "What was she thinking of, expecting you to walk—"

"Nay. She's not so careless with her mama, is Bridie. Not a word did she send. She didn't need to. The girl beat her way t' life beneath me heart. I jest know 'tis her time *here*." Maeve pressed a gnarled fist to her breast.

"You're not from Misthaven lands, are you?" Fallon asked.

"Mary, Joseph an' Jaysus, no, miss. If I was, you can be sure I'd not be trekkin' along dressed like this." Maeve brushed one birdlike hand along her tattered garments. "'Tis jest that grateful I am that me girl's come t' marry one o' Mr. Hugh's tenants. She'll not ever be wanderin' in rags not fit t' keep out the tiniest breeze."

Ciaran looked up at her. "We'll see you to your daughter's."

"No!" Fallon cry startled him. "We can't."

"Sir, ye're most kind, but I can hardly be expectin' a lady o' quality t' be carryin' Maeve McGinty atop 'er pretty saddle."

"It's not that at all," Fallon stammered, dismay shadowing her features. "I would be happy to help if I were riding any other horse in the stables. But Cuchulain would never endure it." She turned to glare at Ciaran. "It's a miracle he'd carry you riding double. But it was worth the risk. We both know how hard your head is. But if he threw Mrs. McGinty she'd shatter into so many pieces even the great and powerful Son of the Mist couldn't put her back together."

Ciaran glowered at Fallon, wanting to shake her. "Damn it, that's not amusing—"

"Me feet'll get me there right enough," the old woman insisted. "I was just catchin' me breath when ye came upon me. The wind—it has a bite in it t'night." A shiver worked through her.

"Little wonder you're cold with what you're wearing," Fallon said. Ciaran helped Mrs. McGinty up, brushing leaves from her threadbare plaid shawl. His face crumpled into a scowl. "I'm not about to just let you walk away, shivering—"

"I have a few coins I could offer—" Fallon began, but Ciaran cut her off with an impatient wave of his hand.

"They'd hardly keep her warm now." At that instant, the wind tugged at the velvet cloak around his shoulders. He hesitated, recalling he had nothing on beneath the blue cloth. He stood there, torn. What kind of a fool would give away the only garment he had? A *borrowed* garment at that. But then, he *had* taken a blow to the head. His fingers went to the fastenings of the cloak. "Here," he said gruffly. "Take this—"

"Oh, no, sir." Maeve thrust her hands behind her back, like a child tempted to filch sweetmeats. "I couldna'."

"But Ciaran," Fallon protested, "you're . . . you're n—"

Naked? The woman didn't need to remind him. He'd be freezing off his hind parts.

"It doesn't matter," he growled, his hands clumsy, his cheeks burning at the prospect of baring himself yet again. "I can't let an old woman go wandering off, cold, when I have this infernal cloak."

His jaw hardened as he slipped the blue velvet free.

Old Mrs. McGinty's eyes went wide as tea plates. "Lad, forgive an old woman fer mentionin' it, but . . . but yer clothes seem t' have gone missing."

Heat surged into Ciaran's cheeks. "I, uh—" Lies obviously came hard to him. Fallon was far more adept at spinning wild tales.

"He had a bit of an accident," Fallon filled in hastily. "He was bathing in one of the streams—"

He supposed he should be grateful. He might have been if Maeve hadn't piped up.

"Bathin' on a night like this? Are ye *tryin'* t' catch lung fever, lad?"

"I happen to like a brisk swim," Ciaran insisted with as much dignity as he could muster.

"He left his clothes on the bank and some animal stole them," Fallon finished. "I found him wandering around without a stitch on, pure begging for help." Damn, she was making him sound three kinds of a fool.

"Did ye, now?" Mrs. McGinty's eyes narrowed, a merry smile dancing across her lips. "With a lad so handsome as this, I'd wager me mam's holy medal 'twas no animal stole his clothes. No, more likely it was a maid such as yerself, eager t' catch a glimpse o' such a fine specimen o' man."

"I—I didn't! I wouldn't! I mean, I've seen quite enough of him already." Fallon tossed those sunset curls as if he were far beneath her notice, but even her thick locks couldn't hide the fact that she was flustered for once.

Ciaran felt a surge of unholy pleasure at her discomfiture. It was about time *she* took a turn feeling like a prize idiot.

"I'd be lookin' t' the lass, here, ye want t' find the culprit," Mrs. McGinty repeated. "But whoever robbed ye, I can't send ye off wearin' nothin' but yer smile, lad, no matter how bewitchin' it might be."

Gnarled old fingers unfastened the threadbare shawl. "This'll keep ye a trifle modest. Though ye've no call for shame, if ye ask Maeve McGinty. An' me, havin' raised seven boys up t' be men." She barely reached the middle of his chest, but she wrapped the shawl around his hips, as deftly as if he were one of her sons.

"I can't take this," Ciaran started to pull the shawl aside, but Maeve's chuckle stopped him.

"Ah, so ye're enjoyin' the effect ye have on the lady, then. Maybe I wronged the girl. Did ye hide yer own clothes a-purpose?"

"No! I—"

Maeve gave the knotted shawl one last tug, then patted Ciaran's cheek. "There, now, don't mind me teasin' ye, the two of ye. 'Tis all we old folks can do when ye put us in mind o' our own young love."

"We're not lovers!" Fallon's outraged cry nettled Ciaran, urging him to indulge in torment of his own.

After all, Mary Fallon Delaney had had the upper hand ever since he'd stumbled into this nightmare. Turnabout was fair play.

"Come, now, Fallon, no need to squawk just because Mrs. McGinty has guessed the truth." And yet, he didn't enjoy the jest nearly as much as he should have. The words had barely left his mouth when a sadness ghosted through him, an *aloneness* too great to bear. A longing never fulfilled. It surprised him, left him raw.

"I'll leave the two of ye to settle yer spat in private. That's always the best way," Maeve said. "But afore I go, lad, I want to say ye're passing kind."

Why did the old woman's words chafe at him so? "No," Ciaran insisted. "I'm completely selfish. I prefer not to spend the next three weeks wondering if you've frozen to death somewhere along this path."

The Irishwoman's work-worn hands grasped the edges

of cloth so lush its worth would feed her family for a year, and she gazed up at him as if he *were* this hero Ciaran of the Mist Fallon kept insisting he was, and he'd just appeared in all his legendary splendor.

"May the dust o' yer carriage wheels blind the eyes o' yer foes," she blessed him. "May ye get the reward in heaven that's been denied ye for yer goodness on this earth. An' may the sons o' yer sons smile up in yer face." Her eyes twinkled as she gave him a winsome smile. "An' once they do, make certain ye take 'em home t' see yer own mam."

His own mother. Pain, wistfulness, it stirred unexpectedly in Ciaran's chest. Was there a woman like this, a mother somewhere, waiting for him, worrying?

He strained, groping desperately into the mist of his mind, but only the most fleeting of sensations, *impressions,* danced just beyond his reach: tears unshed in beautiful eyes, a smile of farewell so brave it broke his heart, a hand letting go of him, when he sensed it wanted to cling tightly, to draw him back. To what? To the boyhood he'd left behind?

Fallon's voice drove back the images, but not the ache of loneliness, of loss. "Mrs. McGinty, let me send one of the grooms back for you. They can take you to your daughter's in a cart."

"Go on with ye now, and don't be worryin' yer pretty head," Mrs. McGinty said. "I'm so heartened by yer kindness that I'll be trippin' up t' Bridie's doorstep before I can say three Hail Marys."

With that, Mrs. McGinty set out again, looking amazingly spry, as if the exchange had worked some sort of enchantment upon her. Ciaran stood, watching the old woman, shaken by the odd sensation stirred up inside him. As if his gaze could clear the path, make it safe for her. As if he should. Should what? Send the storm clouds fleeing? Smooth the path with one sweep of his hand? Fallon's fantastic stories were addling his wits.

"Ciaran," Fallon touched his arm, the awe in her voice raking against his frayed nerves. "Do you realize what you've just done?"

"Raised my odds of catching some sort of fever? I don't know what madness possessed me."

"I do!" Her eyes glistened, her lips parted, ripe with idealism and innocence. "Giving the cloak away is what you were born to do!"

"I can die a happy man," Ciaran groused. "My life's work is complete."

"Don't make a jest of it. Don't you see? This proves you're Ciaran of the Mist. You're one of the Red Branch knights!"

Alarm stirred in his gut. He was unsettled enough. The last thing he needed was another heaping spoonful of Fallon's fairy-tale dreams. He ground one hand against his brow. "You promised you wouldn't harp on that nonsense anymore!"

But she wouldn't be dissuaded. She clung to him even tighter, her face aglow. "The Red Branch had a code, almost like . . . like Arthur's standard of chivalry. No Red Branch knight could ever eat until everyone else had been fed. A Red Branch knight was honor bound to provide for those weaker than he, to give them anything they needed—his spear, his warming fire, the very clothes from his back—just as you gave Mrs. McGinty your cloak!"

He spun around, stalked a few paces away. He winced, realizing the reason her fantasies were so damned terrifying was because she believed in them. "Don't turn this mess into some sort of heroic deed," Ciaran warned. "It was *your* cloak. It didn't mean a damn thing to me."

"But you didn't have anything else to wear!"

Heat seared his cheeks, his mouth curling in a formidable frown. "If I'd been in my right mind, I never would have done it. It was foolhardy. Reckless."

"You would have given that cloak to her no matter what—given her anything, down to your last drop of blood. It's what you were born to do: shield those weaker than yourself."

He wanted to throttle her. He wanted to cover his ears like a witling boy and block out the words. But he only stood, scowling. "I wasn't doing anything except making a complete fool out of myself. Blast, don't you realize how dangerous it was, handing off that cloak like that?"

"No! It was wonderful. Honorable. I knew you were Ciaran—"

He swore under his breath. "I would hope this legendary Ciaran of yours would show more common sense than I did a moment ago! You say it's vital no one knows about me, no one can trace me to Misthaven. Just exactly what do you think will happen when Mrs. McGinty arrives at her daughter's house? Don't you think they'll ask for some sort of explanation as to where she got that cloak? And what will she say? 'From Miss Fallon Delaney and a naked man.'"

He could feel the excitement drain out of Fallon. She stilled, her voice suddenly small. "But . . . But maybe . . . I mean, I can't imagine—"

He plunged on, ruthlessly. "If I *am* some sort of fugitive, my grand heroic gesture might lead this Redmayne person you're so afraid of right to your front door."

"Mrs. McGinty would never do us harm!" She rose to the old woman's defense, as outraged as if she and Maeve were bosom friends and not two strangers who had stumbled across each other on a moonlit road.

"She might not harm us intentionally. But we didn't warn her to keep silent."

Fallon's hand dropped away from him, and he was surprised to find the place it had covered suddenly cold. She caught her lip between her teeth, and Ciaran couldn't help but feel as if he'd kicked a kitten.

After all, crazed though she might be, Fallon had taken him, a complete stranger, under her wing. Invited him into her home. True, she thought he was some magical hero, and yet he'd seen her concern as she bent over Maeve McGinty. Somewhere beneath those dream-addled wits was a generous heart, and a brave one. Who knew how much danger she would incur because of her kindness to him? If it wasn't for Fallon, he'd still be wandering around on that rocky cliff, naked, bewildered, alone.

"Maybe we should go after her. Get a vow of silence—"

Ciaran grimaced. She hadn't said "tell Maeve to keep her mouth shut," or even "ask her to be quiet." No. A vow of silence. As if it were some ancient rite. Legendary heroes, fairy magic, what other nonsense was her imagination stuffed with? Why did some secret part of him almost envy her?

He forced a rare gentleness into his voice. "Chasing after Mrs. McGinty now would only make this seem all the more strange." If it was possible to make things stranger than meeting a naked man and a landholder's sister on a night road.

"No," he insisted, "better to leave it as it is."

He wasn't sure what possessed him to reach out, to touch her cheek. Smooth as new cream it was beneath his fingertips, warm and velvety, scented with heather. So very, very fragile for a world filled with jagged cliffs and battered heads, angry strangers and stormy skies. Her lips parted, her breath caught at that tiny touch, as if it were something rare, something she was unaccustomed to—the brush of someone's fingertips.

Ciaran didn't want to feel empathy for her, but he couldn't help it. Who was she, this fey creature with a woman's body and a child's dreams shining in her eyes? He wanted to cup his palm against her cheek, thread his fingers back into the subtle flame of her hair. But he stayed still, barely touching her.

"Fallon, everything will work out in the end. Maeve's family will be so excited over Bridie's new babe that it will likely take some time for Mrs. McGinty's tale to get back to this Redmayne. We'll just have to make sure that by the time it does, we've discovered who I am."

"Yes. Of course. That's it. Then Redmayne won't be able to hurt you, hurt Misthaven, hurt anyone ever again. You'll understand your destiny. You'll be glad I summoned you back."

Was that what she needed Ciaran of the Mist for? To battle with this Redmayne she so dreaded? What had she done to make such an enemy? How dangerous was he, this Captain Redmayne? And why the devil did he feel a tightening like a noose around his neck whenever he heard that name?

He felt Fallon's hand upon his arm, her grasp eager.

"Just wait, Ciaran. You'll find out who you are, and then everything will be just as I imagined."

"No, Fallon." Ciaran cut her off, turning away from her hope-filled face, unwilling to deceive her. "Then I'll be gone."

CHAPTER

4

ᏻᏯᏒᎹᎤ

Squares of gold lantern light glowed from the stable windows, the musty, warm scent of horses and hay filling Fallon's nostrils as she reined Cuchulain into the shadows at the side of the stables. The horse pricked up his ears, tossing his head as he strained against his reins, eager to return to his oat box and straw bed.

But with each hoof fall bringing them nearer, Ciaran grew more tense, more reluctant.

"Are you sure this isn't going to be a disaster?" he murmured, low in her ear. And she could sense his gaze was fastened not on the stable so near, but rather on the silhouette of Misthaven House on the edge of the hill. "What if someone sees me?"

"If you do as I tell you, no one will. The servants are far too preoccupied with their own work. And Hugh—he'll be locked up in his study or off somewhere tending his precious business interests. There's not the slightest bit of danger."

What was it the priest had said about not daring fate? At that instant, a voice echoed from inside the stables, and hurried footsteps stalked toward the door. "Fallon? Fallon, is that you?"

Hugh! Her stomach plunged, sweat breaking out on her upper lip. What the devil was he doing in the stable at this hour?

She started to shove at Ciaran, warn him to dismount, hide. He'd already sprung from the horse's back with a warrior's instincts. Fallon glimpsed a blur of pale flesh and sinew against the darkness as he dove for the shelter of a hayrick, but it was too late to escape. Hugh stood in the rectangle of the stable door, garbed from head to toe in black as if he were going to a funeral.

Unfortunately, all things considered, it might be Fallon's own. She scrambled to find some explanation as her brother stalked toward her, his usually calm face more thunderous than any of the clouds scudding in from the west. But she was fresh out of good reasons for dragging a half-naked man home as if he were a stray puppy she'd found.

"I–I know this seems odd—" she stammered, "but—"

"Blast it, Fallon, it *is* you, isn't it?" He stepped closer. "I can't see in this benighted dark. Why the devil doesn't Sheehan light a torch or two?"

Fallon sucked in a breath of bone-shattering relief, blessing the head groom for his negligence. Hugh was still blinded, coming from light to darkness. By some miracle, he hadn't seen Ciaran.

Now the trick was to make certain her brother remained ignorant of Ciaran's presence. Desperate to put some distance between Ciaran and herself, Fallon prodded Cuchulain toward Hugh with feigned nonchalance, trying to hide the fact that her heart was in her throat.

"Lovely evening, Hugh," she said, closing the distance. "What are you doing in the stables at this hour? Surely you can't be going out to count your sheep in the dark."

She wanted to taunt him just a little. If he was irritated at her, he'd be less likely to glance around and see something they'd both regret.

Hugh tugged the collar of his riding coat. "There is trouble out at MacDuggan's Quay. With the storm coming, a shipment is in danger."

"Heaven forfend."

Hugh's mouth tightened in a thin white line. "I prefer my sailors on their decks, rather than at the bottom of the ocean. So do their families."

Fallon had the grace to be a trifle ashamed, but she wasn't about to let Hugh know it. His tone was insufferable, quelling, as if she were a naughty child in need of punishment. It only got worse as he continued.

"When I reached the stables, learned that you'd gone out, I was going to ride in search."

Ridiculous notion! The last thing she needed was Hugh trailing after her. It wasn't as if he'd have the slightest chance of finding her! The familiar impatience flared, tinged with shame for her brother. Damn Hugh anyway!

She gritted her teeth, excruciatingly aware of Ciaran hiding behind the hayrick, knowing that the man was listening to the conversation. It made her squirm inside, left her feeling oddly naked. She sought shelter in belligerence.

"You were going in search of me? How strange. I'm amazed you even noticed I was gone. After all, it's not Christmas or my birthday."

Hugh flinched, a heaviness seeming to bow his shoulders. "I know I haven't always done right by you, Fallon, but I was worried. Especially when I heard you were out riding alone at night. The garrison has posted more patrols ever since that Captain Redmayne arrived."

Fallon stifled a shudder at the man's name, and gave a light laugh. "I'll remember to avoid him whenever I'm plotting treason."

"It's not a jest, Fallon. This whole coast has been seething ever since the rebellion was put down. Desperate men, angry men are on the run from the law, men who might hurt you if you saw something they wanted to hide. And that new garrison captain will only make things worse. There's something about him that sets my nerves on edge. He's dangerous. And you're not a child anymore, to run wild around the countryside. Something could happen to you."

Fallon rolled her eyes. "I've met Captain Redmayne. I

hardly think he is the sort who would hurl me down on the heath and have his wicked way with me." But her attempt at humor fell flat as she recalled the probing light in the Englishman's eyes, the way he'd watched her, like a tiger with its prey. Perhaps Redmayne wouldn't fling her down onto the ground to take his pleasure, but he was obviously a man given to more complex, more subtle tortures.

She slid down from Cuchulain and slipped the reins over the stallion's head. "Now, Hugh, if you'll excuse me?"

Her brother stepped in front of her, looming tall and lean, with a quiet intensity. Sometimes it seemed impossible that the same blood flowed through their veins. "Fallon, you can't spend the rest of your life running about the heath. It's time you leave off wild ways. You're twenty-two. A woman."

"You've noticed? Why the sudden interest, brother? Nothing more important to occupy the master of Misthaven's thoughts tonight? No dips in the price of new lambs to fret over?"

She was hurting him. She could sense it in the tightening of Hugh's shoulders, the way his lids lowered to hide his eyes—eyes the color Mama's had been. But blast, she had to get Hugh to leave her in peace. She had to get Ciaran safely into Misthaven House. The longer Ciaran was outdoors, the more danger that he would be discovered.

She couldn't keep the scorn from dripping into her voice. "I've done well enough without your interference in my life thus far, Hugh. I get along fine. You tend to your business dealings, while I—"

"While you what? Wander around the heath barefoot, your hair straggling down like a shepherdess's?"

"It's a little late to start planning teas with the Misses Alberdale, isn't it? Especially considering the disaster it was the last time you stuck your head out of your office long enough to insist I attend one of their fetes."

"You were only eight years old then."

"I was old enough to know I didn't belong there. And the twins never forgave me for dousing their new party frocks in punch." She tried to remember the excruciating pleasure it had given her, to see the golden-curled, pampered darlings of the neighboring gentry dripping in the sticky-sweet mess, red dribbles flowing down their tear-streaked faces, pooling on the exquisite lace their papa had brought them back from Belgium.

Why doesn't your papa bring you back any presents, Fallon? She could still hear their mocking giggles. *Does he think they sticked you in the grave with your mama?*

She'd blamed Hugh for forcing her hand that night, and sometimes she thought he'd blamed himself for the ostracism that followed. Whoever had been at fault, the repercussions of that outing had driven an even deeper wedge between two siblings already impossibly different. Hurt had piled upon hurt until they'd both hoarded their stores of pain in silence, alone, Hugh absorbed in Misthaven, Fallon in her world of legends—two strangers with nothing more in common than a mother's grave.

"Fallon"—Hugh's voice shook her from her dark thoughts—"if you only made an effort, you could charm the gold out of a miser's fist. You're witty and intelligent, and even pretty when you comb the bits of leaf and heather out of your hair. I could try to arrange some invitations. Clarissa Prunty always seemed to like you. You could start by making friends with her."

Fallon grimaced. "That solemn little mouse? She's got all the animation of that bit of barn wood. As for her admiration of me—bah! It was *you* Clarissa liked, Hugh. The way she'd always stand about, blinking those adoring doe eyes at you. It was near revolting."

Color flooded up from Hugh's collar to stain his cheeks. "Don't be absurd," he snapped. "Clarissa Prunty never spoke two words to me."

Fallon gave a snort of disgust. "She never spoke two words to anyone. As for enlarging my social circle, we've discussed this before. I said no. I still feel the same way. You lead your life, I'll lead mine. We're both happy that way."

She shivered suddenly, aware of Hugh's eyes watching her, piercing, strangely haunted. "Are you?" he asked.

"Am I what?"

"Happy?"

The word hung between them, quivering like an arrow's shaft. Fallon was stunned at the sudden lump in her throat. She looked away from him, something in his face leaving her heart raw. "What I am is tired. I'm going up to my rooms to take a hot bath and go to bed."

"You mean you're running away, Fallon. That's what you do every time you race off into the hills. You're just like father, pretending that nothing exists but what you want to see."

Fallon rounded on Hugh, hot fury surging through her veins. "Don't you dare compare me to him!"

"Why not? It's the truth. He just mounted his horse and rode away. Sailed to London and never looked back. God forbid he have to face the fact his wife was dying, his estate was crumbling to ruin and his children were shattered and afraid. I'd wager he was damned relieved when the gin finally killed him."

"I'm not running anywhere! I'm just doing what Mama did. She spent every spare moment wandering about the fields."

"She was going to the cottages, to aid the people there. You could do the same, Fallon. You could take an interest in the estate. Help me. Together we could build Misthaven into something to be proud of."

"Bury myself alive in this place as you do? No, thank you." Fallon led Cuchulain into the circle of light spilling from the stable door. "There is a difference between us, Hugh," she said, passing the reins to an undergroom who loped away with his charge. "You idolize Misthaven. It's your wife, your children, your sister, your friend. For you there's nothing else but the land. Me, I do my best to forget I have any part in Misthaven and all it stands for. This chunk of land isn't worth the price our ancestors paid for it, in my opinion."

"Fallon—"

She turned back to her brother, knowing she should be silent, but unable to be so. The words she had thought for so long, yet never spoken, wouldn't be stopped. "Can I ask you a question, Hugh?"

"I suppose."

"When you ride out over the land with your silver-headed crop tucked under your arm and your boots polished to a gleam, are you ever ashamed? Do you ever think about how the Delaney family betrayed the simple people hereabouts century after century? We're Irish, but we didn't stand with them when they fought for freedom. We compromised, sold our soul, changed our politics. The men, the precious Delaney heirs, even changed their religion when they had to, all to cling to this scrap of land. The glen folk should despise us as much as our English neighbors do."

A lock of dark hair tumbled over Hugh's brow, making him look suddenly boyish, desperately earnest. "I do the best I can to make the crofters' lives better."

Fallon was surprised how much her heart hurt. "How admirable. Of course, it's convenient that their labor keeps a grand roof over our heads, plenty of money in the Delaney coffers and power in our family's hands. Yes, Hugh, you make a praiseworthy sacrifice indeed looking after them."

He looked as if she'd slapped him. But she wasn't sorry—wouldn't let herself be. Everything she'd said was the truth. She only wished that the man still hiding behind the hayrick hadn't heard it.

Hugh turned and walked into the stables. He took the reins of his sturdy mount and swung himself up. "This conversation isn't over, Fallon," he warned. "There are some matters to be settled here. And we *will* settle them." Touching his spurs to the animal's sides, he disappeared into the darkness.

Blast Hugh! She remembered countless times as a little girl when it would have meant the world to her to have her brother's attention for just a little while. But now? Trust cautious, plodding Hugh to wait until it was too late. There was too much hurt between them, and they were both too independent.

Fallon watched in relieved silence until she was certain he was gone and that the grooms had returned to their work. Then she hastened to where Ciaran had hidden.

There was an odd stillness about the man, his lips

69

curved in a thoughtful frown. And she knew, with a sinking sensation in the pit of her stomach, that Ciaran had heard it all, understood it all. She supposed it was against the code of the Red Branch to be disrespectful to one's older brother, no matter what kind of a plodding fool he was.

"Hurry," she urged, leading him through the shadows toward the house. "We can creep in the garden entrance. I always leave it unlocked when I go out wandering. That way, no one will see us."

"Your brother almost did."

Fallon stiffened. "I wasn't worried for a moment," she lied. "Hugh never sees anything that isn't glued to the end of his nose."

They wound through the gardens, redolent with the scent of hawthorn blossoms, holly hedges and boxwood greening. Every shrub and flower was shaped and molded and civilized by the gardener's shears. Yet as Fallon glanced back at the half-naked man shadowing her steps, the trimmed perfection of their surroundings only made him look all the more untamed, as primitive and unpredictable, compelling and perilous as a lion being led about on a blue satin leash.

And as likely to bolt at any moment.

Her brow furrowed, and she cast a nervous glance at Ciaran. The man had been on the verge of running off from the time they were at the castle, in some misguided notion of honor, to preserve her safety. After seeing Hugh and overhearing their conversation, weren't the odds far greater that Ciaran would charge off for the woods the instant he got a chance?

She grabbed his hand, realizing how futile the gesture was. If Ciaran decided to bolt, she'd no more be able to hold him than she could turn the tide. And there was something about feeling that callused palm abrading hers, those long fingers encircling hers, that was devastatingly intimate, stirring an odd heat beneath her skin. A low buzz of tension passed from his hand to hers, tightening her already strained nerves, leaving them humming with discomfort.

At the door, Fallon signaled him to silence, then pushed the panel open. The way her luck had been running, she half expected to find the downstairs maids industriously scrubbing this corridor despite the late hour. But it was reassuringly empty.

Fallon turned to beckon Ciaran inside. She glimpsed his features, so handsome, so still. His gaze was unreadable.

Cautiously, Fallon slipped along the back stairways, astonished at how silently Ciaran traveled along behind her with the stealth of a cat, or was it the hush of a ghost? An odd chill prickled her nape, but she quelled her unease.

Of course he moved quietly. He was barefoot—there were no bootheels to click against the floor. Yet there was something almost unearthly about the way he moved. And something disturbing about his eyes searching, probing as she guided him through corridors with doorways locked shut. Whole wings of the once-elegant manor house were closed up, as quiet and solitary as her mother's grave.

What was he thinking? She felt oddly vulnerable, as if he could draw impressions from the very walls, could feel the unease she had felt as she crept into the chambers as a small girl, certain they were haunted—the holland covers that draped the unused furniture turning into ghosts in her imagination. But not ghosts that rattled chains and shrieked and delighted in terrorizing little girls. No, just shapeless forms that waited as the whole house seemed to wait for Fallon's mother to return and breathe life into them again.

Blast, this was all Hugh's fault. Their rare arguments always made the stillness of the house louder, the emptiness more suffocating, the loss she tried so hard to forget more real.

She bumped into a small table to her left, her nerves leaping at the rattle of china. *For pity's sake,* she upbraided herself. She had to keep her wits about her. What if they ran afoul of a servant while she was woolgathering?

At that instant, she heard a sharp hiss of breath behind her, felt the tension crackling from Ciaran in waves hot as lightning. Panic jolted through her as she wheeled toward him, all but dropping the candle.

She expected to see him surrounded by an army of servants—vigilant footmen with the sights of their pistols trained at his heart, ready to shoot them both as housebreakers.

But the hallway was empty except for her and Ciaran, the glow of the candle, and their reflections doubled in the floor length mirror.

Fist raised as if ready to strike out at some attacker, Ciaran stood frozen, staring at the image of himself—a pale, black-haired stranger glaring back at him from the mirror.

In those astonishing moments at the castle, she'd seen all there was of Ciaran MacCailte—every sinew, every bone, every sleek bit of skin—naked, in all his masculine glory. Yet somehow, the sight of him now made her feel as if she'd intruded, torn back some sacred veil.

She'd seen him angry, seen him confused, filled with pain. But as he stared at his reflection, his long fingers ghosting over the planes of his own face, his eyes raw and searching and hopeless, his very soul seemed laid bare.

The blade-straight nose, cheekbones slashed high like those of a pagan king, square jaw so stubborn, and a mouth that was full and sensitive, sensual and compelling—all might have been carved upon a statue he'd never seen before.

He was a prisoner within that mirror, his very identity held just beyond his reach. And she wondered if he'd looked just so when he'd awakened from eating the enchanted cherries to find himself captive in Tir na nOg.

"Ciaran," she breathed his name quietly, drifting one hand down on his rigid arm. "It's just you—you in the mirror."

His gaze flashed to hers, drowning in hopelessness. "I don't . . . don't remember." The words tore, ragged-edged, from his chest.

Fallon slipped her hand into his, astonished at how cold he'd suddenly grown. "You will remember. Soon.

I'm certain of it. Now, we have to hurry before someone hears us."

It was fortunate they didn't see another soul on their trek to her bedchamber, they were both so shaken by what had just happened.

No maid, no footman, not even a stray mouse stirred anywhere in this wing of the house. She should have been relieved, but the silence only brought home to her how empty the place was, how barren. How dead.

At last, she pushed open the door to her room, and Ciaran followed her in, the dim shadows broken only by the glow of a cheery fire in the hearth.

Fallon locked the door, then fumbled to light a branch of candles, setting the chamber aglow. But the instant the wicks blazed with light, she felt an unreasonable urge to douse them.

It seemed to be a night for stripping the soul bare.

Still ashen, every sinew tense as a whiplash, Ciaran prowled before the silk-papered walls like a feral beast scenting its prey or, more disturbing, a promising mate. He paused to run his fingertips over the dull silver of her mother's hairbrushes, blew softly against the breath of lace at the window.

Edgy, Fallon caught her lip between her teeth, seeing her chamber as if for the first time. The suite of rooms had been little altered since she was a child. There had been no mother to wistfully tuck away abandoned playthings into brass-nailed trunks, no one to guide Fallon through the rite of passage as she became a young woman.

Ciaran's probing gaze skated to where a bedraggled doll, with one arm missing and a badly mended crack in her china face, lay beneath the canopy of Fallon's bed, the plaything resting where it had for seventeen years because the maid had never been given orders to place the doll anywhere else.

Even the bed itself seemed small as Fallon imagined it through this towering man's eyes, the mattress fashioned for a child's length instead of a woman's. What would Ciaran say if he knew the truth—that Fallon could never bear to be parted from it? It had been a gift from her mother, testimony to how well Margaret Delaney had understood her little girl's love of the wild lands beyond her window.

Bedposts, carved to look as if they were saplings, had guarded Fallon's sleep, the canopy draped in clouds of white bed curtains so that she could sleep in a sea of mist. Coverlets the color of heather were crowned with lace-trimmed pillows stuffed with herbs and dried flowers to carry the scent of the hills. Why did the sight of that innocent bed make her cheeks heat with something akin to embarrassment?

Worse still, Ciaran stopped beside a windowseat, its cushions littered with books worn almost beyond repair. Legends and myths, ancient histories and epic poems, they had fed her soul.

Never, in the years since her mother's death, had anyone except the servants entered her room. Not even Hugh. It felt so strange, to have this towering man prowling about, reaching out to touch the gold-embossed cover of *The Ulster Cycle,* an epic tale, one of the oldest poems in the Irish language.

Ciaran had sprung from those pages, alive and vital in her imagination. A man powerful and vulnerable, gloriously handsome. But she'd never suspected he would be imperfect as well, flawed in a way that only made him more appealing.

Fallon winced, almost regretting her decision to bring him here to her room, feeling exposed somehow, as if the very walls were whispering her secrets to him, secrets Hugh had begun to spill in the moonlit stable yard.

She set the candleholder on a piecrust table littered with an army of Gaelic heroes one of the cottagers had carved for her. Suddenly she was eager to distract Ciaran, and herself, from the whisperings of her room.

"I'll just get you settled, then summon up food and a hot bath—" Fallon started to say, then stopped, aware of how intently Ciaran's green eyes were regarding her, his lips curved into a deep frown. She was still stinging from her encounter with Hugh. The last thing she needed was to be pinned by another man's condemning glare.

"What's amiss? You don't care for the color of my room?"

He withdrew his fingertips from the gilt lettering on the book's cover and shrugged. "I hadn't even noticed it."

No. He'd been too busy prying into everything else that belonged to her, touching, examining, sorting her things and her into some kind of order in his mind.

"Then what is it? You look sour as a green apple."

Ciaran's gaze darted to her face, and she wished she'd kept her mouth shut.

"He's right," Ciaran said.

"Wh–what?"

He turned to her, crossing thickly muscled arms over the breadth of his naked chest. "Your brother. He is right. You have no business wandering around alone at night."

It hurt Fallon in ways she hadn't imagined, Ciaran taking up sides against her. *She'd* summoned him back. Wasn't he supposed to have some sense of loyalty to his summoner?

She tossed her head. "I didn't see anyone objecting to the darkness when Hugh decided to go riding."

"That's different."

Her chin bumped up a notch. "Because I'm a woman?"

"No. Because you're a reckless little fool. For all you know, I could be a thief, a murderer just waiting for my chance to strike. Anything could have happened in the time it took us to ride down from that castle. You could be dead. Your brother was worried enough. If he really knew what mischief you've been up to—"

"He'd lock me in a convent school until I was ninety? Don't be fooled by Hugh's illusion of concern. I'm sure it's like an attack of biliousness. It'll be gone soon enough."

"He feels responsible for you. It was obvious—"

"One more burden on the stalwart Hugh's shoulders, another cross to be borne. Bah! I can take care of myself. I've been doing it since I was six years old!"

Unexpected tears stung her eyes. Blinking fiercely, she stalked over to where the secret door was, wanting nothing more than to shove Ciaran inside the priest hole and lock the door. Her fingers trembled with irritation as she worked the hidden latch.

She slid the panel aside with more force than care, the jarring of the door setting the pictures on the wall rattling. "I didn't call you back from the mists of the fairy kingdom to meddle in my private affairs."

"Maybe you should have. It's obvious you're not doing a very good job of managing them yourself."

"I'm not going to discuss my family relationships with you or anyone else, so leave it alone. Just stay in here until I get back."

Yet, as the candleshine poked its fingers into the priest hole, Fallon was tempted to slam the door shut, blocking it from Ciaran's view. If her bedchamber had whispered secret pain, the quiet longings of an abandoned little girl, this hidden chamber fairly screamed them.

Swords made long ago out of sticks stood in one corner, a silver gauze highwayman's mask dangling from the hilts. A crudely fashioned longbow and arrows were cast on the bed beside a dozen crumpled drawings—each bearing the likeness of a rugged warrior holding the hand of a little red-headed girl.

A caricature of the loathsome Misses Alberdale was irreverently tacked to the wall beneath the crucifix, their curls thrusting out as if struck by lightning, their smirks vile, their teeth blacked out by Fallon's pen. An army of bugs brandishing lethal-looking pincers had been sketched trooping up Felicity's arms, while a sly toad peeped out of the tea cake Charity was about to take a bite of.

The bodices of their frilly gowns showed evidence of having been pierced countless times with sharpened-stick arrows, one of which still hung where Fallon had shot it so many years ago.

Even the layer of dust couldn't soften the pain captured in this tiny chamber, pain she'd never allowed another living person to see. The prospect of anyone, especially Ciaran MacCailte, witnessing it was unthinkable.

She was excruciatingly aware of the sudden stillness in Ciaran, and felt his gaze on her. What was he thinking?

She steeled her face into careless lines. "I'll have to lock you in here until I have everything arranged," she said. "The maids will ready a bath."

"Would you mind bringing up something to eat as well? I'm not choosy. Anything that doesn't include a toad would be fine."

It was an attempt at humor. She should have been grateful, and might have been, except that he crossed to the small cot tucked against the outer wall and picked up one of the homemade arrows. He ran his fingers across it, probing as carefully, as insistently as he had to check Maeve McGinty's bones to see if they were broken.

As she slid the secret door shut, Fallon wondered if it was possible to feel the pieces of a little girl's broken heart.

CHAPTER
5

Ciaran paced the narrow confines of the windowless room, his nerves still stinging from the confrontation with Fallon. He didn't know who he was, but in the short time since he'd ridden up to Misthaven House behind a defiant Irish beauty, he'd unearthed more impressions about Mary Fallon Delaney than he'd ever wished to.

A yawning chasm of hurt and loneliness between brother and sister, a young woman lashing out to conceal how badly she needed someone's arms about her, needed to be loved, to belong. A child who had grown into a woman while no one was looking, brave and independent, idealistic and filled with imagination. A stubborn dreamer, determined to grasp her world in her own hands and fight for what she believed in. And she believed in Ciaran of the Mist.

Ciaran closed his eyes, picturing her as she had been when he'd first seen her, surrounded by the shadowy castle walls, almost unearthly in her loveliness, her hair liquid sunset about a heart-shaped face. Her eyes had glowed with passion for life, her lips parted in astonishment, joy—in *welcome*—as if she'd been waiting her whole life for *him*.

She was the kind of woman who needed a hero, not to take her fate out of her grasp, to rescue her from her own helplessness, but rather, to stand at her side as she faced whatever had brought that haunted light to her eyes.

And sometime, during the long ride through the countryside, the encounter with her brother, and the revelations whispered by her chamber—confessions she'd never make aloud—Ciaran had made an incredible discovery of his own.

He'd realized that some part of him, buried deep, wished that he could be that hero for her.

It was a sobering discovery, an unwelcome one. Was it possible that Fallon's fantasies were contagious? That was the only possible explanation for his conflicting emotions.

His thoughts scattered at the sudden sound of the bedchamber door opening, the giggling of two women who must be maids echoing in the room beyond as they busied themselves sloshing what must be hot water into a tub. Ciaran stilled lest they hear him, every sense alert.

"It was a lovely day off work altogether," a rollicking feminine voice observed in a brogue thick enough to spread like sweet cream butter. "In town, I heard the most amusing thing. 'Twas all they're talking of."

"Tell, Sorcha! Tell!" the other maid chimed in.

"Have ye ever heard of old Barrister Fyfe?"

Ciaran rubbed at his temple, his head giving a throb of protest. His brains were muddled enough; the last thing he needed was to be trapped in here listening to servants gossip.

"Who hasn't heard o' the barrister? What a scandal 'twas when he off an married that wife o' his—Vanessa, her name is. Young enough to be his daughter, an' altogether gorgeous she is."

"Not to mention picked fresh out o' a brothel," Sorcha sneered. "Well, Biddy, seems after a taste o' respectability, she missed having company after all those years samplin' men like sweets. She's been availin' herself of any gentleman with breeches that unfasten—even tumbled the Barneses' stable lad, an' he but fifteen years old."

Ciaran's lip curled in disgust, an instinctive recoiling. What kind of woman would dally with a mere boy? Had he known any women like the barrister's wife? If so, he must have felt nothing but revulsion for them.

"Seems Fyfe tired o' being the laughingstock o' Glenceo. Made it known from one end o' the town to the other that the next time he caught a man takin' what was lawfully his, he'd shoot him dead."

"Hope he bought a whole raft o' bullets," Biddy chortled. "He'd have t' cut down half the men in town."

"Arrived home early this afternoon, an' sure enough, heard a commotion. They say she howls like a bitch in heat when she's got 'er legs 'round a handsome man's hips."

Blast, Ciaran thought, would the women never make an end of it and leave the infernal room? Years' accumulation of dust tickled his nose, and he fought to stifle a sneeze. If he didn't, it would be a calamity damned hard to explain. Of course, in a household where legendary heroes could be summoned at a snap of the fingers, a sneezing wall might draw no comment at all.

"Did Fyfe shoot her lover?" Biddy demanded with bloodthirsty eagerness.

"Fired a shot, but he was too fast for the barrister. They grappled, and then the lover leaped out of a second-story window."

"Saints afire! Who was it? Did he break his neck?"

"Nobody knows who it was for certain. A stranger 'e was. But the fall didn't kill him, nor the bullet either. Left a smear o' blood on the pavement. But by the time the barrister got t' the street, he was gone. Fyfe tore about the town, searching everywhere for 'im, but there was no sign o' Vanessa's lover anywhere."

"Probably just melted into the crowd. It would be easy enough to disappear, I guess."

A sly laugh trilled out. "Somehow, I doubt that, lass. See, when the gentleman leapt from the window he forgot something—his clothes. Vanessa's lover was naked as a newborn babe."

Ciaran's breath froze in his lungs, every muscle in his body tight with denial.

"Go on! Ye're lyin'!" Biddy gasped.

"I swear by the veil o' the Blessed Virgin 'tis the God's truth. Those who saw the whole happening did say he was a fine specimen, handsome as sin, with the broadest shoulders they'd ever seen and a shock o' black hair."

Throat thick with revulsion, Ciaran's numb fingers touched the shaggy ends of his own dark mane. No . . .

"But his face—what did he look like?"

"Ye know how particular Vanessa Fyfe is about her gents. Probably handsome as the devil an' twice as wicked. But as for what 'e looked like, well . . . th' only good description they could offer was o' the man's bum. A fine one it was, too. An' don't ye be gaspin' in shock, Biddy Murphy. Tell me true, if ye'd been there on that street an' a bare-naked man had gone runnin' past, where would *ye* have been lookin'?"

Laughter swelled up again amidst a clank of metal. Ciaran felt ill. Was it possible that he was the man in the maid's sordid tale? He closed his eyes, envisioning the scene she'd described far too clearly—the vulgarity of it, the lewdness.

Bedding another man's wife, being caught by the husband, then not even having enough honor to face the man he'd wronged. Instead, leaping from a window and fleeing like the basest coward, naked, through the streets.

The mere thought he might have been involved in such a disaster made his skin crawl. Was it possible that he was the mysterious lover this barrister Fyfe had chased? He wanted to thrust the thought away, deny it, and yet, it was a far more likely explanation than Fallon's story that he was some nine-hundred-year-old hero come back from the fairy mists.

If he'd been shot at and grappled with a cuckolded husband, then leaped from a window, wouldn't that explain how he'd injured his head? And if he'd been fleeing this Fyfe blindly, with no notion where he was going, no need except to get away, wasn't it possible that he might have strayed up to that abandoned castle?

How he'd come to have the Celtic dagger he couldn't guess. Might it have been a letter opener or some such he'd grabbed up from a nearby table when he should have been grabbing his breeches?

He grimaced. He should have been relieved that his plight was making a trifle more sense, that this might be the rational explanation he'd been searching for. Instead, he felt soiled somehow, tainted. He wanted nothing more than to recoil from the thought and blot it from his mind.

In the hours since he'd found himself wandering the jagged cliffs, he'd been willing to sell his soul to find his own identity. It had never occurred to him that he might not like the man he found when he regained his memory.

He winced inwardly, feeling as if he'd failed Fallon already. It was so easy to recall the light in Mary Fallon Delaney's eyes when she'd looked at him, her Ciaran of the Mist, a legend come to life.

What would happen to the unshakeable faith in her animated features if she discovered the truth? If he was the man who had bedded Fyfe's wife, a wastrel whose only virtues were loose morals, lust and cowardice, wouldn't it be best to leave Misthaven House as soon as possible and disappear into the mist from which he'd come before he could hurt her even more? Before he could endanger her brother and all who lived here?

He couldn't stop himself from flattening his palms on the sliding door, wishing he could just shove it aside, stalk past the astonished servants and leave before he ever had to look her in the eye again. But the fates weren't disposed to be that merciful.

"Miss Fallon," Sorcha piped up, suddenly a study in innocence, "is there anything in that bundle I can be helpin' ye with? Some mendin', or—"

"No." There was a hasty click of some sort of door, as if she were shoving whatever she held out of sight. "You needn't trouble yourselves."

He could hear the puzzled undertones in the servant's voice. "Your bath is ready. Let me just help with your gown, and we'll have ye plunged in there in a trice."

"No. I mean, no thank you. I don't need any help with my bath tonight. You can go now."

"But—but your gown—ye can't get it off without help."

"How stupid of me. You're right." Fallon hesitated, and Ciaran knew she was thinking of him, hidden away in the priest hole.

"Miss Fallon, are ye feelin' well? Ye look exhausted entirely."

He could sense Fallon gathering up her frazzled nerves, determined not to alert the servants that there was anything amiss. "I'm only tired. If you'll just help me slip into my dressing gown, I'll have a bite to eat first, then take my bath."

He heard a rustle of cloth, was able to imagine the maids making quick work of the fastenings of Fallon's gown, slipping the fabric off her shoulders, but no matter how he searched, there was no clear image to go with those actions, as if he'd never—what? Undressed a lady? If what the maids claimed was true, he'd doubtless disrobed more than his share.

"If you eat first, the water'll be cool by the time you're ready for it. I could bring some more hot—"

"I just wish to be left alone tonight," Fallon snapped. From the stunned silence on the servant's part, Ciaran knew it was uncommon for her to do so.

"Yes, miss. Forgive me for intrudin', miss."

"I'm sorry, Biddy, Sorcha. But I . . ."

But I what? Ciaran waited with grim irony for her explanation. *I have a nine-hundred-year-old hero locked up in the priest hole, and he's proving to be dashed recalcitrant.*

There was a shuffle of feet, the soft closing of the door. Then, after a moment, he heard the metallic click of a lock being thrown home.

Footsteps marched quickly to where he was hidden, then the panel slid wide.

He hadn't wanted to face her anyway, since he'd come to suspect the ugliness he'd been involved in. But it was even harder as he stared at her now.

The travel-stained gown had been swept away. A dressing gown of sea-foam green draped her slender body. His breath caught in his throat, a crushing yearning taking him completely by surprise. From the instant she'd barreled into his life, Ciaran had tried to shove her away, wanting nothing to do with her. It had been far easier to imagine she was touched in the head somehow, a wild, fey thing he needed to escape from.

But now that he was certain he needed to leave as soon as possible, she stood before him, as fresh and new and beautiful as the first blush of spring—vulnerable despite the stubborn jut to her chin, strong in spite of the fairy tales that dwelled in her eyes. He didn't want to hurt her. He knew that he would.

"It's safe to come out now," she said.

But Ciaran realized with a dull pain that it wasn't safe for him to be anywhere near her.

"There's a tray from the kitchen, a bath ready. Fetching as you look in Mrs. McGinty's shawl, I thought you'd need some other clothes, so I rummaged in the attic and found some of my father's. They won't be perfect, but they're far more likely to fit than Hugh's."

"Thank you." He stepped out into the chamber again, saw the hip bath steaming before the fire.

"I'll just . . . just step in here to give you some privacy," she said, collecting a book and starting toward the priest hole. Yet Ciaran sensed a reluctance in her, as if there were ghosts inside the tiny nook she was too tired to confront. Hadn't she already endured enough discomfort because of him?

"It's cold in there, with enough dust to choke a dray horse."

"I don't mind. I—"

"Don't be stubborn, Fallon. After all, it's a little late to worry about preserving modesty between us. Crawl under your coverlets where you can be warm, and doze."

Filled with longing and discomfort she cast a glance at her bed. It must be damned odd for her, having a man traipsing about.

He forced his lips into a teasing smile. "I'll trust your word of honor you won't take any unseemly peeks at me."

She sighed, surrendered. "All right. I'll just wash up at the basin—"

"I wish you'd take the bath—"

"You're covered in blood and smell like a wet dog. You'll be doing me a courtesy to take a dip in the tub. Call it a gesture of chivalry."

She set down the book, then started across the room to where a white china pitcher and bowl, edged in tiny meadow flowers, stood on a marble-topped stand.

Once her back was to him, Ciaran unknotted the heathery shawl and let it drop to the floor, then lowered himself into the tub. Steaming water lapped against his aching muscles as he folded his long body so that as much as possible was submerged. A washcloth and soap lay near at hand. He should lather the cloth, begin washing away the grime coating his skin.

But no matter how hard he scrubbed, he doubted he would ever be able to wash away the things that were truly chafing him: the stain of the man he likely was, the ugliness he would probably find along with his identity, the feeling that he'd failed this woman, with her generous heart and that fierce believing he envied with every fiber of his being.

He was tired, sick at heart, a knot of dread sinking in his stomach like a stone. And he felt far more naked beneath Fallon Delaney's gaze than any stripping away of clothes could have made him.

He closed his eyes, leaning his head back against the rim of the tub. Restless as his thoughts were, he shouldn't have been able to sleep. But he must have dozed off.

The next thing he knew there was something warm and sweet-smelling and damp gliding over his face: woman's hands plying a washcloth. Why was it that a touch—the touch of another human—was so precious it made his chest ache? He came fully awake with a start, staring into the vulnerable oval of Fallon's face.

"Wh–what the blazes are you doing?"

"Helping you wash."

He grabbed at the washcloth, his cheeks burning, but

not from embarrassment, rather from chagrin that her touch had felt so soothing, so right. And that he knew he had no right to accept it. "I can do it myself."

"You're bruised all over. It must hurt to move. Besides, you can't even see where your head is gashed. You might break it open again. Jesus, Mary and Joseph, but I hate obstinate men."

She surprised a smile out of Ciaran. "I thought that was exactly the kind of man you admired—bullheaded stubborn hero types who would endure any amount of pain for their lady fair."

"I'm not your lady, and bullheadedness isn't heroic. It's annoying." Was that a smile playing about her lips? "I've already seen you wearing nothing but mist. And my brother always insists that I have a rare gift for refusing to see things that are right before my nose if I don't want to. I definitely don't want to see you."

With a groan, he surrendered the cloth again. "All right, you can help around the gash, but that's all." It seemed such a simple thing, a sensible thing for her to do, and surely the pain would distract him from any stirrings of response. It wasn't as if he was attracted to Fallon. She wasn't the type of woman he favored. He grimaced. Of course, he hadn't the slightest idea what type of woman he did find appealing.

She knelt beside the tub, angled so her hands could reach his face easily. Candlelight played across her features—cheekbones astonishingly elegant, a slightly upturned nose sprinkled with a faint dusting of cinnamon-colored freckles, fine black brows accenting eyes deep and luminous as rain-washed violets. Earnest, she was so earnest as she cupped his jaw in one palm and dabbed at his face with the other hand.

Slow strokes, careful strokes, warmed by the heated water. It felt too good, soothing the battered places on his face, reaching deeper still to bruised places, lonely places in his soul.

He was almost glad when she grazed close enough to the gash to cause him pain. A breath hissed between his teeth, and he clenched his jaw, holding himself rigid as she gently probed at the wound.

"I'm sorry. I know this must hurt."

"Heroes feel no pain."

"You're mocking me. Don't. I'm afraid that . . . that this is my fault. I got impatient and threw a stone—"

"You really did hit me in the head with a rock?" His eyes popped open, a surge of hope making him sit up, suddenly eager. If that was true, then maybe he wasn't the lascivious cad the maids had gossiped about. Maybe there was some other, far less repugnant explanation for the predicament he'd awakened in. A grim laugh echoed inside him. An explanation for a grown man running about the countryside stripped to his skin?

"I didn't hit *you* with the rock. Not exactly. When I placed the magic cloak pin on the hearth and tried to summon you, nothing happened at first. No one ever told me how long it would take you to answer the call. I was so disappointed, so frustrated, that I . . . ." She swallowed hard and continued, "I picked up a stone and hurled it at the brooch. That's when it happened—the fire from the jewels, the moonlight shifting, and then you walking out of the mist, your head gashed and bleeding. It's my fault you were hurt."

There was such remorse in her features, Ciaran bit back an oath of bitter disappointment. Damn her for staring down at him, a plea for forgiveness in her eyes.

"You didn't cause this cut. None of this is your fault. It's my own accursed stupidity that landed me in this disaster. If I'd never—" He stopped.

"Do you remember something?" Exhaustion vanishing from her eyes, she plunked the washcloth into the tub, managing to splash a wave of soapy water across the front of her nightgown.

She looked so beautiful, so fragile despite her outward strength. There was no way he could tell her the ugly truth he'd unearthed from servant's gossip. Not even to drive away the guilt that racked her features. The possibility of seeing her hero worship crumble into disgust was more than he could endure.

"No. I don't remember anything. It's just that I'm certain you didn't cause this." He was stammering, tripping all over himself. It was true enough: he didn't remember what had happened at Vanessa Fyfe's bedchamber. But he didn't have to remember it for it to be glaringly true. And it was a truth Fallon must never discover.

Why the devil it was suddenly important to him to keep that light in her eyes was beyond his comprehension. Hadn't he been doing his damnedest to make her face reality from the first moment she'd spun out this impossible legend and pitched him in the middle of it?

She sighed, then dipped the cloth back into the water and freshened it with more soap. Leaning closer, she began on his chest, slick sweeps along his collarbone and down his ribs, sweeps that distracted him with the accidental brush of a fingertip, the side of her hand, against him, skin to skin.

Each slight contact made him edgy, made him want, made him wait for the next touch, the next brush of her breath across his skin, the next teasing whisper of her silky hair feathering against him.

He should stop this. Nothing that felt this good could be right. He would stop her, after just a moment more—a moment to store up the feeling of being touched.

"You will remember everything soon. I just know it." Was there a tightness in her voice? The tiniest tremor? "And once you do, everything will be fine."

"Fallon, I don't think—"

The tender flesh of her inner arm grazed the point of his nipple, sensations jolting through him like a lance. Pleasure. Need. Hunger. It stole his breath away, along with his will to end this subtle torment.

"You must have been some kind of warrior. There are scars."

"There are a hundred less noble ways I could have gotten them." Like leaping out windows to avoid jealous husbands.

The cloth moved from the hair-roughened wedge on his chest, inexorably down the flat plane of his stomach. It was as if she were on a mission of discovery, learning the shape, the planes and hollows of his body at the same time he was. She was quiet now, so very quiet, as if the intimacy of what they were doing had stolen her voice.

Hastily, a little clumsily, she moved to the corded sinews of his calves, his thighs, and as she came to his feet, delicately dabbing at each toe, he was damned sure the woman had refined the art of torture to new heights.

But it was when she began to dampen his hair, to work suds through the longish strands, that Ciaran's meager hold on his self-control threatened to snap altogether.

No cloth, now, between her fingers and his scalp, her full lower lip caught between small white teeth, her dewy soft forehead puckered in concentration as she stroked and smoothed the lather into his scalp.

The sensation—strange and new and precious—took his breath away, an odd reaction for a man so depraved he had just leaped from a wanton lover's window. Yet with his memory gone, this might as well have been his first time beneath a woman's delicate hands. And a part of him wanted, needed desperately to savor it before all the tawdry, cheap lewdness of the man he had been came spilling back to taint his memory.

The scent of her filled his head as she worked. She was so close now, the fullness of her breast was mere inches from his lips. He tried to shove the sight of it from his mind, but his appetite wouldn't be stilled. He trembled with the knowledge that he only had to lean forward just a whisper to taste her through the damp material of her nightgown.

His shaft hardened beneath the meager veil of water. Bloody hell, what kind of lascivious monster was he, lusting after this innocent woman who had taken him in, an angry and battered stranger? This woman who trusted him?

His fingers shot out, manacling her wrist, shoving her away from him. "That's enough."

"But your hair—we need to rinse it."

With an oath, Ciaran ducked his head under the surface of the water. Pity was, the tub was too shallow to drown himself in. Soapy water stung his head wound, but he was damned certain that if he were flogged to within an inch of his life he wouldn't have suffered enough for taking advantage of Fallon this way.

He levered himself out of the water as if it had

suddenly started to boil. Turning his back on her, he grabbed up one of the generous towels and wrapped it around his waist.

Damn, what had he been thinking, letting her bathe him that way? By morning he'd be gone. This was his only chance to be touched by Mary Fallon.

"Did I do something wrong? Did I hurt you?"

"No." Ciaran ground out.

She'd done everything far too right, and given him the sweetest pain he could imagine. More guilt to carry with him when he left—and yet, he couldn't regret it had happened.

Damn, he needed to get dressed, to put sturdy, practical cloth between him and this fairy maiden before—before what? Before he kissed her? Tumbled her as if she had no more virtue than the likes of Vanessa Fyfe?

Drying himself with another towel, he spoke. "You said you'd brought me something to wear?"

"My father's things. I put them in the armoire." She crossed to the piece of furniture and opened its doors. Feminine things spilled out, holding the scent of last summer's wildflowers, as if the cloth itself had steeped itself in the meadows she loved.

Mary Fallon of the Mist—a woman of dreams with legends in her blood and magic stroked into every curve of her face. The name "of the Mist" suited her far better than it suited him.

After a moment, she returned to him, facing him with eyes oddly heavy, misty, lips far riper than they had been before she'd put her hands on him in the tub.

She'd been affected by it, too. The knowledge rocketed through him. How could she not have been—a woman with Fallon's thirst for life, her passion, her quicksilver emotions?

He took the bundle of clothes, dragging on the shirt as if it were made of a chain mail that could banish the feel of her skin against his.

"While I was downstairs, I stopped in the library. There were some medical books there."

"Medical books?" Ciaran dragged on a pair of

breeches. "Don't tell me. You're studying to be a doctor to wayward fairies?"

"No. My father had them sent here when my mother first got sick. I think he hoped he could do something to cure her. When he found out he couldn't, he left Misthaven, left all of us and never came back."

"He never attempted to contact you?"

"I was eleven when we got word he had died."

"I'm sorry."

"Don't be. It should have been more painful than it was. But it was as if we'd already buried him the day we put Mama in her grave." She flushed, looked away. "Anyway, I looked up head wounds in the book, to find out how to treat them, and it says it's important that the patient not be allowed to fall asleep for long periods. Otherwise, you might slip into a stupor."

Her resourcefulness amazed him, her caring awed him, as did the quick intelligence that shone in her eyes. Was there anything the woman hadn't thought of?

Yes, Ciaran thought grimly. She hadn't considered that the "hero" she'd rescued might be a lecherous cad.

Fallon fidgeted with the rose ribbon tied at the throat of her nightgown, and Ciaran had to tear his gaze away from the silky hollow of her throat.

"Reading about that reminded me of the time I fell out of a tree and landed on my head."

"Ah, so that's what happened to you," he grumbled. "No wonder you woke up seeing fairies around every corner."

"Nurse slept beside me all night, awakening me every so often to make certain I was still all right. Not that anyone could have slept, what with the way she snored." Fallon was blushing, suddenly nervous, yet determination was stroked into the line of her creamy jaw.

"You need someone to awaken you tonight. I thought that if you and I slept . . . well, in my bed, that I'd be able to watch over you."

Had the woman lost her mind? "Absolutely not!" Ciaran snapped, imagining all too clearly what a night beside Fallon would be like. Heaven. Hell. Her warm, sleepy body close enough to touch. Dream shadows flickering across her beautiful features. Dreams he could never have.

"You're fully dressed, Ciaran. It's not as if there's any danger of anything happening. You're the most noble knight of the Red Branch Ireland has ever known."

Ciaran winced. If she only knew the truth. No. That was the one thing Fallon must never learn. "I'll be fine in the priest hole. Just get under the coverlets, Fallon. You look tired to death."

"I am tired. That's why I thought it would be better if you were close by, so I didn't have to trek to the priest hole and back so many times."

"You don't have to take care of me any more. I'm fine."

"No, you're not." She looked so sad and wise. "And neither am I. Is it so terrible not to want to be alone for just a little while?"

What had it cost her to let him glimpse the sorrow inside her, the loneliness? This woman who was so brave, so proud, so giving?

He should stay as far away from her dreamer's eyes and her innocent body as possible. And yet, she suddenly looked so small, so fragile, reminding him of everything he'd lost somewhere on those jagged cliffs, of what he would lose the instant he went to Vanessa Fyfe's. Borrowed honor Fallon had given him, a second chance at the innocence he must have squandered long ago.

It would be for only a few hours, until he slipped away. Would it be so terrible to lie down with her for a little while?

"I'll lie with you."

She slipped between the coverlets and reached to blow out the candle.

"No," Ciaran said hastily. "Leave it." *So I can use it to slip out of here the instant you're asleep.* Guilt stung him. What would she think when she awoke to find him gone? How would she feel? Hurt? Betrayed? Abandoned?

He hadn't even asked why she'd summoned Ciaran of the Mist. That in itself should be proof enough that he was no hero. For an instant, the question hovered on his lips, but he crushed it ruthlessly. No. What could he do to help her anyway? He couldn't even help himself. And knowing what troubled her could only make it harder to leave.

He lay down beside her, making certain a hand's width divided them, determined not to so much as brush her with the tip of a finger.

"Fallon, I . . . I just wanted to thank you for everything you've done for me. It's a rare woman who would take in an injured stranger, especially one as surly as I've been."

"It's the least I could do. I mean, I'm responsible for bringing you here. You belong to me in a way."

Belong. Why did that word unleash such a hunger in him? Had he ever belonged anywhere? To anyone? The only thing he was certain of was that he could never belong to the woman gazing up at him with the light of angels in her eyes.

"You deserve a Ciaran of the Mist. I wish I—" he stopped. Damn, there was so much he'd never be able to tell her, and yet he couldn't walk away without knowing she was safe. "You must have summoned this Ciaran for some purpose. You're not in danger, are you? In trouble?"

"No. You could never be called for such a paltry reason. But of course, when you get your memory back, you'll remember that. Your magic is meant for a greater use than just one person's problems."

Relief swept through Ciaran. Whatever was wrong, it wasn't some personal threat to her. She was safe enough, wasn't she?

Fallon smiled, and Ciaran felt it like a lance to the heart. "When Mama gave me the brooch, she made me promise not to summon you to, shall we say, help slip toads into tea cakes. Calling you back isn't without its dangers. If my cause is not deemed worthy, I will have broken my trust, wasted a chance that won't come again for three hundred years. But worst of all, the fairies will be angry, and exact their revenge."

Fairies again. And the woman simply glowed with earnestness. Damn if she couldn't almost make him believe . . . No. He didn't believe in anything so incredible. And yet, there was no question that Mary Fallon Delaney believed everything she'd told him. The fairies and curses and enchanted cherries were as real to her as the pert, freckle-spangled nose on her earnest face.

He couldn't stop himself from probing deeper. "If it's so dangerous, and if you aren't in danger, then why—"

"Why did I call you back? We've fought countless revolutions in Ireland. We've been trying to keep up our courage, our hope. And somehow, no matter what the English did to subdue us, we've managed to do so. But if Redmayne has his way, I'm not certain we will still be able to. Redmayne has devised the most fiendish scheme of all, one that just might destroy the very soul, the will to fight, that we've clung to no matter what the English tried to do to crush us."

"I don't understand. What plan?"

"To destroy anything that might remind the Irish of their past strength. You want to know why I summoned you?" She sucked in a steadying breath. "To save your castle. Redmayne threatened to shove it off the cliff."

"You mean that heap of rubble where you first found me?" He grimaced. "My castle is past saving. Even with my head broken open, I could see that. It looks ready to crumble into the sea of its own accord. What difference can one more tumbledown wreck of a ruin make?"

She looked aghast. "But surely you must know what that castle means to people hereabouts. That's why you returned to build it—so they would never forget who they are, where they come from, that the blood of heroes flows in their veins."

"Fantasies. Dreams."

"When that's all people have left, it means everything to them. Those dreams and the Castle of the Dancing Mist is all they have, all I've had for so very long. Hugh thinks it's a great favor just to preserve their livelihoods. They need so much more. I've always felt as if . . . as if it was my duty to preserve something, too. As if I were the keeper of their dreams."

Ciaran thought for a long moment, then frowned. "Have you ever considered that it might be cruel to these people you love so much, making them cling to everything they've lost, a greatness they can never have again?" If he could have snatched the words back, he would have. Distress rippled across her face.

"You're wrong about that, Ciaran," she said fiercely, but after a moment, the storm in her eyes calmed, understanding and empathy taking the place of dismay. "Don't worry," she soothed. "It will be all right. When you remember, everything will make sense to you." She gave him a brave little smile. "Ireland would not be Ireland without magic. Just think how empty a place it would be without you."

Without him? Ciaran thought bitterly. It would probably be a damned sight better off. And yet, how precious would it be to have the power to believe as Fallon did? As these people she loved did? Tales stored up like riches, a treasure of the heart. Was it possible that such things could be more valuable to Fallon's simple Irish folk than full bellies and warm cloaks?

God, how he wished he understood. But he didn't belong here, with Fallon, or with the folk who dreamed in the castle by the sea. He didn't belong anywhere at all.

Despair rose inside him in a sobering tide, leaving him aching, more alone than ever.

Fallon turned her face up to his, candlelight gleaming in her eyes—eyes that echoed the yearning in Ciaran's own soul.

He gathered her in his arms, her head resting on his chest. He stroked her hair softly, ever so softly, holding her as he sensed no one had held Mary Fallon Delaney in a very long time.

She was asleep far too soon.

Surprisingly reluctant, Ciaran disentangled himself from the sleeping lady and eased himself off the bed. He should have just grabbed up the candle and strode from the room. He should have escaped as quickly and quietly as possible.

Instead, Ciaran surprised himself by leaning over Fallon's sleeping form and drifting a kiss soft as the brush of butterfly wings across lips that tasted like every dream he'd forgotten.

"Good-bye, Mary Fallon," he whispered. "Someday I hope you find your hero." Aching, he straightened silently and slipped from the room, leaving the legend behind him.

CHAPTER

6

Fallon jolted awake. He was gone. Only the hollow in the pillow beside her and the ragged heap of Maeve McGinty's shawl assured her that last night hadn't been a dream.

The living satin of his bare chest beneath her cheek, the throb of his heartbeat, the soothing sweep of his fingers against her hair had been real. *Real.*

He'd been so warm with his arms circled around her, his breath stirring the wisps of her hair. She'd needed to feel his arms around her. And somehow, she'd sensed, he needed her as well.

She should have scrambled to her feet, searched for him, hoping against hope he'd gone back to the priest hole, but she didn't bother to do so. There was no point. She knew he was gone in a way that supplanted sight.

Now, with morning light streaming through the window and the room empty except for the echoes of his voice, his touch, his pain, Fallon felt as though some irreplaceable part of her had been torn away.

God above, had she made some sort of mistake? Broken some sort of fairy rule? Had Ciaran only been hers for that one brief night—and she'd wasted it, lying in his arms? No. He'd managed to build the castle on one of his previous visits. Surely that had taken months—years.

Had the quest she'd offered him been judged unworthy? Her heart sank as she recalled his confusion, his reluctance when she'd tried to explain how important the ruined castle was to the people of Glenceo.

She climbed out of bed, painfully aware that the faint scent of wind and sea, fresh soap and a masculine essence all Ciaran's own clung to the folds of her nightgown. She stumbled to where the heathery shawl lay and scooped it into her arms, pressing it against her breasts. Tears stung the edges of her eyelids. "You promised you'd stay, you'd help me, Ciaran. The legend—"

"Miss Fallon?"

Fallon all but leaped out of her skin as the bedchamber door swung open and Sorcha appeared with a tray of steaming chocolate in her hands.

Unlocked. The door was unlocked! Last night she'd secured it from the inside. That could only mean Ciaran had left that way. Relief and irritation warred inside her at the knowledge that no magic had swept him away. Damn the man. He'd gone of his own free will. But why? And where had he gone to?

She rushed to the window and peered out, hoping . . . for what? To find that he'd left her a trail of polished stones to follow? There was no trace of him—only Hugh's precious green fields flowing on forever.

"Miss Fallon, is there something amiss?"

Fallon stiffened. There was something strange in Sorcha's voice—astonishment, a kind of questioning, and unabashed admiration.

"Yes! I mean, no. I–I just misplaced something." Fallon whirled to face her. The maid's keen gaze fastened on the shawl until it burned like fire in Fallon's hands. She fought the urge to stuff it behind her back like a guilty child.

Instead, she went to the bed and laid it on the tumbled coverlet. Tactical error number two. Could the maid tell

Fallon hadn't slept alone? Two distinct outlines were etched in the feather bed—or was it just her own vivid imagination? Would she see Ciaran there from now on, his dark hair tousled on her pillow, his sun-bronzed body forever imprinted within her bed?

"I, uh, had a rather restless night," Fallon faltered, smoothing up the coverlets, as if by doing so she could obliterate her own imaginings, and any Sorcha might have entertained as well.

But she wished she'd gathered up the whole feather tick, coverlets and all, and stuffed them in the fire when she heard Sorcha's quiet inquiry.

"Miss, there's blood on the edge of the sheet. Did you hurt yourself?"

"No, I just . . . It's my time—" Blast, hopeless. Her flux had come just over a week ago, and there was no hiding such rhythms of the body from one's personal maid.

Disbelief registered in Sorcha's shrewd eyes, but the servant would never dare to question her, whatever she might think. Anyway, she didn't have time to worry about what this particular maid thought of her. She had to get dressed, set out in search.

"I don't care for any chocolate this morning. Just help me dress. And hurry. I–I've misplaced something, and I need to find it as quickly as possible."

Chocolate was abandoned, a froth of petticoats and shift appearing as if by magic in Sorcha's hands. "Would you like me to help you search? If you can tell me what you've lost—"

Six feet four inches of legendary hero who spent the night in my bed—

"No. Thank you. He—" She winced at her slip. "It's a personal matter." Her cheeks flamed, and she dove under the folds of muslin, grateful for a few seconds to compose herself.

"I understand," Sorcha said, so noncommittally that Fallon was suddenly very afraid that she did. Nimble fingers garbed Fallon in a lilac pink walking dress, then fastened the buttons up her rigid back.

As she jammed feet into stockings and half boots, she glimpsed Sorcha's piquant face and saw something new and unexpected in the maid's eyes. Was it admiration?

She barely bothered to brush her hair, just bundled it under a bonnet, then hurried to the door.

"Miss Fallon?"

She wanted to curse at the maid but didn't dare stir up her suspicions any more. She paused, turned, winced at the *knowing* evident in Sorcha's eyes.

"If I were going to search for what you're missing, I would go in the direction of the village."

"You mean you . . . you saw—"

Sorcha lowered her gaze and nodded.

Fallon had always heard the other servants muttering that Sorcha could smell a handsome man a mile away. She should have been appalled that a maid knew she'd had a man in her bedchamber the night before. She *would* be—later. For now, she could only be grateful she had somewhere to begin her search.

"One good thing, miss," Sorcha said. "Something that fine on the eyes could hardly just disappear without anyone noticing him . . . er, it."

That was true enough at least. Fallon turned and hastened out the door, racing toward the stables as if the hounds of the fairy king were snarling at her heels.

Fallon leaned low over her horse's neck, disheartened as the village of Glenceo rose up before her. Not a sign of Ciaran had she seen as she'd ridden along the track of road. She'd hoped against hope she would find him before she reached the town, aware that there would be countless places he could disappear in the maze of thatched cottages and stone buildings, places she might not be able to find him.

And to search for him there would unleash a nightmare of questioning faces, puzzled frowns and whispered rumors. The thought of questioning the townsfolk made her stomach clench.

Did you by any chance see a man breathtaking as a sea cliff in a storm? He left my bed last night, and I haven't been able to find him.

Any query she made about a man would start a deluge of gossip—gossip she could only pray that Sorcha wouldn't feel the urge to embellish.

Fallon shoved away the prospect grimly. She'd find some way to deal with all that later. Now the only thing that mattered was finding Ciaran. But where to start?

She urged Cuchulain forward, scanning the streets and windows. But only the honest, simple faces of the townspeople met her eyes. If a stranger the like of Ciaran had come striding through the village, wouldn't there be some sign of it, some impression? What if he hadn't come this way at all, and she'd wasted precious time on a wild-goose chase?

No. She had to calm herself and make a thorough search of the area. There was time enough to panic if she didn't find him. She was about to rein the stallion down one of the side roads to begin a methodical inspection of the village when she heard the sounds of a commotion a few streets away.

Angry voices, shouts. Her heart sank, and she urged Cuchulain toward the noise. A blur of eager faces greeted her. A sizable crowd had gathered before a redbrick housefront, and an altercation was taking place on its front porch.

From her perch on the horse's back, Fallon could see past the ocean of heads and shoulders to where a distraught woman shrieked and sobbed, and a bantam rooster of a man with thinning, carrot-colored hair battled with all his might against the iron grip of a man twice his size.

Ciaran. Fallon's heart thudded against her ribs in recognition. God above, he was in the midst of a fight! But the thought had barely formed when she realized Ciaran was merely holding his assailant at arm's length by a handful of collar, the planes and angles of his perfectly honed body just beyond the furious little man's reach.

"No! No!" the woman wailed, dragging at the bantam rooster's sleeve. "Norton, stop this madness!"

"I'll kill him! I vow it! You took him to your bed! I saw him!"

Fallon scrambled down from the saddle and started shoving her way through the mob. She'd never spoken to either the red-faced man or his wife, but in that frozen instant she knew who they were: Norton and Vanessa Fyfe, Glenceo's most scandalous couple, responsible for the most feverish bout of gossip the village had ever known. Even Fallon had heard about the notorious appetites of Vanessa Fyfe for handsome men, an appetite unhindered by anything so paltry as her marriage vows.

No. There had to be some mistake. It was impossible that Ciaran knew the Fyfes. Impossible.

"If he hadn't leapt from the window we would have finished it last night!" the bantam's shout rang out. "Bastard! You cursed bastard! Cuckolding Norton Fyfe!"

Fallon shouldered her way past a baker's flour-dusted bulk, a hostler's lean frame, reeking of horse dung.

"I've never seen this man before!" Vanessa's denial pierced the murmur of the spectators. She glimpsed Ciaran through a maze of limbs.

"Are you certain?" Ciaran demanded fiercely, casting the woman a glance that should have shattered the stone wall behind her. "Damn it, I need the truth! I must have been here. It's the only reasonable explanation—"

"Are you out of your mind?" The wild-eyed woman shrilled. "Look at Norton! He'll . . . He'll . . ."

"Liar! Faithless slut! Don't even try to deny—"

"There's a way to prove it once and for all," Ciaran snarled. "The clothes that were left behind last night in your wife's bedchamber. If they fit me, I must be the man you're seeking. And if they do, she can damned well tell me who—"

"That's . . . that's right!" the wife cried. "Let him try on the clothes he left behind! Norton, they'll never fit!"

Fallon's stomach plunged to her toes as Vanessa Fyfe raced into the house. Clothes left behind, a leap from a bedchamber window . . . God above, was there a chance that what Norton Fyfe claimed was true? There could be no doubting the rage suffusing his face, and the pain of his betrayal.

She felt sick. No. She couldn't be wrong. He *was* Ciaran of the Mist. *He was.*

A gasp rose from the onlookers as they recognized her. The villagers parted, making way for Miss Delaney of Misthaven. She burst from the crowd and stumbled, striking her shin upon the stone step so hard tears stung her eyes. "Stop this! Ciaran, please—"

At the sound of her voice he wheeled, a stricken expression darting across his face. He hurled Norton Fyfe away from him and turned away from the man, as if he were so sickened she'd witnessed the sordid scene he would be grateful if the little man plunged a knife into his back.

"Damn it, why?" Ciaran growled low, anguish filling his eyes. "Why the devil did you follow me?"

"Did you think I could just let you walk away?" She choked out, hated herself for the thickening in her throat, the stinging of her eyes. Damn, she wouldn't cry in front of all these people. She wouldn't cry in front of him. "When I woke up and found you gone, I—"

She stopped suddenly, horribly aware of the silence that shrouded the throng, the eager way they were listening.

"What a lot o' fuss an' bother!" a high-pitched voice interrupted. "Let Sarie O'Dowd be settling this once an' for all." Notorious for her enormous bosom and nonexistent virtue, Sarie sauntered up, her hips swaying. "I saw the whole thing meself last night, waitin' as I were for one o' me soldier-boys."

Her blowsy golden curls tumbling about lush mountains of half-exposed breast, Sarie swept pansy-blue eyes from the crown of Ciaran's head to his feet, lingering with feline appreciation. Fallon ground her teeth. If the woman had been a cat, she'd be twined around Ciaran's legs, yowling her eagerness to mate loud enough to bring every tom in Ireland thundering down on her.

"Now, mind, all I saw was his bum," she cooed, reaching out as if to pat that part of Ciaran's anatomy. A roar of laughter erupted from the onlookers. Fallon slapped the woman's hand away.

Sarie's eyes widened. "Now, Miss Delaney, don't

mean to offend yer sensibilities, but if I'm t' help, I have t' take a glance at the part I was seein', don't I?"

Ciaran's fists clenched, white-knuckled. "Am I the man you saw?" he demanded, looking for all the world as if he were in some prisoner's dock, waiting for his sentence to be handed down. "Just tell me, damn it."

"I'd be able t' do it better if ye'd just drop those breeches of yers, handsome. Give Sarie a little peek." She flounced her skirts above trim ankles, drawing a ripple of laughter from the men in the throng.

"Absolutely not!" Fallon dodged between Ciaran and the lightskirt. "Don't even think of it! Just answer the man's question. Unless you'd prefer that my brother become involved."

Sarie's smirk faded, the mere mention of Hugh's name sobering the group. "No, miss. Of course, I wouldn't care to bother Mr. Hugh."

"Tell the truth, then, or it will go badly with you. Is this the man you saw?" She felt as if she were teetering on a blade, the woman's answer likely to shove her into an abyss.

"He had black hair like 'im," Sarie said, examining Ciaran through her shrewd eyes. "An' he was handsome enough. But if he'd looked fine as this specimen here, I would've forgot my soldier an' followed him, naked as he was."

At that moment, Vanessa Fyfe returned, a pair of breeches in her hand—breeches far too small to fit Ciaran's powerful frame.

"There, Norton!" she shrilled. "Is that proof enough for you?"

Fallon wasn't aware of the man's reply. She only heard Ciaran's sigh of relief, felt the uncoiling of her own tangled nerves as she turned toward him, rejoicing. But words of triumph died in her throat as she glimpsed something just beyond Sarie's shoulders—a smear of red uniform, blonde hair, piercing eyes.

Redmayne.

He leaned negligently in the shadows, like Lucifer watching souls stumbling toward the gates of hell, alert to any vulnerability.

Fallon's heart stopped. God in heaven, what if she was wrong? What if Ciaran was the lord of smugglers Redmayne had been seeking? Was it possible the captain already recognized his quarry?

Redmayne's face was unreadable. Only his eyes glittered with faint mockery. For an instant, she wanted to dive in front of Ciaran, block him from Redmayne's view, but she might as well have attempted to conceal the Grenadiers Inn behind her chipped-straw bonnet. The captain sauntered toward them with his lazy, tigerish stride.

"Miss Delaney, imagine meeting you again. I seem to encounter you in the most intriguing places."

She could feel heat rushing into her face, and feared that she must look like a rabbit the instant before a wolf's jaws closed on its throat. Fast as she could, she shuttered her emotions away, but it was too late. She could see by the smirk at the corner of Redmayne's lips that she'd betrayed herself.

As if he sensed her unease, Ciaran moved until he stood between her and the captain. But the instant those sea-green eyes locked upon Redmayne, Fallon could feel a rush of animosity sizzle between the two men, so hot, so sudden, so unexpected it drove the breath from her lungs. Did they know each other somehow? No, it wasn't recognition. It was something far more visceral. Could it be that legendary gift Ciaran of the Mist possessed for sensing evil?

Ciaran turned to her, his voice low, rough. "Let's go, Fallon. We've found out what we needed to know." One arm curved beneath hers, and she was certain he could feel her hand trembling. She wanted to run, bolt like a startled deer toward her horse. Wanted to leave the gaping townspeople, the crooked street, and Captain Redmayne behind.

Instead, she started to move with all the dignity she could muster.

"Perhaps *you've* found out what you need to know, sir," Redmayne charged. "But *I* have not."

"We've no business with you," Ciaran said, and Fallon could sense how much it cost him to keep his tone level.

"That's where you're mistaken. There has been an unfortunate amount of unrest in the area since the rebellion four years ago and I have been instructed to quell it. So you see, any stranger in this part of the countryside is my affair."

The captain fingered the glistening hilt of the saber at his waist. "Tell me, sir. Exactly who are you, and what is your business hereabouts?"

Fallon felt Ciaran's arm tense where it brushed hers, felt him faltering. He was an abysmal liar, doubtless one of the drawbacks of being so noble. If anyone was going to extricate them from this predicament, she would have to be the one.

"I can vouch for him, Captain," Fallon interjected. "He is a close friend of mine. We, uh . . . he was with me yesterday, in fact. At the castle. In the mist."

"Ah, so it was as I suspected when I stumbled across you last night," Redmayne said, the breeze riffling the angelic gold of his hair. "You *had* gone up to the castle to summon back your mythical hero."

Fallon's heart stopped. She heard the sharp hiss of Ciaran's breath. Was it possible that Redmayne knew? That he'd been watching? Listening? That he'd discovered the truth with that unerring gift for discovering an opponent's weakness?

But the officer only glanced at the crowd, chuckling. "Tell me, the lot of you. Does this look like a man who could hurl three dragons into the sea or stop up a flooded river with his bare hands to save a pack of children from drowning?"

He'd meant it as a joke, but the people of Glenceo took their legends seriously. Eyes rounded, a visual battery pounding against Ciaran.

"I'm no damned hero," Ciaran growled, but no one else seemed to hear him.

Obviously delighted with the villagers' reaction, Redmayne crossed his arms over his broad chest. His gaze measured Ciaran as if they were on opposite sides of a dueling field. "However, much as it grieves me, Miss Delaney, honor bids me confess the truth. Considering everything I've heard about your Irish legends, I expected him to be a trifle more . . . impressive."

"Perhaps you'd care to test your skills?" Ciaran challenged, and Fallon could feel the battle heat singing in his blood.

Desperate, frightened, she all but leaped between them, fending off Redmayne's comments the only way she knew how, forcing scorn into her voice, tossing her curls. "You claim to be an officer and a gentleman, Captain. You can't possibly believe in peasant tales of magic."

But those shrewd eyes gave her nowhere to hide. "Perhaps not. Of course, then I'm forced to examine less mystic explanations for this man's presence here, I suppose. I was at the castle last night myself, as you know, but not for some sort of lover's tryst. No. I was there a-hunting. I'd heard reports that a certain lord of the smugglers was in the vicinity, ripe for capture."

"A smuggler?" Ciaran echoed, intensity fairly crackling off his towering frame. "What is his name? Who—"

"They call him Silver Hand, because he is elusive as the fingers of the moon. A particularly slippery fellow who has been giving the garrison here quite a headache of late. Killed my predecessor, in fact."

"If ever a man deserved killing, he did," someone grumbled in the crowd. "Never saw such a man for whippings, wrecking houses."

"I'm afraid the high command disagrees, especially when the dead officer in question is related to a general. General Scargill has made it his personal quest to see the murderer hang."

"So he sent the most vile, ruthless cur he could command t' see to it," the baker groused.

Redmayne actually looked flattered. "I prefer to think he sent the most able man for the job. At any rate, it is only a matter of time. We will run him to ground." He cast Ciaran an assessing glare. "Or perhaps I already have."

"This is no rebel!" Fallon burst out, sweat beading her brow. "His name is Ciaran M—" She hesitated, groping for some name, any name that would serve. "MacDonough. He's my—" Her what? Her friend? Her ward? A total stranger she'd picked up out of the rubble of the castle and adopted like a stray puppy?

"He is your what, Miss Fallon?" Redmayne pressed. "I'm eager to hear the reason you and this man were atop that cliff, in a place known as a gathering point for traitors to the crown."

"Traitors—" Fallon stammered. "I know nothing of traitors, and I've played about that castle from the time I was a child."

"I can't image that you stole up to play at tea party with Mr. MacDonough."

"Don't be absurd!" she said, hating the heat spilling into her cheeks. "Ciaran and I were at the castle because we . . . we needed privacy. Time alone together because—"

She was babbling. God in heaven, she had to get hold of her wits. Redmayne was scrutinizing her so hard it felt as if he were peeling back her skin.

"Because?" Redmayne drawled.

Sweat beaded Fallon's brow. What possible reasonable explanation could she give for meeting a man at the castle? Why would anyone in their right mind trek so far up the treacherous cliffs in the mist at night when one misstep would mean certain death? Only desperation could drive one to take such a risk—the desperation of a rebel, a smuggler, or . . . a lover?

She raised her chin, relief rushing through her as an answer formed. "We were meeting at the castle because this man is my betrothed." She flinched at Ciaran's growl of surprise. She turned to him so swiftly she all but overset herself, her gaze pleading for his silence, warning him not to betray them both. But the tempest she'd unleashed in that fiendishly handsome face nearly made her stumble back a step.

"I—I know we weren't going to tell anyone, my love," she rushed on, clutching his hands. "But you must see we have to tell the captain the truth."

Ciaran of the Mist shot her the fabled glare that had

made the mighty armies of Connaught turn and flee. "He can go to hell! I bloody well don't see why—"

She stopped his words by flinging her arms around his neck and crushing her lips against his in a desperate kiss—a kiss that stunned them both, that branded impressions into her consciousness despite their peril: hot lips that tasted of fury and passion, a living, breathing magic that shot to her toes, and the fierce pulse of a wild creature scenting the hunter closing in.

His arms curved around her, whether to steady her or to shove her away she wasn't certain. Her lips surrendered his, yet she knew she'd been changed somehow, forever.

"Please, Ciaran." She clutched his arm so hard her fingers ached, though they made not a dent in the rigid sheaths of muscle below. Then she angled her face toward Redmayne, praying she would be able to give the performance of her life. "Our engagement was to be a secret. You wondered why I was at the castle last night, alone. Ciaran and I were meeting there, trying to find a way to break the news of our engagement to my brother."

A rumble went up from the onlookers. Fallon's heart sank. This had to be the most idiotic lie she had ever told. Miss Delaney of Misthaven's engagement would be the biggest news the village had heard in years, a juicy tidbit to be squabbled over and dissected in detail for weeks to come. By sunset it would land right back on her own doorstep, where Hugh was waiting. The prospect of Hugh being dragged into this farce made her stomach clench.

"Do you mean to say that your brother disapproves of the match?" Redmayne arched one elegant brow in query.

"He doesn't know about it at all. I told you the engagement was secret."

"Surely you don't mean to tell me you are afraid of your own brother—your only living relative? The country folk claim that Mr. Delaney is the most just landlord who has ever collected rent on this benighted island. In fact, I've found him quite remarkably mild no matter what the provocation." The corner of Redmayne's mouth curled, turning the words into an insult, one that stung Fallon deeply.

Why didn't he just say it? That her brother had all the fire and substance of blancmange? That despite his Irish blood, he was more English than the gentry who had been born across the Irish Sea and had come to rule this island. Stolid, responsible, Hugh possessed all the passion and fairy-touched magic of a Hereford plow horse.

"No," Redmayne continued, "this whole affair still seems most irregular. I fear I must explore it. My duty, you understand. I'm certain that your *betrothed* could have no objection to returning to the garrison with me and answering a few simple questions. No great inconvenience for an innocent man. Just as a precaution, you understand. For example, how did he get that gash in his head? Unless, of course, you are having a particularly rough courting."

"That's none of your damned business," Ciaran snarled, but the captain's gaze didn't flicker from Fallon.

"Also, why wouldn't he go to your brother, ask for your hand as any honorable suitor would?"

Lord, this was getting worse by the second. She could feel Ciaran about to explode, Redmayne circling with the sinister patience of a wolf, searching for the perfect place to sink his teeth.

"He . . . we . . . I mean, I can explain. You see, I . . ." Her gaze snagged on a woman with a babe in her arms. "I was too ashamed to face Hugh. I'm with child."

Why did Ciaran look as shocked and pained as if she'd just driven a knife into his chest? And the villagers—she might as well have screamed that she'd slept with every soldier in the barracks, they looked so appalled. They wouldn't be babbling on about Vanessa and Norton Fyfe tonight.

"Damn it, Fallon, have you lost your mind?" Ciaran demanded as a gasp echoed through the onlookers.

"With child?" Redmayne's cool eyes widened just a fraction, then dipped to her waist so intently it felt as if he could see all the way to her backbone. "A most distressing circumstance for a lady such as yourself. I never would have guessed it. You're still slender as the frond of a willow."

Fallon pressed one hand against her stomach. "I've done my best to conceal it."

"And you've done an astonishingly good job of it. I would never have believed . . ." He let the words trail off, hang between them for a moment as torturous as the rack. "However, all things considered, I am astonished that your betrothed would allow you to be in the midst of such an unfortunate scene as the one taking place here today." Redmayne pursed his features into a moue of concern. "This disturbance cannot be good for you in your condition, Miss Delaney." He said, waving a hand at the milling townsfolk. "It must upset you. Doubtless it would be much better for you if we were to pursue this conversation in the comfort and privacy of my offices."

She wanted to scoop up her skirts, bolt as fast as her feet could carry her, but there could be no escape. The gray stone face of the Fyfe house loomed behind them, the crowd fencing them in on all other sides. What a disaster! She glanced up at Ciaran, the expression in his eyes making her knees shake. Lord, what had she done? He looked ready to bury her instead of marry her.

As if that wasn't bad enough, in trying to conceal Ciaran's identity, she'd just crossed over a dangerous line. It was one thing to help an anonymous traveler injured by the side of the road, and another thing entirely to lie to the authorities on his behalf.

She might be certain Ciaran wasn't one of the smugglers Redmayne sought, but what if the captain decided to press the issue? What alternatives would she have? Ciaran had lost his memory. There would be no way to prove that he was *not* Redmayne's quarry. And she could sense, with every instinct, that Captain Lionel Redmayne believed none of the lies she'd spun and that he had no intention of letting a prime suspect go, once Ciaran was in his grasp.

Following the captain to his lair like lambs to the

slaughter was too great a risk. There was only one thing to do. She had to make certain Ciaran bolted the instant the chance presented itself.

The captain made a sweeping gesture with one hand, the crowd dividing as if he were the Celtic sea god Mannan MacLir commanding the waves to part. Then he turned his back on them, walking with deceptive negligence toward the place where his horse was tethered.

Fallon's hand shook where it gripped Ciaran's. Her first instinct, whenever shamed or scorned, had always been to thrust up her chin, donning the hauteur of a captive queen and never allowing anyone to glimpse weakness. But much as it pinched at her pride, she did the opposite, burying her face against Ciaran's shoulder, feigning embarrassment. Doubtless an emotion the crowd felt was natural enough. After all, she was now a fallen woman in the eyes of everyone present.

"Run," she whispered for his ears alone. "The moment we're in the clear, you must run."

"Abandon the mother of my child?" She'd never heard such burning scorn. "What kind of a coward do you take me for?"

Her head jerked up so fast her neck all but snapped. She glared at him. "Don't be a fool," she mouthed the words, saw understanding register in Ciaran's eyes— eyes mystically green as a fairy field.

God above, didn't Ciaran realize Redmayne was offering them a perfect opportunity to . . . to what? Cudgel the captain over the head? Make a break for open ground?

At that instant, the anguish and fury in Ciaran's eyes seemed to shift, and it was almost as if she could hear what he was thinking through some mystic connection of their minds.

Redmayne *was* offering them a perfect chance, but not the one she would have embraced so recklessly. Rather, he was attempting to lure them in, to confirm the suspicions that had been lurking in his eyes from the moment he had seen Ciaran.

She glanced up into Ciaran's tempestuous face as they

edged through the crowd, and in his gaze she could see a dozen plans for escape hastily formed, then discarded. Why? The answer was as obvious as her penchant for disaster: because she was entangled in this mess, and he would die before he left her to fend for herself. A fist closed about her heart, and she gathered up her courage, her resolve.

"It will be all right," Fallon whispered. "We just have to . . . to brazen this through."

Angry as he was, he tightened an arm about her and cast her a glance that stripped away any delusions. In that instant, she glimpsed splashes of red against white-washed walls. An escort of a half dozen soldiers stood at the ready just beyond the Grenadier's Inn, awaiting their commander's pleasure.

Or, Fallon wondered, did the soldiers believe they were waiting for a far more vital reason—to spring a trap upon the lord of smugglers who had eluded them for so long?

CHAPTER

7

Instinct—deeper than memory, more potent than anger—a cipher engraved deep into every fiber, every sinew, every breath that he took. It stirred, awakened, came to life inside him—a piece of the man he'd lost.

Ciaran grasped it as the Celtic hero Cuchulain had grasped the enchanted spear Gae Bulga, clutched it with the same fervor with which Arthur Pendragon had taken the mighty sword Excalibur in his hands—for it was his only weapon against the adversary he now faced.

This adversary endangered the woman who had found Ciaran wandering amid the ruins and taken him in, offered him safe haven, a place to gather up the scattered fragments of his memory. Fallon, with her legend-brightened eyes and her courage, and the secret lonely places in her heart.

It would take all his wits, now, to save her from paying a terrible price for protecting him. But, half-blinded as he was by his own ignorance, did he have the strength? The cunning? He'd pleaded with the fates to give him that power during the miles he'd ridden, Redmayne's soldiers clustered in a loose chain about him, a hangman's noose woven of men, ready to jerk tight at the first sign of an attempt to escape.

He would need every resource at his disposal to best Redmayne, that much he knew. Because the Englishman was watching, gauging every movement, every fleeting expression during the miles they'd traveled from the Fyfe house.

Ciaran had been all too aware of Redmayne gathering information about him from the instant he'd gotten up on Fallon's mount and cradled her before him. The Englishman had marked Ciaran's discomfort on a horse and noted the subtlest nuances of emotion. Every scrap of information might be invaluable in what was to come.

A duel of wits.

A duel that could have dangerous consequences for the woman who had spun such desperate lies on his behalf, if he should lose. But despite all his vigilance, Ciaran had learned precious little about the officer who now held Fallon's fate in his hands. He hoped like blazes he would discover something now.

Awkwardly dismounting, he turned to lift Fallon down, felt the trembling in her, the fear. The need to protect her, to shield her, clawed like a living thing in his vitals.

"If you will follow me?" Redmayne invited, as he cast the reins of his mount into the hands of one of his inferiors. "We will get through this as quickly as possible, in deference to Miss Delaney's delicate condition."

Ciaran's jaw clenched against the instinctive denial that rose in his throat. Their lives were in peril. Why the devil should it matter so damned much to him that any man—especially a cur like Redmayne—thought he had violated Fallon? But the fact ate at Ciaran's pride, seared him like liquid fire, as if taking this woman's virginity, dishonoring her so, was a betrayal of everything he believed, everything he was.

He swore inwardly, yanking his attention back to the situation at hand. He had to keep alert, focused, or he'd come awake to find Redmayne's blade at his throat, figuratively if not literally.

He paced after the captain, taking in their surroundings. Flags and sabers lined the walls of the military post. Artist's renditions of men's quests for glory brightened the walls like blossoms of blood on the chest of a dying general.

Each nook and cranny of the building was decked out like the soldiers themselves, every inch of uniform that could be emblazoned with some medal or award or trophy was crammed tight with something glittering. With every step, Ciaran attempted to memorize what he saw, in an intuitive attempt to know the enemy he now faced.

Redmayne ushered them into his private office, a place far different from the corridors they'd just passed through. Ciaran's hope of learning of some weakness in the man died.

The chamber was like a secret, tightly guarded.

The walls of Captain Redmayne's study were bare, everything else in the room so precisely in its place it bespoke a man who left no detail to chance, no avenue unexplored. A man this merciless in ordering his quill pens in their box would be even more ruthless in trying to bring order to the suspicions in his mind, Ciaran thought grimly.

The door closed behind them, and with a look of concern, Redmayne ushered Fallon to a chair as if she'd suddenly turned invalid. "You mustn't tire yourself, my dear. We would not want anything untoward to happen to your baby."

Ciaran sensed that Fallon's nerves were stretched so taut she could barely keep from pacing the room like a caged tigress. "I prefer to stand," she said.

"But I must insist." In Redmayne's voice there was something as forceful and irresistible as a hand on her shoulder, nudging her down. She sat, looking suddenly terribly young and vulnerable in her soft muslin gown.

"Now, let us begin at the beginning," the captain said. "Where did you and Mr. MacDonough meet?"

"You can have no interest in such a tedious story, and such a personal one," Fallon began.

"I assure you, I am interested in anything concerning

your . . . betrothed." There was the tiniest hesitation, yet Redmayne's doubts screamed along Ciaran's nerves. "Where and how did you meet?"

"I . . . we . . . I was on my way home from visiting the widow Treacle. I met him on the road. My horse had bruised its fetlock on a stone."

"With his talent for riding, it's obvious to the most untutored eye that Mr. MacDonough is exactly the man you'd wish to have on hand when you were having difficulties with a horse. An *expert* equestrian."

Ciaran tensed at the blunder, but Fallon covered it neatly. "I didn't say he was able to help me with the horse, only that I met him when Cuchulain began to limp. But once I did see Mr. MacDonough, I was glad enough to walk the rest of the way, as long as he was at my side. You see, we—"

"You what?" Redmayne prodded.

"We fell in love at first glance."

That much was true, Ciaran thought, wincing in discomfort. The woman had gazed on him with embarrassing adoration the minute he'd walked out of the mist. But then, it must be easy to fall in love with a legend rather than a mortal man. Why did the knowledge give him a twinge?

The captain laid one finger along his jaw. "Miss Delaney, I wish I could believe you. But there is something in your countenance that troubles me. Where exactly are you from, Mr. MacDonough?"

Ciaran shrugged. "Nowhere. Everywhere. I travel where I'm needed."

"Or where you are able to find a hot bed in which to plant the seed of rebellion? Smuggling goods in defiance of the Crown? This ground would be as fertile as Miss Delaney's womb, I assure you."

"Captain Redmayne—" Fallon started to protest, but Ciaran cut in.

"Keep your crude comments regarding my relationship with Fallon to yourself, Captain," Ciaran warned. "I am no rebel, Redmayne. I have no family, to my knowledge, and no place to call home. That is no crime, that I'm aware of."

"You were raised in a poorhouse then? A foundling home?"

Why couldn't he think of something to say? Why couldn't he fabricate one of the tales that tripped so glibly off Fallon's tongue, desperate as she was?

"You seem most reluctant to impart simple information, Mr. MacDonough. Is there something you're concealing—not only from me, but from the lovely Miss Delaney as well? Something you are ashamed of? Perhaps you are not a fit mate for a lady such as she?"

Fallon thrust her chin in the air. "I don't care if he was born in a cow byre! I love him, and I will have him!"

"You've made that quite plain. And as for you, Mr. MacDonough, considering your past, I can see much more clearly why the *attractions* of Miss Delaney were irresistible to you. It would be enough for many men that she is lovely, spirited, a promising filly to tame. Add to that the fact that she is an heiress—"

"I don't give a damn about her money!"

"Of course you don't," Redmayne said slyly. "You wish to marry her no matter what the cost. It is merely a happy chance that the two of you will be able to live on her fortune. Yes, a most romantic epic."

Rage flared, but Ciaran wrenched it under control. The captain was up to something. Closing for the kill. Ciaran could all but feel the wolf's breath at his throat. But how? How would Redmayne attempt to bring him down?

"Mr. MacDonough, that is a nasty gash on your forehead. How did you come by it?"

"His horse stumbled," Fallon leapt in. "He fell."

Ciaran cast her a glare. "I was in such haste to get to my beloved." Could that tender word sound more like an epithet? But Fallon latched on to his arm, forcing a smile.

"You've mentioned his clumsiness on horseback," she said. "Surely such an accident couldn't come as much of a surprise?"

"Not the most dashing of entrances in such a romantic tale." Redmayne steepled long white fingers, tapping them against his chin. "We must make certain there are no more such blunders along the path to true love. And I would guess that the most dangerous obstacle is even now in his study at Misthaven House working on his ledgers. A great man for detail, your brother is, madam. If I were to guess, I would say that it will be difficult indeed for you to avoid the censuring hand of Hugh Delaney. Quite a weighty problem."

"I'm certain Hugh will come to agree once he understands that Ciaran is the love of my life. That I would die without him."

It was a damned uncomfortable thought that if she kept these lies up much longer she'd be more likely to die *with* him, on the gallows.

A chuckle erupted from Redmayne, his eyes narrowing. "We cannot run the risk of such a tragedy." The captain's voice dropped low, the purr of a cat about to snap the neck of a mouse. "Miss Delaney, what would you say if I confessed to you that I have a tender spot in my heart for young lovers?"

"I'd say you were an accursed liar," Ciaran began, then stopped as those shrewd eyes flashed to his.

Redmayne sketched him an infinitesimal bow. "A rather ungenerous label to apply to your benefactor, Mr. MacDonough. You see, I've devised the perfect way to be of service to both of you. Your child will carry its papa's name before this night has flown."

"Impossible—" Ciaran began, but Redmayne cut him off with a feral smile.

Redmayne crossed to the door, opened it. "Crimmins, Dalton."

Two soldiers, one hard and hairy as a blacksmith's hand, the other proudly sprouting his first whiskers, entered and came to attention. Ciaran could see that there was a wariness about the men, as if they weren't yet certain what to make of their new commander.

"Aye, Captain, sir," Crimmins saluted. "The battering rams you requested are almost finished. Sturdy as we can make them, sir. They'll be ready before two weeks are out, just as you ordered."

"Good. They'll be put to hard use in the next few months. The castle on the cliff is only the beginning. One needs sturdy equipment to sweep the whole of a county clean of this ancient stone refuse."

Even distressed as she was, Ciaran could see Fallon flinch at Redmayne's talk of destruction. Two weeks. He was to begin his campaign of demolition in two weeks. But how could the infernal woman be so worried about a heap of crumbling stone when both their lives hung in the balance?

"However, at the moment I have another mission for you, gentlemen. Sergeant Crimmins, you will ride to the bishop's and secure a special license for a marriage between Miss Fallon Delaney and Mr. Ciaran MacDonough. And Dalton, you will fetch a clergyman."

Ciaran felt as if the man had snatched the earth from under his feet. His head reeled, nails digging deep into his palms. *"What?"*

"You are both perishing to wed. Such devotion should be rewarded. No chance must be taken that your babe will be born a bastard, Mr. MacDonough."

"But I don't . . . There is no . . ." Ciaran glanced wildly from Fallon to the soldiers to Redmayne, and the protests died on his lips.

"There is no what, Mr. MacDonough?"

Ciaran swore under his breath. Mother of God, the man was diabolical in his genius. While Ciaran had been watching, bracing for attack from other, more obvious quarters, Redmayne had slipped up behind him and thrown a noose around his neck. Trapped. They were trapped. Damn Fallon for her tangle of lies. They'd only bumbled into an even worse disaster than before.

Marriage? It was unthinkable! For all he knew, he already had a wife somewhere, waiting for him. Yet the infernal captain had manipulated it all so neatly. What were Ciaran's choices? Marry Fallon, or confess the truth? He glanced down at Fallon, saw her eyes saucer-wide, her lips parted in a gasp. Could Redmayne and his soldiers possibly misinterpret shock as joy?

He half expected Fallon to cry off her tale, to say "never mind" and make a dash for the door. "This isn't necessary, Captain Redmayne," she stammered. "I would not want to place you or your men in the middle of a family argument. It wouldn't be fair."

"For two lovers all but dying to pledge their vows, you are both astonishingly patient. Why this cooling of your ardor? Or perhaps it never burned as hotly as you wish me to believe?"

"Yes!" Fallon stammered. "I mean, no! Please send your soldiers on their way . . . to the bishop and—"

She sounded as shaken as if Redmayne had just fired a cannonball into her chest. And who the devil could blame her? Ciaran felt as if a whole battalion of artillery had just thundered across him.

"How could we possibly thank you?" Fallon asked a little faintly.

"By allowing me the pleasure of watching your faces as you take your vows." Perfectly chiseled lips spread into a lethal smile. "After all, it is not every day one has the chance to make a dream come true. Then, after the ceremony, I will ride with you to Misthaven House, to help smooth things over with your brother, Miss Delaney. With luck, we can all raise a toast to the newly wedded couple before the night is past."

Ciaran could feel Fallon's panic. Her face was ice-pale. "Kind as your offer is, I don't think that would be a good idea. My marriage will come as quite a shock to Hugh. Better to face him in private."

"I must insist on having my way, Miss Delaney. Trust that I know what is best. The presence of a stranger in such a crisis will serve as a calming influence upon your brother."

Did Redmayne see the tiny spark in Fallon's eyes— heartbreak, hopelessness? It wrenched at Ciaran. "Again we are in your debt," she said. "I only hope someday we can repay you."

"I shall be looking forward to my just reward, my dear. Now, forgive me. I have some pressing business to take care of before Crimmins and Dalton return. There is a washbasin in my adjoining chamber. You are welcome to tidy up a bit if you wish." Redmayne's uncannily piercing gaze skated over the tendrils of Fallon's hair, wild and windblown. "After all, this is your wedding day. A day you'll remember the rest of your lives. A bride should look her best. Allow me to lock the door to assure your privacy while you prepare yourselves."

Ciaran gritted his teeth. No doubt the bastard allowed prisoners to prepare for hanging as well. Wouldn't want one's hair mussed when the noose was slipped over one's head.

With a crisp bow, Redmayne exited the room. The instant the door clicked shut, Ciaran charged to the single window, hoping to find some avenue of escape. He couldn't marry this woman. No, fleeing this place would be better. Whatever had estranged Fallon from her brother, Ciaran had seen the love in Hugh Delaney's features. Her brother would help her somehow.

But as he peered through the glass panes, his heart sank. Curse Redmayne to hell, the devil had thought of everything. If there had been one guard, even two or three below the window, Ciaran might have risked a fight. But just as in the village, a half dozen men lounged about, pretending to clean their weapons while they stole surreptitious glances at the window.

Fury and helplessness raged through Ciaran's blood. He rounded on Fallon. "There's no way out. Damnation, you've gotten us into one hell of a disaster with your accursed lies!"

Color flooded her cheeks, her eyes overbright. "If you hadn't run away from Misthaven like a brainless idiot, I wouldn't have had to lie! Why didn't you tell me you were leaving?"

"I've been trying to do nothing *but* leave you ever since I met you, woman! But no. You think I'm some accursed hero—some stupid myth. A legend you were going to keep like a pet dog to perform tricks at your command. I'm not Ciaran of the Mist or the Sea or the Cow Dung! I'm just some poor sonofabitch who got cracked on the head. Damn it to hell, why couldn't you just let me leave?"

Her eyes widened, a wounded light flickering in their depths. "If I hadn't found you, you wouldn't be in

Redmayne's office, you'd be in a gaol cell, or Crimmins and Dalton would be trying to beat answers out of you!"

"I would have preferred an honest lash to Redmayne's brand of torture! The man damn well knew what he was doing—stalking us, trapping us in your infernal web of nonsense strand by strand. By God, you made it so easy for him."

"So this is all my fault, is it? I'm sorry that things got so tangled, but I couldn't think of any other way to calm his suspicions."

"Tangled? That's the understatement of the century. We're not talking about ruined hair ribbons here, madam. We're talking *marriage*. How the devil can I marry you? I barely know you—hell, I don't even know myself. What if I have a wife somewhere? Children?"

She looked as if he'd slapped her. "Nowhere in the legend is there a wife mentioned. No children. Ciaran was always alone."

He wanted to throttle her. "Damn it, I'm not—"

"If you're not Ciaran and you have another wife"— she paused, swallowed hard—"then whatever happens between us in the next hour won't matter. The marriage won't be valid."

"But you'd have me make the vows anyway? *Sacred* vows laid upon my honor? Knowing I will discard them?"

"Why should it matter so much? To hear you talk, you don't even know if you have any honor. You're no one. Nothing. But perhaps you've discovered something you loathe in addition to Redmayne even more than my hero tales—the mere idea of marriage."

He wished it were that simple, wished that it were true. But as he glared down into the soft oval of her feminine face, all peachy tints, ripe and sweet with the scent of new cream, he knew with sudden certainty that he had always been alone.

As alone as her precious Ciaran of the Mist had ever been.

Ciaran probed beneath the dark veil that was his past. Had he chosen to be solitary of his own free will? No. He could feel the tug within him, an ache more familiar than his own face.

He'd wanted a bride. He'd wanted to hold a woman's hands tight in his, feel them tremble as she pledged her love to him, the souls of their unborn children dancing dreams in her tear-misted eyes. He'd imagined taking her to his bed, stripping away her garments piece by piece, unraveling the mysteries of their bodies together.

He could remember nights that seemed to stretch out forever—the sweat dampening his skin, the yearning in his body, in his soul, so fierce it all but drove him mad, the need to touch, to hold in his arms someone who belonged to him, only to him. He knew the stark despair, the feeling it was impossible, forever beyond his reach. He'd stared up at the stars, raging . . . at what? At whom? The fates or his own idiocy?

And now this fresh-faced woman who had braved so much for a dream stood before him, willing to cast her life into his hands. Didn't she know she'd be giving him the power to destroy her?

Anger drained away, leaving desolation. "Fallon, I can't let you do this thing. I can't let you sacrifice yourself for me. What if I'm some kind of monster? Someone more evil than Redmayne himself?"

Her voice was small, broken, and yet, so very, very sure. "Don't you know, Ciaran? Honor shines, like the armor of the knights in the Arthur tales. It can't be hidden by darkness, or danger, or doubt. You *are* a hero."

"The kind of hero who could get you killed if we're not careful. If I *am* proved to be this smuggler, this Silver Hand person, and you're my wife, what the devil would happen to you? If I am involved in some kind of skulduggery, you'd be in it up to your neck."

Her gaze met his, heartbreakingly valiant, unbearably innocent. "I'm not afraid."

"You should be. No matter what happens with Redmayne, I would destroy you. I can't stay here, Fallon. I don't belong here. That's the only thing we both know for certain. A marriage between us wouldn't be any more real than your pretty myths and legends. I don't love you. You don't love me." The simple truth shouldn't have made him ache so much. "I will leave whenever this is over. If you were my wife, pledged to me, bound to me, you'd be alone for the rest of your life. There could be no husband to love, to fight with, to grow old beside. No children."

One delicate shoulder shrugged, and she smiled up at him. It was a brave smile, and it broke his heart. "I never expected to marry anyway."

He frowned, feeling an unexpected twinge. It couldn't possibly be disappointment. "You didn't want to marry?"

A flush pinkened her cheeks. "I didn't say I didn't *want* to. But some things just aren't destined to be. You might want to pluck the moon as if it were a silver lily. That doesn't mean you can reach into the night sky and do it."

"You're a beautiful woman, Fallon. Brave, resolute, generous to a fault. Why the devil should marriage be impossible for you?"

"I'm a lot like you, really. There's no place I fit. Hugh and I are loathed by the other landowners, though they pretend to tolerate us. Our Irish blood is sin enough. The fact that I refuse to grovel at their feet is unforgiveable. The way they abuse their tenants—they sicken me. They are gluttons for pleasure no matter what it costs the crofters who work their land."

"Like the twins in the drawing on your bedchamber wall?"

She flushed. "They know how I despise them—all of them. I'd rather die than wed one of the English, an enemy. It would make me a traitor to everything I believe in. And, though I love the crofters dearly, they are a little afraid of me—fairy-kissed from my cradle, the landlord's daughter. Not even the bravest among the young men would dare even think of loving me the way a man loves a woman. I belong *to* them. But not *with* them."

Pain, yearning, and resignation rippled through her voice, echoed in the glistening of her eyes. Ciaran wanted to touch her cheek, offer comfort. He understood. By every river that tumbled through Ireland, he understood the loneliness she felt.

"Even you don't quite know what to do with me, Ciaran." Her smile wobbled and she gave a little laugh. "You think I'm mad. Not the most attractive quality in a prospective bride."

"*Mad* is too strong a word. You have a unique view of reality, I'll admit, but at least you remember your own name." Ciaran meant it as a joke. He'd never felt less like laughing. He cupped her cheeks in his palms, as if she were the moon-lily she'd spoken of, to be treasured, longed for, impossible to possess. Soft, petal-soft, her skin warmed his hands, tendrils of coppery hair kissing his knuckles. "You deserve better than what I can offer you, Mary Fallon. I wish—"

Wish what? That he could give to her all the dreams hidden in the rosy curve of her lips? That he could open his arms to her, gather her against his chest and give her a place to belong? Or were his motives far more selfish? Did he want this woman who had already given him so much, risked so much for him, to teach him that sometimes fairies did make magic, and heroes could walk from the mist? That sometimes moon-lilies could be gathered by a mortal's hand?

Tears glittered, diamond-bright, on the thickness of her lashes. "Be very careful of wishes, Ciaran," she said, with such sorrow it crushed his heart. "I wished you here, and there's been nothing but pain for you ever since."

"Not all pain, Mary Fallon," he whispered, knowing it wasn't true, because it hurt so damn much to want, to wonder, and not to taste. But she was hurting, too. Alone. If only there were fairy-kisses that could drive away the hurting, drown the ache. But there were no fairies here, no magic. Only the two of them, lost and alone.

If she was to be comforted, it would have to be his lips that touched hers. She'd kissed him before—that fleeting moment when she'd used her mouth to stop up his words, to keep him from betraying their lies. He'd been stunned, angry, ready to throttle her.

MAGIC

This time was worlds different.

Slowly, he lowered his mouth, saw her luminous eyes widen in surprise, then flood with fierce emotion. Thick lashes fluttered down, concealing summer-sky blue. Her lips parted, sought his, eager. A tiny cry rose in her throat. And the knowledge that she wanted this kiss as much as he did humbled him, inflamed him.

She tasted of the nectar of the wildflowers she'd wandered in. She offered herself up with the generosity of the mother goddess who had once given life to all Ireland. Her hair burned warm red, with the immortal fire of bardsong, her courage and strength as humbling as that of Deirdre of the Sorrows, who had risked everything for the love of heroic Naosi.

Why was it that the mere thought of that ancient tale filled his own chest with such sadness and anguish, like a wound still raw?

A shiver of surprise rippled through him. He remembered the story. Bits and pieces that tantalized, asking far more questions than they answered. Love, that greatest of all beauties, the most lethal weapon of destruction, the bronze blade that could cleave comrades in arms, brothers in spirit, into factions of enemies.

Had he ever tasted of love before? Ever understood its power? He didn't love Mary Fallon Delaney. Couldn't possibly love her when he didn't even know himself. But the forces her kiss unleashed in him were the most honest, most potent thing he'd ever known.

His tongue traced her lips, then slipped between them, tasting her deep inside. But even that wasn't enough. Not for him. Not for her. Desperate sounds filled the chamber, kittenish, hungry, as her hands glided over the taut muscles of his arms, the cords of his neck, the planes and hollows of his chest.

Was danger an aphrodisiac? Or was there something else at work here? Fallon's own unique brand of magic?

He drove the fingers of one hand back into the lustrous cascade of her hair, his other arm catching her about her waist, dragging her closer, until her breasts flattened against his chest. Her skirts tangled about his legs.

She was soft, delicious, exotic. He reveled in all the

127

things that made her a woman, exploring her as if she were some creature spun of moonbeams and sea foam and his own restless fantasies.

He was agonizingly aware of the twin pearls of her nipples, hardened at the center of her pillowy breasts, the musky hollow where her femininity was hidden, the soft swell of her belly igniting a living fire in that part of him suddenly rigid with an arousal so fierce he couldn't breathe.

He shut his eyes tight, but that didn't stop him from wanting to scoop up a handful of soft muslin, slide it up the slender column of her thigh and the lush curve of her hip, bunch the fabric around her waist so that his fingers could go questing for secret, satiny places beneath.

Places he'd yearned to discover. Places he was suddenly certain he never had discovered.

There had been no other woman. Not ever.

Why? The question reverberated through him.

Was there something wrong with him? Some fatal flaw he couldn't remember? Was there a sacred vow barring him from this devastating pleasure? Or a past mistake so terrible that he'd turned his back on the possibility of feminine softness filling his arms, hot, eager, honey-tinged lips filling his senses? He couldn't be certain.

He should break away from Fallon, surrender the magic of her body beneath his hands. He had no right to touch her. But did he have the strength, the courage to let her go? Her hero of the mist would have done so. Her hero was a damned fool. And yet, Ciaran felt his kiss gentling, hunger shifting to tenderness, passion to a reluctant yielding. To honor? He didn't know. But Fallon was certain he possessed it.

He drew back because of her belief in him, not his own. And when the moist heat of her lips came away from his, something tore deep in his chest. Reality spun into focus again—the sterile room, the voices of guards beneath the window, the suffocating scent of danger.

"Blast it, Fallon," he ground out. "I must have been out of my mind."

She flinched, for an instant the mask of bravado slipping away to reveal the girl who believed that magic and fairy tales and heroes truly existed. But there would be no happily ever after for her. And Ciaran hated himself for putting the shame and the hurt in her eyes. "You can always blame your sudden impulse to kiss me on the blow to your head. After all, why else would anybody—"

"Damn it, it's not because I kissed you," he tried to amend. "I mean, I had no right. And—"

"And it's against the code of heroes with amnesia to kiss women they think mad?"

"I don't think you're mad, just a trifle . . . hazy about reality now and then. And right now our reality looks dashed grim. What if Redmayne had walked in while you were in my arms?"

Rose-petal lips, still swollen with his kisses, tipped into an ironic smile that almost obscured her pain. "Then the insufferable captain would be far more likely to believe all the lies I told. In fact, maybe we should listen for his footsteps and stage the whole kiss again."

"The hell we will!" Ciaran roared. He'd rather let Redmayne flay the skin off his body one knife stroke at a time than allow the Englishman to witness something so intimate, so forbidden, so . . . *beautiful.*

The word echoed through him, reverberating like the shaft of a spear that had suddenly pierced his chest. And he knew that he'd made a terrible mistake when he'd succumbed to the temptation of kissing Mary Fallon. Every fiber in his body was still sizzling like a lightning bolt, damned uncomfortable in its intensity. And she looked so bruised, so tired suddenly, so sad.

He groped for the right words to make her understand. It was too dangerous, too painful, this quickening in his heart. If he cared for her, loved her, it would give Redmayne yet another weapon to use against them. And what would happen in the end, when Ciaran had to walk away, back to the life he couldn't remember? "Blast it, Fallon, listen to me—"

"We don't have anything more to say to each other," she said, a catch in her throat. "Except wedding vows."

She turned, walking into Redmayne's chamber. Ciaran could hear her splashing water from the washbasin as she bathed her face. But he could have told her it was hopeless.

Nothing either of them could do would wash away the danger that had glittered like an assassin's stiletto in Redmayne's cunning eyes. And there was no way to scrub away the taste of the kiss that had altered Ciaran forever.

CHAPTER

8

◦━━━◉

Fallon stood in the shaft of light beneath the stained glass window, the fragments of color filtering down over her in a chaos of broken rainbow, that wild disorder reflecting the anarchy in her heart.

It was as if she'd stepped into a bizarre dream—the musty chapel, Father Gerrard intoning gentle warnings about the sanctity of marriage, Redmayne hovering near, with the fiendish patience of a spider enjoying the struggles of the prey trapped in its web.

The whole improbable scene unfolding here was so unreal it might have been woven during the time when the triple goddess still ruled in Ireland, when bardsong and hero tales were new, and anything from sorcery to sea monsters to star-crossed love was possible.

She was marrying Ciaran of the Mist, becoming the bride of a legend. But the man who stood so rigid, so grim beside her, his hand closed protectively over her own, was real. She could feel the warm coursing of his pulse beneath her trembling fingers, the scent of him— sea wind and uncertainty and reckless honor—filling her senses.

His eyes, those green eyes she had seen glittering with

131

rage, eclipsed with confusion or softening with vulnerability, now darkened to the hue of a primeval forest as he gazed down into her face. Confused. Hurting. Desperate to do right. Knowing that somehow he had failed her.

The image seared itself deep into her heart, ached there. And she wanted to comfort him, wanted to tell him everything would be all right. Because it was *him* she was marrying, as if their union had been destined before time began.

How could she begin to explain that she finally understood why she'd never dreamed of wedding rings and bridal trips, or kisses beneath the rose arbor?

When other young girls had been in a romantic dither over the county's most handsome beaux, thrilling to fox hunts and waltzes and the dashing tilt of high-crowned beaver hats, Fallon had been curled up in the topmost tower of Ciaran's castle. Hour after hour she'd listened to the waves piercing their breasts on the cliffs below, hurling themselves against the rocks in an effort to possess something they could never have.

She'd felt one with those waves as she devoured the tales in books whose pages were near worn thin. She'd dreamed of bold Celtic heroes in horse-drawn chariots, spears flying, magic swirling, immortality beckoning with gossamer wings.

She'd fallen in love with the *idea* of Ciaran there, perched on the crumbling ledge of his castle, and once she had, no man of flesh and blood could ever challenge his hold upon her heart.

And now, she was to be his bride. She would have the right to touch him, to share his body, his bed, his inmost thoughts for as long as the fates allowed. A dream come true. *If,* a voice whispered inside her, *if he is truly the Ciaran of legend.*

"Mary Fallon?" Father Gerrard's voice made her start, and she turned her gaze back to the priest who had offered Margaret Delaney such comfort during the weary years of illness. He was as familiar to Fallon as the tiny chip in her front tooth, and she paid as little attention to him. Yet the good father had baptized Fallon and done his best to offer spiritual guidance to a girl far more intrigued by the pagan than the saintly.

The priest's face had always reminded Fallon of an old shoe, misshapen and leathery, the scuffs of countless years' journeying gouged into its surface. Yet it was a face oddly more comfortable than anything shiny and new and stiff.

Somber new lines now carved about his mouth, and she knew she'd been the one to put them there. "This is a very serious step you are taking, albeit a necessary one for the coming child," Father Gerrard said. "Yet I fear you haven't heard a word I've spoken."

Heat stung Fallon's cheekbones. For an instant she feared he'd demand that she repeat whatever he'd said, as he had while attempting to get a wild, wayward girl to attend to her catechism. "I'm sorry, Father. I'm just so . . . happy it's hard to think of anything else." As a child she'd always felt as if God had put an invisible window in people's foreheads so that Father Gerrard could see inside. She prayed now that she'd been wrong.

"Mary Fallon, I wish you would send for your brother. Let Mr. Hugh share in your joy. A wedding is a time for family."

"Now, Father Gerrard," Redmayne chided. "I thought we'd discussed all this before you even came upstairs to meet with our bride. The couple is somewhat shamed by their circumstance. They wish to be wed before they face her brother. It is understandable, I think. In your ministry, I would imagine you've stumbled across irate fathers or brothers, ready to revenge themselves on the rake who had seduced an innocent young woman. And explain it as you may, the fact is that Miss Delaney is carrying this man's bastard."

"It's none of your blasted business, Redmayne," Ciaran snapped.

Redmayne's taunts had been infuriating enough to Ciaran when only the three of them were present to hear them, but now, with Father Gerrard here, they were intolerable.

Always, the priest's goodness had shone through—unshakable faith, nobility of spirit, unfailing compassion. That this decent man should think Ciaran capable of an act so vile obviously seared like acid.

She could sense how much Ciaran wanted to proclaim the truth to the priest. That he'd never violated her. That he would rather have died than taken a woman's honor when his own was so precious to him. But he was helpless to do so.

"Captain Redmayne," Father Gerrard said, "I must ask you to keep your comments to yourself."

Redmayne's eyes narrowed a fraction. In grudging admiration for the priest's courage in reprimanding an English officer? Fallon wondered. Or had Father Gerrard just made a dangerous enemy?

But the priest had turned back to Ciaran, his voice gentling. "As for you, my son, your anger does you credit. It's obvious you are angry with yourself, that you regret that you have sinned. But you must forgive yourself for your mistake. I've always felt that showing our love with our bodies as well as our souls is a gift God gave us. In return, he asks only that we use that gift reverently. Wisely. Appreciating both its beauty and its power. There are those who would disagree with me, I know."

Disagree? Fallon was certain there were those who would have Father Gerrard defrocked for such a view. And yet, her affection for the old man grew, for he stared full-faced into reality, loving the earth with all its wonderful flaws, instead of trying to mold his parish into a replica of heaven.

The priest smiled. "In a perfect world, we would have the patience to wait until vows were spoken. But we are none of us perfect, I fear. Perhaps you were not patient, my son, but you are making it right, giving your child your name. You love Mary Fallon, and in the face of that love, God will forgive you. You must forgive yourself also, no matter what others might say."

"Hugh Delaney, for instance," Redmayne observed. "If Miss Delaney were *my* sister—"

"But she is *not.*" Father Gerrard frowned. "And Hugh Delaney is not just any man! He understands human

134

frailty, that people make mistakes. And he's never attempted to make them pay for it. He deserves better than this, to be banned from his only sister's wedding. Mary Fallon, child, I beg you to reconsider—"

"No, Father. Miss Delaney and Mr. MacDonough have made it perfectly clear that they do not wish Hugh Delaney's presence. Now, will you begin with the vows, or should we wait until Miss Delaney's belly swells big enough for all of Glenceo to see?"

White-hot violence. She could feel it rise in a wild tide inside Ciaran. Lightning fast, he spun, his fist knotting to smash into Redmayne's smug face, but Father Gerrard lunged between them. The priest had spent seventy years gauging the emotions hidden in men's souls. His voice rang out, clear, sharp. "Mr. MacDonough!"

Ciaran froze at the last moment, and Fallon could feel every muscle in his body vibrating with the force it took to rein in his fury. "Enough! Mr. MacDonough, would you have blood spilt at your wedding?"

Blood? As long as it was Redmayne's, Fallon was certain that nothing would fill her bridegroom with more delight.

"This is God's house," Father Gerrard warned. "Show proper respect. I've never believed in caning unruly schoolboys, but considering your behavior, I might be tempted to try it if you don't stop this nonsense."

"Not another word, Redmayne," Ciaran snarled, murder in his eyes, "or I vow, I'll drive them down your throat with my fist, wedding bedamned."

Redmayne flicked an imaginary speck of dust from the gold braid decking his uniform. "Miss Delaney, your bridegroom shows a distressing lack of manners. And this tendency to fits of temper. Most unappealing. Perhaps you should reconsider."

Fallon shook as she grasped Ciaran's arm, dragging him back. Lord, at this rate, Redmayne wouldn't have to prove Ciaran was a smuggler to hang him—the man was a heartbeat away from murder. "Please, Father. Let's just get on with it. You can see that everyone's nerves are on edge. And as for my brother—you must know that Hugh and I are . . . are not close."

It had chafed her when those aged eyes had been soft with gentle disappointment, astonished her when they sparked with anger. Now a very real mourning stirred beneath sparse gray lashes. "It would grieve your mother so very much to know that, child. Before I offered her last rites, she sent for Hugh. Her last words to him before she died were a plea that you would love each other, take care of each other for her sake."

The priest might as well have shoved a thorn beneath Fallon's skin. It stung and burned. Mama had sent for Hugh, wanted to see him, speak to him one last time. But she'd left Fallon without even saying good-bye. "A pity Mama never mentioned her wish to me," she said. "But it's a bit too late to worry about it now, I'm afraid. I wish to get married. At once."

The aged priest had seen that stubbornness in her features often enough to realize that imploring her further would be futile. She could see the surrender in his eyes, and the regret. With an almost imperceptible sigh, the priest turned the full light of his saintly eyes upon Ciaran.

"And you, sir. Do you wish to be married as well?"

Oh, yes, Fallon thought with grim irony. Her bridegroom was so eager he was all but grinding his teeth to dust. "Yes," Ciaran grated.

"And your faith?"

The quiet question raked Fallon's already battered nerves. Blast, more tangles? Fallon grimaced. What faith was Ciaran? Most likely a pagan who had reveled in the mysticism of the druid's sacred groves long before St. Patrick ever set foot upon Irish shores. But she could hardly tell Father Gerrard that. The poor old man would never recover. The theology of this wedding was beyond comprehension.

"My faith?" Ciaran echoed. Anger faded just a little, and he cast a wary, bewildered glance down at her.

It took more effort than she could imagine to force her most mischievous smile. "What do you think, Father? That he is a pagan?"

The old man flushed. "This is not a joking matter, Mary Fallon! I must know . . ." She felt crushing guilt when the priest gave a rare chuckle. "Child, you are incorrigible. All right then. I'd best marry you before you get into even more trouble, or your gentlemen friends turn the sanctuary into a boxing salon."

Clearing his throat, fumbling with his prayer book, the old man took his place at the altar. "Come, young sir," Father Gerrard beckoned Ciaran. "It is time for you to decide what you wish more—to fight with the captain, or to make this lovely young woman your bride."

For a moment she couldn't breathe. There was no question in Fallon's mind which Ciaran would prefer. He seemed to consider for a long moment. But in the end, he stepped up beside her.

Clearing his throat, Father Gerrard opened his worn prayer book. Fragments of rainbow danced across the tarnished crucifix above the altar and the faded black folds of the priest's cassock, bits of color glimmering like those that had flared from the ancient moon-struck brooch what seemed a lifetime ago.

Words that had joined lovers into one flesh for all eternity wove about them. She'd told Ciaran that they were words, just words. But from her earliest memories, Fallon had sensed that words held their own special magic. And none were more powerful than those she was about to exchange with this man beside her.

I promise to love, to honor, to cherish until death do us part. But death wouldn't part them. Their bond would be broken by the return of his memory, when he'd go back to his former life, or on the day he finished his quest here and disappeared back into the mist of legend.

It shouldn't have seemed so *real*. The ceremony. The vows. Her heart shouldn't have thundered, her gaze clinging to the fierce warrior's face beside her. But as Father Gerrard gently guided them through the rite he'd performed countless times, the old priest infused it with a fresh new wonder, a sense of timeless beauty, a beauty Fallon suddenly wished she could draw deep into herself, to treasure forever.

"I, Ciaran, take thee, Mary Fallon, to my wedded wife. To have and to hold, from this day forward, to love and to cherish—" His voice roughened, torn upon the vows.

His eyes seemed to probe to the deepest reaches of her soul. Asking for what? Forgiveness? Understanding? A hundred answers she didn't have. But suddenly she wished she did have them, could give Ciaran whatever he was seeking.

"Do you have the ring?" Father's query made her start.

"Ring?" Ciaran echoed. He looked so tense, so bewildered. Whatever faith he was—if he was any—Fallon was certain it wasn't Catholic.

The troubled crease deepened in Father Gerrard's brow. "The wedding ring. As a symbol of your love for each other."

"This was all so sudden. We . . . we didn't have time to get one." Fallon started to stammer.

But at that instant, Redmayne swooped near, his lips curling into that hawkish smile she wanted to smack from his face. "I was so concerned that this wedding take place without any . . . unfortunate snags, that I took the liberty of securing a ring." He extended his long white fingers, a wide gold band caught in their grasp.

"The blazes I'll take his—" Ciaran started to snarl, but Fallon's fingers clenched so hard on his it was a wonder she didn't draw blood.

"It will do until . . . until we can get our own, Captain Redmayne. Thank you." The words might have choked her if she hadn't been so preoccupied with keeping Ciaran from throttling the officer. Not that the image wasn't tempting. At least it would shut Redmayne's infernal mouth.

For the blackguard had shattered the dreamlike haze that had warmed the ceremony, made it beautiful, almost real. Ciaran did as the priest bid, said the proper words and shoved the ring on her finger. But the tenderness, the uncertainty, the reaching out that had been in his gaze had vanished.

Did Father Gerrard see it? Sense it? Why was there sudden sadness in his voice as he spoke the words, "I now pronounce you man and wife. What God hath joined together, let no man put asunder."

Shaken, aching somewhere deep within, Fallon looked down at her finger, the ring glittering there. And she tried to think of something to say.

The angels themselves must be shaking their heads over this union, St. Peter adding these latest sins to the endless, blotted tally beneath Mary Fallon Delaney's name. Not to mention the fact that she doubted the fairy king would be amused that she'd married his high champion. Doubtless, she'd broken some cosmic rule, and Irish fairies weren't the gossamer-winged, nectar-sipping kind that granted children's wishes. No. They could be a damnably spiteful lot.

She supposed it was a good omen, though, that the roof hadn't been split by lightning, Father Gerrard hadn't been transformed into a goat, and Ciaran hadn't disappeared in a puff of smoke.

"MacDonough, are you going to kiss the bride?" Redmayne drawled. "Or have such pursuits lost their appeal now that they're under papal sanction?"

There might have been another fray, but before Ciaran could move, the chapel door flew open, crashing against the inside wall. Fallon wheeled toward it, the other men following suit. What she saw there made her stomach plunge to her toes.

Disheveled from riding, her brother raced into the room, his eyes wild and haunted. "Thank God I got here before it was too late! Stop this . . . this wedding at once! I object! Isn't that the way of it? If anyone objects—"

"Yes. The wedding must be halted," Redmayne purred. "However, I'm afraid we're well past that part, Mr. Delaney. You are just in time to kiss the bride."

Hugh staggered, gripping the edge of one of the pews with a white-knuckled hand. "Fallon. My God, what have you done?" It was the anguish that made her furious. How dare he pretend to care so much when she knew the truth: that she'd been nothing but one more burden to him, to be endured since their mother had died?

"I'd think it obvious, Hugh. I've gotten married."

Hugh's gaze darted hopelessly to the priest's somber

face. "Father Gerrard, this can't be. Surely there is some way to undo it. An annulment! There is still time! The marriage hasn't been consummated."

Redmayne chuckled. "I should love to hear you plead your case. Perhaps if you convince the pope there is to be another virgin birth?"

"What the devil?" Hugh blazed.

"My son, there is something you should know," Father Gerrard said gently. "Mary Fallon is expecting this man's babe."

The words seemed to age her brother twenty years. His gaze flashed to Ciaran, loathing, fury, helplessness warring in his features. A scream tore from Fallon's throat as Hugh swung his fist at Ciaran's face. Ciaran didn't even attempt to deflect the blow. It connected with a sickening thud, making him stagger back a step.

"Hugh, for God's sake! Stop it!" Fallon shrilled, diving between the two men.

"You bastard!" Hugh roared. "You sonofabitch! What kind of cur are you?"

"He's my husband, Hugh! I love him!" It wasn't a lie. That fact suddenly terrified her.

"How . . . how could this have happened?" Hugh demanded, dazed. "I've never even seen him, didn't even suspect you were involved with a man."

"Perhaps you thought I was playing pattypans up at the castle all this time," she fired back. "You're gone all the time. I got tired of being alone."

Hugh flinched. "Fallon, this can't be . . . I can't believe—"

"I'm a woman grown now. Is it so impossible to imagine that a man could want me?"

Hugh looked as if she'd slapped him. "No! Of course not! It's just . . . I never even knew this man existed. I know nothing about him at all. Why didn't you tell me?"

She was stinging with guilt, hurting inside, raw with regret and the fresh wound of loving Ciaran, a wound that opened countless other gashes left on her lonely heart. "You've always seemed far more concerned with your estates and your ships and your infernal ledger sums than with me. I didn't think it would be of any importance to you."

"Fallon, that's enough!" A hard hand gripped her arm, and Ciaran whipped her around to face him. A bruise was purpling the side of his jaw. Damn, he'd been so anxious to fight with Redmayne, why the devil didn't he pound Hugh back? But there wasn't even anger in his features when he looked at her brother, only fierce intensity and burning shame. She wished they'd both pound each other to pulp. That way she wouldn't have to see what a disaster she'd wrought.

"Your brother has every right to be angry," Ciaran ground out. "He feels responsible for you."

"Well he's not. Not any more! I'm a married woman now, and—"

She might as well have been yelling at the stone walls of Ciaran's castle for all the attention either man paid to what she'd said.

"Mr. Delaney, I know that I deserve nothing but your contempt. Even so, would you be generous enough to talk privately with me so I might explain?"

"Explain?" Hugh raged. "You ruined my sister! Took advantage of an innocent young woman. She's carrying your child. *Your child.*" Hugh's voice broke. He turned away. But not before Fallon saw his features contort in anguish. "Why the devil am I blaming you?" he muttered, broken. "This is my fault."

"My dear son," Father Gerrard reached out in comfort, but Hugh jerked away, burying his face in his hand with a strangled sound akin to a sob. Silence fell. Even Redmayne was eerily still. After what seemed an eternity, the priest urged gently.

"Go back to Misthaven, the three of you. Speak, with forgiveness in your hearts, and understanding. Heal this breach before it scars you further."

"They cannot possibly leave yet," Redmayne inserted. "I must insist we share a glass of wine, make a toast to the happy—and fruitful—couple."

"We're leaving," Ciaran snarled. "Now." With that, he grasped Fallon's hand and hauled her toward the door.

"But I must insist—" Casually strolling in front of them, Redmayne blocked the exit with his own uniformed shoulders.

Green eyes locked with ice blue, sizzling like the metallic hum of clashing blades. "Am I under arrest, Captain? The only way you're going to keep me here is in chains. I'm taking my *wife* back to her home. Your involvement in this affair is over."

Fallon's stomach lurched. What was Ciaran doing? Begging to be taken into custody? One gesture from the captain would bring half the garrison down on their heads.

"Chains? Arrest?" Hugh's head snapped up, and he stared at the two men. "What the devil?"

"It's nothing, Hugh," Fallon insisted. "Just a mistake."

"The question is, who made it?" Redmayne purred, his gaze never leaving Ciaran's face. Astonishingly, in the end it was Redmayne who backed down. In surrender? Or was he manipulating this as well for some dark purpose of his own?

With fiendish carelessness, the captain strolled away from the door and leaned against the wall with a long-suffering sigh. "I was warned that the Irish are an ungrateful lot, even when one attempts to do something for their own good. I see now that it is true. I suppose we can talk later, Mr. MacDonough. I still have a number of questions that need to be answered. But we're civilized men, are we not? We can wait until after I've asked them to decide whether or not to add chains to your apparel."

The threat vibrated through the room. Redmayne turned to Fallon.

"As for you, Miss Delaney, it is a little-known fact that I adore children."

Fallon grimaced. Doubtless he liked to eat one or two lightly toasted with his breakfast each morning.

"I shall await the birth of your child with great anticipation. Considering all my efforts to get you wed today, you might even consider me for the position of godfather."

Ciaran snarled out an unintelligible oath, but Fallon

couldn't keep from shuddering. The thought of Redmayne hovering near any child—even an imaginary one—chilled her blood.

She said nothing, only swept out behind Ciaran. The ride back to Misthaven gave a new meaning to the word "torture." Hell, Fallon learned, wasn't fire and brimstone and shrieks of agony. It was silence, tension strung fiendishly tight until she wanted to scream just to end the torment.

But she said nothing. It was difficult enough battling to ignore the rigid fury of the man mounted on the horse behind her, while keeping her gaze as far away from the devastated features of her brother as possible.

When they reached Misthaven, she wanted nothing more than to stumble up to her room, fling herself facedown on her bed and pull the covers over her head. Not that she'd cry—devil if she'd do that. Just time to gain a little peace, time to think what to say, what to do.

When she climbed down off Cuchulain in Misthaven's carriage circle, she staged a dramatic little stumble for effect. Hugh winced, but Ciaran only hauled her upright none too gently.

As they entered the house, a thousand questions etched in the haggard lines of Hugh's face, but he only dragged his fingers through his hair. "Perhaps you should just go to bed, Fallon. After all, this upset can't be good for . . . I mean, we have to . . . to think of . . . your child." It was obvious the words twisted like knives in her brother's chest.

Fallon could hear Ciaran's teeth grinding. "She is a great deal stronger than you think," he insisted. "We need to have our discussion now."

"Wh–what discussion?" Fallon glanced up at him, dread thudding in her chest as she saw the mulish jut of his square jaw. "Hugh's right. I'm exhausted. And there's nothing more to say, at least, nothing that can't wait until tomorrow."

"It can't wait another blasted minute," Ciaran insisted.

"But you and I need to . . . to discuss what we're going to tell—"

"The truth, Fallon," Ciaran snapped. "We're going to tell him the truth. That is, if we can even sort it out from this infernal tangle we've made."

Hugh's brows etched upward in question, but he strode down the corridor and opened the door to his private study. Fallon would sooner have entered a lion's den.

"I don't think this is a wise idea," Fallon drew back, stammering. "Surely Hugh understands that we need some time alone—" But Ciaran grasped her wrist, all but dragging her into the chamber where her brother had spent so many hours.

In their father's day, the curtains had always been drawn to protect eyes from too much brightness after an evening of excessive wine. The chamber had been scented with the smoky tang of tobacco and brandy, the walls decked with hunting prints, the tabletops more likely to hold silver-handled riding crops or lists of horses to be sold at fair. Pamphlets about races and scandal sheets from London had littered the desktop—a country gentleman's pursuits, uncluttered by anything so vulgar as actual business affairs.

But all evidence of their father had been swept away. The new blue draperies at the window were flung back to let the sun spill in. The massive mahogany desk was weighed down with papers and heavy ledgers.

The only picture in the room was a portrait of their mother, dressed as simply as any shepherdess, while three-year-old Hugh twined heather in her hair. Her cheeks bloomed, rosy and plump, and her eyes sparkled. Jealousy jabbed at Fallon. The woman in the portrait was a stranger to her, an image lost during the years, replaced by the fragile, hollow-eyed mother who had lived in the sickroom. But Hugh had known the woman in the portrait. He could remember . . .

"Fallon, what is this all about?" Hugh demanded. "When young Kevin Dunne came dashing up, telling me the priest had been fetched to the garrison, that you were getting married, I scarce believed it. And now to find out you're bearing a child? How could you be so reckless?"

"She *was* reckless," Ciaran said. "So much so I've

wanted to throttle her a dozen times since I first met her. However, she was also generous and brave."

"Ciaran, no," she protested. She wasn't certain what she would say to Hugh, but whatever it was, it would be a sight easier without Ciaran in the room. Could she possibly shove over six feet of male out the door as if he were a hunting dog? No. Reasoning had a far better chance—infinitesimal instead of none at all. "This is really something between my brother and me. Why don't you go upstairs, and leave Hugh and me to speak alone?"

"So you can keep sheltering me?" Ciaran looked as if the very thought of any more deception made him want to retch. "Keep digging yourself into deeper and deeper trouble with lies? No. It was one thing to lie to that bastard Redmayne. Your brother deserves the truth."

She couldn't have summoned back a *reasonable* legendary hero. No, she'd had to call back the noblest of them all. She'd just never realized how damned inconvenient honor could be until now.

Ciaran turned to Hugh. "Your sister found me wandering near some castle ruins last night. I was damned helpless. Head gashed, my memory shattered. She claimed she'd been working some sort of magic, trying to summon up some long-dead hero."

Hugh blanched. "My God. Fallon, you couldn't . . . you didn't really believe the legend?"

Ciaran grimaced. "I know. It sounded preposterous to me, even with my head bashed in. Worse still, I could have been dangerous and she damned well knew it. She'd encountered Redmayne at the castle earlier. He let her know that he was prowling around that area searching for someone."

"At the castle ruins?" Hugh scowled. "Who was he searching for, a ghost? The one thing you can be certain of is this: whatever fairy tale Fallon was chasing, the captain wasn't out trying to find some accursed legend that probably never even existed."

"He was searching for a man they call Silver Hand."

Hugh blanched, fingers closing, white-knuckled, on the edge of his desk. "The smuggler?"

"He's been plying his trade up and down the coast—"

"I know what he's been doing, damn it!" Hugh stared at Ciaran, stricken. "Redmayne believes that this man is Silver Hand?"

Panic fluttered in Fallon's throat. It wasn't too late for Hugh to fling Ciaran out the door. Charity was one thing, but sheltering the rogue Silver Hand would be suicidal. And Hugh had proved time and again he'd surrender anything to protect Misthaven land. "You know Redmayne and his kind, Hugh," she pleaded. "You've seen what they're capable of. With all the furor over bringing this Silver Hand to justice, they won't be overly cautious about who they hang. And who better than a stranger who has lost his memory? No one in Glenceo knows him. No one would care if he lived or died. I had to find a way to keep Redmayne from arresting Ciaran and flinging him in jail. So I pretended that he was my betrothed."

"Pretended?"

"That he was my secret lover. That we were going to elope because we feared your disapproval. It was the only logical explanation I could think of to explain why no one had ever seen Ciaran before. But Redmayne—it was as if he knew it was a lie. He kept pushing, probing, twisting everything I said around until I was desperate. I had to find some way to calm his suspicions." She swallowed hard. "I claimed that I was pregnant."

"But you . . . you—"

"There is no babe," Ciaran said.

Relief washed over Hugh's face, draining him so completely he sagged down in his chair. "No child? You were pretending to be engaged. There is no child." Hope brightened his eyes. "Does that mean that the marriage is a sham as well? It was damned clever of you to—"

"No. The marriage is real. Redmayne trapped us into it. I think he suspected Fallon was lying. He put her to the test, thinking she would break. Once we'd started the deception, there was no way to escape the trap he'd laid." Ciaran spun out the story, from beginning to end. "So now you know the whole of it. There is no way to be certain who I am. My memory is gone. You should know that there's a good chance I might be the man they're seeking." Ciaran's lips twisted in an ironic smile. "Unless you're like your sister, and believe in this magic spell, this Ciaran of the Mist story."

Hugh rose, crossing to where a cut-glass decanter stood on a marble-topped table. Withdrawing the stopper with a trembling hand, he poured himself a generous measure of madeira and drained the glass in one gulp. "Fallon, this is unbelievable. You're married to a man you met one day ago. You don't even know who he is. Hell, *he* doesn't even know who he is!"

"The last thing I wish to do is put you and your sister in further danger." Ciaran interjected. "You've both risked too much already on my behalf. You'll be wanting me to leave, and I don't blame you."

"No!" Fallon protested. "Hugh, please. For once, drag your nose out of your infernal accounts and have a little courage! You can't just let him go charging off this way."

"Fallon, your brother is only trying to protect you. He's responsible for everyone on this whole estate. And he can't be expected to risk everything for a man who might be a criminal, a rebel. A man he doesn't even know. Just let me leave as I should have done the first moment I saw you."

Fallon thought his leaving would be like tearing out a piece of her heart. "You can't leave! Hugh, stop him!" She had no hope that her brother would. Cautious Hugh would be all too eager to show him the door. She braced herself for a battle of wills, but Hugh turned to Ciaran, his voice low.

"No. Fallon's right. I can't let you risk leaving Misthaven."

Ciaran gaped, incredulous. "Are you as mad as your sister? Do you have any idea of the danger you could be in? If I *am* Silver Hand, you could lose everything! You could hang!"

Hugh yanked at his neckcloth, as if he could feel the rough kiss of the noose. "We don't know that you are this smuggler. But even if we did, it wouldn't change my decision. What if you tried to leave and Redmayne had his men watching the house? They'd arrest you, and Fallon would be trapped by her lies—condemned for aiding a fugitive from the law! No. No matter how grim things seem, better to follow through on this charade you've begun for now. We'll work to discover who you are. Then, once we get everything settled and the danger is past, we can have the marriage annulled."

"Hugh, I don't necessarily think we should—annul the marriage, I mean." Fallon protested, astonished by the depth of panic she felt at the thought of the marriage being dissolved. How could something that had seemed such a calamity become so precious in such a short time?

Hugh's brow furrowed beneath the lock of sandy hair that tumbled across it. "There is no babe. As long as the union is never consummated, this can still all be untangled in the end. But for your own safety, the servants—and everyone else in the county—will have to believe that you're wed. That means adjoining bedrooms." A slight flush buffed Hugh's cheekbones. "And you will have to be seen together, as a couple, at local assemblies."

"But what if someone recognizes me as this . . . this Silver Hand?" Ciaran demanded. "You could be in grave danger."

Hugh's jaw hardened, the masculine equivalent of Fallon's own stubborn expression. "That's a chance I'm willing to take."

"Why? Why would you do this for me?"

"You heard my sister. Our family is notorious for bending with the winds to hold on to our lands, no matter what the cost. Perhaps it's time I had a little courage."

"You have nothing to prove to me. To anyone," Ciaran said.

Hugh turned away. "You ask why I would help you. What would you say if I told you that, in a way, I envy you, Mr. MacDonough?" Hugh paced to the window, shoulders bowed with unutterable weariness as he stared out across the fields of green. "There are times it would be a relief to lose my own memory," Hugh said softly. "I've seen enough innocent people suffer to last me a lifetime."

CHAPTER

9

Fallon grimaced, raking her mother's silver-backed brush through her hair. As long as she could remember, the act had comforted her somehow, as if it drew her mother closer. But she'd nearly brushed her scalp raw, and tonight it only coiled the tension, the restlessness inside her, tighter still.

Her wedding night. She'd never expected to have one, but if she *had* imagined one, it would never have resembled the trial she'd been through tonight. She had stood with a smile plastered on her face while Hugh announced the "happy tidings" to the household staff.

The stunned servants had offered uneasy congratulations. The whispers and blushes and confused glances told Fallon that rumors about her supposed pregnancy had already reached the house. And theirs was a mild reaction indeed in comparison to the ordeal that would await her when news of her hasty and most unusual marriage reached the neighboring gentry.

And no matter how fiercely she'd argued with Hugh once they'd again sought the privacy of his study, he insisted that once the wound on Ciaran's head had completely healed, the two of them must go out and face the infernal lions. In the end, they'd given her two weeks' reprieve. A paltry victory. Hugh's insistence had been infuriating enough in itself, but it was made far worse by seeing Ciaran coming down solidly on Hugh's side—a nasty surprise.

It still stung—the respect that had darkened Ciaran's eyes as her brother had spoken, the way he'd embraced Hugh's cautious plans. She'd felt betrayed and hurt, and she loathed the sense that her brother had somehow stolen away Ciaran's loyalty—something that should belong to her.

Unable to endure it any longer, she'd stalked from the room, half-certain that neither man had noticed her leaving. But she'd always had a knack for hurling herself from a bad situation to a worse. For Sorcha, her eyes gleaming with the wisdom of a Celtic Eve, had prepared a bath scented with some mystic charm a white witch had given her, one that promised to make the flower-spangled bridal bed pure heaven.

'Twill bewitch any mortal man, me granny promised, till he'll fall desperate in love with ye, Sorcha had sworn.

But there wouldn't be a bridal bed. And Ciaran had been bewitched by far greater magic than any white witch could make. Fairy chains already bound him to another world. And neither the chains of the marriage vows nor the chains of some herbal charm could change that.

Fallon had wanted to thrust the maid out of her chamber bodily, but Sorcha had stubbornly insisted on dressing her in her finest nightgown, dabbing on essence of lavender—preparing her for a wedding night that would never be.

Sorrow rippled through her, and she gently lay her mother's brush down on her dressing table, unable to face the image that stared back at her from the mirror.

The wild, hoydenish girl who had struck terror into the hearts of the prim county misses was gone. Even the stubborn, headstrong woman who had resolved to take a chance, to summon back Ciaran of the Mist, had vanished. A stranger wore her soft oval face, her lightly freckled nose, her unruly fall of red hair. Someone achingly new stared out of her eyes, shadowing them with a vulnerability she never would have believed possible.

Wincing, Fallon turned away and paced to the window. She unlatched it and pushed it open, hoping to find herself in the whispering of the hills she loved so well.

Night was singing its song to the moon, the wind plucking at branch and blossom and silvery cloud like a bard's fingers on a harp. Fallon leaned out as far as she dared, wishing she could slip onto the ledge, spread her arms like a nightingale's wings and drift through the sky, one with the darkness and the wind and the whispering of legends that seeped into every fissure and rock, cliff and glen of Ireland. But even that had changed.

Why had she wandered out so many times in the years since her mother had died? What had she been seeking? She'd never been quite sure. Fairy magic, enchanted castles, mermen who kept drowned sailors in Soul Cages at the bottom of the sea—so many things mere mortals could never see, could only believe deep in their hearts. But she'd never suspected the truth. She'd peopled her world with stories and myths and possibilities so that she wouldn't have to be alone.

But none of her questing had changed that sense of isolation. She'd huddled under a varicolored quilt of a thousand dreams spun by an entire people throughout a thousand years, the same way a frightened child huddled under a blanket to keep out the dark. Because legends could never die. Fairies would never leave you. She'd just never realized, until now, that the dark was still out there. And the loneliness.

She'd never guessed the truth until Ciaran had come stumbling out of her dreams and into her life. In an instant, everything had changed forever. The danger was that everything could shift again in a heartbeat. Mortal or fairy-kissed champion, Ciaran could disappear from her life forever—*would* disappear, once fate had played out her game. Once the castle was saved, the quest was finished. The legend always ended the same. The mist and the magic. And the vanishing.

A chill worked through the thin fabric of her night-gown. It was only a question of when. And even if he wasn't the Ciaran of legend, he'd leave. He'd return to the life he'd known before her, the people he'd cared about . . . maybe a woman. Unthinkable. Fallon tried to shove the notion away.

Who could say when he might disappear? He'd already tried to leave her once. It was possible he might slip away at any time in another misguided fit of heroics, attempting to shield her and her brother, to keep them from further danger.

Dread dropped like a cold stone into her belly. She hugged her arms tight against her middle—that place where no babe grew. Where none would ever grow. And she was stunned at the sudden feeling of emptiness, of loss.

She crossed to the door that separated their rooms. Such a thin barrier. And she stiffened at the sound of someone entering the chamber beyond. Heavy footsteps, as if the weight of two worlds were upon his shoulders.

Ciaran. She sensed his closeness in every fiber of her being. Sensed his weariness. His confusion. His regret. And even her earlier irritation faded.

Relief flooded through her at the certainty that he hadn't disappeared. For now, he still belonged to her. It stunned her to realize how much she needed to touch him, assure herself he was real. But what could she bring as a peace offering?

Mustering her courage, she crossed to a table Sorcha had draped in white linen and covered with countless delicacies: rich pastries and jewel-like wine, sweetmeats and the ripest fruits. "A lover's feast," the little maid had said brightly. Fallon smiled as her gaze locked on a crystal bowl all but lost among the treats. One tidbit about Ciaran the legends had passed on was his favorite sweet: the fresh cherries the fairy king had used to enchant him so long ago.

Fallon scooped up the bowl and held it against her breasts, then crossed to the door. She grimaced. It would be a miracle if Hugh hadn't slipped up and nailed it shut for the night. But the handle turned easily. Not pausing to knock, she eased the door open.

Her breath caught in her throat. Ciaran stood, stripped to his breeches, his naked back gleaming in the candlelight. He turned, surprise darkening his gaze. "Fallon. What are you doing here? Do you need something?"

I need to touch you. To beg you never to go away. I love you. The words bubbled up inside her, but she didn't dare say them aloud. He already thought her half-mad. Her cheeks burned. "Hugh kept insisting it was important to act as if we were married, so I thought . . . I mean, the servants left a table full of food, and I can't possibly eat it all myself." She was making a mess of things. Desperate under the intensity of his gaze, she thrust the crystal bowl toward him. "I brought you these. Cherries are your favorite."

He glanced down at the red fruit, but instead of hunger or pleasure, his features tightened with aversion. He drew back as if he thought they were poisoned. "I don't eat those."

"But you do—the legend says—"

"Fallon!" He snapped. "I'm no legend. Damn it, why won't you believe me?"

She set the bowl down, aching inside. And suddenly, the truth spilled out. "Because if you're a legend, you can belong to me. At least, for a little while."

"Fallon." His voice was gentle, filled with quiet yearning. "It's all make-believe. It isn't real."

"But you're here, aren't you? I called you back and you came."

"Only by chance. I'll be going away as soon as possible. We both know that."

"Yes." Fallon blinked hard, fighting back the hot tears that burned her eyes. "Ciaran," she said after a moment, "there's something I need to ask you. A favor."

"I'd do anything in my power to repay you for what you've done for me, Mary Fallon."

"Promise me something. That you won't just vanish—leave without saying good-bye. Promise you'll tell me when you're leaving."

"I can't promise that. If there's some sort of disaster, I might not be able to find you and tell you." His gaze intensified on her face. "Why is it so important to you?"

Fallon sucked in a shuddering breath. Did she dare to trust anyone with the wounded corner of her heart? "Too many people have disappeared from my life already. Papa rode away, and I never saw him again. And Mama—I woke up one morning, and she was gone. Ever since, I've loved the hills and the castle, the stories and the legends and the sea cliffs. I've never let myself care about anything or anyone who could leave me."

A stillness settled over his features, an unutterable longing. He closed the space between them, cupping one hardened palm gently against her cheek, and she wanted to reach up, stroke away the lock of hair that all but concealed the healing gash. "Ah, Mary Fallon. I understand what it's like to be alone."

"Because you've lost your memory? Everything is strange and new?"

He shook his head. "No. I've always been alone. I don't know how I know that, but I do." His thumb stroked a tiny arc across her lips. "And I didn't want to be. I wanted . . . somewhere to belong. Someone to wait for me."

"Are you starting to remember?" She didn't know if the thought relieved or frightened her.

His eyes slid closed. "Just impressions. Shadows. The ugliness of battle, the stench of death, suffocating."

"You were a warrior, then! I knew it!"

"I fought. That much I know."

"Can you see what kind of clothes the other men are wearing? That way we could tell if it was hundreds of years ago."

"No. I can't remember that because it wasn't important to me. All that mattered was what happened after the battle was past. The sun shining. Other men laughing as women flung themselves into their arms, sharing fierce kisses, not caring that the whole world was looking on. That *I* was looking on. Tears. The women crying, touching the faces of their husbands and lovers as if to make certain they were real. And children clambering about, clinging to their fathers' legs, tugging at their hands, their little voices . . ." His voice cracked.

"Time—there would be time for tales of glory later. Admiration, respect. I'd get the hero's share. But none of that mattered. I didn't want that—didn't need it. I needed . . . someone's arms around me. Someone's tears dampening my chest. I needed . . ."

Fallon's throat tightened at the image he'd woven. In all the years she'd pored over her myths and legends, learning Ciaran's tale by heart, she'd never considered what it would have been like to be high champion, separate from other men because of his honor, his noble deeds. And there had been no woman waiting. For all that he was beloved by his people as a hero, Ciaran the man had always been alone. "I would have kissed you even if the whole world were watching. In fact, I already did, outside the pub."

Ciaran's mouth tipped up in a heartbreaking smile. "You did. But you seemed far more likely to kick Redmayne in the shins than to stand by, helpless, weeping pretty tears."

"I–I'm not very good at crying. I gave it up soon after Mama died. What's the use when there's no one to hear?"

Silence hung between them, a long, aching moment. It squeezed Fallon's heart. Then Ciaran's voice, so low, so tender.

"I'm listening, Mary Fallon."

Damn him. Just four tiny words, and she could feel the burning beneath her lashes. This time, all the stubbornness she possessed couldn't keep the tears from spilling free. He gathered her in his arms, her cheek pressed to the beating of his heart. They were the tears of a lonely little girl, the tears of an angry young woman, the tears of a dreamer awakened and afraid.

And he held her in the strength of his arms, warming her, stroking her hair, murmuring soft words against the crown of her head.

She wanted to stay there forever. In the end, she had to pull away. Scrubbing away the traces of tears with her fist, she gave a nervous laugh, suddenly and hideously uncomfortable that she'd revealed such weakness to anyone.

"I have to stop this," she said. "This is supposed to be our wedding night. It won't do for the maids to see my eyes all puffy and swollen from crying."

"Perhaps they'd think these were tears of joy." He grasped her chin, turned her face up so that he could look full upon it. "And I—I would think they were beautiful." He skimmed his fingertip along her cheek, gathering up the droplets and hiding them in his hand, as if they were liquid diamonds, a treasure too precious even for the cache of the fairy king.

She peered into his eyes, suddenly breathless. Yearning softened the sensual curve of his mouth. "Would you kiss them away? If they were tears of joy?"

"Any tears. All your tears."

"Show me."

He hesitated just an instant, and Fallon sensed that he was ready to pull away. But then he threaded his fingers back through her hair. Slowly, as if he'd imagined this moment a thousand times and wanted it to last forever, he lowered his mouth to her tear-damp face.

Warm, tender, moist, his lips skimmed along the salty wet path trailing down her cheek. His breath wisped against the fragile skin beneath her eye, then he kissed her lids closed. A tiny whimper rose in Fallon's throat, as his mouth melted the hard lumps of pain, of grief, of loneliness she'd hoarded through the years in her soul.

Unable to bear the sense of opening, of unlocking for another moment, she shifted her own mouth until it was under his.

He stilled, and she could feel the wild lurch of his heart. "Fallon, we shouldn't—"

"You promised to kiss away all my tears, Ciaran. There are still so many left deep inside me. *Here.*" She gathered up his fingers in her own, then pressed them against her heart. The soft mounds of her breasts yielded beneath the gentle pressure of his palms, his long, strong fingers curving along the edge of gossamer fabric that skimmed low, his thumb pillowed on fragile, velvety skin.

"Fallon," he said hoarsely, "this isn't real. No matter how much we might wish that it was. We shouldn't—"

"What isn't real? My tears are. And your loneliness. And the vows we spoke today before Father Gerrard. *With my body I thee worship*. Such beautiful words. And just a moment ago you said you wanted . . ." She nibbled at her bottom lip, heat spilling into her cheeks. "But maybe . . . maybe you don't want me. I know I'm not beautiful. And you must be used to fairy maidens, so bewitching they can steal a man's soul."

"No fairy maid could weave the kind of magic you've spun. Ever since I saw you, there in that ridiculous castle, parting the veil of mist like some lady spun out of moonlight, offering me her hand, to lead me . . . where, Fallon? Where are you taking me? Into some beautiful realm of illusion? One so strange and wondrous I'll never want to leave? But they're your dreams, Fallon. Your legends. Your magic. They can never belong to me."

"But tonight can. Our wedding night. No matter what else comes after."

He thrust her away from him, torment racking his features with agonized longing. "No. No matter how much I want you, we can't be together."

"How can you be certain? Maybe I'm wrong. You're just a man, alone." She didn't believe it, but she didn't care. She only wanted to erase the stubbornness, the resolve that was darkening his eyes, hardening that mouth that had been so tender against her own.

Ciaran frowned. "I just know I can't stay with you. Those fragments of images, those emotions, those shadows—the feeling was so strong in me. No matter how much I wanted, it was impossible."

"I never even dreamed of marriage, of someone to hold me, to kiss me, to take me to his bed and love away the loneliness. You think I'm a dreamer, with my head in the clouds, and yet, I looked out over my life and I knew no love would ever find me."

"Why would you think such a thing? You're brave and generous. And beautiful. Not in the common way—all rosy perfection, like some goddess carved in marble. You're far too warm, too much of earth and sea and wind and wildness, to be contained in the boundaries that short-sighted men draw around the word 'beautiful.' Some day, a man will come who deserves you, Fallon. Who sees what I see. The strength, the power in you, the tiny flaws that make you like no other. Your face—the way it changes like the sky above the sea. And the way your spirit calls out."

"What does it say?"

"Believe. If you dare. But I'm afraid I don't have that kind of courage."

"Maybe I believe enough for both of us right now. In all the legends I've ever read, one thing is the same. Fate spins out, like a ribbon of silk, linking everything together—every fear, every challenge, every quest and reward. Destiny. Ciaran, isn't it possible that I was meant to find you on the cliffs? That we were meant to wed? And that tonight—just for tonight—we've been given a chance not to be alone?"

He sucked in a shuddering breath. "If it were only that simple—"

"It is. We've even spoken the wedding vows. I'm your wife." And would be forever if they lay together this night. The marriage could never be annulled, wiped away as if it had never existed.

"We'll be wed for only a little while, Fallon. Until this disaster is over. It's not as if you love me. It's a phantom you love—a figment of your imagination, not a man."

"I don't know how to love a man. Teach me."

"I can't," he ground out. "I don't think I've ever . . ." A flush darkened his cheekbones. He glanced down at where a blue satin bow gathered the neckline of her nightgown at her breasts. "From the moment you kissed me it felt so . . . unexpected. So new. As if it were the first time."

"It was. My first time, I mean. It made me wish . . ."

"Wish what?"

She trembled, feeling so wanton, needing him so much she didn't care. "That you would touch me. On my skin. Beneath my nightgown. That you would let me touch you."

He swore, low, his hands knotting into fists. "You already did. When you were bathing me, sliding your hands across my skin. It felt so damned good. I was lost, but when your hands were on my body I didn't care where I'd come from, why I was wandering. That's one of the reasons I had to leave before you awakened. So you would forget all about me."

"Even if I'd never seen you again, I would have remembered forever. Your body is so beautiful, Ciaran. Hard and warm. I couldn't help but see." She reached out, touching his bare chest, running her fingertips along the curves and hollows, where the shadows clung. "But even your body isn't as beautiful as what I saw in your eyes."

He gave a snort of self-disgust. "Confusion? A tangled mess?"

"No. Sadness and courage. Honor and pain. The same loneliness I've felt forever. I never thought I'd find someone who could understand. I never thought I could find anyone at all." Her lips curved, tremulous. "I know I may just be . . . borrowing you for a little while. But maybe, just maybe, we could make that enough."

"You give so much, Mary Fallon. And you ask so little in return. How can I—"

"Like this." Her fingers went to the ribbon tie, pulled it loose, the fabric opening to reveal the shadowy cleft between her breasts. His gaze burned her, seared her, touched her more deeply than fingers ever could. He swallowed hard.

Bewitched. Enchanted, by something more powerful than even the fairy king's cherries. Were there rules against making love to the king's champion? Fallon suddenly wondered. What would the cost be for seducing Ciaran of the Mist? What forfeit would the fairies demand? For in every tale, every legend, every whispered story the crofters told before their peat fires, the fairies were a vengeful, jealous lot who guarded what was their own.

But she didn't care if she had to spend the rest of forever sorrowing as Deirdre had when Naosi was hunted down, or as the princess Isolde had when she'd been separated from her beloved Tristan. It would be worth any price to be loved by this man tonight.

Fallon grasped the edge of the delicate muslin, and started to slide it down her shoulder, to bare herself to that hungry gaze.

"No," he rasped, catching her fingers tight in his, stopping her. And shame flooded through her, regret clenching about her throat. Rejection. She should have expected it. Should have known he would turn her away in the end.

She should go back to her own bedchamber. She had to do it before the tears came. But before she could move, he whispered.

"Let me do it."

Hunger sang through her, passion drumming to an ancient rhythm in her blood. She arched her head back, giving him access, felt his fingers awkwardly fumbling with the garment. He eased the cloth off her shoulders and halfway down her upper arms, but the edge snagged on the burning tips of her nipples. With unsteady fingers, Ciaran dipped between the cloth and her skin, drawing her breast out from beneath the gown. Something warm, slightly rough abraded the point of her nipple. His finger. He traced the circle of her aureole in a wonder of discovery.

"Like peaches. So pretty. So sweet," he murmured, gliding the fabric beneath her other breast. The night-gown bunched beneath the velvety mounds, held in place by his big hand.

"Let the gown fall," she whispered. "I want you to . . . to see me."

"No. We've both waited so long, Fallon. I want to savor every inch of you—slowly, so slowly. Too precious to rush." It seemed to take an eternity as he revealed her, a sliver at a time, marveling, murmuring praise, caressing her with his hands and his eyes and his voice. He discovered her body an inch at a time, awakened every nerve and stirred it to life with the lightest brush of his fingers until she was burning with desire for him. And when at last he let the nightgown drift like fallen petals about her feet, Fallon could scarcely breathe, she needed him so desperately.

Scooping her into his arms, he started to carry her to the big bed that was supposed to be his. But she stopped him, remembering Sorcha's promise: the bed sprinkled with flower petals and rare herbs that promised devotion, the scent of the water she'd bathed in, a magic elixir that would drive a man mad with love.

And she wanted Ciaran mad with love of her—wanted it more than she'd ever wanted anything in her life. "Please . . . my bed. I want us to be in my bed tonight."

Wordlessly, he turned, and carried her into her chamber. A bridal chamber alight with banks of white wax candles, bundles of wildflowers, the coverlet turned back. Gently he laid her down on the sheets. Her body crushed the velvety petals, her warmth releasing their essence.

He kissed her mouth. Then stood, unfastening the breeches that strained over the hard ridge of his arousal. She'd seen him before, naked in all his glorious masculinity. But this time was different.

She tried to memorize the width of his shoulders, the cords of muscle, the dusting of dark hair that formed a perfect vee on his chest. His stomach was ridged with hard muscle above a soft line of dark down that arrowed from his navel into the shadows where his clumsy fingers worked the fastenings. It was as if he'd never seen buttons before. And maybe he never had. Embarrassment stained his cheekbones as he struggled.

Fallon smiled and caught his wrist, not wanting him to feel anything but thick, honeyed pleasure. "Let me do it," she echoed the words he'd said to her. "I want to savor you, the way you did me. Make you feel delicious."

"I don't know if I can . . . can stand much more. I want you too much."

She knelt before him, her hair a shimmering curtain about her shoulders, and stripped the breeches down his hips, past his straining erection, then down the length of his legs. She kissed him. His thigh, the inside of his knee. Awed by the beauty, the *rightness* of it all. Ciaran's lady. Ciaran's wife. Bride of the mist and the magic. But like the mist, this was so fleeting. The burning sun of reality threatened to snatch it away.

She circled her arms about his thighs, wanting to hold him forever, knowing she never could. The tousled silk of her hair swirled in a veil about his legs in the most intimate of caresses, and she pressed her cheek against him—the flat plane of his stomach, the hard ridge of his shaft. A low groan tore from Ciaran's throat at the intimate contact.

He gathered the mass of coppery curls in his hands, let them fall in a cascade of liquid flame. Then he stepped out of the breeches and drew her up—up the long, granite-honed landscape of his body, to where his mouth was waiting, fierce with hunger.

"Mary Fallon . . . beautiful . . . so beautiful. My wild fairy maid," he breathed, gathering her against him, soft, feminine swells and hollows pressed to a wall of muscle as rugged and primitive as the sea cliffs where she had found him.

Even now, the ancient tales she'd loved spun silken rainbows about her. Was this what Deirdre of the Sorrows had felt when her forbidden lover Naosi had taken her in his arms? This wild need, this power beyond the earth and sky and sea? If so, Fallon could understand why the Celtic beauty had turned her back on Connor MacNessa, the king of Ulster, to run away with her love.

For this was a feeling beyond right or wrong. Two souls crashing against each other like the waves below the Castle of the Dancing Mist, battling for an instant, then blending into one in a glorious flash of shimmer and foam.

Every part of her trembled as she smoothed her palms up the thick caps of muscle that formed his shoulders, then along the cords of his throat to the thick waves of his hair, dark as the night in which he'd come to her.

She thought she'd die of wanting before he lowered his mouth to hers, but then he took her lips in a kiss so hungry, a moan rose in her throat. His hands were everywhere, charting the delicate ridges of her spine, smoothing down the flare of her hips, cupping her bottom and pressing her tighter against that part of him that throbbed between them, hard as the shaft of Cuchulain's enchanted spear.

He eased her back down on the bed where she'd lain alone so many years, dreaming. Now she was alone no more. He followed her there, filling his palms with the creamy bounty of her breasts and feasting on the berryred tips as if they were the cherries that had lured him to immortality. Hot, wet, eager, he tasted her, suckling her nipple in his mouth. A shower of sparks ignited beneath his lips, driving down into her woman's core, setting it burning.

And she wanted him. Her husband. Her lover. Her dream. Wanted him to be a part of her forever. For no matter what happened in the future, nothing—not Redmayne's plotting or reality's cold blaze, not fairy kings or memories reawakened—could ever steal away from her the beauty of this one night when Ciaran belonged to her. Only to her.

His fingers played her body with the awe of an ancient bard touching the harp strings for the first time, plucking at her nipples, strumming the delicate ridges of her ribs, circling the slight swell of her belly. Her breath caught as his fingertips stirred the dark auburn curls of her femininity.

"Open your thighs for me. I want to touch you, Fallon. Let me . . ."

Swallowing hard, cheeks burning, she eased her legs apart, knowing she'd open her very soul for this man if he but asked it of her. In a way, she already had. She'd surrendered pieces of herself she'd never shared with another soul. The surrendering of her body was far easier. She fitted her hand atop his, and pressed it, tight against the place that was afire for him.

She gasped as those strong fingers threaded through warm ringlets at her urging, then dipped deeper still to sleek satin. One callused tip brushed a tiny ember where all sensation seemed centered. The eye of the storm, where all magic was born.

"Soft." Ciaran groaned, exploring her, teasing her, learning her secrets by touch. And she was shaken to the core by the wonder of his discovery. His first time. Hers.

"I never knew a woman was so soft and damp, like rose petals in rain. I want to bury myself in that heat. In you."

"I'm your wife, Ciaran. I . . ." *Love you,* her heart cried, but she dared not give voice to the words, words that might well wound this honorable man, make him desert her for fear he'd leave her heart bleeding when he walked away. "I . . . feel so empty, deep inside. I need you."

"You need to be ready—ready to take me inside you. There'll be pain the first time you lie with a man."

"I don't care. I need you too much."

"I wish I could take that pain for you."

They weren't idle words, Fallon knew, her heart full. This was a man who would suffer any anguish for those he loved, bear any burden, sacrifice with joy. It humbled her, made her love him all the more. She rose up, kissing the pale shadow of bruise just visible beneath the silky fringe of his hair.

A sheen of sweat glistened on his brow. His mouth contorted in pleasure as his fingers followed that satiny path down to where the wet wanting was centered. Gently, so gently, hand trembling, he eased his finger into her tight passage to open her, ready her for what was to come.

The joining. His body buried in the softness of her own, reaching deep, to the mouth of her womb.

"Hot," he breathed. "You're so hot and tight and damp with wanting."

"You. Only you."

"Passion. I saw it in your eyes from the first . . . craved it. I'm so damned lost now, Fallon." His eyes blazed with desire, glittered with a vulnerability that wrung her heart. "Find me."

She did. Her fingers curled delicately around the white-hot length of his shaft, guiding him to the portal of her woman's body. He hesitated, the blunt tip nudging the burning center of her. "Fallon, are you certain? I don't even know who . . . who I am. What I am . . ."

"I know. You're my husband. My first lover. My only." She rolled her hips upward toward him, a silent plea, a reaching out of years of heartbreak, years of hope.

Then, with a low growl of surrender, ecstasy, Ciaran drove his shaft deep. She clenched her jaw against a cry of pain, but his mouth closed on hers, his kiss drowning it in thick, hot pleasure.

He was a warrior—from whatever time, whatever place, whatever magic had brought him here. A man fierce in his honor, his passions, his needs. She could feel the urgency to take, to conquer, the raw, physical power his instinct demanded that he unleash. But he held it in check, struggled to grasp at some fragment of gentleness for her.

"Fallon," he rasped, his arms trembling, holding most of his weight off her body. "Are you all right?"

Tears stung her eyes. How could she ever tell him how she felt? Heavy, hard, thick, he stretched her delicate passage, filling her completely—her body, her heart, the aching places in her soul.

Not trusting herself to speak, she closed her eyes, and glided her legs about his hips, moving against him, drawing him deeper.

"Please, Ciaran," she begged. "Please . . ."

With a growl of eagerness, hunger, he thrust, setting a powerful rhythm that stirred her blood. It was the wild, sweet throbbing of Celtic dreams, of the bodhran, the battle drum from ancient days that now pounded out the beat of the dances where feet flew and spirits soared. It was the throbbing of the hearts of lovers whose passion was so great it spilled through the centuries. And she couldn't get enough of it, enough of his loving as it spun her deeper and deeper into a whirlwind of magic.

"Everything, Ciaran," she pleaded. "I want everything. All of you." She strained against him, her own hips meeting his in a desperate quest for fulfillment, her mouth nipping gently at his shoulders, his chest. By sheer accident, her tongue skimmed the hardened point of his flat male nipple, and she was stunned at the shudder of exquisite pleasure that racked him.

Remembering the pure heaven of his mouth suckling her breast, she fastened her lips about that small nub, nibbling at it, soothing it with her tongue.

A fierce cry tore from Ciaran's lips as he drove himself

into her body harder, faster, as if he could split the hard shell she'd built around her heart, send it crumbling down like the battered walls of the castle he'd built beside the sea.

Something cinched tight, low in her belly, squeezing her in a vise of pleasure, of need, a questing for something that shimmered within the mist. Something she'd always sensed was there, if she had the courage to reach out, to take it. A searing ball of flame that might consume her.

But she didn't care as the wild creature within her rose up, eager to embrace it, no matter what the cost. She could feel her passion enveloping Ciaran as well, the elemental part of him rising to match all that was untamed in her.

"No," he ground out. "I don't want this to end. Don't want it ever to end." But they could no more slow the force between them than they could catch the mist in its flight across the hills.

Her fingers dug into the flexing muscles of his buttocks, urging, taking, giving. And then she shattered, raw animal cries tearing from somewhere deep inside her as she writhed against him. She was drowning, rivers of molten silver rushing through her, carrying her to a place where heroes never died, where love burned eternal, where no one was ever lost or alone.

He thrust once more, as if he would embed himself in her very soul. He flung back his head, the tangle of midnight hair glistening around features harsh with agony sweeter than any pleasure could ever be. Waves of fulfillment racked him, again and again, a guttural cry of ecstasy breaching his lips as he spilled his seed deep inside her.

Ciaran buried his face against her hair, fine tremors still echoing through his powerful body, his arms shaking as he clutched her tight, so tight.

She wanted to hold him there forever, stroking his broad back and the sweat-dampened tangle of his hair as his breath slowly eased, his heartbeat steadied. But at last he rolled to one side, flung one arm over his face.

Still. He was suddenly so still. So quiet. Joy faded,

concern making her catch her lower lip between her teeth. Did he regret what had happened between them? Or had she done something wrong? Had she been too eager? Ciaran MacCailte, high champion, most honorable of all the knights of the Red Branch, would have nothing but scorn for a wanton.

But he was her husband. She had wanted to give him all of herself, holding nothing back.

"Ciaran?" she said softly. "What is it?" He shook his head, his face still hidden from her gaze. Dread tightened inside her. Anything was better than this uncertainty. She slipped her fingers into the cup of his hand, drew his arm away.

She couldn't breathe as she gazed down at him. His eyes were closed tight, dark lashes fanned against his rugged cheekbones. His jaw clenched, his mouth still reddened from their kisses. But what stunned her, moved her, was the tiny trickle of moisture that charted a trail from the corner of his eye to the fine hair at his temple.

A tear?

God in heaven, he'd probably be furious that she caught a glimpse of such stark vulnerability. This strong, powerful man, with his honor and his fierce pride, his courage and his confusion.

She didn't know what to do. Should she pretend she didn't see it? But then it would lie between them forever, a tiny, aching secret. No. This was one time she couldn't pretend. She remembered his words before they'd made love, tender words that she'd carry forever in her heart.

I'd kiss your tears away. All of your tears.

No one understood the pain of solitary tears better than Fallon did. Or the danger in them.

Leaning over Ciaran, she pressed her lips to the glistening trail. He tasted of salt air and broken dreams, the secret sorrow of a wanderer who yearned for a place to belong. But wasn't it possible—just possible—that he could find it in her arms?

A harsh moan rose in his throat.

"Ciaran, what is it? What's wrong?"

"I've lost so much along with my memory. Know so

little. But now I know this, Mary Fallon," his voice cracked. "If this is madness, I never want to be sane again."

He opened his eyes, and they seemed to plumb her very soul. "Tell me, Mary Fallon, about the world I glimpse in your eyes. Your dream places, where everything is as color-bright as your fiery hair and heroes shine, even their defeat glorious. Where love echoes, untouched even by the grave."

"You mean—"

"I know it's impossible, but I almost wish that I could be your hero."

She cupped his jaw in her palm, the faint roughness of his beard warm against her skin. "You already are. You gave me tonight. A gift so beautiful—one I never expected to have."

"You're the one who gave me a gift. My first time, and yours. Perfect. It almost made me believe—"

"What?"

"In the tales you spin, my weaver of dreams." His lips curved into a smile, astonishingly tender, soul-searingly beautiful in its vulnerability. "Can you tell me how the story ends? The tale of your warrior Ciaran?" His fingertips caressed the full curve of her lips. "When his quest is finished, does he win his lady love?"

Such a simple question.

Such a painful truth.

The words snagged in her throat, and for the first time she wished he were right: that she was blinded by her vivid imagination, that he was nothing but a mortal, simply a man who could belong to her.

She buried her cheek against his chest, unutterable sorrow clenching her heart. "It ends just as it began. Ciaran walks into the mist." Her voice quavered, broke. "Into the mist, alone."

CHAPTER

10

Stripped to shirt and breeches, Lionel Redmayne lounged in the chair before the fire, staring into the flames, the rustlings of his aide-de-camp, Kenneth Barton, irritating as the incessant scraping of a wind-shaken branch against a windowpane.

"Captain, sir, is there anything else I can do for you before I retire?"

Redmayne arched one sardonic brow and cast a glance from the shards of his broken shaving bowl to the gold braid torn from his uniform. "No, Barton. I believe you've done quite enough for one evening."

The young man flushed, even the faint blond shadow of his beard seeming to take on a pinkish cast in embarrassment. In the month since Barton had come to him, Redmayne had mused that it was a pity the army didn't give a medal for blushing. The twenty-year-old Barton would have been sure to win it.

"Captain, I'm sorry I was so clumsy tonight. I can't think what came over me, sir."

The same thing that seemed to *come over* everyone when in the presence of the unnerving Captain Redmayne, Lionel thought wryly. He had only to enter a room for people to begin dropping things, breaking things, stammering and stumbling.

He usually found such bumbling far more amusing than he had tonight. It seemed his sense of humor had gone a-begging sometime during the moments when Mary Fallon Delaney had become a bride.

Lionel glanced at the unopened bottle of fine claret he'd intended to use to toast yet another victory once he'd broken the woman's resolve, gotten her to admit— what? That her absurd tale of a secret betrothal and a bastard in her belly was a lie? That for some reason she was struggling to protect this Ciaran MacDonough? Perhaps because he was the criminal Redmayne was seeking.

It had seemed such a simple plan, there in the street with the crowds all around. Easy enough to outwit one headstrong female with a temper far too easy to stir, and every emotion painted on her face as brightly as the rouge on a ha'penny harlot's cheeks.

Yes, it should have been as simple as teaching a raw beginner a lesson in swordsmanship. Cut past all the pretty trappings of loyalty, generosity, and even patriotism until one struck that most elemental need in the center of any living creature—the will to survive.

Self-preservation. He'd seen men barter their own souls to grasp it. Watched them betray their comrades, their mothers, their wives and children when they felt the kiss of the blade on their own throat. Mary Fallon Delaney was no different.

He'd been so very certain. Give Miss Delaney enough rope, and she would hang herself—and her companion, too. It had been rather entertaining, toying with his prey when he'd been sure of victory. There had been times he could almost taste her fear, her indecision, her panic, and the hot fire of anticipation had risen in his body, a feeling akin to passion.

He'd even made certain the woman couldn't rationalize her actions away. No, nothing so simple that she could unravel it when the time suited her. He'd made damn certain it was a marriage by the laws of man and her nuisance of a God. A true marriage, with one of her

Catholic priests presiding, and her claim that she was carrying a child driving away any possibility of annulment.

He'd watched and waited throughout the ceremony for the inevitable shattering, sensed the roar of emotions in the man who stood beside her, rigid with outrage and fury. Once, in the West Indies, Redmayne had seen a runaway Scotsman fresh from the convict ships caught in a mantrap, the savage jaws mangling his leg. Personally, Redmayne abhorred such crude measures. After all, had the master of the ship done his job correctly, manipulated the convict's will, the fool would never have run.

But still, he remembered the Scot. For despite the pain, the devastation that would cripple him for life, the man had glared at his captors as if he were an embattled king, refusing to admit that the fierce metal teeth of the trap were grinding his flesh. Ciaran MacDonough reminded Redmayne of that man.

Fool. Damned fool. Hadn't MacDonough realized he was helpless? Redmayne had wondered, waiting for either bride or groom to break down. But the couple had spoken the vows despite Redmayne's most expert goading. Ciaran MacDonough had slipped the ring on her finger, and suddenly the thing was done.

Redmayne had battled to keep the smirk on his face, his eyes as devoid of emotion as the silvery surface of a mirror, but a blue-hot frisson of anger had squeaked past his control, sizzling along his nerves like a bolt of lightning no one else could see.

But he'd known it was there—anger, for the first time since he'd been a boy.

Unnerving. In the space of two days Mary Fallon Delaney had accomplished the impossible. And it was damned disconcerting.

"Sir?" The aide-de-camp's voice cracked just a little, and the captain turned back to Barton. It was all Redmayne could do not to grimace. A fine sheen of sweat now beaded the young man's upper lip.

"I thought you were gone," Redmayne said, irritation prickling him. He damn well didn't like anyone hovering about when he was *thinking*.

"You didn't dismiss me, sir. Not officially."

Sometimes Redmayne thought Barton wouldn't dream of breathing unless he'd given the man permission. There were times Lionel had almost been tempted to give the order. *No more breathing until I give the command.* Unfortunately, he should have thought to give it half an hour ago. That way he'd have gotten a little peace.

"You're dismissed, Barton," Redmayne enunciated so clearly most men in his garrison would have been bolting out of the room as if a flesh-eating monster were at their heels.

"Sir, I was wondering, sir."

"A dangerous pastime."

The youth's Adam's apple bobbed twice in his scrawny throat. Did Barton have any idea how easily he betrayed himself to anyone with half an ounce of wit? Grandfather would disapprove. How many times had the old man made Lionel stand before a mirror until the boy had smoothed out any ripples of emotion to his satisfaction?

Reveal nothing.

The motto had been newly carved into the mantel above the fireplace at Rawmarsh, the slashes upon the new marble reminding Lionel of a fresh scar. Perhaps he should send Barton to grandfather for schooling. Doubtless the old man needed a new pupil. But Barton wasn't intelligent enough to match wits with Paxton Redmayne. His brains would be seared to ash before a fortnight was past.

And there was a distressing overabundance of puppyish eagerness in his face, despite all Redmayne's efforts to quench it. He feared Barton behaved as if life were an adventure to be enjoyed instead of a nasty jest to be mastered.

"Sir, I happened to see some men building battering rams, and I thought . . . I wondered . . . Are you expecting a fight? There don't seem to be any strongholds to storm hereabouts."

Heaven save him from men hungry for their first blooding. It was so inconvenient when they realized it was *their own* blood likely to be spilt. He wondered what Barton would say if he told him the truth. That the enemies they'd soon be attacking would be more apt to cause injury by toppling over on them than by returning fire.

"You mean, you failed to see the great castle upon the sea cliffs? Your powers of observation leave much to be desired."

"The—the one that's tumbling down, sir?" Barton asked, astonished. Then his chin dropped a notch, as if suddenly believing his commander had just made a joke at his expense.

Irritating puppy, acting hurt. Redmayne had told him the truth. It was Barton's own fault he was too dense to realize it. "My plans and strategies are none of your business," Redmayne said. "Your duty is to keep my things in order, to make certain my uniform is pressed, my sword is sharpened so that when the time comes, all is in readiness."

"Yes, sir. It's just that all the preparations, the battering rams and such, and the lady who was married here today—it was all so odd. Made everyone wonder if they might be linked somehow."

Redmayne merely stared into the flames without acknowledging a word of what Barton had said.

"We couldn't help overhearing it was supposed to be a . . . a kind of trick. No one believed the wedding would ever really happen. But in the end, she did marry."

She had. It had been one of the boldest countermoves Redmayne had ever witnessed. It had stunned him utterly, and he'd not been surprised for a very long time. Something very like admiration had stirred in him. Doubtless that explained the ragged edges he couldn't quite smooth out. He was unaccustomed to being thwarted. And Mary Fallon Delaney seemed to be making a career out of doing so.

But the game was far from over, and she was far too passionate to move wisely for very long. He only needed to wait until her rashness betrayed her. It was just a matter of time. And Redmayne had cultivated the art of patience into a weapon far more lethal than a pistol.

The question was, how far would the lady go in her attempt to win? Had she just cast the rest of her life into the hands of MacDonough? Was she even now sharing a bridal bed with her unexpected husband? Redmayne's eyes narrowed a fraction. No. Pretenses would have to be kept up, but there would be little purpose in actually bedding him—unless, of course, Redmayne had posted guards at the bedposts. Then, doubtless, Mary Fallon would do whatever she deemed necessary to convince him. She was a most determined woman.

"Captain, sir, do you think Miss Delaney was telling the truth? Perhaps she is in love with Mr. MacDonough."

The fine muscles of Redmayne's face tightened just a fraction. He was unaccustomed to misjudging his opponents. "Don't be a fool, Barton."

"But why else would she do what she did today?"

Redmayne's voice was barely above a whisper. "Do you think, perhaps, I should discuss strategies with you, Barton? Might your stunning intellect uncover something I have missed?"

The young man's face washed pale. "No, sir. Of course not, sir. I . . . Forgive my impertinence. I'll leave you now." He hustled to gather up the uniform in need of mending and the shards of porcelain to be disposed of. Redmayne hoped the infernal fool wouldn't cut himself to ribbons on them in the meantime. If he bled on the captain's uniform it would be the outside of enough.

"Good night, sir," Barton said with a ridiculous salute, then stumbled out the door and closed it behind him.

With a grimace, Redmayne crossed to the bottle of claret and opened it. After filling a goblet, he took a sip.

Barton was a fool, but he had given voice to the material question.

Perhaps she is in love with Mr. MacDonough. Why else would she do what she did today?

"Why indeed?" Redmayne muttered. He'd pondered over that question countless times in the hours since Mary Fallon Delaney's new bridegroom had hauled her away.

It had been aggravating, watching Hugh Delaney and MacDonough tow Fallon away before he was done with her, before he'd peeled back whatever pretenses, whatever veils she'd drawn over her motives. For an instant he'd wanted to draw his sword and block her way, force them to stay until he gave them leave to go. A ridiculous display of power, saber-rattling between men. It would have been a grave tactical error. And one thing Lionel Redmayne never made was a mistake.

Even so, the woman had flashed him a glance in the last moment before she swept from the room. One tiny glance that had taunted him, tempted him. It was exhilarating. It was unthinkable. But then, Mary Fallon Delaney was completely unpredictable, with courage any general under siege would kill to possess. Still, Redmayne had found that courage came easily enough when one underestimated one's opponent. And Miss Delaney, with her sheltered, gentry life here in the wilds of this barely civilized land, could have no idea what kind of a man she'd just crossed swords with.

Or did she? He recalled her animated features the night he'd found her wandering about the castle ruins, when he'd told her of his plan to destroy the circles of standing stones, the hulking shells of castles, the dolmens the Irish thought fraught with mystic powers.

She'd understood his theory with a quickness that surprised him. No sense slashing at the body of an enemy when one could cleave straight to the heart. And the horror that had flooded her eyes had told him everything he'd needed to know.

He'd found the jugular of these ungovernable people who had caused nothing but trouble for England since the day they'd first been conquered. And if his threat had upset Mary Fallon Delaney so much, what would it do to a man like Silver Hand?

Most smugglers in England would be thrilled at the thought of the authorities being distracted. They would probably begin building dolmens of their own to occupy the soldiers. But there was something different about Silver Hand, something Redmayne had sensed from the beginning. It wasn't greed that motivated the smuggler.

There was something else. And the instant his men began the destruction, they would smoke the rebel out.

A brilliant move. One worthy of a master.

Redmayne set down the goblet of claret and crossed to his trunk. Opening it, he removed the tiny wooden box that he'd hidden in the farthest corner.

How many times had he almost thrown it into the fire? Every time he'd been transferred to a new command he'd resolved to do so.

It was dangerous to allow the clutter from one's past to accumulate, his grandfather had always said. Nothing could betray a man faster to his enemies. Weaknesses, secrets, tiny clues could be forged into a weapon. And Redmayne had made more than his share of enemies in his stellar rise through the ranks before a clash with a fool had plunged him into obscurity here in Ireland. But despite his best intentions, in the end he had always returned the box and what it contained to the trunk.

He lifted the lid. Candlelight flickered into the depths of the tiny chest. Slowly, Redmayne withdrew a lone game piece, the figure garbed in medieval splendor.

Why had he kept it? As a sentimental token of the years he was raised by his grandfather? Some grand appreciation of artistry or beauty?

No. He couldn't fathom the reason. But even as a boy, during the endless games his grandfather had forced him to play, something in the carved features had fascinated him, intrigued him. Like the woman who had left hours before. And when he'd left Rawmarsh, it was the only thing he'd taken with him.

His thumb ghosted over the delicately crafted countenance of the most powerful piece ever to grace a chessboard.

The queen.

He gazed down into her exquisite face. "You may think you have escaped me," he murmured aloud, "but your surly knight and pawn of a brother won't be able to guard you forever." He perched the piece on the table top. "It's time to raise the stakes, unearth your husband's secrets, lay out a most irresistible trap for this

Silver Hand. And if, in the process, I happen to capture you . . ." He gently flicked the chess piece with his finger. The queen toppled, lay there, exquisite, vulnerable, conquered.

"The next move is mine, Mary Fallon." His lips twitched into a half-smile. "And I never lose."

CHAPTER

11

Exhausted, Ciaran sagged back into the chair he'd drawn into the thin stream of light that pierced the divide between the curtains, his hands still, his task finished at last.

It had taken him longer than he'd imagined, though he'd started soon after Fallon fell asleep, had slipped from the bed where he'd made her his own to work by the flickering light of the fire with whatever makeshift tools he could find. When the fire had died, he'd shifted to the window so that the first watery rays of dawn could filter down over his work as he labored.

He'd worked until his hands ached, and his fingers were raw and bleeding. But he didn't care. He had wanted it to be perfect. Perfect. He grimaced. The only thing he'd managed to do was to make himself feel like a perfect fool. He stared down at the trinket he had made, as it lay cupped in the palm of his hand. A pitiful offering. Yet, it was truly his. His gift. His token, to be given to the lady who lay sleeping still.

A smile curved his lips, and a wistfulness tugged at his heart as he glanced over at her, a drowsy water nymph afloat upon foamy coverlets. She'd gobbled up the space on the bed, adorable in her greediness. Her arms and legs had sprawled over him, her fingers curling in his hair. He'd never felt anything more precious than her slight weight against him. And no matter what happened in the future, he knew that just before he closed his eyes in death, her face would be the face he'd see, her eyes, her mouth, just as they'd looked when he'd made love to her this first time.

He closed his eyes, recalling the flickering images he would carry with him forever, memories that he was certain would never lose their luster. Petal-pink lips parting in gasps of pleasure, the dainty column of a slender thigh, so pale in contrast to his own rough, tanned hand as he'd slid his fingers from the sensitive inside of her knee, higher, higher, to a cache of downy red curls.

Those incredible eyes that had flashed open, wide, when he'd touched damp satin, surprise and awe at the sensations his intimate explorations unleashed between them making her seem almost luminous. The flame of a red-gold candle, destined to lead him out of darkness.

He might never have known another woman's body, but still, he knew that if he'd taken a hundred to his bed, none would touch his soul as deeply as Mary Fallon had. She was the rarest kind of treasure. Unspoiled as a wild doe tamed to his hand, the rivers of passion that shone in her face untapped by any other man. As if she had been waiting for him forever.

She had offered her maidenhead with the same generosity as she'd offered him her help there upon the sea cliffs. She'd opened herself to his possession as eagerly as she'd embraced the magic in her legends. No maidenly shyness, no cloying coyness, no fear. Only courage and faith, passion reduced to its most essential element.

The spirit of wind and sea, the kiss of fire and earth that stood at the beginning of all life. They had consumed him when he was in her arms.

And in that precious moment when he had thrust deep into the dark haven of her femininity, he'd felt as if worlds as yet unseen were being born in this single, magnificent act. That no man had ever loved a woman this way before, and never would again. He'd wanted to remain there forever, in the petal-spangled bed.

But now, reason was returning as inexorably as the rising of the sun, tainting the beauty of what he and Fallon had shared with a niggling of guilt.

What had he done? He had taken something he had no right to. Yes, Fallon had offered herself to him—a trembling sylph garbed in gossamer white, his lady of the mist with magic in her eyes. But she couldn't understand the danger.

No. That wasn't true. Ciaran brought himself up grimly. Fallon did understand. But she stared danger in the face, not flinching, not turning away, brave as any hero in the midst of battle. He'd seen the evidence of her courage time and again since she'd entered his life.

Still, he should have turned her away when she came to his bedchamber last night. But how? How could a man close his eyes to his first glimpse of sunlight after an eternity in a night-dark prison? How could he refuse to drink from a stream of crystal cold water when parched by a killing thirst?

How could the first solitary man who had had the spark of life embedded in his chest have walked away from the mate the powers of creation had fashioned just for him—to fit his hands, his mouth, join with his body?

Fallon had claimed he was a hero. Last night was proof she was wrong. But it was too late to change what had happened between them now. They had taken an irrevocable step when he'd carried her to the bed. And truth to tell, no matter what the danger, what the cost, he would not have changed one moment of last night even if he could. It had been too precious, too perfect, holding this brave, vulnerable, stubborn, generous lady in his arms.

Even now, as he watched her slumbering, the need for her boiled in his veins, a hunger he could never sate. And yet, was it fair to surrender to it again and again? Plunge deeper into this storm of emotion between them? It didn't matter that the laws of Fallon's priest claimed bedding was a husband's right. It didn't matter that the more primitive laws linking man to woman since the beginning of time compelled him to bury his seed in this woman's body, plant his child in her womb.

A fist clenched his heart, crushing him with yearning. *A child.* Outside the pub, with a crowd looking on, she'd claimed he'd already put his babe in her belly. He'd been enraged, furious at the insult to his honor. Or so he'd believed. The truth was, her words had taunted him, dangling before him a joy he'd sensed intuitively he could never have.

But what if he was wrong? What if their lovemaking resulted in a tiny son or daughter with Fallon's fiery curls and intrepid spirit? His pulses tripped at the possibility.

Fool! A voice jeered inside him. And what would you give to Fallon and her child? You have nothing—no fireside to keep her warm, no bed for her to sleep on, not even a name to give her. It's even possible that the loss of your memory might be a blessing. When the curtain parts, who knows what ugliness might be revealed?

What if you really are the smuggler Silver Hand, that cur Redmayne is seeking? There could be no question about what fate Captain Redmayne had planned for the enemy he hunted. Ciaran winced. Even the myth Fallon had spun around Ciaran of the Mist ended in sadness— no joy, no love, no reward, just one man, alone until the end of time. Perhaps that was an omen, a warning.

Slowly, he got to his feet and crossed to the bed. Grief coiled tight in his chest, his blood afire with the need to awaken her, make love to her until the world beyond this room crumbled to dust. But no. He dared not touch her again. Until he unraveled the mystery of his identity, until he outwitted Redmayne, he could give Fallon nothing but pain. He couldn't kneel before her and offer her, not a knight spun of dreams, but rather a man, hopelessly flawed, imperfect in body and in soul.

But for this moment, she was still his slumbering goddess, his lady of enchantments. His.

Gently, he took up her hand. Such a delicate hand, compared to the rough bronze of his own. Redmayne's ring was just a little loose, an abomination glistening there on her finger. Ciaran hated it. It was a symbol of the Englishman's cunning, the shrewd and dangerous web he had woven to trap them. He couldn't bear to see it in place another moment.

Ciaran eased the ring over Fallon's limp finger, wishing he could toss it into the fire. He dropped it on the coverlets instead, but at that moment he felt her hand twitch. He looked up to see wide blue eyes peering at him, solemn, yet so soft. The eyes of a woman newly made.

"My wedding ring," she protested, loss darkening her gaze as she gathered the sheets against her bare breasts.

"No. The ring was Redmayne's." He wished he could explain to her how he'd felt, the fierce possessiveness, the fury it had raised in him that anything belonging to the Englishman touched her in any way. "This is mine."

His cheeks burned, his pride badly stung that this paltry gift was all he had to give. He couldn't meet her eyes as he poised his own offering at the tip of her finger, slid it into place. She'd think him mad. Ridiculous. He braced himself for the slightest flicker of scorn.

But her face glowed, lovely, intent as she peered down at the only thing she was wearing, the lace-work of gold wire he'd labored over throughout the night.

"It's beautiful! Celtic interlacing made of gold. Wherever did you get it?"

He felt an irrational urge to shove his hands behind his back, to hide the myriad of tiny gashes he'd cut into his fingers as he bent the gold wire to his will. *I plucked it from a fairy's wings. I stole it from the god whose task it is to light the sun each morn.* He wished he could spin her a beautiful story, far from the mundane truth: that a clumsy, fiercely jealous man had struggled with the gold wire and his own torn emotions throughout the night.

"I made it," he admitted gruffly. How could he explain that the intricate designs had risen up from some secret part of his soul?

"You made this? But how? Wherever did you find such a delicate thread of gold?"

"It's mine," he said almost fiercely.

Her delicate brows lowered in confusion.

"I uncoiled it from the hilt of the dagger I was carrying when you found me."

"Your dagger! But, Ciaran, it was priceless! You didn't have to do this."

His jaw hardened, stubborn. "The dagger is the only thing that belongs completely to me. You're my wife. My ring will be on your finger."

He'd determined to keep some safe distance between himself and Fallon. But how could any man resist the picture she made, gazing down at his ring. Her eyes glowed as if he'd just offered her the most precious jewel from the fairy king's crown instead of a tangled bit of wire. "It's perfect," she murmured, then flashed him a soul-stealing smile. "Look, Ciaran. It fits exactly."

And it did. No heavy gold band, no chunk of jewel could ever capture the essence of Mary Fallon as well as the ring of gold lace could. For all his resolve to keep his distance for her own good, Ciaran felt himself drawn to her, irresistibly as the tide to the shore.

"This is an ancient Celtic art—this weaving that you've done," she said, her eyes sparkling with enthusiasm. "Let me show you!"

She scrambled up from the bed and Ciaran's heart lurched at the beauty of her lithe body as she snatched up a dressing gown and slipped it heedlessly about her nakedness. Subtle shadows, flashes of velvety skin tantalized as she hastened over to a table and grabbed one of her well-worn books. Bringing it to him, she curled up beside him as if she belonged there. She leaned against his shoulder, one full breast brushing his arm with its tempting softness.

Opening the volume to one of the pages, she pointed to the border of one of the illustrations. Ciaran stared. The lace-work ring was nearly a replica of the intricate frame surrounding an exquisite picture.

"Ciaran, don't you see how important this is?" Fallon said eagerly. "You must have some memory of interlacing, some link with it, or you could never have created this beautiful ring."

But he'd forgotten interlacing, forgotten the ring, forgotten everything as he stared at the delicately tinted image on the page. Two lovers lay upon on a platform made of stone, the woman slumbering, wrapped in the folds of her lover's mantle. Even at a glance, Ciaran could see that they were being hunted. The man guarded the dark-tressed beauty, watchful, as if at any moment some unseen force might snatch her away.

"Who are they?" Ciaran couldn't help but ask, some sense of kinship tugging at his vitals.

"Deirdre and Naosi—the most tragic, most wondrous lovers ever to wander Ireland's hills," Fallon said. "They defied a king because of their love. They divided the loyalties of the knights of the Red Branch—a breach that could never be healed. And yet, their story has haunted the hearts of all Ireland ever since. She's said to be the most beautiful woman ever born, but that isn't how she is remembered. She's called Deirdre of the Sorrows, because in the end, Naosi was betrayed by his enemies."

The words slipped like an icy blade beneath Ciaran's skin. He stood, paced to the window, wishing it was as easy to shove aside the feelings Mary Fallon stirred in him, the needs she unleashed, the promises in her lovely face.

"This is one of the most haunting poems ever written," she said softly. "Deirdre's Lament."

Her eyes slid closed and she recited by memory.

> *"The lions of the hill are gone,*
> *And I am left alone—alone—*
> *Dig the grave both wide and deep,*
> *For I am sick, and fain would sleep!*
>
> *The dragons of the rock are sleeping,*
> *Sleep that wakes not for our weeping:*
> *Dig the grave, and make it ready;*
> *Lay me on my true-love's body."*

The words of the poem resonated through Ciaran's whole being, like the shaft of an arrow that had found its mark. True love. Was it possible that he and Fallon had found a love so beautiful, so complete? Because he did love her. The realization pierced his soul. Love had been the force that had driven him to take her in his arms last night, to strip away her nightgown and worship her moon-pale body with his hands, his mouth. Love clenched in a fist about his heart, exquisite, terrifying, the most beautiful anguish a man could ever know.

He raised his gaze to Fallon's face, saw the tiniest glisten of a tear at the corner of her eye as she traced one slender finger over the lovers on the page. "They killed him before her eyes," she said, softly, as if she were Deirdre, mourning.

It was a shadow, just a shadow of grief over lovers long dead, lovers neither he nor Fallon had ever known. Why did it feel so fresh, so new?

Because for the first time Ciaran knew what it was to love, what it would mean to lose.

He wanted to tell her—tell her everything she meant to him. Wanted her to know that she held his heart in her hands. But he crushed the words, his jaw knotting with the effort. She was in love with a legend, not a mere man. And yet, even if love's incandescent light should glow in her eyes just for him, he couldn't tell her how he felt. His gaze moved sorrowfully to the image of the dark-tressed woman clasped in Naosi's arms. Had Deirdre known there was so little time before destiny claimed him, and death stole Naosi away?

What would happen to the dreams in Fallon's eyes if she watched *him* die as Deirdre had watched her lover?

Love was like a blade, and it had been forged between them in fires hotter than any Ciaran had ever known. Beautiful as it was, it could bring wounds—terrible, gaping wounds of the heart and soul.

He wanted to take her in his arms, hold tight to whatever time the fates allowed them. He was tempted to scoop her up, to do as Naosi had done, to carry her into the wildlands where Redmayne's treachery could never touch her.

But the danger in running was that once you began, you were doomed to run forever. And wandering thus, one step ahead of the huntsman, was no life for a woman, romantic as it might seem when captured in bardsong. There, you couldn't feel the bite of winter winds, the hunger gnawing in your belly, nor realize the pain in sacrificing everything you'd ever known. What kind of man could ask that of a woman, no matter how desperately he loved her?

He took the book from her hands and closed it, the illustration suddenly too painful to look at. As he carried it back to the table, he gathered up the pieces of his spirit her loving had stripped raw. With fierce resolve, he hardened them against the rare vulnerability, the mystical beckoning in her eyes.

"What happened between us last night was a mistake, Fallon. A dangerous one."

A weaker woman might have been hurt. Fallon only raised her chin a notch higher, her sea-blue eyes shining with certainty. "No, it was beautiful, Ciaran. For both of us. I saw it in your face, felt it in your touch. You were as shaken by the power of our lovemaking as I was."

Ciaran felt as if she'd torn open his chest, gazed full into his very soul. "That may be. But it doesn't change anything. I won't be touching you again." *Not until I unravel the mystery of my identity. Until I find a way to render Redmayne harmless.*

She rose from the bed, her dressing gown streaming around her, her hair a nimbus of sunset curls—a woman, infinitely generous, heartbreakingly brave. If Deirdre had looked at Naosi thus, Ciaran understood why the warrior had cast caution to the winds and carried her away.

"You're not making any sense," Fallon insisted. "We've already made love. It was beautiful."

Ciaran ground his teeth. "Beautiful"? It was too small, too common an expression. No word had yet been invented that could reach the depth and breadth of the wonder that had happened between them. But he quelled the thought, his voice harsh.

"It was a distraction. A dangerous one. From this moment on, I intend to focus on what I should have focused on from the beginning: discovering who I am, if I'm dangerous, if somewhere, somehow, I have responsibilities. Am needed."

Curse her for the understanding that softened those rosy lips. "Of course. We'll find the answers together."

"No, Fallon. The answers are mine, and I'll find them

myself. I'm going back to the castle, to find some way to track this Silver Hand to his lair."

"But you could be killed!" she burst out. "They're desperate men, the smugglers. They will do whatever is necessary to protect their secrets."

Ciaran thought he'd almost enjoy bashing a few smugglers, sweating out some of the frustration, the raging emotions that were roiling inside him. "It's a risk I'll have to take."

He winced at the sudden squaring of her shoulders.

"I'm going with you," Fallon insisted. "I'm known throughout Glenceo. Even the most desperate men hereabouts would never dare to hurt me. They trust me, after a fashion."

The thought of Fallon hurling herself into danger again on his behalf made Ciaran's gut clench. "Absolutely not. You'll have plenty to do on your own while I'm gone."

"Ciaran—"

He wheeled on her, lashing out the only way he knew how. "Don't you think we should get to work, trying to save your castle, Mary Fallon? Neither one of us can keep playing at fairy tales forever."

She flinched as the words lashed her, and he hated himself for striking at such a soft, vulnerable place in her spirit. But she only confronted him with stony resolve. "It's been a little difficult to concentrate on anything except hauling you out of trouble for the past few days. If you hadn't run away, I might have had a chance to begin considering—"

Ciaran cut her off with an impatient gesture. "We've been through all that. It doesn't matter anymore. It's time to focus on the task at hand. You did summon Ciaran of the Mist from the fairy kingdom for a reason, I presume."

"Of course! I told you what Redmayne threatened to do. That he was going to destroy . . ."

Castle ruins, tumbledown circles of stone, the ancient dolmens like those on which Deirdre and Naosi had slept. Shattered remnants of ancient glory—ghosts of a time that could never come again. Why the devil shouldn't he stand back and let Redmayne and his kind shove the infernal eyesores into the sea?

Because tearing them apart would be like tearing the very heart out of Mary Fallon. And no matter what Ciaran himself believed, that was one thing he couldn't bear. The least he could do was preserve some part of her dreams, to keep the light of magic sparkling in her eyes after he was gone.

"While I'm searching the coast for this infamous Silver Hand, you need to dredge up information about these stone wrecks you want to save. Whose property are they on? Does Redmayne have the owner's permission to tear the things down?"

Fallon bristled. "Caislean ag Dahmsa Ceo doesn't 'belong' to anyone. Neither do the fairy rings of stone. It's impossible to own the soul of an entire people."

Perhaps that was true, Ciaran thought, but he was discovering it was possible for a woman to hold a man's soul in her hands. He dared not let Fallon suspect— what? That he loved her? That he would walk through fire for her? That despite the tragedy that had given birth to a legend, he envied the long-dead Naosi for what little time the ancient Celtic lover had had with his lady? He battled back the raw emotions with his own anger.

"If the monuments can't belong to anybody, why did you go to all the trouble of summoning Ciaran of the Mist in the first place? Why didn't you just storm up to Captain Redmayne and tell him that? Your problem would have been solved with a lot less trouble."

Her cheeks flamed. Her embarrassment stung Ciaran, her anger chafed him, but it was the hurt in those eyes that had glowed with passion such a short time ago that undid him. "I know what you're trying to do, Ciaran. You're just trying to distract me—keep me busy, like a troublesome child, so I won't insist on going with you to find Silver Hand. But it won't work. Hugh hasn't been able to control me since our mother died. And you won't be able to keep me from doing what I know is right, either."

The woman would have made a glorious warrior

queen, marching off to disaster, her head held high. Not waiting for a man like Naosi to do battle for her, she'd fling herself into the fray, to take the sword thrust meant for him. Not once would she stop to count the cost to herself. If legends could still be born in manor houses instead of castles, Fallon was the kind of woman who could play the heroine in one. Naosi should be grateful his Deirdre accepted his shelter, allowed him to protect her. Fallon never would.

"Fallon," Ciaran said, low. "It's true that I don't want you near these smugglers. But that isn't why I'm asking you to stay behind. I've asked you to perform vital tasks, tasks that might hold the key to whether or not the Castle of the Dancing Mist falls. If we could find out who owns the property, we might be able to reason with them, talk them out of destroying something so ancient."

"And exactly how would we do that? Most of the landlords would be thrilled to rid themselves of the ruins. They mock the crofters for their superstition, but you won't catch one of the pompous idiots with the nerve to walk into a fairy ring at night. The stones are a reminder that Ireland might not be subdued, but only sleeping. That it might awaken at any moment and scatter its conquerors to the winds."

Ciaran frowned. To someone logical, like Captain Redmayne, Fallon's image might sound absurd, yet Ciaran couldn't discount it. Even in the brief span of a few days, he'd felt the undeniable pulse of this land, as if rivers of enchantment flowed just beneath its surface. Every stream or pond sparkled with water nymphs, every hidden glen was a haven for magic, an unearthly power he sensed was unique to this island.

To anyone who hadn't been bred here, it must be not only beautiful but also a little frightening, as unpredictable as the weather that cast rain across the heather, then an instant later set the drops sparkling with sunshine.

"You claim that the gentry are uneasy?" Ciaran prodded.

"Squire Harry Biddleston once claimed it was like being stalked by a ghost whenever he rode past one of the standing stones in his parkland. Doubtless, the ghosts of all the people his family starved out, abused, stole from. Every family in the county has some sin to haunt them."

Ciaran scowled, mulling over Fallon's comments. Fear—it could be far more powerful than a sword. Because it was an enemy that had already breached the walls, one that lived inside you. "Perhaps reasoning isn't the answer. There might be another way," Ciaran mused slowly.

"What are you saying?"

Ciaran crossed to where her sketchbook and pencils lay. He gathered them up and brought them to her. "Draw up a map charting all the ruins you want to protect. Add the names of the landlords who hold sway over them. Note down anything about the landlords that might be useful—skeletons in their family closets, secrets they might have, any weakness we might be able to use."

"Use for what?" Fallon asked, as she pressed the sketchbook to her breasts.

"You've almost managed to make me believe in this nonsense—a nine-hundred-year-old hero called back from the mist. Isn't it possible that we can make them believe it as well?"

"Make who believe? The gentry?"

"Why not, if they're as vulnerable to suggestion as you seem to think. But I'll need every weapon you can give me, every detail from this legend. After all, if Ciaran of the Mist is to walk again, he'd better not be bumbling about as I have the last few days. It's damned hard to be intimidating if you don't even remember your name."

"You? Portray Ciaran of the Mist?" She nibbled at the full curve of her bottom lip, perplexed. "It's a wonderful idea, but isn't it too late? The servants already know you as my husband. And the rest of the neighborhood soon will if Hugh has anything to say about it. One ball or soiree, and they'll all recognize you."

"I'll deal with your brother."

She forgot to be angry about the bond between the two men, the knowledge that Hugh would listen to Ciaran when he wouldn't listen to her. All thoughts were banished except her sudden realization of the import of Ciaran's words.

Her eyes widened, her features fiercely intent. "Wait. This plan. Does it mean . . . Do you mean you believe? That you're Ciaran?"

He should tell her not to be absurd. The whole story she'd spun was ridiculous. No sane man would believe it. Instead, he turned away, loving her, wanting to be a hero for her, fearing he never could be.

"I don't know what I believe anymore," he said with searing honesty. "But I don't have to believe it, Fallon. As long as they do."

CHAPTER

12

She'd married the stubbornest man in Ireland, Fallon thought grimly. And if he didn't fall off an obliging cliff or get his throat slit by some amiable smuggler, she just might murder him herself. Once she managed to catch up with him, that is.

She urged her horse to a faster pace, eyes searching the dirt road for signs he'd passed this way.

Blast the man. He'd lulled her into thinking he was going to lock himself away with Hugh to discuss his plans. She'd relaxed a little then. By the time Hugh, the ever-cautious, decided to go after a nest of smugglers, the thieves would have died of old age. But Ciaran had only used the ruse as an excuse. In reality, he'd slipped outside to the stables when she wasn't looking. The insufferable wretch! The High King of Brainless Honor, Sir Noble-Peat-in-His-Head had ridden off without her.

She might still be pacing the garden, trying to sort out the wild tangle of emotions Ciaran MacCailte had unleashed in her if young Talesin, the groom, hadn't slipped away from his tasks long enough to warn her.

"While I was readyin' his horse, yer husband said he's that determined t' be wrenchin' information about Silver Hand from the first crofter he meets. I warned him 'twasn't a wise idea," the groom had said. "People hereabouts are still stingin' suspicious of anyone poking about, asking questions, ever since the Sassenachs put down the rebellion. Plenty o' people still see the whippings, the hangings when nightmares come upon 'em. An' now, with that new devil, Captain Redmayne, about—got everyone on edge, he does."

The groom hadn't needed to say more. Anyone desperate enough to take up smuggling wouldn't shrink from silencing one inconvenient, meddling stranger to protect their secret.

She'd rushed to the stable herself and ordered up her horse. Within a quarter hour she was mounted and searching. But even the riding that had once freed her mind and soothed her spirit had been invaded by Ciaran MacCailte. She shifted her weight in the saddle, a slight tenderness in the delicate tissues between her thighs reminding her all too vividly of the night before.

Her cheeks burned at the memory of her wantonness, her complete abandon in Ciaran's arms. Who would have believed that the mere touch of a man's hands, that possession by a man's body, could alter the very soul? Could make her crave his bed, his arms, the unforgettable fire of his passion? But he had turned his back on their lovemaking and vowed not to touch her again. A distraction, he'd called it. The pain at his rejection had been fierce, but she'd clung to the emotions she'd glimpsed in his eyes: desperation, need—*love?*

The possibility was too painfully beautiful, too precious to bear. He'd been raw with that torrent of emotions. They made a man ready to lash out, heedless. And such recklessness now could mean his doom.

She suppressed a chill and eyed another crescent shape cut by a horse's hoof. God knew what she'd find when she finally ran him to ground. She could only hope that the fates were with her and that he hadn't stumbled across anyone yet.

But that hope was dashed as she suddenly saw someone approaching. Burly Tom Dunne was carrying one of his nine children in his brawny arms. Almost from birth,

Caitlin's escapades had kept the whole parish in gales of laughter. "Pleaded wi' the Blessed Virgin t' give me one daughter, after havin' eight sons," Tom would say fondly, shaking his head. "Man craves a touch o' gentleness, says I t' My Lady. But seems the mother o' our Lord has a sense o' humor they don't catch in the holy statues, 'cause she sent me a girl who could whip all eight o' her brothers, an' me atop it."

Now, little Caitlin's blond hair straggled about her deliciously naughty face, the child wet as a half-drowned kitten. Fallon might have feared she was hurt if it wasn't for the brazen smile displaying a winsome gap where one front tooth had been.

"Top o' the mornin' to ye, Miss Fallon," Dunne called, but Fallon scarcely heard him. Caitlin was smirking like a cat in the cream pot as she stroked the shimmering green cloth that bundled her slight body. Ciaran's cloak. At least she was on the right track, Fallon thought.

"Caitlin, what happened?"

"There was a man askin' Da questions forever an' ever, an' I got in-patient, so I creeped away. There were diamonds on the water an' I tried to catch 'em an' fallen in. An' it was terrible cold. But the man wrapped me up. He gave me this to keep." She flicked reverent fingers across the elegant fabric.

Ciaran. Fallon's heart squeezed. Her nerves calmed just a whisper. He obviously hadn't clashed with Dunne. Perhaps he wasn't racing into calamity after all. At least not the one she'd anticipated. She shook her head, a pulsing of tenderness washing through her. Of course, by the time she found him, he'd probably be wearing nothing but an old shawl again.

"And what did ye learn from yer mischief, ye disobedient miss?" Caitlin's father demanded.

Caitlin gazed up at him with sparkling blue eyes. "That I should've been wicked sooner, 'cause Liam O'Hara got the sparklies from the man's shirt first."

Dunne tried and failed to stifle a laugh, and Fallon couldn't help but smile at the audacious little mite.

"An' what would you be doin' with a gentleman's shirt studs, I'd like to know?" her father demanded.

"I certain-sure wouldn't waste 'em tradin' for new boots like Liam is, even if I was a peddler walkin' monstrous far. I'd poke holes in my dresses to stick the sparklies through when I went to mass of a Sunday, an' then Francis an' Joseph an' Kevin would all be jealous enough t' burst, I'd be so fine." Her brow crinkled, and she nibbled on her plump bottom lip. "Papa, I think I must be wicked much more oftener if I want another pretty."

Fallon didn't even hear Tom's chuckled reply. Her throat tightened with envy at the child's utter confidence in her father's acceptance, his love, the certainty that even "wickedness" would never make Tom turn away from her. How many times had Fallon wondered if she might have changed things with her own papa. If she'd been pretty, like the daughters of his hunting friends, if she'd been sweet and biddable, and never wicked, might he have stayed?

"What direction did the man who gave you the pretty go?" she asked, suddenly wanting desperately to get away from the loving father and the child who took him so for granted. As it should be, Fallon knew. As it should be.

"That way." Caitlin gave an airy wave of her hand. "I liked him, Miss Fallon. Da says he's yer husband. Could you ask him to wear a red cloak next time? I'm berry partial to red."

"Ye're incorrigible, lass! I'm that ashamed of ye," Dunne said, but he took the sting from the words by smacking the child's cheek with a hearty kiss.

Fallon felt a sting of regret. Had her own papa ever kissed her? Carried her in his arms? If he had, she couldn't remember. She could only remember him riding away, turning his back on all that was painful, drowning it in drink and dissolution until he died of it. He'd wanted to make everything he'd left in Ireland disappear. And it had worked. He had made Fallon and Hugh disappear from his life.

But if Ciaran MacCailte ever loved, he would never walk away from his wife, his child, Fallon knew intuitively. He'd be their strength through whatever tragedy they faced, and if death came to one of his family, he would hold their hand until the angels came to claim them, so that even as they slipped into eternal sleep, they wouldn't feel alone.

"Miss Fallon," Caitlin's voice intruded. "Da says there won't be any wedding party. Is that true?"

Fallon flushed, glancing from Caitlin to Dunne, wondering if the crofter had heard the story of her unusual marriage. She winced at the vision she had of whispers around firesides, the sorrowful shaking of heads, the disappointment. For doubtless the story of her wedding had flown through Glenceo, along with the story that she was pregnant with Ciaran's babe. But even worse than the embarrassment that stung her was the sudden longing for what might have been.

What might it have been like to wed Ciaran with these people who loved her looking on? The liquid sparkle of fiddles dancing cares away, the yearning cry of the uilleann pipes filling the soul to bursting? Tin whistles seducing until no one's feet could stay still, while the rhythm of bodhrans stirred the blood? A night to remember forever, with cakies for little Caitlin Dunne, and dreams of a future for Fallon to treasure.

Fallon swallowed hard. How was it possible to feel the loss of something you'd never thought you'd have? Marriage vows wreathed in beauty and awe instead of forced by the hand of a master strategist, dancing and celebration instead of a grim scene in her brother's study. A day of enchantment, where every time her eyes met Ciaran's, they filled with anticipation of the time when they'd be alone at last, when he would come to her, and make love to her, with no shadows, no doubts between them.

"There wasn't time to have any sort of celebration," she faltered. "No time to plan one, I mean."

Caitlin heaved a sigh. "Then I'll get no cakies this week, I s'pose. It's most dis-tressing."

"I'll have Cook send over a basket full of cakies next time she bakes them," Fallon promised.

She started to spur her horse on its way, but Dunne managed to catch the reins, his eyes kind and wise. There was no judgment in them, Fallon realized, only deep affection. "I only wish we'd been able to sail you off into marriage the way the folk hereabouts always wanted to—with the grandest bridal celebration ever to grace Ireland's shores."

"It doesn't matter," Fallon lied. "It would just have been a lot of trouble. It's most likely better this way."

But Dunne peered up into her face, and she was certain she hadn't fooled the man for a moment. "Ye're our own kind o' princess, ye know. Ye're the closest we'll ever get to Maeve the Fairy Queen."

But I'm failing you, a voice inside her cried. *What if I can't stop Redmayne from destroying the castle? The standing stones? What if . . .*

"I have to go," she said, the tiniest of quivers in her voice. "My husband is probably halfway to the castle by now."

"The castle? Caislean ag Dahmsa Ceo?"

"Captain Redmayne was searching for signs of the smugglers there. That's where my husband is headed."

Dunne frowned. "Miss Fallon, some things shouldn't be meddled with. It's not always good t' be pokin' into things. Sometimes ye find things ye wished ye never had."

"I know."

"Miss Fallon," he said again, his frown softening. "It's not me place t' say, I know. But it's glad I am ye're not alone anymore."

Fallon nodded, urged her horse away, wondering if Thomas Dunne, with his loving wife, Oonagh, and bevy of children, realized how dangerous that could be. She'd been alone forever, had almost embraced her solitude. But now, now she'd tasted what it was like to let someone into her heart. What would it be like once the inevitable happened, and she was alone again? When there was no one to answer the most secret echoes of her soul?

She'd ridden past three more rolling hills and around a ruined abbey when she reined her horse to a halt, the dread she'd managed to calm during her talk with the Dunnes returning full force. She groaned as she saw the spur of road Ciaran had taken. He couldn't have chosen a worse place to begin his prying if the devil himself had whispered in his ear.

Once upon a time, Ferghall Moynihan had been famous hereabouts as the hardest worker in three counties, a wizard who could fix anything that broke, cure any lamb that was sick, coax music out of the most battered fiddle in Glenceo. But all that had changed when he'd collided with something he couldn't make right, no matter how desperately he'd tried.

Grief had banished his legendary patience, rage at the English had sharpened his temper, and helplessness had burdened his spirit until he did his best to drown his pain in drink. But all the whiskey in Ireland couldn't blind him to the anguish in his wife, Siobhan's, eyes, or make him forget the two empty spaces at the family fireside.

Two of their large brood had been sacrificed to the ill-fated rebellion: Samuel gunned down at Vinegar Hill on his seventeenth birthday, nineteen-year-old Michael transported to the convict colonies across the ocean, most likely a slower, more tortuous path to death.

Sickly, pale and rail-thin with mourning, Siobhan was expecting another babe despite the fact that she was well past her forty-first birthday. The doctor Hugh had sent out was grim, and Ferghall was nearly out of his mind with worry. The last thing the Moynihans needed was someone prying about after Silver Hand. Even the gentlest probing could bring disaster. For if, by some chance, Ferghall thought Ciaran was one of Redmayne's informers, God alone knew what might happen.

Digging her heels into her mount, Fallon started down the road at a dead run. She wasn't certain what she expected—Ciaran's hands clamped around Ferghall's throat as he tried to shake loose the information he sought, Fergall swinging the wicked blade of a scythe at Ciaran's stomach, Siobhan and her brood terrified. But no such dreaded image met her eyes.

She drew her horse to a halt, her heart squeezing as she peered down at the scene below her. Ciaran the warrior who had stalked from her bedchamber with fire in his eyes was transformed. He was on foot, all signs of his gentleman's garb vanished, his dark hair gleaming, his shirt hanging open to bare a slice of his chest.

He led his horse toward the Moynihan cottage, his handsome features softened, while atop his mount sat Siobhan Moynihan, her stomach so swollen it seemed ready to burst, exhaustion lining her once lovely face. Still, she managed to have the dignity of a queen. A toddler was perched in front of her, sporting the handsome frock coat Ciaran had worn this morning. Balanced between Ciaran's other arm and his hip was a rough-woven basket brimming with freshly washed laundry.

Fallon watched as he drew rein at the cottage door, set down the basket, then lifted down the child and pressed coins into his hand. The few coins Hugh had doubtless given him the night before.

Sioban started to struggle down herself, but he stopped her, and, gentle, reverent, sorrowful as if she were the Holy Mother herself, Ciaran lifted Siobhan into his arms and gently set her on her feet.

In that instant, he glimpsed Fallon watching on the path, and the expression on his face awed her, stunned her, broke her heart. It was as if all the tears shed, all the pain endured, all the dreams lost on this embattled island gathered into the soft green of Ciaran's eyes. Understanding—stark, complete. A sudden meeting of souls more intense in its way than any physical union of their bodies could ever be.

Without a word he carried the basket into the tiny cottage. Fallon watched as he went to the well, drew up a fresh bucket of water, and took it inside.

Then he mounted his horse and came toward her. He'd never looked so strong, so honorable, so beautiful.

"I was afraid you would get into trouble," she said, her voice unsteady. "Searching for Silver Hand."

"I meant to find him. But then—"

"Then you found Caitlin and her da, and Siobhan and her babies."

"I looked around me, and I saw . . ." He stopped. Swallowed hard. "I couldn't even remember why I'd ridden out. I could only . . . How do they survive, Fallon? All those children—and this soil so harsh, so barren, for all its beauty. How can they believe in fairy songs and bard's hero tales?"

How could she ever explain? She looked down at the tiny cottage. Its thatch gleamed, rose vines clambering up to weave among the straw. "The stories feed their souls. The tales are their lifeblood. Every time they trace the ogham script carved into a standing stone, every time they enter a fairy ring of stones, they remember that they're part of something greater, more powerful, more beautiful than anything their conquerors have known."

Ciaran's voice dropped to a soft murmur, his solemn gaze meeting hers. "That's why you called me back."

She trembled at the enormity of what he'd said. "Called . . . called *you* . . . Does that mean . . . Ciaran, do you remember something?" She hovered on the brink of something wonderful, something terrible.

"I'm not certain. It's just . . . impressions. Bits and flashes. Feelings. But I have to go back to where it all began. The key has to be there, Fallon. Whether it's tangled with Silver Hand's smugglers, or wrapped in your dreams." His eyes darkened, the mysteries of the ages in their depths. "Take me there, Fallon. To the castle."

She nodded and turned her gaze toward the hills, to where limitless possibilities lay waiting. Wasn't this what she'd wanted? For him to believe in heroes that walked out of the mist, in fairy rings and magic. And yet, she'd never imagined what that belief might cost her. For if he *was* the Ciaran of legend, nothing could hold him. Not the chains of marriage vows, not even a woman's love.

CHAPTER

13

⌒◡◡◠⌒

A delicate web of mist snagged on one green hilltop, shimmering in a puff of transparent silver, an island of mystery, of magic, floating in the heartbreakingly blue sky. It was as if Eire had polished and preened and garbed herself in her finest raiment to welcome Ciaran of the Mist home.

Ciaran's horse picked its way to the top of the hill, where the tower castle still stood sentinel after so many years, and he wondered how many times over the centuries beleaguered Irish had turned their gaze toward the stone walls, drawing courage from a past almost more real to them than their present. Was he a part of that legacy? Or was he sinking ever deeper into Mary Fallon's beautiful dreams?

He glanced at her, so regal atop her own mount that she might have been Maeve the Fairy Queen herself. Her hair glowed, the red highlights burnished into exquisite ribbons by the fingers of sunlight, her chin tipped up, neck arched with an innate pride no mere mortal could humble. And her crystal blue eyes shone with the dreams of ages past and the hope of the future to come. A hope hard-won, Ciaran now realized. Wrested from the crushing grasp of those who had conquered this island so many generations ago.

His throat tightened, his fingers clenching on the reins. Where was she leading him, his fairy queen? One thing he was beginning to be certain of: destiny had cast him into her arms. Perhaps it didn't matter whether or not he was the legendary hero she believed him to be. There was something in these people that echoed through his soul with the exquisite resonance of a familiar, haunting tune plucked from the strings of a harp.

He brushed his fingers over the healing gash in his head. The low throb of headache was all but gone, leaving him with nothing but questions. What lay beyond the veil of his lost memory? Skills, tools, knowledge that might help him in this quest? And he had no delusions: Redmayne was a formidable foe. To match wits with the Englishman, to defeat him, would take every resource at Ciaran's disposal.

He struggled to open himself to the flickerings of impressions, sifting through the shadows for any scrap, the tiniest spark that might light some candle of memory, illuminating everything. Gradually it came, in tantalizing glimpses.

Small—he was very small. Sorrow was crushing the breath from his lungs, while tears flowed down porcelain-smooth cheeks. Beautiful—the most beautiful lady in the world, and someone was taking him away from her. He wanted to kick and scream and run back, to stay with her forever. But he knew the men would only take him anyway, with their hard hands and their fierce eyes. And her tender heart would be bruised forever by his cries.

"I'm not a baby anymore, to be clinging to a woman's skirts." He forced his best scare-the-dragon smile, but it couldn't scare away the dragons uncurling scaly claws of fear in his own chest. *"They have swords."* He'd jabbed a grubby finger at what looked to be a giant forest of thick-muscled legs and bone-cracking fists. *"They promised to teach me everything, how to lop off enemies' heads. I'll fight an' fight an' . . ."*

Sobs cut him like the sharp stone he'd stepped on once

*in a stream, the sound made far worse because she fought
so hard to silence it. Then the biggest man of all roared.*

"You robbed me of my wits for a little while, woman.
Bewitched me. But I came to my senses. Rid myself of
you. I can only be grateful I discovered what else you
stole from me, thief that you are! My son!"

Ciaran's mother cried. "The marriage between us held
nothing but hate! I feared you would hate him, too. He's
innocent. A child. I beg you—"

*But no plea on earth could have stopped the big man.
Ciaran knew it though he'd never set eyes on that
towering figure before.*

"The boy is mine," *the big man snarled.* "You'll never
see him again."

*One beefy hand closed on his arm, pinching so tight
that the next day a bruised ring would be marked into his
skin. Then he was being dragged away. Rage, helplessness
welled up inside him. He was a boy, but he wouldn't be
dragged about. A man—they were determined to make
him a man. Then his first act would be to make certain his
mother remembered him standing tall.*

*He kicked his father in the leg with all the force he could
muster, pain exploding in his toes. But it was worth it.
The big hand released him in surprise. He straightened
his spine and stalked ahead, leaving of his own free will.
Leaving everything warm and safe and loving.*

"I will make you proud of me," *he vowed as he walked
out of the doorway.* "I will come back someday, Mother,
I promise."

The words were so clear, and the emotions as vivid as
a new scar against white skin. He struggled to picture
some detail, anything that might give him some visual
idea of where he'd been taken from, what his mother had
been wearing, or what the men who came to take him
away looked like. The tiniest detail that might give him
some idea as to when it had taken place. Thirty years
ago? Or was he mad enough to consider the possibility
that it had been nine hundred years since his mother and
his father had turned to dust?

His struggles were futile. He could only feel the pain of
the small boy he had been awakening again in the

darkest, most hidden reaches of his heart. Is this what regaining his memory would be—an excruciating journey with all the pain he'd suffered made new?

"Ciaran?" Fallon's gentle voice reached out to him, and he turned to her, every emotion still in his eyes.

"They took me away from her. And I never . . . never saw her again."

"Never saw who?"

"My mother." He searched Fallon's face, almost desperate, as if he might hold the answers to the questions welling up inside him. "The legend, Fallon—does it say anything about that?"

"Ciaran's childhood is lost. It was as if he'd merely stepped from the mist a man, a warrior."

"Do all the hero tales begin that way?"

"Usually there is something special, some story that marks a man a hero from boyhood. Cuchulain killed a ferocious wolfhound that attacked him, then stood watch over the household it belonged to until another hound could be trained. His name means Cullen's Hound."

"But there's nothing about Ciaran?"

"Only that he had no ring fort of his own, nowhere he returned to when the fighting was over. The high king tried to reward him with the finest of conquered lands, but Ciaran refused. He said he had no need of a home."

Because his mother was dead. She'd been so fragile, outcast for his sake. Every day he'd spent away from her he'd fought, struggled to hone himself into the best, the finest, the boldest fighter of all. He'd wanted so much to bring her someplace safe and care for her. But by the time he'd been old enough, strong enough to wrench free of his father's grasp, it had been too late. She'd died, weak with hunger, sick with fever. Alone.

Guilt crushed him in its fist, and he wanted to shove the memories away, longed for the blissful oblivion where he could begin again, with no mistakes, no regrets to haunt him.

Yet the memory wouldn't be halted. It charged on, despite his pain. A cloth-wrapped bundle thrust into his hand by the crabbed old woman who had buried her.

He closed his eyes, seeing his trembling fingers fold back the material. And for the first time he saw—actually *saw*—a fragment from his past: the ancient dagger, gleaming there, gold and exquisite.

Anger, outrage, confusion mingled with tearing grief.

"Why did she not sell it? It could have kept her fed, warm, until I came to find her!"

"Some things are without price. No man who ever fought with the dagger fell to an enemy. She believed it was magic."

Magic. More magic. He wanted to rage at her, bellow at the fates. He wanted to fling the dagger away.

"She tried to cling to life, to give it to you, certain you'd return because you'd promised you would. She spoke about you every day, watched the horizon. 'He cannot keep my son from me forever. My son vowed he would come back to me. He vowed it.'"

She'd been waiting for him all this time? While he'd been piling up brave deeds, proving himself again and again to men who meant nothing to him. While he'd been reaching higher, higher, no honor he'd attained enough. If he could just master one more art of swordplay, one more contest of the intellect, she would be so much prouder of him.

The truth crushed him, the knowledge agonizing. He could have come to her so much sooner, if he'd not been attempting to prove himself to the father he despised. He'd been a vain fool, and it had cost his mother her life.

"Fling the dagger into the fire. What do I care about it after all it has cost me?"

"Do you not see, you brainless boy? This dagger was all she had to give you. Her only legacy. She loved you beyond any price—her honor, her life, her very soul. She wanted to give it to you, when you returned. This symbol of her love you can carry with you forever."

But he'd wanted her. He'd wanted to see pride shine in her eyes. He wanted a chance to tell her that no matter what cruel things his father said, he'd never forgotten her gentleness, her courage.

"We were poor," Ciaran said aloud. "My mother and I. But I never realized it. When they took me away, I had everything I could want, and yet I had nothing. Does that make any sense?"

A tiny crease appeared between Fallon's brows. "All my life I've lived in a mansion, with every servant at Misthaven House at my beck and call. Hugh would buy me whatever I wished—gowns and trinkets and sweetmeats. I never went to bed hungry. And yet, sometimes I would go to one of the cottages. They'd give me sour milk and potatoes in a crude bowl by the peat fire. And I'd look around at the faces—a ma and da, brothers and sisters, a lazy cat dozing by the fire. And I would have traded everything I owned just to have the chance to climb up on someone's lap and feel their arms around me."

Their eyes met, held. Understanding. So complete it was terrifying. He wanted to stop the horses, to go to her, slide her down until she was in his arms. He wanted to stroke her hair and tell her she would never be alone again, his brave, generous-hearted Fallon. There would always be someone to hold her when the night grew too dark, the cry of the wind too lonely. *He* would be there to hold her. But those were promises he couldn't make, no matter how much he might wish it. He couldn't be certain . . . And now, he knew with heart-shattering clarity how high a price such uncertain vows might cost him.

"The dagger—my mother gave it to me. Where would a gentle lady have gotten such a weapon? It might have been handed down through the family, I suppose. Or collected, somehow. But—"

"But?"

"It would have been far easier if—" He stopped. Was he utterly mad to even consider the possibility? Yet she was peering at him with those eyes, her soul shining through them, ancient, wise as the first winds ever born, yet at the same time as gloriously new and fresh with wonder as a babe's.

"If what, Ciaran?"

"If she got the dagger when it was . . . new."

He saw a tiny shiver work through Fallon, but not the unrestrained joy he might have expected. He was admitting there was a possibility her wild tale was true, that he *was* the man she'd said he was from the beginning. Yet her pleasure was tarnished with something akin to resignation, and a soft kiss of sorrow on those lips that had tasted so sweet, so right beneath his when he'd claimed them with his own.

Because if he *was* the legendary Ciaran, she could never follow him into the kingdom beyond the mist. Did she realize, though, his bold, beautiful lady, that that might be the least painful sort of parting? A far worse one would be to walk away from her as a mere mortal man, to wander the world, a hunted fugitive, a smuggler, a dishonored criminal, gazing up at the heavens every night and knowing that Mary Fallon might be watching the night clouds dance with the stars, might be thinking of him, yearning for him, the way he yearned for her.

He tore his gaze away from Fallon, already feeling that rending of his spirit, and was stunned to see the walls of the castle ruin rising up before them. Caislean ag Dahmsa Ceo, Fallon had called it. Castle of the Dancing Mist. And the mist did seem to dance about it, ethereal, exquisite, until the shattered walls became oddly graceful, the slender fingers of stone seeming more powerful in their destruction. The single soaring tower that had escaped whole was a triumph.

Fallon had found him here, battered, confused. Whatever secrets shrouded his past, the key was here.

Ciaran drew rein and dismounted, tying his horse to a low-lying branch. Then wordlessly he picked his way through crumbling stone softened by wisps of grass, delicate clouds of wildflowers, all the sharp edges worn away by wind and rain and the loving hands of time.

Did he belong here somehow? To this place? To this land that had cast a spell upon his heart? Or was it only that he suddenly wanted to, for Fallon, for mischievous, elfin Caitlin Dunne and Siobhan Moynihan with a babe in her belly and grief for two sons shadowing her lovely eyes?

"This castle—it isn't ancient enough to have been built when Ciaran first lived," he said quietly. "You say Ciaran returned to build it centuries after he'd first been bewitched. Why would he do such a thing? He couldn't live in it, Fallon. He had to leave it behind, empty. What could he hope to accomplish?"

"The legend says that each time Ciaran was summoned back to the land of mortals, his heart bled. He could see that three hundred more years of pain, of suffering must pass before he could return again."

Ciaran looked around him, knowing what the hero of legend must have felt—the helplessness, the anger, the same emotions he himself felt whenever he thought of leaving Fallon behind.

"He argued with the fairy king, fought with him, tried every means he could think of to outwit him. But the king was too cunning. At last, in desperation, Ciaran came up with a plan, a way that the people could feel his presence even when he wasn't able to help them, a way that he could shelter both their bodies and their spirits."

"By building a castle? Fallon, I don't understand how that could make any difference."

"This is holy ground, Ciaran, from long before St. Patrick brought Christianity to Ireland, even before the triple goddess and the horned god of the druids. There are places like this, scattered about the earth, places where the pulse of all life can be felt. Men give it different names throughout time. Call it what you will— Olympus, Eden, the druid grove, like the one at Chartres—but if you open your heart, trust your senses, you can *feel* it."

He could. The pulse traveled from the earth, tingling through his boot soles, sending rivers of sensation up his legs. It seeped into every fiber of his being, a sense of union with every creature who had lived before, every joy and sorrow, betrayal and love. Echoes of life.

"There were caves beneath this place, secret passages since time began, where generations had stored their treasures. There were paintings of men hunting on the walls, bits of pottery, gold torques, bronze ax blades. Crosses have been carved in the stone, and messages written in ogham script at the time when the standing stones were new. Ciaran built his castle here as a shelter, to protect the treasures of ages from being plundered. All treasures. Not only objects, but people, too."

Ciaran reached out, gliding his fingertips over a carving in the stone, as if he were trying to memorize a lover's face.

"There was a time here when bards were outlawed, hunted. The English claimed the sounds of the harp and the pipes stirred up the spirit of rebellion." Her lips curved in an aching smile. "It may be that they were right. Yet, all of our history, every tale of love and valor, the very soul of a whole people, was twined in the threads of that music, Ciaran. It would have been more merciful just to sink Ireland into the sea than to try to steal the tales and the music away."

Tales like that of a hero bewitched away to Tir na nOg by enchanted cherries, loves like the star-crossed Deirdre and Naosi, brave deeds of Cuchulain. Was it possible that Fallon was right? That such stories were far more precious than any gold or jewels or land that a conqueror might plunder?

"A man could be killed for playing the harp or the pipes—even for speaking Gaelic, their own language. Just one more of countless attempts to turn them into proper English subjects."

"A murder of the soul," Ciaran said, turning toward her.

Fallon's delicate brows rose, and she nodded, slipping her hand into his. "A woman named Eilish Fallon was the keeper of the brooch then. She summoned you back—Ciaran back—and begged him for help. She was an artist, they say, and couldn't resist capturing his face on canvas. It's said she memorized one feature at a time while he worked on the castle, and spent every night trying to capture it, failing, then trying again. He disappeared before she was finished. I saw the portrait once when I was a little girl."

"You saw it? Then you know what Ciaran looks like?" Every muscle in Ciaran's body tensed. "Is he . . . Am I . . ."

"In the end, Eilish couldn't capture the likeness well

enough to satisfy herself. So she began again. In the only image that survived, his face is half-turned, the mist swirling, so you can't see all his features."

Ciaran couldn't stem the bitter sense of disappointment. "Then the thing is worthless."

"No. His expression in the portrait is so wistful, it broke my heart. It made every woman who saw it want to love him, and every man who saw it want to become a hero. Ciaran built the castle over the labyrinth of caves and added his own maze of souterrains—tunnels—beneath. It's said that no enemy of Ireland can escape it once he enters, and no one who loves the land can ever be lost. Fiachra O'Riordan, one of the greatest bards who ever lived, took shelter here. For fifty years he taught his students here, passing on the epic poems, the ballads, the history. Legend says that he went blind from being in the darkness so long, and yet he didn't mourn the loss of his sight. He said that within the heart of Caislean ag Dahmsa Ceo, he found a brighter light than any he'd ever known."

"But didn't the English hunt him here? You can't keep such a place secret for hundreds upon hundreds of years."

"Once, it's said, the soldiers attempted to find him. But he merely wound through the passages, drifting out notes to lure them after him. One passage leads to the sea, a dropoff so sudden that you don't know you've fallen until you strike the rocks below. So skilled was Fiachra with his harp, he hurled the notes beyond that opening, made them dance upon the air. The soldiers followed and crashed to their deaths. Sometimes, when the moon is full, people say you can still hear the faint sounds of his clarsah's strings being plucked. But you mustn't follow, lest you join the soldiers who crashed to the stones.

"Then, when Cromwell came, he *slighted* the castle, bombarded it, wanting to turn it to rubble. His Roundheads butchered everything, everyone in their path. A woman took shelter in the souterrains here, and as the cannons pounded, she gave birth to a son. When her son grew to manhood, he became the savior of the people

Cromwell had left to starve in Connaught. He banded them together, taught them how to grow food on the barren, rocky ground, kept the fire of hope alive inside them."

"And now this place is a den for smugglers? Common criminals like this Silver Hand?" The thought sickened Ciaran, as if something holy had been defiled. The fact that *he* might have defiled it was almost unbearable.

"In some ways, Silver Hand is a hero. He smuggles out the wool the English won't let us sell. They've blocked our trade in an effort to protect their own farmers— shackled us by that means as they have so many others. Because of Silver Hand, people are able to survive."

It made Ciaran feel a little better. He turned his gaze out to sea.

"If the assizes ever catch him, or Redmayne's soldiers—"

Disaster, again, for these brave, beleaguered people, Ciaran thought. But the greater danger was losing this castle with the hopes of the ages woven through its broken fingers of stone.

What would happen if Redmayne succeeded in tearing it down? The captain's plan was diabolical, brilliant, the possibility that he might succeed unthinkable.

"I'll stop Redmayne, Mary Fallon," Ciaran vowed. "I swear it."

"I know you will. That's why I summoned you back."

He wanted to kiss the wistful rose of her mouth, wanted to draw her into his arms, to keep her safe, the dreams in her eyes untarnished. Instead, he turned to the stones.

"Have you ever ventured beneath the castle? Through the souterrains?" he asked, then grimaced. What a pointless, absurd question. "Never mind. Just show me the entrance and I'll go down into the labyrinth."

Her chin tipped up at that resolute angle he was coming to dread. "Not unless I come with you."

"Blast it, Fallon, what if we stumble across someone dangerous?"

"If there *is* someone hostile down there, they wouldn't need to bestir themselves to do away with you. You'd just bumble around until you fell through one of the holes or stepped from a hidden dropoff. The one thing I can guarantee you is this—you'd never find your way out."

"And Fiachra might lure me to break my body on the cliffs?"

"He might. Ciaran, I had started to hope . . . believe you were beginning to understand. The magic of this castle, the magic that summoned *you* was entrusted to me. This is my quest, too."

Ciaran wanted to deny it. There must be a dozen ways to keep one obstinate woman out of the labyrinth and safe. Any sane man would make use of one of them. And yet, she'd been so determined, so brave from the very beginning, a lonely and desperate young woman who had known too little love in her life, a dreamer with the courage to test a legend, have faith in magic—not realizing that the real magic lay in the fact that after all she'd seen, all she'd suffered, all she'd endured, she was still able to believe so fiercely in the power of good over evil, right over wrong, love over hate.

She stood before him, regal as a warrior queen, magnificent in her strength. And he knew, in that instant, that to leave her behind now would be a betrayal of the worst kind.

Besides, Ciaran reasoned, wouldn't she be in as much danger out here, with Redmayne and his men prowling about? Perhaps she was safer beside him.

Ciaran peered down into those lake-blue eyes. "You're right. This is your quest, too."

Despite the tension, the uncertainty, the possibility of danger, her face glowed, suddenly incandescent. Ciaran's heart lurched. She'd offered him so many gifts since he'd staggered into her life. He was certain that this act of his—trusting her abilities, acknowledging her strength— had returned a small measure of what she'd given him. He wanted to touch her, smooth his fingertips over the soft curve of her cheek. But if he did, he might never have the strength to pull away again. He curled his fingers into his palms and turned away.

"Show me the way," he said quietly, realizing she'd been doing just that, time and again.

She crossed to an overgrown section of the castle, where vines wove an exquisite pattern of lace against the wall. Fallon knelt down, her slender fingers easing into a crack outlining a stone block. She slid it free, revealing a nook beyond. He marveled at what it contained: a length of rope, several torches, a bundle of candles and a battered tin candleholder, a tinderbox containing flint and steel. She lit the torch within moments, and he eased the stone back into place.

Holding the flickering light before her, she led him to the secret door Ciaran of the Mist had fashioned centuries before. He followed her, his enchantress with hair like a sunset and the fire of ancient Celts still coursing in her blood. And if she'd guided him through a window in time, to this place, this Tir na nOg she'd spoken of, he'd not have been surprised.

Ciaran felt at his waist for the hilt of his dagger. He would find answers here. He had to uncover his past life before he could hope for a future. He had to find some way to shelter the time-worn stones, the fairy rings, the mist-touched souls of the people Fallon loved.

Once inside, he and Fallon sealed the entryway again, so none could follow. Darkness closed about them, held back only by the circle of golden glow from the torch. Down Fallon led him, through winding passages where, here and there, lay the treasures she'd spoken of.

An iron axe head from ancient times was tucked on a ledge of stone, part of its wooden handle still attached. A sword, its once sharp blade eaten away by time until it had the appearance of iron lace, lay on a bed of embroidered linen so fragile it looked as if the merest touch would make it disintegrate.

Perhaps the labyrinth *was* enchanted, for he could almost hear the whispers of all who had sought shelter here, feel their presence pressed into the stone.

Was this the kind of place Silver Hand would choose for his lair? It felt as if no man since Fallon's Fiachra the bard had dared these narrow passages.

Fallon's torchlight ran orange-gold fingers of light across the rough walls, and Ciaran saw carvings here and there. *May God have mercy on our souls,* the plea was etched in an uneven scrawl, names carved alongside—Aisling MacConnell, Michael Moriarty, Fr. John Donnelly. How had they chipped the names into the stone? It must have taken forever. Had they wanted to immortalize themselves? Leave the writings as a testament to their suffering? Or had they chipped into the wall slowly, painstakingly during the time they were trapped here, to keep themselves from going mad?

The path was leading downward, the man-made tunnels opening into caves carved by nature's hand. Fallon edged around gaping holes in the floor, guided Ciaran past ledges that beckoned to certain death—cunning traps, set by the desperate, who had tucked bits of crude gold jewelry on the far side of the openings to tempt the greedy.

As they wound deeper, Ciaran saw a cradle, carved with interlacing, tucked into one nook. Was it here the savior of Connaught had been rocked, taught the resourcefulness that would save at least a few from being crushed beneath Cromwell's boot? A kettle for boiling lay overturned, a gaping hole staved into its bronze belly. A primitive stone quern for grinding grain stood silent beside it. Ciaran wondered how grain had been brought to that quern—at what price in danger? Had it belonged to the woman who had rocked the cradle? Had her husband, her lover, stolen out after darkness to find food for her and the little one? Had he carried the horrible knot of terror in his gut, the agonizing question—what would become of his wife and child if he was killed?

The musty remains of a makeshift bed made Ciaran's chest hurt. What would it be like if Fallon were that woman? If the cradle held *their* child, and he was all but helpless to protect them? An enemy stalking, hunting them?

A sound shattered his thoughts, and in an instant the dagger was in his hand. But Fallon laid gentle fingers on his arm.

"It was only loose pebbles," she said. "You grazed them with your boot."

It was true. His heartbeat slowed, but that did nothing to calm his self-disgust. This time it had been only pebbles, but it might have been Silver Hand or his men, and he would have been caught completely by surprise.

Fool, he berated himself. No matter how the ghosts in these souterrains clamored for his attention, he had to remember there was more immediate danger. Redmayne. Silver Hand. Maybe his own undiscovered past.

He searched, his gaze newly focused as they continued, saw the print of a man's boot heel, a broken bottle that smelled of madeira, tufts of wool snagged on rough stone—the tiniest signs that someone other than Fallon's fairy spirits had wandered here of late.

He tried to concentrate, tried to fit this place into his memory, grasp something familiar. But all he got for his efforts was a fierce throb that made his head ache again. He could hear a roaring in his ears.

No, by thunder! He could feel a sudden dampness in the air, and the roaring was the sea! Grabbing Fallon's hand, he charged toward the sound. A few minutes more, and they were standing in a high-ceilinged cave, a miraculously calm crescent of water lapping at its exit. Boats, pristine and well cared for, were overturned on the ground, neat bales of wool stacked in dry alcoves. Beside them were wooden boxes, unopened. Ciaran wondered what they were. Expensive laces or liquors so the rich could pinch a few more of their precious coins?

He stalked over to the boxes, grabbed a long iron bar, and pried off the nearest lid. Had a captive mermaid sprung from its confines, he would have been no more startled.

Fallon leaned over, bringing the light with her. She gasped. "What . . . what is this? Simple crockery, foodstuffs, leather shoes. Surely no smuggler in his right mind would risk his neck to bring such things to Glenceo."

"Why? What should he smuggle in, Fallon?"

"Laces. Wine and brandy. French silks. Whatever the gentry might buy when the excise men have their backs turned. But this—not one grand family in the county would let such pedestrian wares cross their threshold."

"Then perhaps the wares aren't *for* anyone grand." His gaze met hers over the top of the box. "Blast, this is so strange. Smugglers ply their trade for money. They dare the noose for wealth, not for such paltry things as these."

"But there must be something here that can help us if we search hard enough. Ciaran, does anything here look familiar?" Abandoning the crate, Fallon began to look around. But there was nothing that could lead them to Silver Hand or give them any clue as to who might be lurking behind the elusive smuggler's carefully concealed identity.

Blast, it was just one more mystery. Their journey through the souterrains only raised more questions. Fallon was still searching doggedly through the last of the crates, and Ciaran was almost ready to curse the place to the blazes, when he noticed something white tucked beneath the prow of the farthest boat.

He knelt down, slid out a slip of paper and scanned the bold scrawl. *Tuesday next.*

A rush of triumph jolted through him. It must be mean some sort of rendezvous for Silver Hand and his men. He and Fallon would have to return Tuesday. He glanced at her, intending to share his find, but as his gaze locked on her face, he hesitated.

I was hoping you were beginning to understand, her voice echoed in his memory. *This is my quest, too.*

It should be so simple—Fallon deserved to know everything. She was brave, bright, resourceful, and she knew this land, understood these people better than anyone else living. She had traced the paths of this labyrinth countless times. Yet, could he really bring the woman he loved into danger? Gamble her life?

His jaw tightened, and he thrust the message back into place. He'd rather take a beating than tell a lie, but, there were other ways to conceal—half-truths, things left unsaid.

"Enough, Fallon."

She turned, shadows from the torchlight flickering over her face. Guilt seared him. "Surely you want to keep looking—"

"You were right. If we keep poking around, what will we find? More sturdy boots and cooking pots? There is nothing here that is familiar to me." It was true. The casks, the boxes, the boats—none of them whispered to him of all that he'd lost. Yet the souterrains themselves, the tunnels, the things fugitives had left behind—they resonated, plucked chords deep inside him.

Shoving a wisp of hair away from her brow with the back of one hand, Fallon gazed at him intently. "I'm sorry you didn't find anything to help you here. I know it must be difficult, feeling as if you've lost yourself."

Could she make him feel any more the bastard, Ciaran wondered. She did. She reached out, touched his hand with the slightest butterfly's wing of a touch, her mouth sweet with sorrow. Something in that mouth made him realize the truth. Yes, he was worried about Fallon's safety. No, he didn't want to risk hurling her into the midst of a nest of angry, possibly vengeful smugglers. Even smugglers with such common wares to protect could get ugly when their lair was invaded. They might shoot first, ask questions later.

But there was another reason, even stronger, that had driven him to thrust the note back beneath the boat's prow. A reason that shamed him. To take a smuggler's bullet, to die in front of his lady's eyes would be terrible beyond imagining. But it wouldn't be half so chilling as watching Fallon's eyes flood with disillusionment, revulsion, if the mystical hero she'd summoned was transformed into a common criminal. To watch her dreams die.

No. Whatever he had been before he met her, whatever mistakes he'd made, however he'd failed, he'd been changed, forever altered, by the faith in those sea-blue eyes. When Tuesday came, he would find his way back to this cave, confront these men who might know his secrets. But he'd do it alone. And in the meantime, he'd do what he could to make certain Fallon and the people she loved, this castle with its secrets and its living soul, were protected.

And he would love her. For whatever time they had left. He would fill the empty spaces in his memory with every nuance of her expression. He'd memorize the warmth of her hand, the texture of her fiery hair, the sound of her voice.

Fallon tried to pry loose the torch she'd jammed between two stones. Ciaran crossed to her, tugging it free himself. "I'll find the way out," he said, hating himself for deceiving her.

"It's too dangerous—"

He forced a smile. "You're the one who claimed I couldn't do it. Come, Fallon, you don't think your hero of the mist could resist such a challenge."

"But—"

"You'll be right there to call out before I step into oblivion."

She sighed. "That's true enough. It's not as if you'd be attempting it alone."

Not this time, Ciaran thought grimly. But when Tuesday came . . .

With a warrior's instinct, he focused every fiber of his being, every sense and instinct he possessed to mark the path. What was it Fallon had claimed? No friend of Erin had ever been lost in the maze, and no enemy had ever returned alive.

When he returned, perhaps the legend would tell him what his memory would not: whether he belonged to the mist and the green hills, the singing winds and the delicate interlacing. Whether he belonged to Ireland, and to the woman who had invaded his heart.

CHAPTER

14

∽◉∽

Thank God he hadn't attempted the labyrinth alone, Fallon thought, relieved as they neared the entrance at last. She'd pulled Ciaran back from the brink of disaster a dozen times as they'd wound their way back through the souterrains, and the strain was beginning to fray her nerves.

But what troubled her now was far more complicated than a mere journey through twisted tunnels. It was the labyrinth of her own emotions she was beginning to fear. Everything had seemed so simple when she'd taken the ancient brooch to Caislean ag Dahmsa Ceo on Beltane.

Even after Ciaran had appeared she'd known what she wanted. Perhaps his memory was obscured. Perhaps he wasn't exactly what she'd expected. And perhaps there had been unforeseen complications to deal with. But the one thing there had been no question of was what results Fallon wanted. The castle safe. Redmayne stopped. For her life to go on as it had, year after year, filled with legends and bardsong, the scent of heather and the warmth of the peat fires in the cottages she visited. Dreams that had always been far more real to her than the world of shipping ledgers and livestock and crops, ballrooms and military reviews and foxhunts. The ancient past had always seemed far more alive to her than the present. Because it was safe.

The realization struck her, astonishing her. She'd always considered herself an adventurer, like Maeve, the woman so strong she'd matched wits with Cuchulain, had been his greatest adversary, or Grainne O'Malley, queen of the pirates, who'd bedeviled England's Elizabeth I. Was it possible that she'd been hiding, as deeply in her own way as Hugh was when he buried himself among his ledgers and business affairs?

And yet everything had changed since Ciaran had come into her life. She knew what it was to love a man, to feel callused, eager hands on her naked skin instead of the caresses of mere phantoms, taste the fierce tenderness of his kisses instead of just imagining what it must be like.

Now she understood the real tragedy Deirdre of the Sorrows had faced. Deirdre hadn't cared about legends or the laments bards would sing about her one day—she'd only wanted Naosi's arms around her, wanted to sleep with her hand pressed against his chest so she could feel the precious beating of his heart.

Deirdre had never been given a choice between becoming a thread in the tapestry of legend and embracing the lot of a mere mortal woman—a woman who would awaken with her lover throughout a long life filled with simple joys and sorrows, aggravations and triumphs, arguments and the honeyed pleasure of healing the breach once tempers had cooled.

Fallon's throat tightened as she watched Ciaran near the opening that led back out into the world of blue skies and mist, a place where destiny still awaited them and the fates held uncertain futures in their hands. She would be given no choice either—be it myth or reality—however the next weeks played out. But if she could choose—between Ciaran of the Mist, the magic that would protect what was irreplaceable to her people, and Ciaran the man, who had taken her to wife, who had awakened her to the glory of simple things, a rumpled bed, a drowsy smile, the possibility of a cradle of their own, filled with a child created out of their loving—how would she choose?

In her heart, the darkest, most secret places of her heart, she had betrayed the legacy of the brooch already. If he were only a man, he could love her.

Ciaran turned at that instant, reached for her hand. She clung to his strong fingers as they stepped back into the light. It was only the glare after so much dimness that made her vision blur, her eyes sting, Fallon assured herself, not the battle even now taking place in her heart.

It took Ciaran mere moments to extinguish the torch and return it to its hiding place. Carefully he erased all signs of their presence, instinctively doing his best to protect the entrance to the souterrain from Redmayne's keen eyes.

Despite her most valiant efforts, Fallon couldn't drive back the tears, even when he turned back to face her. She needed so much for him to touch her—to know that, for this single moment, this tiny, infinitely precious window in time, he was real. He was hers.

She could see the emotions warring in his face, the need, the resistance, the surrender. Without a word, he came to her, gathered her in his arms. She clung to him, the wind whispering Deirdre's lament, the sea that had always sung to her, jeering now. *If you could choose . . .*

He never belonged to the fairies—they stole him. He never wanted to be their champion. Why shouldn't he be allowed to love?

But without the betrayal of the fairy king, without the enchantment of the cherries, there wouldn't have been the magic. The battles he'd fought through the centuries for those too weak to defend themselves, the castle, the souterrains that had offered haven, even when the greedy otherworld had kept him prisoner.

Why can't he be mine? A voice cried in her heart as his lips skimmed over her temple, down the curve of her cheekbone to the corner of her mouth. *Why can't he . . .*

His finger hooked under her chin, raising her mouth to his, and he kissed her with such tenderness, her knees melted, her heart burst. She delved her fingers back into the dark thickness of the hair at his nape, and with a wounded moan made fierce love to his mouth, as if this were the last kiss they would ever share.

She could taste the passion in him, the pain, the yearning, and the fear—the same fear she herself knew: that the time they had left was running between their fingers like sparkling drops of water cupped in a child's hand.

She wanted him to drag her down onto the mossy bed in the lee of the stone, wanted to strip away the layers of clothing that separated them, wanted him to make love to her with such immortal passion even the fairies across the divide in Tir na nOg would weep at its beauty. The heartless, greedy creatures would be unable to part them, even when his quest was past.

She slid her hands into the opened front of his shirt, felt the ripple of hot muscle, the soft swell of her belly cradling the hardening evidence that he wanted her as much as she wanted him. Then, suddenly, Ciaran's whole body stiffened, his mouth stilled.

She gave a tiny cry of protest as he drew away. "Fallon, wait."

God in heaven, she couldn't bear it if he turned away now. She tightened her fingers in his hair, strained on tiptoe to meet his mouth. But he only shook his head, his voice roughened with unappeased passion.

"We're not alone."

Her heart leaped into her throat. Saints above, had Redmayne or his minions followed them? Had they led the Englishman here? She wheeled. What she saw stunned her. Heat spilled into her cheeks, and she pressed her fingertips to her kiss-stained lips.

No soldiers emerged from the faint wisps of mist that always seemed to cling about the castle. Rather, beloved, familiar figures—the country folk from around Glenceo.

The Dunnes were the first she recognized—gawky stair-step boys who never backed down from a fight—Dermott Mahon with his flock of pretty daughters, old Brian Loughlin who had buried his wife and children and grandchildren when fever had swept through their cottage eight months ago, Siobhan Moynihan, her stomach swelling, a toddler's hand in each of her own. And others—a dozen others.

What could have driven them to come here? Some catastrophe? The soldiers raiding the countryside as they had so many times before, sweeping up supposed rebels to fill their jails and wet their whipcords with blood?

"What is it?" Fallon ran toward them, sick with apprehension. "Is something wrong?"

"Not a'tall, miss!" Tom Dunne cried as she reached them, his uilleann pipes tucked beneath one beefy arm, a grin on his face. "Caitlin an' me, we thought ye an' yer husband should have a proper weddin' celebration," he said. "So we summoned up the lot o' those who love ye, an' brought 'em here fer a charmin' time. 'Cept, o' course, seems as if ye had other plans." A merry twinkle lit his eyes. "'Tis a fine place fer a lover's tryst, though ye'd have t' be careful not t' get pebbles in yer . . ."

"Thomas!" Dunne's blushing wife, Oonagh, jabbed him with one elbow. "That's enough o' such talk! Nothin' like a wedding, Miss Fallon, t' bring out the bawdy in a man."

"Shoes! I was just goin' t' say shoes, woman!" Tom feigned indignance. "'Tisn't me fault that yer mind runs wicked!"

Fallon stammered something, she couldn't remember what. But even embarrassment at being caught in such a compromising position faded next to the glow of happiness, of affection in these people she loved so well. They were people of the earth, with an innate understanding, respect and awe for the seasons of life—death and birth, courtship, marriage and mating.

"Thomas," Ciaran said gruffly, his gaze flicking to the bundle of food Oonagh Dunne was busily spreading on a flat stone. "You shouldn't have gone to such trouble." Fallon glanced up at Ciaran's face, saw how deeply he was moved.

Little Caitlin swept up, still resplendent in Ciaran's cloak. "*I* wanted to wait till Mammy made up me dress all shimmery. Then Miss Fallon could sit on the Lady Stone, like it was a throne, an' we could bring our presents, an' I'd be so pretty me brother's eyes'd all pop out o' their heads like they do when I punch 'em in the belly."

"I think that's a grand idea, treasure," a stooped figure slipped from the crowd, wise old eyes shining, her slender shoulders wrapped in the cloak Ciaran had given her. "Not the punchin' o' yer poor brothers, mind. But perhaps Miss Fallon's husband would take her t' the stone."

A smile spread over Ciaran's face. "Maeve! Maeve McGinty."

"Aye, 'tis me, lad. Wouldn't be missin' this fer the world. Now, do as young Caitlin says, an' take yer bride t' the Lady Stone.

"Lady Stone?"

"The man who built this castle long ago, he never had a love because o' a fairy spell. But many's the lady would've given her very soul away for a chance t' win his heart. Not wantin' the ladies t' suffer the pain he did, Ciaran did three impossible tasks for a fairy maid. In exchange, the fairy placed an enchantment on a stone where the wind whispers most sweetly, an' the sea sings its song. An' any lady who sits upon it will dream o' her one forever-love."

Fallon saw the shadow cross Ciaran's face at Maeve's tale, felt the yearning in him. But he did as the old woman bade. He took Fallon's hand and led her to the stone Maeve pointed to.

The Lady Stone. Even Fallon had courted its magic once, lowered herself upon it to watch the sea roar and the mist dance. But no dream of a true love had spun out inside her head. Instead, as always, her imagination had filled with images of Ciaran of the Mist.

Her eyes locked with Ciaran's for a long moment. Then she eased down onto the stone almost gingerly. His hand, so strong, so warm, so vital and real, curved atop her shoulder. And in that instant, it was as if a jolt of something shot through Fallon, a sense of rightness, of destiny, of fate.

But she didn't need the stone to tell her. This man was her husband. Her love.

MAGIC

Maeve placed a crown of wildflowers on Fallon's curls. Their fragrance filled her senses—yarrow and fairy grass, cherry blossoms and tiny sprigs from a rowan tree.

Family after family came forward, dressed in their shabby finest, their faces alight with anticipation and joy. Work-roughened hands pressed humble gifts into her grasp. Moira MacConaghy brought a baby dress stitched from her wedding gown: "Had enough cloth fer two, an' the one I made for my first babe was so pretty, I couldn't resist sewing up the other. Was savin' it fer somethin' special. An' now, I'm so glad I did."

Caitlin brought her family's offering, a twig with a few straggly leaves on it, the roots wrapped in a damp cloth. " 'Twill be a cherry tree when it grows up, like the one in the story ye always loved. The one with the 'chanting cherries an' the fairy king. An' someday, if ye're lucky enough t' have a girl like me, ye can sit under the tree an' tell her, oh, everything magic."

Fallon cradled the little seedling in her hands, such a small, fragile thing on which to hang a legend, such a tenuous link to a dream—the dream of a daughter with Ciaran's glen-green eyes, his heart-shatteringly beautiful smile.

The last to approach was Siobhan Moynihan. She glided up, took something from her pocket. A lumpy bundle of soft, heather-colored homespun, a lump of sugar loaf inside. "My grandmother gave me this on my wedding day." A soft rose stained her cheeks. "She was a healer. She said . . ." Siobhan's voice broke a little. "She said it was a charm to help me remember the sweetness of love when trouble came. And there *is* sweetness," she said fiercely. "I only hope my man remembers it some day."

Fallon wondered if the Madonna had looked thus before her son had died—lovely, fragile, yet so strong, the hope of the world shining through the pain in her eyes.

How could she begin to thank them, these people who had opened their hearts to her? Their generosity, their selflessness, their courage humbled her. They had sacrificed so much, had so much stolen from them. But not their dignity. Not their warmth. Not their innate beauty. And Ciaran—Ciaran understood.

Fallon's eyes filled with tears, until their faces blurred before her, their gifts as hazy as images from the other world. But no fairy treasure could have been more precious to her. And no memory could hold more beauty than that of Ciaran, his handsome face flooded with emotion, his eyes grave with gratitude as he thanked Siobhan and little Caitlin, Tom and Dermott, pausing to press the women's hands with gentle chivalry, ruffle the curls of the children, talk to their men.

It was so beautiful, tears burned Fallon's eyes. It was Tom Dunne who saw her swipe one surreptitiously from her cheek.

"Here now, we can't be havin' this, Miss Fallon. 'Tis for joy only, this day. Time for a bit o' music, I'm thinkin'." He turned to Ciaran. "Ye may not know it, but yer bride can dance like the wind. Never saw anythin' more wondrous than Miss Fallon dancin'. 'Tis pure pleasure t' watch her, it is."

Ciaran's gaze found hers. "Would you, Fallon? Dance for me?"

There was such hunger in his eyes, a need to know all of her, every facet, every secret, every sorrow and joy before it was too late. Fallon sensed it implicitly, for she felt the same driving need.

But was it possible to dance with a lump of suppressed tears in one's throat? When all one's emotions were far too tender and close to the surface? Wasn't there a danger of revealing too much? Everything she was? Everything she felt? Everything she needed—from Ciaran, only Ciaran.

But it was Ciaran who asked this of her, his ageless eyes beckoning her from a thousand dreams.

Slowly she stood. Tom Dunne perched on a ledge of stone, cradling his set of uilleann pipes with the same infinite tenderness he lavished on his little daughter. Fallon saw her beloved glen folk fall back into a circle, smiling delight, encouragement. The first notes spun out, sizzling down Fallon's spine, igniting some irresistible force within her with their hauntingly beautiful strains, quivering there for a long moment, before Tom Dunne made the melody dance.

Since time began, the Irish had poured joy and sorrow, passion and pain into their music and dance, distilling life to its purest essence. She closed her eyes and embraced it, letting it flow through her. Her feet moved in the steps of the dance.

How many times had she done this? Shared this with the country folk? Delighted in it? Yet this time was far different. She'd watched others courting, wooing through the movements, watched passion ignite in the eyes of other lovers as the freedom of the dance unleashed inhibitions, overcame shyness. And some secret part of her had envied them for having something she could never know—the freedom to love.

But this time *she* was the one dancing for her beloved, feeling his gaze hot upon her, as certainly as she'd felt his caress the night before.

Someone brought out a bodhran, and the ancient Celtic war drum kept a beat as primal as the pulsing of the earth's very heart. Fallon felt a vulnerability—stark, terrifying, and yet oddly exhilarating as well—born of complete trust, absolute surrender, a crashing down of inner walls that had protected her battered heart since the day her mother had died.

Her blood quickened, raced, her steps became faster, as she dared to let her lashes flutter up. She knew the others were there, but she saw only him, Ciaran, standing so tall, so proud, his eyes hot as coals, his mouth fierce with hunger and yearning. Her gaze locked with his as she poured everything she was into the dance.

The dance . . . Ciaran couldn't breathe, couldn't move as he watched her whirl about, her skirts caught up to her knees, her trim ankles flashing, white-stockinged, delicate, lovely. Light as will-o'-the-wisps, her feet darted to the rhythm. Airy, otherworldly as the mist, she moved as if the merest gossamer threads bound her to the earth.

Her hair tumbled down from its pins, a luminescent, silken cascade, and Ciaran felt as if the wind itself had plucked the pins free, unable to bear any trappings of cold civilization, prim English ways that might taint this wondrous, fey creature. Ireland seemed to be claiming this woman as its own.

But she was *his*, Ciaran thought with savage possessiveness. *His bride*. For now, this enchanted moment, Mary Fallon belonged to him.

Her eyes sparkled, her cheeks flushed rose, every movement of her supple body beckoned him, seducing him, enthralling him. He glimpsed Maeve nudging one of the bold crofter's lads. With a smile, the young man came into the circle and began to dance facing Fallon, a strong, handsome youth, as much a part of this place as Fallon was. Ciaran felt a hot tide of jealousy raging through him, unreasonable anger at both Maeve and the other man. Before he could stop to consider, Ciaran strode into the ring of clapping glen folk. The youth took one look at his face, and backed away. Ciaran saw Maeve's winsome dried-apple face smiling at him, then she turned in a swirl of blue cloak and started down the mountain.

Blast the old meddler! Where the devil was she going? But there was nothing to do but brazen this out. A hush of expectancy hung over the crowd, the only sound the dancing of the pipes and the rhythm of Fallon's steps.

Defiantly, resolutely, Ciaran stared down at Fallon's feet, not giving a damn if he made a complete fool of himself, wanting only to share this with her, this rite of earth and sky and wind, this melding with things ancient and eternal.

Hands on his hips, he forced his feet to move. Awkward, clumsy, he felt like a plodding plow horse beside an ethereal butterfly. Yet the stomp of his boot heels against the ground caught the rhythm. Heat flooded his cheeks, sweat beaded his brow as he fought to keep up with the relentless beauty of Tom Dunne's piping.

Then his gaze caught Fallon's, and he drowned in the fey blue depths. And in that instant, Ciaran believed in the power of enchantment. Like a swift current, she swept up his soul, shaking free every inhibition, awakening something that had been sleeping within him. Steps that had seemed impossible were no longer so. His was no dance of air and sunbeams and light, his was one of earth and fierce masculine desire, the pulsing of battle drums, the primal need to protect one's mate.

Gasps of awe rose from the crowd, but he barely heard them. He only saw the astonishment, the rising tide of pride and joy in the eyes of his bride. In that instant something sizzled between them, a challenge as old as the first wild mare who had tossed her mane—teasing, tempting—and raced away across the hills from the stallion she desired.

Fallon's chin tipped up, her neck arched at a proud angle. Impossible as it seemed, her feet flashed even faster, the steps intricate as the web of lines in the interlacing she'd shown him in the pages of her treasured book. Breathtaking, beautiful, she paused for an instant, daring him to echo her dance.

He wanted to grab her, crush her in his arms, bury his lips in hers. He wanted to lay her down on the moss, bunch her skirts up about her waist and take her with all the primitive passion that had been building between them.

Instead, he matched her step for step, move for move, his boot heels pounding in answering rhythm to the tightening in his loins. Astonishment lit her face, drove her to dance faster, leap higher as the pipes worked their enchantment, but he'd not let her outstrip him, pushed her to greater lengths, until their breath rasped, their skin glowed with sweat, their hearts raced, and their eyes answered each primal call in a language neither could mistake.

When her tongue flicked out to lick a tiny bead of sweat from her upper lip, Ciaran couldn't bear the torment any more. He had to touch her. In a heartbeat, he lunged, sweeping her into his arms. She cried out in surprise and delight as he tossed her high above him, the flower crown flying from her hair in a shower of petals, her skirts rippling, her face glowing. He caught her as she came down and whirled her around and around in his arms until they were both dizzy, so dizzy that he collapsed on the turf, taking her with him.

The firm curve of her bottom landed on the rigid

length of his staff, her breasts, heaving with the exertion, trembled against him where his shirt hung open. He remembered suckling those soft globes, watching her nipples respond to his merest touch.

The world stopped, nothing existing in that instant but Fallon's face, blossom-bright, turned up to his, love luminous in her eyes, her lips dewy and eager and ripe with hunger for him—only for him.

No force on earth could have kept him from claiming her. His mouth devoured hers, drinking in the flavors that were Fallon's alone, bewitching, intoxicating, wild, and yet fragile and sublime as fairy wings.

His wife—his bride. Could any words spoken by any holy man ever forge the bond that joined them together? Or was this something timeless, immortal, beyond the grasp of mere vows, something so fiercely exquisite that it broke Ciaran's heart? He kissed her, every vulnerability stripped raw, every need throbbing at the surface, nothing held back from her, nothing concealed. Nothing existed except the two of them, and the power and the passion between them.

He didn't notice the hush fall over the crowd, the sudden stillness. Only the low purr of a voice that pierced through him: "Such deplorable lack of finesse, MacDonough. Much more enthusiasm, and I fear you'll suffocate her."

Redmayne.

CHAPTER

15

⟨⟫⟪

Awareness of the Englishman slid beneath Ciaran's skin like a cold blade. He jerked away from Fallon and glared up into the faintly amused eyes of his nemesis. Where the devil had the man come from? It was as if he'd appeared in a puff of brimstone, like the devil he was.

In a heartbeat, Ciaran was on his feet, Fallon drawn up beside him. He stepped in front of her in an effort to shield her as she shook her tangled skirts into place, and tried to conceal the vulnerabilities so stark on her face.

Ciaran's gut churned at the knowledge that the English bastard had witnessed such a precious, intimate moment—between Fallon and her beloved glen folk, between the mist and the castle, between Ciaran and his bride.

But now the darkness crawled with shadowy figures, Redmayne's soldiers, prowling like a pack of wolves. How could he have been such a fool, not noticing Redmayne's minions all but surrounding them? He'd been too intoxicated by Fallon, the lithe movements of her body, the invitation staining her mouth, the need that had driven every instinct from his mind except the need to mate with her. If Redmayne had come to massacre these people, he'd have been oblivious until the first pistol shot rang out.

"What the devil are you doing here, Redmayne?" he snarled.

"It's a little known fact that I adore dancing. Allow me to say that I've rarely seen anyone perform the art with more grace than your bride. By the stars, she almost seems to float on a cloud of air." He sketched Fallon a bow, peering at her a little too intensely beneath hooded lids. "Under other circumstances I might be tempted to request the honor of partnering her myself."

"The devil you will! She'd sooner dance with a rabid dog!"

"'Tis a private celebration, this is," Tom Dunne put in. "On their weddin'. No place here fer Sassenach soldiers. Unless, o' course, the Crown's made dancin' a hangin' offense."

"Only clumsy dancing. There's nothing more repulsive. But this is a wedding celebration, you say?" One brow rose a fraction in mock astonishment, as he turned back to Ciaran. "And I wasn't invited to this little fete? How embarrassing. And after all my efforts on your behalf, getting you wed." Redmayne shook his head in feigned sorrow, and it was all Ciaran could do not to slam his fist into the man's face.

It was a violation, this man's presence in the shadow of this castle, amid the glen folk. An abomination. Ciaran wanted to rip him out, fling him away from this place, this night, these people.

Redmayne sighed. "You show a regrettable lack of a sense of humor, MacDonough. All this uncontrolled rage and passion—it grows wearying. It addles a man's wits, exposes his weaknesses. The first rule of strategy should be to conceal—"

"I don't need any lessons from you, Redmayne."

"I could argue with you, but I never waste time—a precious commodity. And it's obvious you can't be taught. Truth is, I have two missions to accomplish tonight. I have several army engineers examining these ruins to discover their weakest point—where to plant the explosives to blast it to rubble. A far less amusing pastime than dancing with so lovely a lady as your bride, MacDonough."

Fallon glared at the Englishman, her face contorted in loathing. "I'm certain if the castle falls, you'll be the one dancing in victory, devil take you!"

Ciaran expected laughter, more of Redmayne's urbane mockery. Instead, the captain's eyelids dropped lower, as if he had something to hide. His voice was suddenly strange. "Oddly enough, I doubt the destruction of this place will afford me much of a sense of triumph." The words were scarce out of Redmayne's mouth before he gave an edgy laugh, creases forming in his brow as if he'd surprised even himself. "Of course, I don't know what one could expect. A soldier can hardly hope that defeating a pile of rubble would compare to the pleasure in conquering a worthy human foe. In any event, this will all be over soon. Squire Butler has given us permission to commence the castle's destruction. Actually, he's quite anxious to get it over and done."

"Butler?" Fallon echoed, her fingers gripping Ciaran's arm so tight her nails cut his flesh.

"It seems he had a bit of difficulty during the last rebellion. Made him rather . . . excitable."

"If ever a man deserved t' have his roof pulled down on his head, 'tis Phineas Butler!" Tom Dunne snarled. "Conspired t' kill 'is own brother, 'e did, so's he could get 'is hands on the estate. All o' Glenceo knows it to be true, even if none 'ere could prove it! An' ever since, Butler's people are all but starvin'. Rich as Croesus, 'e is, but every ha'penny he spends goes t' gamblin' an' drink an' fancy women. Yet even that wasn't entertainin' enough for that craven coward. No, th' divil-spawned bastard had t' start ruinin' decent girls as well, fillin' up their bellies whether they said yea or nay."

Dunne cast a pain-filled glance at a tow-headed girl of scarcely fourteen, her stomach protruding just enough to be suspicious, her face ducked low with shame.

A bantam rooster of a man, red-haired and red-faced, staggered forward, reeking of whiskey. "Ye needn't be blatherin' about me wife. Squire seen that we were wed right proper, an' he'll be payin' handsome fer the raisin' o' this babe. We'll be bathin' in coin, won't we, me darlin'?" He pinched the girl's buttocks. "Bran MacGrath knows how t' strike a bargain, 'e does!"

Ciaran wanted to yank the man away from the girl, beat him senseless, make certain MacGrath could never touch her again.

When his gaze flashed back to Redmayne's, Ciaran was surprised to see something flicker in the Englishman's eyes. Disgust? Distaste? As if Redmayne were repelled by MacGrath and by what Butler had done? In an instant, the spark of emotion vanished from Redmayne's face, leaving behind that cool marble mask.

"That is the beauty in dealing with Squire Butler. A man careening from one disastrous mistake to another is all too easy to . . . influence, is he not, Mr. MacGrath? I could scarce believe my good fortune when I found the squire owns this spit of land. He's only too glad to get rid of this eyesore, especially since I informed him it's a suspected den of smugglers. His family has been beset by an unfortunate string of accidents already, courtesy of this Silver Hand—warnings regarding the squire's, er, appetites, as it were. Butler has no desire to find a knife blade pressed against his throat anytime soon."

"Blade might be *in* 'is throat if he lets anyone topple so much as a stone from this place," one of the Dunne boys muttered, but Redmayne ignored the comment.

"I would advise against any attempt to follow through on that threat. Mr. Butler's home is quite protected. I've seen military encampments less prepared for battle. Pistols everywhere, footmen hired for skill with weapons instead of more civilized graces. It's a wonder some poor scullery maid hasn't been blasted into eternity coming down to stir up the morning fires."

"'E won't be able t' hide forever," Gerald Sullivan snarled.

"That is the material point, is it not?" Redmayne observed. "No one can hide forever. Not the squire, and not even the elusive Silver Hand. You see, destroying the castle might be my main goal, but my commander,

General Scargill, has another priority—hanging the man who shot his nephew. It's a dangerous pastime, shooting the relative of a general, no matter how unsavory his character. And Silver Hand is guilty of that crime."

"Aye, bless 'is kind soul!" someone deep in the crowd said.

"He'll need all the divine intercession he can get," Redmayne observed, glancing at the intrepid old woman. "Even now, my men are combing the area for signs of the rogue. An unmarked ship was spotted in the storm the other night. It disappeared in this area. There must be some sort of smuggler's nest nearby. I will find it."

Ciaran exerted every fiber of his will to keep his expression frozen so as not to betray what he had found in the souterrains below—an entire world Redmayne must never discover. But an insistent bubble of panic pushed at his throat. Had he and Fallon left any sign? The smallest scrape of a footprint, a broken twig, a bit of crushed underbrush that might betray the entryway to the hidden world below Caislean ag Dahmsa Ceo?

"No smuggler in his right mind would use this place as a lair," Fallon scoffed, stepping up beside Ciaran. "The sea is too wild, the cliffs too perilous. Silver Hand would seek someplace calm and hidden."

Like the tiny inlet they'd discovered below the castle, Ciaran thought. A place so unexpected, it would take a miracle to find it. Then why did his gut knot with dread at the intensity in Redmayne's eyes, the intelligence, sharper than any blade ever forged, and—most terrifying of all—the chill resolve untainted by emotion? It was as if Redmayne were something not quite human.

A smile ticked up one corner of Redmayne's mouth. "My dear Miss Fallon, *any* smuggler who would ply his trade in a territory assigned to me must be . . . how did you say it? Out of his mind? A man ruled by anger, I would judge. One who surrenders to primitive passions instead of his intellect. A man very like your new husband, I would guess."

"A man with blood in his veins instead of ice?" Ciaran snapped.

Tom Dunne stepped up, the Irishman's eyes glittering with hate for Redmayne, but more so for the uniform the man wore, the eternity of oppression it stood for. "I can't imagine why ye think ye can capture this Silver Hand, whoever he is, Captain. He's been outwitting the garrison and excise men long before ye came here. There's none can touch 'im, the rogue Silver Hand."

Damnation, didn't Tom realize it was dangerous to poke a sleeping tiger with a stick? Redmayne's eyes narrowed. "You seem to have great faith in this criminal. From personal knowledge, perhaps?"

A tiny cry tore from Oonagh, and she leaped before her husband. "Please, yer worship, my Tom, he's just in a blather because o' the celebratin'. Braggin' like all men do—"

"Enough, woman," Tom snapped. "'Tis just the truth I'm speakin'. Easy enough for anyone with eyes t' see."

"I'm most interested in your . . . range of vision. All of you." Redmayne cast a glance about the silent, hate-filled crowd. He drew a purse from his pocket, emptied it on the turf. The coins clinked against each other, rolling to the bare feet of the crofters. "There is far more where that came from. Anyone who provides information leading to the capture of Silver Hand will earn a hundred pounds in gold."

He prowled to where little Caitlin Dunne stood and started to kneel down. Ciaran saw Tom lunge for his daughter, but Ciaran reached her first, scooping the child up into his arms.

"Contrary to popular local myth, we English don't eat children—at least, not unless they are seasoned with the proper blend of spices." Redmayne chuckled, straightening. "Do you know what you could do with a hundred pounds, little girl?"

"I could use it t' choke yer throat, ye bloody Sasse-nach!" the babe spat, from her safe haven in Ciaran's grasp.

"Caitlin!" Oonagh cried in alarm.

But not so much as a flicker of anger sparked in Redmayne's eyes. He caught a fold of the cloak Ciaran had given Caitlin between long, white fingers. "You could wear silk every day of the week. You could buy pretty dolls."

Caitlin's mother rushed over, snatching her babe away from Ciaran, carrying her back into the crowd of Caitlin's stalwart brothers.

Undeterred, Redmayne's gaze flicked to Siobhan, her belly distended, her babies clustered around her. They were far too thin, and Siobhan's face too careworn. "With a hundred pounds you could fill your kettle with meat night after night, and your children would never be hungry."

"Mr. Hugh gives us all our fill. 'Tis just I haven't stomach to eat of late."

"You could have the finest doctors in all Ireland to deliver a babe."

"Hugh will make certain she's cared for!" Fallon declared, but Redmayne's gaze never wavered from Siobhan's.

"You could even use the money to sail away to America, where your man could forget the call of the whiskey."

Redmayne chose his prey with the fiendish skill of a predator, homing in on the most vulnerable. It sickened Ciaran, made his blood run cold, that this monster should know gentle Siobhan's pain and use it as a weapon against her.

"Leave her out of this, Redmayne," Ciaran snarled, stepping forward to shield her, but Siobhan stepped forward with infinite dignity.

"I'll not be taking your blood money, sir. My Sean died trying to drive your kind from these shores."

"Ah, but you have another son. Michael."

Siobhan flinched. Redmayne was Lucifer, fiendishly beautiful, cunning, tempting, preying on her motherly heart, her grief, her loss.

"The Crown sent him to . . . Barbados, was it? All that gold might be able to find him, buy his indenture."

Siobhan went white, one hand trembling almost imperceptibly. "I . . . Michael would not want me to—"

"To free him before the fever and the heat rot his body and his sanity?"

"Leave her alone, you bastard!" Ciaran roared, lunging for Redmayne, only Tom Dunne's strong arm stopping him.

"I was merely attempting to ease her sorrow. Even you can't object to the prospect of reuniting a mother with her son, MacDonough."

"You twisted cur! I should—"

"Should what? Kill me? For what, MacDonough? Offering these people a chance to build a new life, away from the poverty, the dirt? I am only offering someone the opportunity to become a rich man or woman."

The officer's unsettling eyes locked on Ciaran's. "Silver Hand will hang. And I will be the one to tighten the noose about his neck. With your help, or without it. But the opportunity I'm offering you is a limited one. You'll never have the chance to earn such riches again. Anyone with information to sell knows where to find me."

"No one here'd tell ye the time o' day, if ye flayed 'em alive!" Tom Dunne roared.

"Is that so?" Redmayne's eyes widened a fraction. "Let me give you a bit of advice. Be very careful what you say, Dunne. Some men might be tempted to take up such a challenge."

"Leave him alone, Redmayne," Ciaran snapped, misliking the glint in the officer's eyes.

"You needn't arouse all that righteous wrath, MacDonough. I won't put your friend upon the rack. I deplore such crude tactics. There are other ways of getting the information I seek." His voice dropped low. "Every man has his secrets. And every man has his price. It's merely a question of discovering the key." He reached up, skimming his fingertips along one of Fallon's tumbled curls, the tiny gesture poisoning Ciaran with rage.

"Keep your hands off her!" he blazed.

Something flashed in Redmayne's eyes. "You see. We've known each other a matter of days, and I have found your weakness already." He sketched Fallon an insolent bow.

"Until we meet again, madam." With military precision, the captain turned and strode from the crowd.

Silence was a deafening roar behind him, the magic of the night stripped away, anger and fear and helplessness left behind in Redmayne's wake.

Without a word, the glen folk were beginning to melt away, all except for Tom Dunne and his family fleeing to their own hearthsides, the cottages that gave some small illusion of protection.

Ciaran couldn't blame them. His stomach churned, dread gnawing at his nerves, his whole being possessed by a fierce need to scoop Fallon up, carry her as far away from the sinister Englishman as possible. Keep her safe.

Safe? As Siobhan's sons had been safe? As Caitlin and Tom Dunne were safe? Could there be safety in a land under Redmayne's boot heel?

But almost more dangerous than the Englishman's threats were the temptations he had dangled like sweetmeats before starving children. More coin than they could earn in a lifetime, coin that could restore lost sons, set whole families sailing to a new beginning. If it were Ciaran's child suffering somewhere, his sons and daughters lost to poverty and hunger and sickness, might he betray . . .

No. But Redmayne had played the scene like a master spider, catching them all up in his web. Under the crushing pressure of threat or temptation, chances were that someone would break.

He heard the crunch of a footstep near him, Tom Dunne's voice low, rough, hate-filled. "Redmayne—he's a devil, is that one, an' 'twould be the finest day's work 'e ever did if Silver Hand were t' cut 'is throat."

"Why doesn't he?" Ciaran demanded, itching to have the knife blade in his own hand. "Why doesn't he rid the countryside of the accursed soldiers?"

"He's tried it, right enough. Rid us of the commander 'afore Redmayne, 'e did. General Scargill's nephew, it was, an' a viler man ye've never met. But the English only send another man t' fill 'is boots. An' one a hundred times more dangerous. I'd wager Silver Hand figures better to outwit the one we've got than to stir things up so much the English come crashin' down on Glenceo the way they did after the rebellion. None too choosy about who they trample in the process, the English are."

Ciaran's eyes narrowed, something in the Irishman's voice driving him to question. "This Silver Hand—do you know him?" Ciaran asked. But Dunne's features closed, hardened.

"In a way we all do. He belongs t' us, like your Fallon does. She keeps hope alive, dreams and hero tales, a bit o' the ancient magic we can touch. Silver Hand keeps bellies full, roofs over heads, clothes on children's backs. Without 'im, the people hereabouts would've starved, lost everything after the rebellion. If there be such a thing as guardian angels, then the angel o' Glenceo sails a smuggler's ship an' wears a pistol 'stead o' wings. No one I know of 's ever seen his face, but 'e's there, always there, when we're in need."

Ciaran looked into Dunne's eyes, bright with intelligence, inborn wariness veiled by quick humor. Doubtless the man could spin tales that Fallon's saints themselves would believe, but Ciaran didn't think the Irishman was lying now. He didn't know who Silver Hand was. Even if he did, he'd not betray it.

"If ye're thinkin' o' lookin' for him yerself, ye might as well save yerself the trouble. 'Tis as if he doesn't have a face. If it weren't for the shoes that end up on me doorstep, or the warm coats or books fer me boys, I'd say Silver Hand was as much a legend as Ciaran o' the Mist. Even our Fallon, here, has done her best t' find Silver Hand, but she failed t' find 'im, same as all of us. Take yer bride home, MacDonough. Finish what ye started before we all came chargin' in on ye. Celebrate life, love, happiness. 'Tis far more fragile, far more fleetin' than ye know."

Dunne was wrong, Ciaran thought. He did know. Knew in his very soul, every time he looked into Fallon's eyes, felt the enmity in Redmayne, remembered the vulnerability of his own lost memory.

"Tom." Fallon's voice was quiet, shaken, as she pressed the Irishman's strong, hoary hand. "Thank you, for tonight. Don't think Redmayne could spoil what you did for us. I'll always remember . . . the beautiful part. The pipes, the dancing."

Dunne's face reddened, his voice gruff as that of one of his sons caught in some sentimental act. "Wanted it t' be perfect fer ye. Blasted English cur came t' ruin it."

"The English tried to destroy this castle, too, but it's the broken edges that make Caislean ag Dahmsa Ceo so beautiful." She smiled at Tom and his family clustered about, and Ciaran had never loved her more. "Redmayne could never taint the gifts you've given us."

"Ye're a fine one, Mary Fallon Delaney MacDonough. A fine one," Dunne said, and Ciaran saw tears glisten in the brawny man's eyes. "But have a care, girl. I'm that fearful fer ye. There's somethin' in Redmayne's eyes when he looks at ye."

It was true, and it made Ciaran's blood run cold.

"Nothin' can hurt Miss Fallon!" Caitlin declared, pushing forward, her face upturned, her eyes fierce with believing. "She can just call Ciaran o' the Mist back, an' he'd crunch Redmayne up in a million bits! She has magic!"

Magic. Could something so ephemeral triumph over a man like Lionel Redmayne? Over a race of conquerors like the English? Or was Redmayne right? Would time run out? Would some weakness be exploited, some vulnerability discovered? Would someone desperate turn betrayer?

Ciaran's arm tightened about Fallon.

"Ye'll take care o' her for us, MacDonough?" Dunne asked fiercely.

"I would die for her," Ciaran vowed before the castle wreathed in legend, before Dunne and Caitlin and the echo of the music from the pipes, and before the eyes that watched them beyond the mist.

Dunne nodded. "Me boys will see yer gifts get delivered up t' Misthaven. Ye jest be takin' our Fallon home."

Dunne gathered up his daughter, his sturdy sons taking up the humble offerings that were so precious. Then the family made their way down the tangled path. Ciaran felt Fallon's hand grasp his arm. He looked down into her face: the ethereal joy had vanished, the bright challenge, the hunger that had driven him nigh mad with wanting her. Her fairy-kissed features were subdued with worry, her eyes heavy with quiet desperation.

"Now that he has Butler's permission, Redmayne won't wait to start destroying the castle. Ciaran, what are we going to do?"

Ciaran's mouth hardened, grim. "I think it's time the squire had a visit from Ciaran of the Mist."

CHAPTER

16

∽

Only a miracle could have allowed Ciaran to reach this room, guided him through twisted corridors past drowsing footmen, helped him thwart locks no master thief should have been able to break through. But he'd begun to believe in miracles ever since Fallon had entered his life. And tonight he needed all the help he could get.

He grimaced. No high king's tomb could have been sealed more tightly than Phineas Butler's bedchamber, Ciaran thought as he slipped into the room, but then, a man who would murder his own brother and rape a defenseless child like Ailis MacGrath had much to fear—a fact that could only work to Ciaran's advantage. A grim smile twisted his lips.

Butler's massive bed stood like a fortress amid a sea of discarded clothing, spilled wine and half-eaten food. Thick wooden posts jutted to the ceiling, the old-fashioned bed curtains drawn tight despite the warmth of the night.

The air was too thick to breathe. It reeked of brandy, was weighed down with the heavy scent of Hungary water, sweat, and a woman's cheap perfume, the mustiness made far worse by windows all but nailed shut, as if fresh air were some sort of invading army attempting to breach the walls.

The master of this rotting elegance huddled under masses of satin coverlets, his face bloated with dissipation, his balding pate gleaming with sweat in the flickering of the firelight, a dribble of wine staining the front of his nightshirt.

The debris made it clear a woman had been part of the evening's entertainment, but she was gone. It seemed Butler liked to sleep with a more deadly mistress—the cold steel of the pistol just visible beneath his pillow.

Had that weapon been there when Butler had dragged Ailis MacGrath up to this chamber? Ciaran wondered as the hopeless, shame-filled woman-child's face rose in his memory, her delicate body swelling with Butler's bastard.

He glared down at the man in the bed, poisonous hate welling inside him. This was the craven monster who had forced Ailis into his bed, then when she was pregnant with his child, had tossed her to the crude, greedy dog of a crofter. She'd been no more to Butler than the scrapings from the plates littering the room, a surfeit of delicacies to be devoured, then disposed of to the dog scrabbling at his feet.

It must have been laughably easy for Redmayne to get Butler to agree to his scheme. If the man was willing to destroy the lives of young girls like Ailis, why wouldn't he be eager to see the castle tumbled into the sea?

Disgust, loathing, revulsion filled Ciaran as he drew the ancient dagger from the belt at his waist. He pressed the blade to Butler's throat, and it was all he could do not to slash it deep.

Butler would have awakened screaming if he could have drawn air into his lungs. Instead, his eyes bulged, his mouth gaping open on a hoarse, choked cry.

The myriad sins the man had committed were written in his eyes. Terror and confusion contorted his features, as if he were groping through the filth of his life, trying to decide which wrong his assailant had come to revenge.

"No! Don't kill me! For the love of God!" Butler

croaked, his gaze flicking from Ciaran's face to the costume Fallon had put together—billows of linen shirt, belted at the waist, a flowing mantle, the ancient cloak brooch's cabochon jewels gleaming like red eyes.

"Wh-who are you?" Butler choked out. "Wh-what do you want?"

Ciaran had rehearsed what he was going to say to the man, plotted it with Fallon. What would Ciaran of the Mist say? What would he do? What would most terrorize this craven cur with the dagger at his throat? Yet as Ciaran stared down into that bloated face with its eyes gluttonous from selfish pleasure, every speech vanished from his brain, leaving only a red haze of rage.

"Who am I?" Ciaran echoed. "I am your worst nightmare—the reason you keep that pathetic pistol beneath your pillow at night, set guards at your doors. Did you really believe such paltry measures could keep me away?" Was it possible for the man to blanch any whiter?

"J–James?" Butler stammered, shrinking back. "No! No, you're not . . . I've never seen you before!" Was there the tiniest hint of relief in the man's face? "Then why—" Butler hesitated.

"You've committed crimes aplenty, Butler. There are many who would fight each other for the chance to put a dagger in your heart, as you well know."

"The guards! Wh–what happened? What did you do to them—kill them?" Sweat slickened his jowly features. "The house must be crawling with rebels."

"I come alone."

"No lone man could get into this room! It's impossible! I made certain—"

A brutal laugh tore from Ciaran's lips. "If you had an army, they could not stop me from fulfilling my quest."

"Q–quest? Who are you? What do you want?"

"I come to give you a choice, Butler. Leave my people in peace, keep their bellies full, their bodies warm, and I might decide to let you live."

"Your people? Y–you have family on my estate? I–I'll give them the best cottage on my land . . ." he babbled eagerly. "Anything you want . . . if you'll just tell me who they are."

"Not one family. All of them. Every poor soul unfortunate enough to live on Butler land."

"All the crofters? You can't be serious! They're like animals—filthy and constantly breeding—"

The dagger bit deep. A line of blood welled above the bright edge of the blade. "Not too filthy for you to take to your bed. Innocent young girls, barely more than children. You rape them and—"

"Not rape! Never rape!" The spark of offense in Butler's eyes nearly cost him his life. "I gave them a choice—"

"Submit to your pawing or have their families flung into the street to starve on the open road? I will give you the same kind of choice. Do as I tell you, or I will carve up your rotting carcass the way you carved up the souls of those girls."

"Wh–whatever you say! I swear, I'll—"

"You lying scum. Even now, you are thinking about what you will do the instant I leave this room. If you live through this ordeal, you will hunt me down like a dog. You and your army of cowards will take the knife and—"

"No! You're wrong!" Butler protested, but the hot flush on his cheeks betrayed him.

"Do you think you could capture me? You and your partner, Captain Redmayne?" Ciaran sneered. "Is it possible to imprison the mist?"

"The mist? Silver Hand! You're the smuggler—"

"No."

"Then who . . ."

"I am the man who built the castle you and Redmayne are plotting to destroy."

Butler swallowed hard. "You can't mean . . . can't possibly be . . ."

"Ciaran of the Mist."

Butler's eyes all but bulged out of his head. "You're mad! That's impossible!"

"Is it?"

"It's nothing but a legend . . . make-believe. A pack of fairy tales."

"My castle is real, is it not? And this dagger at your

throat—surely you don't think it is *make-believe?* Perhaps we should test the blade against your throat to see—"

"No! No! I just . . . Why would you come here? To me? There . . . there are worse men—far worse landlords in Ireland. Why, Squire Biddleston, he—"

"Squire Biddleston hasn't agreed to demolish my castle, has he?"

"I–I didn't wish to! Captain Redmayne is a most forceful man. He coerced me shamefully, or I would never have agreed to such a plan."

"You would've had your army of footmen out there with hammers and chisels if you'd thought of the idea first, Butler."

Something sly crept into Butler's eyes, the expression of a man who would barter a three-year-old to the hangman to save his own neck. "The castle is about to crash down on its own. I–I only wanted to keep some innocent crofter's child from getting hurt. I am trying to protect my people."

Ciaran's fist knotted in the front of Butler's stained nightshirt. "Like you 'protected' Ailis MacGrath, and who knows how many others? You're the soul of compassion, Butler. But hear me now, and remember this. If so much as one stone of the walls of Caislean ag Dahmsa Ceo is toppled, if any 'accident' befalls the place, if Redmayne and his vultures chip away a single flake of stone, there will be no place on earth you can hide from me."

"I give you my word." So fast, so simple, the vow was made. Ciaran was sickened by it.

"Why should I trust a craven cur like you?"

"I'll do whatever you want! Forbid Redmayne to demolish the castle—"

Ciaran gave a bitter snort of laughter. "You *forbid* Redmayne—I'd like to see you try. No, Butler. I know exactly how it would be. You'd be a tower of strength, most resolute, until you're face-to-face with the captain, and he's the one you fear most." He frowned, considering. "I think I had better kill you after all, and make certain."

"No! No, please!" Butler's eyes rolled, wild. Sweat ran down his face. "Mercy . . . I'll do anything you say! Write it in blood—"

Ciaran glared down at him for a moment. "Butler, you might just have saved your worthless life."

Relief shot across the man's swollen features.

"Write to Redmayne, refusing him permission to destroy the castle."

"O–of course! So simple—"

Ciaran could see the gleam in Butler's eyes, as if the man were already plotting what he would do once he escaped.

"No. Not quite so simple. I'm not certain what I mistrust the most—your cowardice, or Redmayne's ability to bend people to his will. This is the bargain I offer you, Butler. Pen a letter to Redmayne, then disappear."

"D–disappear? I don't understand."

"I think you do. Leave these lands in the hands of a generous steward, sail away from Ireland and never come back."

"B–but I've nowhere else to go!"

"I'm certain if you search hard enough, you'll be able to find some other hive of debauchery—willing women you pay for, plenty of wine to keep you in a drunken stupor. Unless you're so attached to this land you wish to be buried here."

"No. I'll do as you say."

"You will. Or die." Ciaran released Butler. The balding man scurried to a writing desk in the corner of the room. With one arm, he swept away an assortment of crumpled cravats and tall crowned beaver hats. He rummaged about, took pen in hand. After a moment, Butler sanded the missive, sealed it.

Ciaran stared into the man's face. What he saw there both disgusted him and reassured him—a coward, desperate to save his own skin, a man weak-minded enough to believe in ghosts and avenging angels and nine-hundred-year-old heroes called back from the land of the fairies. Butler couldn't wait to put as much distance as possible between his villainous carcass and Ciaran of the Mist.

"One last word of warning," Ciaran said, easing the dagger away from Butler's throat. "By the javelin of Cuchulain, and the tears of Deirdre of the Sorrows, I curse you, Butler."

"No!" Butler wailed. "I've done what you want! I've done what you asked! Don't—"

"If you ever set foot on this land again, I promise you that you'll suffer torments beyond anything your image of paltry Christian hell could imagine. At my hands, Butler—the hands of Ciaran of the Mist."

He left Butler quivering, sobbing in the loathsome bed like a terrified child, too shaken to even think of raising the alarm. Quietly, cautiously, Ciaran eased through the corridors he'd passed through earlier, then let himself out into the gardens.

A ghostly pearl of moon sailed on a drift of clouds, turning the garden path into a silver ribbon, the cascades of flowers and hedges hovering like specters in the shadows.

The castle was safe. The quest was over, Ciaran thought. He should be elated, relieved. He should feel triumphant. Instead, he felt an odd emptiness, an ache, as if he had lost . . .

Lost what? His sense of purpose? The hope that he could somehow shield the woman he loved? Be the legendary hero she'd wanted so desperately? He closed his eyes, remembering her face as he'd left her behind. They'd both known that if anyone on Butler's land had seen them together while he was garbed as Ciaran of the Mist, their plan would be ruined. Yet, she'd looked so small and lost and alone.

"Ciaran?"

The soft voice made him freeze, his heart hammering first in alarm, then in recognition. She slipped from the shadows, her gown pale as the robes of a fallen angel, her face kissed by moonlight, desperate, fragile, vulnerable, the faint gleam of tears on her cheeks.

"Fallon? What the blazes are you doing here? We agreed you shouldn't come."

"I know, but I couldn't . . . couldn't bear the waiting. I thought you'd . . ." She hesitated but an instant, as if trying to leash some force inside her. He could almost hear it snap free. She ran into his arms, a ragged sob tearing from her lips. "Thank God," she choked out, her fingers tracing the planes of his face, his hair, the muscles of his chest. "I've been so afraid!"

"Of Butler?" he asked, holding her, reveling in the precious feel of her in his arms. "Surely he was no match for Ciaran of the Mist! Especially considering all the other heroic deeds the legend claims I've done."

"Don't!" She cried fiercely, burying her face against his chest. "Don't mock me."

Ciaran felt her fear and pain twist about his heart. Had she really been so afraid? His bold, brave Fallon.

"Don't cry, my love," he murmured into her hair. "It's over now. Everything is all right. The castle is safe. Redmayne can't destroy it."

"I'm not crying about th—the castle. I was afraid I'd never see you again. That you'd vanish into the mist."

The words struck something cold into Ciaran's belly, a dread so deep his grip tightened on Fallon until he feared he might bruise her. What would it have been like, to be swept away from this land, this woman? Unthinkable. A wound that would never heal. "I'm still here, my love."

"Yes. You're here. I can touch you. Feel the beat of your heart." She gave a broken laugh and raised her face to his. "It's so strange. When I found you that first night, I wanted so desperately for you to be the Ciaran of the legend. I made myself believe . . . But now, I'm so glad that you aren't Ciaran of the Mist!" She looked up at him, so hopeful, so fragile, this woman who had defied Redmayne, taken in an injured stranger, danced in the arms of a wild Irish night.

She didn't realize that he could still be taken away from her. That he had a rendezvous with his own destiny in the confines of the labyrinth they had traveled together. "You can't be the Ciaran of the legend, or you'd be gone, wouldn't you?"

"Yes. I can't be Ciaran." Blast, what was the matter with him? He'd spent every minute he'd been with Fallon trying to convince her it was all some pretty nonsense, that he was no legend spun over hundreds of years. He was a man. Just a man, like any other. He should be relieved that the charade was over, that the dream-dust could fade from her eyes and she could see him for what he was: a man. A man who had lost his memory. A man who might never even remember his own name. Her husband—but not one woven of hero-tales and her own vivid imagination—a far more commonplace husband. One hardly worthy of a fairy-kissed sprite like Mary Fallon.

But her fingers were threading through his hair. Her lips trailed against his jaw. "I'm so glad you're not the Ciaran of legend! I want so much to keep you with me, to love you. I want it more than magic, more than saving the castle. Is that so horribly selfish?" She peered up at him with wide sea-blue eyes, as if he held all the answers, when suddenly he felt more lost, more adrift than ever. Stark realization pierced him. He didn't want it to be over. The dream. The magic she'd poured into his doubting hands.

"You could never be selfish, Mary Fallon. You, who give everything, all of yourself to me, and to the crofters on Misthaven land."

"B–but the legend—it gives people something to believe in."

"Just because I'm not the Ciaran you summoned from the land of the fairies doesn't mean he doesn't exist somewhere, beyond the mist." It cost Ciaran more to say that than he could have imagined. Her perfect hero, the mythic man she claimed she had loved her whole life, might still be drifting in the place where dreams were kept.

But for now, she belonged to him. His wife. His lady. His love. A fierce need swept through him, born of the danger he'd faced entering Butler's fortress home and the sense of foreboding that seemed to whisper to the night. Legends never died. But a mortal man could never be certain how many precious hours of his life might remain. The image of the smuggler's den rose in Ciaran's memory, the salt sting of the sea in his nostrils, the bold scrawl of the note he'd hidden from Fallon beneath the belly of the overturned boat. Suddenly he couldn't get close enough to her. The thought of not being able to touch her even during the ride back to Misthaven was unbearable.

He took her hand, led her to where he'd tied his horse. Her own mount cropped grass beside it. "I want you to ride with me, Mary Fallon. In my arms." He traced the elegant curve of her cheek.

"Cuchulain will follow." She slipped the bridle from the horse's head, whispered something in Cuchulain's velvety ear. Those wise equine eyes met hers with complete understanding.

Then she turned to Ciaran. He mounted his own horse, held out his hand to her. With fairylike grace, she eased onto the horse's back, settling into the curve of Ciaran's arms.

He'd been an abysmal rider from the first, but tonight it was as if the keeper of the Castle of the Dancing Mist had drifted an enchantment over him. Or was it Fallon, with her special brand of magic that turned the dirt path into a ribbon of beaten silver, the trees into sentinels from other ages, warriors still brave and strong, untouched by English swords?

Ciaran should have carried her back to Misthaven House, the safety of her brother's walls. He wasn't certain what force guided him onto a different track, winding upward along the cliffs.

Why? There was a warm bed, a fire, waiting in the room where he'd first made love to Fallon. And the truth that he was not the hero of legend she'd sought still left him feeling oddly raw.

She nestled against his chest, infinitely precious, the only thing in his life that was real. He couldn't help remembering the tale she had spun for him—the tale of Deirdre of the Sorrows and her lover, Naosi. Had Naosi held her in his arms thus as they fled from the high king's wrath? Had he been uncertain of his powers to protect her? Feared that he would disappoint her somehow? Fail her?

MAGIC

But Ciaran had fulfilled the quest Fallon had set for him. He'd made certain the castle was safe, hadn't he? Why did he feel that something vital was unfinished? Why was he restless, disappointed in himself? Why did he suddenly need the healing power of jagged stone walls reaching up into the sky, of sea spray and gull cries from the ocean crashing beneath the cliffs? And why did he need Fallon there, in his arms?

This was insane. The place had been crawling with soldiers when he'd left it the night before. Beneath the castle lay a den for smugglers, Silver Hand and his men. Why did it feel as if the tumbledown castle belonged to him? Now, when he was finally certain that Fallon's whispers of magic and legend were what he feared—the beautiful imaginings of an embattled people?

Or was it that he needed to be as close to Mary Fallon as possible just once before he traversed the labyrinth alone, and walking into Caislean ag Dahmsa Ceo was like entering her very soul?

She said nothing, but he sensed when she realized where he was going. She melted even closer against him, her breathing soft and light, as if the castle had had the power to calm her spirit the way the hand of Mannan MacLir, the Celtic god of the sea, could smooth out the most raging of waters.

Ciaran reined his horse to a halt just beyond the wall, his cheeks heating with embarrassment and confusion. "I must have lost my mind as well as my memory. Bringing you to this place. What if Redmayne has set men to watch it?"

"No one is here. The spirits would whisper warning."

She sounded so certain. But how much trust could one place in things unseen—in intuitions and in dreams, in things you couldn't touch? Yet something had compelled him to ride to this castle. His heart? Or an enchantment spun out like a fairy's thread, drawing him to the cliffs and the age-worn stone?

"I just . . . had to come here. I don't know why."

"But I do." Her breath, warm, moist, feathered across his jaw. She drew away, shifting in his arms until she

253

could gaze up into his eyes. And he knew in that instant that if the goddess of enchantment had a face, it looked exactly like Mary Fallon's—delicate features filled with possibilities, eyes brimming with the power of believing, lips full and tempting, impossible not to taste. The silky waves of her hair brushed against his throat, her scent— meadow blossoms and sea wind and peaches in new cream—filling his senses.

"Come with me." She slid to the ground, held out one hand, small and white in the light of the moon.

"Fallon," he grated. "I don't think—"

"This place isn't about thinking, Ciaran. It's about *feeling*—so many things. Joy and pain, despair and triumph. And love, Ciaran. Always the power of love. Ciaran of the Mist's love for his people, the love that drew him to build this place to shelter them. The love of freedom that began countless rebellions. The love of the mist for the sea. Now, it holds something even more precious to me. This is where I found you. I feel . . . want . . . I need . . ." her gaze flickered away for a moment, and in the moonshine he could see a blush stain her cheeks.

"What, Fallon?" Ciaran's voice roughened with need. "What do you need?"

"You. Your arms around me. Your heat against my skin. Your mouth and your hands." Her gaze found his, and his heart wrenched at the hint of uncertainty that made her voice tremble. "I was so afraid tonight that I would lose you forever. Make love to me, Ciaran. Here, in this place where I've dreamed forever."

His whole body hardened with savage need, the passion he'd battled to keep in check since their wedding night jolting through him in jagged streaks like lightning.

Blast, he'd sworn he wouldn't touch her again. He still didn't know who the blazes he was. His past hovered out there somewhere in the mist—something that could be dark and ugly, a past he might find on Tuesday when he descended into the labyrinth alone.

But her words reverberated through him, soft, tremulous with a trust that lanced his heart. *I was so afraid I would lose you forever.* Mary Fallon, woman of magic and moonlight, courage and dreams. She had been alone for so long. And she wanted him. His lady of the mist. She was everything brave and beautiful, nurtured here, in the shelter of these stones. And tonight, he felt it, too. The power of this place. Tonight the spirits of Caislean ag Dahmsa Ceo would hold the shadows at bay for this woman, the daughter of the magic here.

Ciaran peered down into Fallon's eyes, then dismounted, tying the horse to a low-hanging branch. Then he swept her up into his arms. "Where?" he murmured into the fall of her hair. "Where should I take you?"

"The tower. That way." She waved her hand. He moved toward the ancient stairs that ascended the curve of wall. Astonishment, awe rippled through him.

Enchantment? The wind sang of it. Magic? The air was scented with its perfume. Love? The pulse of it echoed through his very soul.

He was certain that the stones of the castle must still be jagged, the walls half tumbled down. But as he cradled his love against him, he saw the place through Fallon's eyes, in all its former glory—bold towers thrusting skyward, thick walls defying enemies, the souterrains beneath newly carved, offering haven to the weak.

And he wished, as he bore Fallon skyward, that he was Ciaran of the Mist, bringing home the bride who had broken the cruel enchantment and won his hero's heart.

Skyward he carried her, up stone steps that seemed to soar to the darkened heavens. The arms of Caislean ag Dahmsa Ceo reached out to embrace them. At the crest of the stairs, the single tower room stood intact, its circular walls pitted but unbroken, the sky its only ceiling. It seemed right to be here, in Ciaran's arms. He carried her into the chamber where she had played as a child, dreamed as a woman.

Slowly, he lowered her to her feet. Her breath caught at the sight of him: the billows of the saffron shirt accenting his broad warrior's shoulders, the glow of the brooch holding his rippling mantle, the cabochons seeming to hoard ancient mysteries. He looked as if he had just strode out of another century, daring to breach the gates of time to find her.

He said nothing, but she could feel the heat of desire emanating from his every pore. A desire magnified by her own need for him.

Tangling his hand in the silky cascade of auburn at her nape, he tilted her head back on the delicate stem of her neck and drank of her lips with the tenderness of the first awe-touched man who had ever made love to a woman. Fallon melted, pulsed, her breasts afire where they brushed his chest, the place between her thighs aching with emptiness only Ciaran could fill.

Her fingers went to the brooch, working the heavy fastening free. The cloak started to slide from his shoulders. Ciaran broke their kiss, caught the woolen fabric, then knelt to make them a bed. And Fallon was certain she would be happy forever, with nothing more than this—an Irish sky above her, the music of the sea below, a crumpled mantle for a bed and Ciaran's kisses to feast upon.

Her heart lurched as he shifted, kneeling before her, like a knight from a beloved fairy tale. Scooping up one of her feet, he placed it on his upraised knee, then with deft fingers worked the ribbons that held her slipper in place. His touch whispered about her ankles, unbearably intimate, sensual. His dark head bent over the rose-colored satin enclosing her foot. After a moment, he slipped his fingertips beneath the slipper's opening and eased it from her foot. Then, his eyes burning, intense, he trailed his fingers upward, along the silken trail of her stockings, until he found the tender, secret velvet of her inner thigh.

The ribbon garter slipped free, and he rolled the stocking downward, pressed between his two hot palms, his thumbs skimming thigh and the sensitive skin behind her knee, down her calf, to the dainty bones of her ankle, then off her foot. She could scarcely bear the sensations racing through her, but he wasn't finished with his tender torture. He cupped her foot in his two hands, brought it to his lips. Then he began again, conquering the intimate curves of her leg, but his mouth now seemed hungry for the taste of her. He raised the hem of her skirt, and pressed hot kisses on the inside of her knee, the soft white of her thigh. "Beautiful," he murmured. "So . . . beautiful."

Her own hands tugged at his shirt, longing to unveil his magnificent body. But he stopped her, his voice low, pleading. "Not yet, *mo chroi*. Not yet. Let me."

He rose again, so tall, so proud, his big hands impossibly deft as he stripped away her clothes layer by layer, treasuring each part he unveiled, soothing her nakedness with his mouth and his hands.

There was something ragingly intimate, excruciatingly sensual as he peeled away her chemise, letting the last of her garments drift to the floor. He was still fully garbed, yet she stood before him, naked except for the moon-light. But she needed nothing to warm her except the wild heat in his warrior eyes.

He stared at her, as if to burn her image into his memory for eternity. Her nipples pearled, her knees trembled, a heavy, thick pulse beat in the wind-stirred auburn down nestled between her thighs.

His hands skimmed the line of her collarbone, dipped into the hollow at the base of her throat, then he filled his palms with the lush globes of her breasts.

"I've dreamed of you touching me there," she confessed. "Your mouth suckling, as if . . . as if you could draw life from me somehow."

"Don't you realize I have? Drawn everything I am from you, my lady? Everything good and beautiful, until there are times—" He broke off the words, creases forming between his brows.

"Until what, Ciaran?"

"Until I never want to know any life but this—the one I found in your arms."

"Is that so terrible?"

"It might be. For you. What if—damn, who knows what kind of man I used to be? My past—"

"Don't you see? It doesn't matter who you used to be. What matters is who you are now. My husband. The man I . . ." she hesitated. "The man who convinced me that it might be possible—that we might be able to have a future together." Her voice dropped low. "That is, if you want one."

"Do you think I haven't thought of it? Dreamed of it? I can't stop. I imagine your belly swelling with my babe. Children with your fiery hair, your courage, your generosity of spirit. But even if I dared, I'd come to you with nothing, Fallon. No money to provide for you. No home to shelter you. No name, and no memory."

"But I had all those things—wealth and a grand house, a name I could trace back generations, and so many memories, I only wished I could forget some of them. But none of that mattered. What I came to you with was far sadder than a lost memory, Ciaran. I came with an empty heart."

"Empty? Your heart is brimming full with courage, with generosity, with the love of this place and these people."

"But that was safe, that love. Different. I didn't have to trust just one person, believe in just one person. The castle would always stand here. And the people—there were so many villagers, they would never all leave me. You awakened me, so I could care for something, someone real, instead of pretending my life away. I know that you never intended to stay, but isn't it possible that instead of being lost, Ciaran, you were meant to be found? Maybe . . . maybe you could be happy here."

His face contorted in anguished longing. "Fallon, there is nothing I want more than a future with you. But—"

"Hush!" She laid her fingers across his lips, stopping him. "You're the one who gave *me* life, brought me out into the world again after years of living in a land of dreams."

"It was a beautiful world, Mary Fallon."

"But a lonely one. I'd not go back to it again. Would you? Return to that other life? The man you were before?"

"I don't know who I was before, but one thing I can tell you." He traced her cheek with his fingertips, gazing at her as if she were something holy. "If I were Ciaran of the Mist, with all eternity before me, I would trade immortality in a heartbeat for just one lifetime to love you."

His face was so raw, so vulnerable, so tender. If he had stood before the fairy king, striking this bargain before him, she couldn't have felt his sacrifice or his passion more keenly.

"Ciaran," she whispered. "Ciaran, I love you." Something ignited in his eyes, as if he'd waited twenty lifetimes to hear those words. The emotions in his face were so strong she nearly stumbled back beneath the force of them. Then he was stripping away the billows of his shirt, casting it away. Naked, he gathered her against him, the hot lance of his arousal pillowed against the soft swell of her belly, his mouth devouring hers, his hands skimming across her hip, her back, her breast, her buttocks as though he wanted to touch her everywhere at once.

And she gloried in it—the silky hair spanning his chest rasping against her nipples, the sinewy bands of his arms, the hot satin of his skin, so different from her own. *This* was the honeyed elixir Deirdre had cast aside a kingdom to taste. *This* was the primal magic that had made Naosi, the warrior, betray his king. A power beyond reason, an intoxication of the spirit, a fierce pull of destiny, of fate that no laws of man or of heaven could deny.

Gathering her up, he laid her on the nest of mantle he'd made for her. "Do you know how much I wanted you while you danced? It all but drove me mad—the music pounding, your body swaying, swirling, taunting me."

"I wanted to drive you mad—make you crave my touch the way I craved yours. I was dancing for you, Ciaran. Just for you."

With a low growl of need, he trailed kisses down her throat, found the burning point of her nipple and took it in his mouth, suckling, nipping, soothing the tiny sting with the sweep of his tongue. His fingers charted a path downward, along the faint ridges of her ribs, into the tiny dimple of her navel, then down, into the silken lace of auburn curls. She parted her thighs, and the callused tips of his fingers found silken petals. When he dipped into her core, she arched, cried out.

"Ah, Fallon . . . so hot, so damp . . . needing me . . ." he groaned.

She tugged at his bare shoulders, trying to squirm under his body, craving the hard contours of muscle and bone and sinew melding with her own yielding softness. "Please, Ciaran," she begged. "Fill me . . . I need you to fill me . . ."

But he resisted her—hateful man. His voice was low and rough and ragged. "Patience . . . Don't want it to be over . . . so soon. Your Ciaran of the Mist had . . . eternity. Never thought to envy him . . . until now. Fallon. Ah, Fallon. Want this . . . to last forever."

Then he was kissing her—the vulnerable underside of her breast, the sensitive skin of her belly, and then lower. Moist warmth stirred her secret curls. A tiny cry of surprise breached her lips as he pressed a hot kiss there, in the place that was nearly wild with wanting him.

Pleasure broke over her body in crashing waves that tossed her higher, ever higher, until she felt as if she would shatter. Until she wanted to shatter—craved it, as Ciaran worked his spell upon her with his dark, forbidden kiss. She tossed her head, her hands clutching at the midnight silk of his hair, but just as the crest nearly carried her away, he rose over her, his shaft plunging deep. A low scream tore from Fallon as he buried himself inside her, filling her with thrusts that seemed to pound at the very gates of her heart. Again and again, he came into her body, murmuring hot words of love, of passion, of need against her throat.

She could feel it building between them—quicksilver, a storm to sweep them both away. But it was his words that shattered her, hurtled her into a world beyond mist, beyond magic, beyond believing.

"Fallon, I love you." He plunged deep, spilling his seed into her body, and his heart into her hands.

He collapsed atop her, breath rasping, heart thundering, then rolled to one side, carrying her with him. Tenderly, he drew the folds of the mantle about her.

So precious, the gift she'd given him—not only her passion, the bounty of her lovely body, but far more than that. Something that glittered in unbearable beauty just beyond his grasp. A future to replace a past he no longer cared about. A love powerful enough to banish any ghosts. A chance to begin again.

He stroked her hair, his gaze on the sky. Thunderclouds scudded toward them from the sea. He would make one last effort to discover who he was—journey into the labyrinth that wound its way beneath this enchanted castle. He'd find out whether he was the smuggler Silver Hand. And if he was, he'd put an end to it, once and for all.

After Tuesday, he would stop searching for his past. Instead, he would look to the future. A future with Fallon, a future of believing in the happily-ever-afters she'd dreamed of. He'd grasp the gift the fates had given him—a chance to be born anew in the love that graced his lady's eyes.

CHAPTER

17

⟨⟨⟨⟩⟩⟩

Ciaran watched the candlelight trickle in shimmering rivulets down Fallon's hair to pool on the velvety bank of her collarbone. Her brow was creased with concentration, her gaze earnest as she stitched at the shirt in her hands. It was for him, Ciaran knew, his heart squeezing.

There was no logical reason why she needed to prick her fingers until they bled, laboring over the fine piece of linen.

A small army of seamstresses had been employed to make him a decent wardrobe at Hugh's behest. And Fallon was as ill suited to the task of stitching as a woman could be. He couldn't help but smile. He'd never know how she'd learned to sew in the first place, restless as she was. But he'd never forget the shy gleam in her eyes when she'd confided to him that she wanted to make him something with her own hands, a gift of love from a wife to a husband.

Precious. So infinitely precious was every moment he'd spent with her these past few days.

Nights filled with lovemaking so fierce and tender and drenched in wonder, as if both he and Fallon had been trying to make up for too many years alone.

Days when his hungry gaze couldn't get enough of watching her, eagerly drinking in every nuance of emotion that crossed her animated face, the lilt of her voice as she read to him from her treasured books of legends. The sparkle of her humor as she gave him riding lessons that ended most often in both of them tumbling to the heather, where they schooled each other in lessons of another, more primal kind—a kind that ended in the beauty of his name on her lips when she cried out in fulfillment.

His throat tightened. From the moment he'd staggered into awareness in the shadow of Caislean ag Dahmsa Ceo, time had slipped through his fingers at an alarming pace, no matter how desperately he'd tried to hold it. And since the night he'd found the smuggler's note, it had fluttered, then flown away like spring's first butterfly caught in a child's hands.

The joy of loving Fallon, the glittering possibility that he might be able to love her for all time, filled his every waking moment, and he wasn't certain if that fierce pleasure was tainted or if it was made even more intoxicating by the knowledge that when Tuesday came, he risked losing her forever.

Fallon—so brave yet so fragile in the deep reaches of her secret soul. Fallon, who had gifted him with her generosity, illuminated his mind with her treasured imaginings, and trusted him with her grief and loneliness. A woman so confident in his honor, she didn't care that he didn't even remember his name. Such courage, such faith deserved a happy ending, didn't it? And yet, so many of the tales of great love she'd spun out for him—Deirdre and Naosi, Diarmad and Grainne, Tristan and Isolde—had ended in heartbreak. What if their own love was swallowed up by tragedy as well?

No. He shoved the thought away, along with the shadowy sense of foreboding that had tormented him since he left the smuggler's cave. He would do everything in his power to make certain Fallon would have joy instead of grief, a lifetime of love, his kisses, warm with life instead of cold with death.

Time and time again, he'd lain beside her, sated with

lovemaking, cradling her so close it was a wonder she could breathe. He'd watched her sprawl over him like a drowsy kitten, tousled, naked and warm, and he'd told himself he was a fool. Why even make the trip to the labyrinth and Silver Hand's lair? Why tempt fate to snatch everything away? She didn't care who he'd been in that life before.

But he did.

He'd searched through every fragment of memory, sifted through the images that had come back to him, plumbed for emotions—love, hate, fear and valor, things he must have felt. There had been pathetically little to grasp: being wrenched from his mother's arms by a father he loathed, grief when he'd returned to find her dead.

Honor. Respect. And loneliness. No love to pull him back. He wondered who he had been. He felt curiosity, but no driving need to plunge backward anymore. Yet he was warrior enough to know the harsh realities of life. You didn't have to reach back into your past to have it overtake you. Sometimes your past could surprise you, catch you from behind when you least expected it and drag you under a current of danger, of old hates and betrayals, greedy to snatch up anyone you dared to love as well.

A shiver of unease trickled down his spine, the need to protect this woman he loved savage inside him. No, Ciaran resolved. He couldn't risk that Fallon might be endangered any further than she already had been because of her love for him. Nor could he bear that Hugh Delaney might be at risk for offering a stranger safe haven, endangering everything he owned for no other reason than generosity and a code of hospitality that stretched back a thousand years.

If Ciaran *was* Silver Hand, he needed to know the truth before he plunged deeper into a future with his lady love. And if he was not Silver Hand, he needed to warn the smuggler that Redmayne was determined to see him hang. His jaw clenched at the memory of Tom Dunne's words: the books on the doorstep to fill the greedy minds of his children, the shoes left for those in need. Silver Hand, a guardian angel, hunted now by the most ruthless of men. There must be some way to keep him alive.

He glanced at the window, the sky beyond tinted with the first lavender ribbons of twilight. He needed to slip away from Fallon without her suspecting what he was up to. But how? They'd lived for each other, these past, precious days. He'd barely been able to endure letting her out of his sight.

Now how was he supposed to explain the fact that he didn't want her anywhere near him for the next few hours? After a moment, he cleared his throat, but that didn't change the bitter taste he had in his mouth because he was about to lie. "Fallon, love, I thought I'd ride out for a bit, see if I can find Hugh. He said he was going to Tom Dunne's to talk about adding another room onto their cottage."

She let the stitching fall to her lap. Her eyes brightened. "I'll ride with you. If you'll wait just a moment—"

"No!" His voice sounded brusque even to his own ears. He saw her eyes widen in surprise, a hint of hurt about her lips. "Fallon, forgive me, it's just . . ." He paced to the window, groping for some logical reason to explain his snappishness. "It's time I took my place here, on Misthaven. Found some sort of . . . work to occupy myself. I've been lounging around on your brother's charity far too long."

Her laugh was a little ragged about the edges. "You've only been here a few weeks," she said, setting her sewing aside. "Give yourself time to settle in. Hugh doesn't mind."

"Perhaps not, but *I* do. I need something useful to do. To feel as if I'm giving something back in return for food and shelter, the new clothes, everything you and Hugh have given me. I need to take care of you myself, provide for you as a man should. Is that so hard to understand?"

"No. But that still doesn't explain why you don't want me to ride with you," Fallon said softly. Trust his lady of the mist to cut straight through his babble to the main point. For such a dream-spun maiden, she could be practical at the most inconvenient times. One delicate hand drifted down to rest on his arm.

Ciaran pulled away, driving his fingers back through his mane of hair, hating himself for this ruse. Yet it was based on truth, wasn't it? Could Fallon even guess what it cost him not to be able to give her a home, provide her with the things she needed, books filled with adventures for her to dream upon, sweets to tempt her with as he eased her down onto a bed he had provided for her, a cradle where she could sing Gaelic lullabies to the babes given life from their love.

Yet, to use that truth, that need in order to manipulate her sickened him.

"This is something Hugh and I need to work out between us ourselves, Fallon." He tried to gentle his voice, failed. "It would shame me to have you hovering over me as if I were a helpless boy."

The hurt in her eyes deepened, and Ciaran hated himself for putting it there.

"Fallon, Fallon, Fallon," he breathed, drawing her into his arms. "Don't you know I'd rather surrender my last drop of blood than hurt you? But I have to make my place in your world if I am ever to be able to stay. I have to make it alone."

He could feel her reluctance, the stiffness in her spine, a subtle resistance, but after a moment she shrugged. "Men. You'll probably get lost if you go to search for Hugh, and—"

"If I do, it's my own problem." His mouth hardened, doubtless Fallon thought from stubborn male pride. "I won't have my wife trailing after me. Blast it, I've felt so inept ever since you found me, I need to do this alone."

He wished she would yank herself away from him, storm off in a temper. He wished she would tell him he was an ungrateful wretch and could go to the devil. It might have made him feel a little better to get the dressing-down he deserved, and his lady wife could tear anyone down to their knees when she had a mind to.

But she dealt him a punishment infinitely worse.

Trusting, vulnerable, more than a little hurt, she gazed up at him, and he loathed himself for lying to her. "I–I suppose I have been demanding all of your time, and there's nothing more annoying than a clinging wife. It's just that, it's so wonderful having someone to talk to, someone to smile at, someone to touch, that I suppose I got greedy."

"Fallon—" Ciaran protested, unable to bear the raw wound she'd shown him, her sudden aura of uncertainty. For a moment, just a moment, he considered telling her the truth. Only the fact that she'd follow him into danger stopped him. He traced the sweep of rose darkening her cheekbones with shyness, maybe even a little touch of shame. And he wished he could scoop her up into his arms, carry her to their bedchamber and love every shard of doubt away with his hands and his mouth.

"Fallon," he breathed, his voice ragged. "You're more than I could ever deserve in a wife. Please, just try to understand."

She brushed a lock of hair back from his brow, the slightest touch of her fingers infinitely sweet. "All right. I'll stay home and stitch like a good wife." She made a wry face. "I have to pick apart this last seam anyway. I stitched the armhole closed."

She surprised a laugh from him, one filled with love, with pain, with the sudden fear of losing her. "You don't have to do anything to be my wife except . . . love me." He cupped her cheeks in his palms, and tasted her lips— their flavor so familiar, yet always so wondrously new.

When he drew away, she gave him a tremulous smile that struck through to his heart. "Strange," she said, "who would have believed that after only two weeks, I would have forgotten."

"Forgotten what, treasure?"

She touched his lips, her eyes full of emotion, of honesty. "You've made me forget how to be alone."

Could any words have cut him more deeply? Ciaran drew away, strode from Misthaven House, hating himself for the lies he'd told, the hurt he'd caused, the wounds he'd unwittingly opened. And the trust he was about to betray. As he spurred his horse into the deepening twilight, he vowed that once this night was over, he'd make it up to Fallon. He would come to their bed, take her into his arms, and spend the rest of forever loving her.

But tonight—tonight belonged to the shadows, the subtle sense of danger. Tonight he would confront the smuggler Silver Hand. He only hoped he didn't discover that the dread lord of smugglers was himself.

Violet shadows spread in thick pools about the underbrush, the first faint glimmer of stars barely visible in the evening's veil as he dismounted outside the castle and found the hidden entryway. Torch in hand, from Fallon's store of supplies, he made his way into the souterrains. Yet the winding passages seemed far different without his lady leading the way, like a fairy maid guiding some ancient hero away from an enchantress's cave. The objects were still where he remembered them, treasures of other lives in other ages. But this time, his footsteps seemed to echo through the tunnels as he drew closer to Silver Hand's hidden lair.

Twice he nearly fell into traps set centuries ago, and once he barely avoided stepping on something alive as it scurried past. But he scarcely noticed. He could hear something, down in the bowels of the place. Low, tension-filled voices, the scrape of boots, the thunk of what must be the boxes full of goods he and Fallon had found there days ago.

Ciaran swallowed hard. How did one announce oneself to a band of smugglers without them doing something rash like blowing one's head off with a pistol ball? He might have figured out some sort of smuggler etiquette in time, but something slammed down on the back of his head.

Pain exploded through his skull, the torch flying from his hand in a rain of sparks. He plunged face-down on the ground, a black tide of unconsciousness trying to pull him under as a cacophony of sounds rang in his ears—angry shouts, the hastening of footsteps.

"Should'a jest killed 'im—saved the trouble o' havin'

t' throw 'im int' the sea t' drown," a voice snarled. "Cursed spies pokin' everywhere!"

Another voice, younger, objected. "An' have Silver Hand take me own head? Ye know how he feels 'bout the killin'.'"

"What 'e don't know won't hurt 'im, I say. Somebody has t' see 'e doesn't hang! Too soft fer his own good, is Silver Hand. Roll th' blighter over an' see who 'e is." Rough hands closed on Ciaran's shoulders, and with a brutal yank, he was on his back, staring up into faces garishly lit by his own torch.

"You!" The younger of the two gasped. "Holy mother o' God, Moran, ye fool! 'Tis ye who'll be hangin' now, an' Silver Hand'll be tyin' the noose!"

"How was I t' know—" The burlier of the two protested in alarm.

"You . . . know who I am?" Ciaran choked out, a sick twisting in his stomach. His worst fears were realized: he was somehow linked to this place, these smugglers, a criminal to be hunted.

"O'–o' course. D'ye take me fer a fool? I'm passin' sorry this happened, sir. 'Tis calamity, this is. Pure disaster."

What was a disaster? Ciaran wondered through the thundering haze of pain that used to be his head. Cracking the smuggler king over the head with the butt of a pistol? Why the devil couldn't he remember he belonged here?

He struggled to sit up, and the younger of the two was quick to help him, brushing the dirt off his clothes with the eager desperation of a rambunctious boy who'd just overset the parish priest in his mother's dustheap.

"It's true, then." Ciaran's shoulders sagged, and he stared at the ground, fingers pressed to his nape, warm with his own blood. "I am . . . Silver Hand."

The sudden crunch of a boot sounded behind him, and a low voice, stunningly familiar, reverberated through the cave. "No. I am."

Ciaran tried to wheel toward the sound, but the world still heaved and swayed. For a heartbeat, he didn't believe his eyes. But his vision cleared, the image still remained, standing tall, with world-weary eyes the color of Fallon's.

"Hugh," Ciaran breathed in disbelief.

Hugh Delaney moved farther into the light. He was garbed all in black, face smudged with soot. Twin pistols were shoved into the waistband of his breeches, and a sword hung from his side. How many men had felt the bite of that blade, Ciaran wondered. But even here, in his lair, Hugh looked distinctly uncomfortable in the guise of Silver Hand.

"It's all right, Martin, Moran," Hugh said in a tired voice. "Fetch my brother-in-law a cold cloth for his head."

The two men hesitated for a moment, reluctant, and Ciaran could see by the hero worship in their eyes that they would plunge headfirst into a school of sharks before they'd betray their leader. Loyalty. A fierce protectiveness. Yet, also a blind faith that made Ciaran's throat tighten. The look of men who would follow their leader through a wall of fire, and gladly. Memory flickered. Men had peered up at Ciaran that way once—as if he could work miracles, defeat dragons. The responsibility had awed him. Terrified him.

Ciaran contained himself until the pair of smugglers disappeared deeper into the cave, then burst out. "What the blazes are you doing here, Hugh? A smuggler? Blast, I still can scarce believe it."

"I know it's difficult. Stolid, boring, plodding Hugh Delaney is Silver Hand." Hugh gave a laugh, half bitter, half amazed. "I can scarce believe it myself. The question is, how did you find me here? Did you follow me?"

"Fallon brought me through the labyrinth the day after we were married. This is where she found me, and we both thought that I might be Silver Hand."

"Of course Fallon brought you." Hugh shook his head in affection and irritation. "Blast that girl, she's made it pure hell from the beginning trying to keep my identity a secret. She can be damned tenacious."

Realization dawned. Ciaran straightened, staring at his brother-in-law as if for the first time. "You knew from the first that I wasn't the smuggler. That is why you allowed me into your home."

"You'd make a far better lord of the smugglers than I do, that's certain. It's a position that calls for a sense of the dashing, the daring I could never hope to achieve. But I could hardly let Redmayne hang you in my place for the sake of appearances."

"Why risk hanging in the first place? You have to know what kind of danger you've put yourself in. Redmayne is hunting you. He'd sell his soul to see you on a hangman's gibbet."

"Doubtless he'll succeed eventually. Or someone else will. Until then, I do what I have to do."

"Do what you have to do? That makes no sense! The master of an estate like Misthaven turned smuggler. Why?"

"I'm certain Fallon hasn't told you about our father—"

"She said he deserted you after your mother died."

Hugh's eyes widened in surprise. "She's never spoken of that to anyone I know of. Especially not me. She's pretended none of it mattered—Mother's death, Father's desertion. I always worried about her, keeping all that hurt locked up so tight inside her heart. Thank God she trusted somebody enough to give them the key. I–I was never very good at comforting her."

"You're a fine brother. A good man."

"No. We were always different, Fallon and I. She was flame, hurling herself into life headlong. While I . . . I'm cautious, stoic, considering every step I take a dozen times before I dare make a move."

"That is called wisdom. It's the only reason your tenants have survived."

"It cost me the love of my sister—something I wanted more than you'll ever know. Grief can do terrible things to people, Ciaran. I was so raw and Fallon was so angry. I suppose I thought time would heal the breach between us, once the pain softened. I was wrong. By the time I realized it, it was too late."

"I don't believe that. It can't be too late."

"I failed her. Nothing can change that. Worst of all, I couldn't make her understand. Fallon hated our father, never understood it was love of our mother that drove him away. He couldn't bear to see her suffer, and once she died, he tried to forget Misthaven existed, the land she'd loved so much. Tried to forget about me, and about Fallon who was so much like her. He ran, that's true. But Fallon doesn't understand the real tragedy of our father. He wasn't running away from us, he was running away from himself—his own weakness, grief and pain."

"I'm sorry," Ciaran said, knowing the words were futile. Wishing he could reach out, touch this man he'd respected from the first, a man he was beginning to love like a brother.

"By the time I inherited, the estate was on the brink of ruin. England had locked up Ireland's trade so tightly there might as well have been iron bars surrounding us. Most of the gentry had lands in both Ireland and England. They bled the Irish lands white, and would've been happy enough to see the whole island starve if it meant English trade was protected."

"But what about the people, the crofters who live here. How are they supposed to survive?"

"The same way they always have—clinging to life as tenaciously as the heather on the cliffs. They've struggled to keep body and soul together for centuries. This is just one more skirmish in a battle without end. Their resilience, their courage astonishes me, humbles me."

Ciaran remembered his own visceral reaction to the people he'd met—Maeve McGinty with her ageless eyes in a face wrinkled and tart as dried apple, Tom Dunne and his irrepressible daughter, Siobhan Moynihan, a lady of sorrow and courage, tending her flock of babes. And the others, so many others who had brought him bridal gifts and clapped as he and Fallon had danced in the moonlight.

Hugh paced to where the boats stood, upright now, their bottoms lapped by the water. "I fear I'm a most unnatural landlord. You see, I can't stand by and watch my people go without—without shoes, clothes, food, books for their little ones, decent cottages for shelter. I had to do something."

"So you put your own neck in the English noose. Risked your life so children could be warm in winter, have shoes on their feet, food in their bellies."

"Don't make it sound like some epic act of heroism. I just didn't know what else to do. Things grew so bad, I got desperate. I promised myself I'd do it just one time—smuggle a shipload of wool to France and sell it, get what was necessary and bring it back. I was scared as hell. If the ship hadn't been buffeted by the devil of a storm from the north, I might have turned back a dozen times."

"You wouldn't have turned back if the whole English fleet lay in the channel," Ciaran said with quiet certainty. "As for your courage—the only man who isn't afraid is the man who has nothing to lose."

"Stands t' lose ever'thing 'e owns if the Sassenachs ever catch 'im," Moran grumbled under his breath as he and Martin melted out of the shadows, a rag in hand. "They'll take 'is land, 'is house, an' the fates o' every soul on Misthaven."

"That's enough," Hugh snapped, obviously uncomfortable with his cohorts' adoration. "The two of you take yourselves off and get busy. We've got all that cargo to disperse."

"Aye, sir." Moran cuffed young Martin in the shoulder, and they returned through the tunnel. Hugh took Ciaran's arm, led him around a tight curve into the chamber he and Fallon had found days ago. Torchlight bled down the walls. The boats, righted and in the water, were packed so full they looked ready to capsize.

Hugh's men had already started rummaging through several of the boxes, Moran keeping up his constant grousing. "Hurry up, ye young fool, or by the time we get this box t' Tom Dunne, those boys o' his'll already have outgrown the fixin's Silver Hand's brought 'em."

"Ciaran—" Hugh said after a moment. "Fallon must never know about this."

"Why? Why not tell her? She's so hungry to love and

to be loved. Not only by a husband, but by a brother. She loves these people as much as you do. If she knew the truth she might—" He stopped, apalled at what he'd almost betrayed, the hurt he'd nearly dealt the good man standing before him. But Hugh finished his sentence with brutal honesty.

"She might feel something for me besides contempt?"

Ciaran could sense exactly how deeply Fallon's scorn had injured this man, how much suffering her rejection of him had caused. But there was no blame, only sorrow and understanding. "Hugh, give her a chance to know you. Who you really are—"

"No. That's impossible."

"But why? Why can't you—"

Hugh held up one hand. "Her contempt is a small price to pay for her safety. Think, Ciaran. Headstrong, brave as she is, defiant and honest—what would happen if she ever flew into a temper, accidentally let slip that she knew something. The fact that she's a woman wouldn't protect her. The authorities would wrench a confession from her any way they could, and then, life as a virtual slave in a penal colony would be the best fate she could hope for. What would you give to keep Mary Fallon safe?"

"The last drop of blood in my body. Anything. No matter what the price. I thought . . . Fallon and I thought I might be Silver Hand. I'm not. I may never know who I really am. But I know this. What you're doing here is a brave thing. A just and noble thing." Ciaran let the bloody rag fall from his hand. "Let me help you with your work here."

Hugh ran his fingers back through his hair, his jaw hardening. Yet Ciaran could see the longing in his features, too. He sensed how much Hugh wanted someone to share this with—the fear, the crushing responsibility. Like his sister, Hugh Delaney was a man too often alone. But he shook his head in denial.

"No. You've already helped me in a way far more important. When I took the identity of Silver Hand, my greatest fear was that I might die and leave Fallon alone, with no one to care for her. I don't have to be afraid of that any longer. I'll thank God forever that he sent you to guard my sister, to love her." Hugh reached out, clasped Ciaran's hand.

Ciaran's chest ached with affection and admiration for this man—a hero, in a way he never could be. If only Fallon could know. How proud she would be of her brother.

"I pledge to you that I'll do all in my power to keep her safe. And this land, these people, they'll be my people, too." Ciaran began, then froze at a blood-freezing sound—a shriek of terror from somewhere back in the labyrinth, then the sound of flesh and bone slamming into rock far below, the scream cut off as if someone had slit the sufferer's throat.

"Someone's in the tunnel—" Hugh's face paled, his mouth hardened, as voices erupted—English voices, shaken, angry, one clipped, military voice above them all.

Redmayne.

"Forward, you fools, before they escape!"

Ciaran turned to Hugh, stricken. "They must have followed me." Close, they were so damned close, he realized with cold certainty.

"Sir, hurry, t' the boats! We have t' flee—" Martin choked out, alarmed. But there wasn't room for all of them in the small vessels packed with smuggled goods. Even if there were, they'd never have time to launch the boats and get away. The little vessels were too heavy, too cumbersome.

"A passageway—there's another passageway—" Martin piped up. But even that wouldn't save them.

There was no time. Ciaran knew it instinctively. Redmayne would only close the gap between them, destroy everything—these brave men, the land that Fallon loved, her brother. The fates of all the people in Misthaven were in the hands of Hugh Delaney. If he died . . .

"Go, damn it," Ciaran snapped. "I'll stay behind and delay them. It's your only hope."

"They'll kill you!" Hugh snarled. "I won't leave—"

Ciaran swore, surrendering to the inevitable. He drew

back his fist and slammed it into Hugh's jaw. His brother-in-law's eyes widened in surprise, then rolled back as Silver Hand collapsed, unconscious, his head cracking against the stone floor as his men clustered around him.

"Get him the devil out of here," Ciaran ordered. "Or do you all want to hang?"

Moran hoisted his master up, slung him across burly shoulders, the thunder of English boots drawing perilously near. "Sir, I . . ."

"Go!" He watched them vanish down another tunnel, Martin easing a stone before the opening. Ciaran could only pray that by the time the English found it, they'd be long gone.

Time. He had to find a way to give them the precious time to escape.

He closed his eyes for a heartbeat, the shouts drawing nearer, the footsteps closing in on the cave. In that frozen instant faces danced behind Ciaran's closed lids—memories, infinitely sweet, new memories, precious ones. Fallon dancing in the moonlight, Tom Dunne with little Caitlin on his shoulders, Maeve placing the flower crown on Fallon's sunset curls, Siobhan Moynihan offering the bit of sugar rock, telling Fallon that love, that life could be sweet, despite the quiet suffering in the Irishwoman's eyes. And Hugh, who had risked everything with quiet heroism.

All these people belonged to Ciaran in a way that brought out all that was best in his soul. He had found himself again in their eyes. Fierce love, crushing loss burned in his chest.

There was only one way to save everything, everyone Fallon loved. She had tried to summon a hero back from the mist, needed a champion to fight for her. He prayed he had the courage to be that man for her now.

Ciaran turned to face the entryway, his shoulders squared, his jaw hard as Redmayne and his soldiers poured into the stone chamber. He knew exactly what he had to do.

"MacDonough." The slightest hint of triumph curled

Redmayne's lips. "I knew if I waited patiently enough, watched carefully enough, someone would lead me to the smuggler's lair."

Ciaran let go of any dream of forever with Fallon and stared into the face of his nemesis. "My lair, Redmayne. *I* am Silver Hand."

CHAPTER

18

Waiting was driving Fallon mad. She glared out at the darkness, apprehensive about the strange restlessness that pulsed through her blood. Hugh and Ciaran had been gone for hours. Dinner had been readied, a valiant battle fought to keep things warm. But after two hours, even Misthaven's stalwart cook had been forced to surrender, carting the ruined feast back to the kitchen in high dudgeon.

Not that Hugh's absence from the table should have alarmed her. He frequently missed meals because of business affairs that stretched long into the night. But he'd always made certain the servants knew beforehand, and sent his apologies to the kitchen. Yet tonight, not so much as a word had been carried back by some crofter lad. The silence made Fallon skittish as bedamned.

Blast, there was no way to even know if Ciaran had found her brother. For all she knew, he might have taken a wrong turn and ridden off a cliff, she thought, struggling to make even the vaguest jest about the situation. But her attempt fell flat, her uneasiness cinching tighter and tighter within her.

Only the echo of Ciaran's words kept her from going out searching herself.

I'll not be shamed by having my wife trail after me.

How could she have been so insensitive, and not realized how difficult the situation must be for a man with Ciaran's pride and sense of honor? Not even to be able to provide for his own wife. No meaningful work to fling his heart into. No place to feel useful.

In penance, she'd tried to respect his wishes, damn the man. She'd spent the long hours making bargains with herself. They would be home by the time she finished stitching an inch of seam for every day she and Ciaran had been married. They would return when the shadow from the moon crossed the rose in the center of the Aubusson carpet. They would be home in ten minutes more.

But neither Hugh nor her husband would be conjured out of the night, no matter what she did.

When the clock struck one in the morning, she couldn't bear it another moment. Shoving her needlework aside, she grabbed her cloak and plunged into the night. When she reached the stable, Padraic, the new head groom, was in one of the stalls, poulticing a horse's leg.

"Mistress?" the gnomelike man stared at her in surprise. "Is there somethin' I might do for ye?"

"Saddle a horse and tell me exactly where my brother was going."

The little man's face shut tight as a miser's purse strings. "Miss, if I let ye ride out this late an' alone, yer brother'd turn me out without a farthing, an' I'd not blame 'im."

She glared at him. "It's nearly one in the morning. I'm afraid something is wrong."

"With the master? No. Ye know how 'e is. Allus ridin' about, turnin' his hand t' whatever needs doin'. More'n likely he and yer new bridegroom are sittin' watch over the birth o' Tom Dunne's calf, or helpin' thatch a roof what's leakin'. An' those ships o' his—tends 'em like a mama duck wi' a raft o' wee ones."

"My husband hasn't returned either, and he doesn't

know the countryside at all. Now, saddle my horse, or I'll—"

The sudden sound of horse's hooves made her stop, and she pressed her hand to her heart in relief. "They're back."

"Aye, miss. Told ye there was no use in worryin'—" Padraic began, but suddenly, he stilled. "'Tis a wagon I'm hearin'. An' it's comin' fast. Master Hugh an' yer husband were on horseback."

Alarm tightened in Fallon, and she turned, ran out into the torch-lit stableyard. What she saw made her knees tremble. Young Martin Feeney, white-faced, driving the horses like a madman, while bulky Phelan Moran sat in the back of the cart, pistols drawn, his gaze searching the road behind them.

"What is it? What's wrong?" she cried.

Martin yanked on the reins so clumsily the horse shied, nearly oversetting the wagon. "'Tis Master Hugh. He's hurt."

Fallon's stomach plunged. "Hugh!" She scrabbled up into the back of the wagon, saw her brother there, face ashen, a wicked, purpling bruise on his jaw.

"Padraic, send someone for the doctor—"

"No. No. Can't . . ." Her brother grasped her arm. "F—Fallon. Oh, God, no." The sight of her seemed to stir him. He struggled to sit up. "Moran, why bring me here?"

"Where else would he bring you? Hugh, you're making no sense."

"Dangerous . . . too . . ."

"Nothin' else t' do but bring ye here," Moran snapped. "All Glenceo is crawlin' wi' soldiers, an' ye know damned well they'll end up here eventually. An' ye'd better be in yer nightshirt an' cap when they come."

"Soldiers? Redmayne? Did they do this to him?"

"Nay," Moran said, climbing out of the wagon and dragging Hugh into his arms as if he were no more than a boy. "'Twas yer bridegroom what done it. Wicked right cross t' the jaw, an' 'is lights blinked out like somebody snuffin' a candle."

MAGIC

Fallon tried to grasp the crotchety Irishman's words. "Ciaran did this? Why? Where is he?"

Hugh struggled against Moran's iron hold, agitated. "C–Ciaran. We have to . . . to help him. Won't let him . . ." Hugh's unsteady gaze snagged on Fallon's face, and his features contorted in anguish, fear and regret. "Sorry . . . so sorry . . . I tried not to . . . let him . . ."

Fallon could scarcely breathe. The night was closing in, her fears clawing inside her. "Hugh, where is Ciaran?"

"Get dressed. I'll take you t–to him. Promise . . . won't let him die."

"Die? God in heaven." A sob broke from her throat. "Tell me where he is!"

"Redmayne captured him. My fault . . . all my fault. Took him prisoner."

"But why?"

Martin climbed down, his beardless face young and frightened. "We heard on the way here, miss. Yer husband—he confessed t' bein' Silver Hand."

"Confessed? Silver Hand?" Fallon echoed, reeling. "But . . . but he said he was going out to help Hugh."

Hugh struggled from Moran's grasp, stood braced against the crude wagon, wobbling on his feet. A chill worked through Fallon as she looked into his face, so pale and grim. "He . . . did find me, Fallon. In the lair under the castle."

"I told him how dangerous it was! Told him not to—" She tried to claw through her confusion. "But y–you? But why would you be there?"

"I am Silver Hand," Hugh admitted, his tormented gaze finding hers.

She gripped the side of the cart so hard that splinters drove into her palm, but she barely felt the sting. "You? Silver Hand? I don't believe it!"

"The soldiers overran the cave, intending to capture me. Ciaran . . ." his voice broke. "Ciaran sacrificed himself in my place."

Fallon's stomach churned, horror reeling through her. Impossible. This was impossible. Some sort of mad nightmare. Hugh couldn't possibly be Silver Hand. And Ciaran—Ciaran couldn't be at the mercy of Lionel Redmayne.

But Hugh said he'd confessed—confessed to being the smuggler half the king's army was fighting to bring to the gallows. Her blood iced, hands trembled. Dear God, they would hang him.

"No," she cried, pressing her fist to her mouth. "No—"

"I won't let him hang for me, Fallon." Hugh grabbed her, held her with one shaking hand. "I swear it on my life. I'll go to Redmayne. Tell him the truth."

"Then you'll die in Ciaran's place?" Tears spilled down Fallon's face.

"It's my crime. I'll take whatever punishment the Crown sees fit to give me. I knew the risk. But I won't let an innocent man die for my sins. Get dressed. I'll have my valet help me. We'll go to Redmayne's."

"And what? Sign your death warrant? Hugh, I can't—"

"Fallon, since you were a tiny girl, I had my chance to . . . to love you. To give you what you needed. I wanted to, but . . . I just couldn't seem to do it. This man loves you. You love him. I won't let him die, leave you alone again."

"Oh, Hugh!" Her voice caught on a sob. She flung herself into his arms. Her brother held her as he never had before, and there, in his arms, she realized how much the child she had been had wanted this, needed this—to know her brother loved her. It wasn't fair that she'd just found him in time to lose him to the hangman. "There m—must be another way. Some way to save you both!"

"There isn't time, sweetheart. Come. We have to hurry. I'm afraid—" He stopped, glanced away.

The dread pounded more insistently inside Fallon. "Afraid of what?"

"Redmayne won't be satisfied with just Silver Hand. They'd rather have a gibbetful."

"What do you mean?"

"Just that . . . I don't know how far Redmayne might go to get the information he wants."

Fallon swallowed hard, gazing up into her brother's bruised, tortured face. Hugh might not know how far Redmayne might go, but Fallon did. It was there in the Englishman's burning eyes, the intensity that radiated from him in hot waves. It was in the curl of his lips, the biting wit of double entendres that made the simplest words an enigma.

Redmayne had hated Ciaran from the moment their paths crossed. His loathing had only grown sharper, more intense the night she'd danced at the castle.

Redmayne would go to any lengths to triumph.

Ciaran was at his mercy.

Fallon.

He drank in the coolness of her name, imagined her in his arms, her face blooming and luminous with laughter, as the soldier's fist slammed into his gut again and again in a hellish rhythm. How long had it been, Ciaran wondered, his bound hands knotting into fists—two hours? three?—since the beady-eyed sergeant had dragged him into this cell and made it his personal mission to beat the prisoner to a pulp?

Twice he'd been so near the blessed release of unconsciousness he'd felt its dark, cool fingers sliding over him. Twice one of the sergeant's men had dashed icy water into his face, forcing him back into a red haze of pain. Doubtless Redmayne had given orders that the prisoner shouldn't miss so much as a twinge. Not that he wanted blood on his own hands. He hadn't said a word on the journey from the castle to his headquarters, only paced into his own chamber, leaving Ciaran to his underlings.

"Names!" The sergeant roared so loud Ciaran's head threatened to split. "The captain wants names o' all the scum under yer command!"

Ciaran sucked a breath into lungs that were sacks of fire. "Go . . . to the . . . devil."

"Not as soon as ye will! Drummond, give me the cat-o'-nine-tails. We'll lash the answers from the bastard's hide."

The sergeant's hand closed around the wicked-looking weapon, its whipcords braided around heavy iron balls. Ciaran stiffened, waiting for the first blow.

Fallon. He had to think of Fallon. Fallon by moonlight, ribbons of fiery red gleaming in her hair. Ciaran heard the door to the room open. Someone else to give an expert opinion how to wield the lash?

"Sergeant, what is going on here?" Redmayne's voice.

The soldier drew back, his jaw jutting out, defensive. "The men haven't been able to find a single one of the others what escaped. But he knows their names. Where they're holed up. I'll beat it out of him, I swear."

"Without your commanding officer's permission?"

The sergeant's face turned brick red. "You want that information 's much 's I do! I just . . . I assumed . . ."

"A dangerous pastime. I fear you're experiencing delusions of grandeur, assuming that you can read my mind." Redmayne heaved a heavy sigh and shook his head. "Really, you need to use better judgment. How many times have I told you to *think*. Use that paltry mind of yours before you go charging in, flailing around like an imbecile. You could beat this man until doomsday, and all you'd get for your efforts is a damned tired arm. Flay the skin off his body a knife blade at a time and he wouldn't tell you the sky is blue. No. Mr. MacDonough is an *honorable* man. Sergeant, the rest of you, leave us. I wish to speak to the prisoner alone."

The soldiers fled the chamber as if their coattails were afire, the sergeant not even daring to cast Ciaran a mutinous glare.

"What . . . kind of game are you . . . playing, Redmayne?"

The Englishman had the gall to look injured. "You have a most suspicious nature, MacDonough. Haven't I always shown myself to be your friend? Not only did I release you the first time I held you here under suspicion, I single-handedly arranged your marriage to Miss Delaney. When my sergeant, here, would have beaten you, I took the lash from his hand."

"I like his methods better. At least they're honest. I know where he stands."

Redmayne's mouth curled in amusement. "But what is the sport in that? Surely, you didn't marry the beautiful Fallon because she was predictable."

"Leave my wife out of this," Ciaran snarled, fear thickening in his belly.

"I find that astonishingly difficult. She's the most extraordinary woman I've ever met." Redmayne drew something out of his pocket, a palm-sized figure of a queen. His fingers traced the carved features. Why was it Ciaran wanted to snatch the tiny woman from his hands? "One can never tell what she will do next. The only thing you can be sure of is that she will move with the daring of a master strategist, bold, quick, willing to risk all to gain victory. If only she could be taught to channel her passions, control them, she would be a most formidable opponent."

There was something in the Englishman's face that terrified Ciaran, as if Redmayne were attempting to peel back Fallon's spirit to see what lay inside—weaknesses, vulnerabilities, raw places where he could probe.

"Leave Fallon alone or I swear I'll—"

"I implore you, MacDonough, don't weary me rattling at your chains, hurling threats," Redmayne said, tucking the chess piece back in his pocket, something unreadable in his eyes. "I loathe such uncouth scenes. All I require from you at the moment are details regarding your villainous escapades. Something to include in my report to my superiors. The officer who preceded me was General Scargill's nephew, and he has taken a personal interest in seeing his murderer brought to justice."

Details? Ciaran gritted his teeth, realizing the flaw in his plan to play the role of Silver Hand. He didn't know the details of Hugh Delaney's missions. There was nothing he could give Redmayne. What if the Englishman wanted some sort of proof that he was the smuggler as he claimed? Would Redmayne be overly concerned about the guilt or innocence of the man he executed? Or would the allure of being the officer who delivered Silver Hand to the general be so appealing he wouldn't care?

"I've confessed to being Silver Hand. That's all you need to know. My deeds . . . speak for themselves."

"Why, oh why are you determined to make things difficult?" Redmayne asked with insufferable patience. "What would you say if I offered to make you a bargain? I am willing to let the rest of your ragged band go. Without you, your men will be rudderless, and if we make a proper example of you, they'll be far too afraid to ply a smuggler's trade."

"Why? Why would you do such a thing?"

Redmayne shrugged. "My explorations into the escapades of Silver Hand have revealed a good deal to me. A smuggler, not particularly brutal, rather eccentric, in fact, by all accounts. Hardly a big enough problem for the revenue cutters to trouble themselves with. In fact, he probably would have been left in peace forever if not for the unfortunate incident with General Scargill's nephew."

He flicked a bit of lint from his sleeve. "Others might wish to run about, sweeping up the dust that fell from your boots, but I see no purpose to it. You are prize enough. I am striving to be reasonable with you, MacDonough."

"I wouldn't trust you if you said your coat was red," Ciaran snapped.

"You would prefer I turn you over to the less civilized guardianship of my sergeant?"

"I don't give a damn what you do with me."

"That may be. But I would wager someone else cares. Your bride, perhaps?"

A timid knock at the door sounded.

"Enter," Redmayne said.

A young soldier poked his head in. "Begging your pardon, sir. But there are two people come to see the prisoner. Mr. Hugh Delaney and his sister."

Fear throbbed through Ciaran at the mere thought of Fallon anywhere near Redmayne. The look in the officer's eyes when he spoke of her filled Ciaran with dread. And Hugh—what was he doing here? Blast the man— there could only be one reason, Ciaran thought, considering the kind of man Delaney was. Ciaran was willing to give his life to keep them both out of this mess. Why couldn't they just stay away?

Redmayne was watching him intently. "MacDonough? Do you wish to have a word with them? In private, of course. Permit me to point out that I am, once again, a most obliging gentleman."

What he wanted was to shove Redmayne's teeth down his throat, carry Fallon away to the fairy castles she was always talking about, a fortress where he could keep her safe. Since that was impossible, he'd have to talk some sense into the two of them himself. But what kind of game was Redmayne playing? And why was he making such a magnanimous move? Out of the goodness of his heart? If Ciaran were wagering, he'd bet the captain didn't *have* a heart. Yet, what choice did he have but to play along?

"Yes. I want to see them." Ciaran glanced down at his battered chest, then hesitated, all but choking at the prospect of having to ask Redmayne for anything. Only the thought of Fallon seeing him this way and the pain it would cause her allowed him to speak. "My shirt," he ground out. "First let me put it back on."

Redmayne's gaze flicked to the bruises his soldiers had left, and Ciaran thought for just a moment that disgust glinted in his eyes, something akin to regret. Then it was gone. "I suppose the misplaced enthusiasm of my sergeant has left you a trifle unsightly for a lady's eyes. And those ropes." Redmayne gestured toward Ciaran's bound hands. "So unnecessary." He sliced through the bindings with a knife. "Escape is impossible, unless, of course, you could enlist the aid of one of the local heroes. I might suggest that legendary one whose castle I intended to destroy, since he's made an appearance recently."

"Is that so?" Ciaran gingerly eased his shirt over his bruised ribs, hoping the pain would disguise the sense of triumph he felt. But Redmayne was too canny to miss even the slightest twitch of his lips.

"You might tell your bride that my plans for the castle have been temporarily abandoned. It seems Phineas Butler left Ireland—and on a particularly stormy night.

But not before he'd withdrawn his permission for the demolition of the castle."

Ciaran's eyes narrowed. "You can't touch it without his permission."

"Not when it belongs to a proper English landlord, I'm afraid. But there are other castle ruins, other rings of standing stones. Even Ciaran of the Mist can't protect them all."

"Someone else will."

"I'm certain you're right. I've found these people most tenacious. Some might even call such determination in the face of such odds heroic."

Ciaran stared at the officer, astonished by his words.

Redmayne strode toward the door, then stopped and turned to cast an inscrutable frown at Ciaran. "Whoever terrorized that pathetic wretch Butler played a master stroke. It quite astonished me. And I am rarely surprised."

"I suppose your powers of omniscience don't stretch to untangling magic."

"Magic." Redmayne rolled the word off his tongue as if he'd never heard it before. A smile played about the corners of his mouth. "There are times this land could almost make a man believe in it—until he comes to his senses." With that, Redmayne exited the cell.

Ciaran's numb fingers were still fumbling with the shirt buttons when the door opened again. He looked up, swallowing hard at the sight of Fallon, her lithe body garbed in primrose yellow, her face pale and taut, her eyes filled with torment. And love, Ciaran realized with stabbing pain. Love.

Hugh's strong arm was around her waist in comfort, as if some new and precious bond had been forged between them. Ciaran's throat tightened at the sight of it.

"Ciaran!" Fallon raced to close the space between them. She flung herself into his arms. Ciaran winced, but made no sound as waves of hot fire surged beneath his rib cage. Instead, he cradled her close, drinking in the clean scent of her hair, the satiny caress of her cheek against his jaw.

He looked up to see Redmayne in the doorway, the

captain's eyes piercing, intense, something unexpected softening his mouth. Envy? Impossible.

"Captain," Hugh Delaney said. "There is something I need to discuss with you."

Ciaran started to protest, then stopped, trapped. He couldn't afford to betray anything to Redmayne. "Hugh, wait. I owe you some explanation for all this."

Hugh wanted to refuse. Ciaran could see the stubborn jut of a Delaney jaw he'd witnessed all too often in Hugh's sister. What could he do if Hugh walked out that door with Redmayne? There would be no way to stop him.

"Please," Ciaran said, silently pleading for help from every wandering spirit, every roving fairy, every ghost who called Ireland home. The safety of so many teetered in the balance. It seemed an eternity before Hugh spoke, his face grim, reluctant.

"All right. For a moment only."

Redmayne's gaze sharpened. "I'll await your pleasure in my quarters, Mr. Delaney," the captain said, sketching a bow. The cell door closed, the bolt rasping as it slid into place.

Fallon drew away from him, her hands on his face, tears glistening in her eyes. "How . . . how did this happen? Why didn't you tell me you were going through the souterrains? Didn't you trust me?"

Ciaran winced at the anguish in her face. "I trust you with my life, lady, but I couldn't put you in any more danger. You would have insisted on coming with me, and if you had—Fallon, if you had, you would be locked in this cell."

"Maybe not! I could have . . . have helped somehow. Done something to stop this madness. God in heaven, Ciaran, they plan to hang you!"

"He's not going to hang, Fallon," Hugh said, his voice steely. "I'll be damned before an innocent man dies in my place."

Ciaran glared at his brother-in-law. Hugh was standing stiff, resolute. "And what about all the innocent people who will suffer and die if Redmayne puts the noose around your neck, Hugh? Fallon says the English have been attempting to take Misthaven away from the Delaneys for generations. And this—this would be the perfect opportunity for them to do so."

Hugh's Adam's apple bobbed convulsively in his throat, his eyes darkening with guilt. "I wish there were some way to hold the land. But there's no help for it."

"Yes, there is. I die as Silver Hand. You *live.*"

"Ciaran, no! I . . . oh, God, it's an impossible choice!" Fallon sobbed, tears streaming down her cheeks. He'd never loved her more.

"No, Fallon. It's a hard choice, a painful one. And you know, deep in your heart, that it's the only choice we can make." He held her, stroked her hair. "What would happen if your brother died? The land taken away from you, put in the hands of some greedy fool like Phineas Butler? Think of how his people suffer under his rule. He's bled the land white, turned his tenants into starved shadows, with nothing to shield them from the winter except rags."

"God in heaven, don't—" she begged for mercy. He could have none. He went on ruthlessly, tearing away any illusions.

"Hunger, hopelessness, even eviction. That's the fate that will befall every person on Misthaven land if their master hangs as a smuggler, a murderer. Is that what you want, Mary Fallon? To condemn them all to death? Siobhan and her babes? Tom Dunne and little Caitlin?"

"No! Of course not! But—"

"Their survival has depended on your family for hundreds of years. You've never failed them. Can you turn your back on them now?"

"This is hopeless!" Hugh ground out. "How the devil can I live with myself if you hang because of me—my rashness, my stupidity?"

"Your courage?" Ciaran said quietly. "You held this estate together when it was on the brink of ruin. You risked your neck to give the people under your protection decent lives. And you'll spend the rest of your years doing the same thing—sheltering them from monsters like Butler and Redmayne, giving them a chance to watch their children grow up, fed and warm and healthy. Every soul on Misthaven will bless you for it. So will I."

"God, what can I do? Desert the people who depend on me, or . . . or allow you to sacrifice yourself?"

"I choose this path of my own free will. It's my sacrifice. My honor to do this for a man I respect above all others."

Hugh attempted to speak, but it came out in a ragged groan, half oath, half sob. "But Fallon . . . what about Fallon? I've done this to her. Hurt her again. Failed her."

"Not that," Ciaran denied fiercely. "Never that. You love her, and you love this land enough to do the only thing you can. Live."

Torment contorted Hugh's face, his eyes anguished, desperate. "I won't surrender in this. I'll find some way to save you. I swear it."

Panic bit deep. "Don't do anything foolish, or all this will have been in vain," Ciaran said fiercely. "We'll both die, Misthaven will be lost, and Fallon will be alone. I need to know that you'll be there to comfort her after . . ." He hesitated, not able to put it into words. A loss so great, a love too new, a pain too fresh. "Promise me."

Hugh swore under his breath, then nodded. "I won't endanger Misthaven. That vow I give you. But I'll move heaven and earth to try to get you free."

Ciaran reached out, grasped Hugh's hand tight. "I'm proud that you were my brother even for a little while."

Hugh closed his other hand over Ciaran's, holding it in both his own. "When you and Fallon married and I found you in the chapel, I all but went mad thinking it was a disaster. I didn't realize that you were the only man in Ireland who could be worthy of her love. I only wish I'd had a chance to know you better. Wish things could be different." Hugh broke off with a strangled sound, his eyes overbright.

"I know," Ciaran glanced from Hugh to Fallon, his heart full. "Hugh, leave us . . . a moment."

Ciaran could see exactly how much it cost him to turn away, this man of nobility and courage who had risked so much, given others so much. It was almost impossible for him to accept anything in return. But loyalty to the people under his protection would bind him, keep him safe. And his brotherly love for Fallon, freed after so many years, would help to heal her.

Hugh crossed to the door, knocked on it. The soldier beyond let him out. Ciaran watched him disappear, feeling a bond with this honorable man, love for him, regret. And he prayed that Hugh would find a way to make peace with the sacrifice that had to be made.

Ciaran turned back to the woman he loved, her tortured eyes cutting his heart. He forced a smile. "I fear I'll have to have a word with these legend weavers of yours, my love. Redmayne lost a soldier or two charging down into the labyrinth, but he came out unscathed. The enchantment promised that any enemy of Ireland—"

"Don't make a jest of this! And don't ask me to . . . to watch you die!" Fallon choked out. "I don't think I can do it—even for the people I love."

Ciaran peered down into Fallon's eyes, engraving every line and feature on his memory to carry with him like a talisman when the noose bit into his neck. "I came to you with nothing—not even the memory of my own name. You made me fall in love with you, Fallon, and with this land. The way the mist shimmers atop Caislean ag Dahmsa Ceo, the tales of courage and bravery, love and triumph spun by bards generations ago. And the people, with their dreamer's hearts and their work-battered hands, their haunting music and simple wisdom."

He feathered his thumb across the creamy velvet of her cheek. "From the beginning, I wasn't certain why I'd come here—what unseen force had led me to this castle. Why the fates brought me here. Now I know."

"You came to teach me how to love again," Fallon said. "To make me remember . . ."

"I'll always be grateful for our time together—an infinitely precious gift. But the fates didn't put me here only to love you. When Butler fled, and I knew the castle was safe, I felt so restless, as if . . . as if something was left unfinished. Now I know why. Don't you see? *This* is why I'm here. To die in Hugh's place. To shield the people of Misthaven from ravenous wolves like Redmayne. The night you went to the castle, you tried to conjure up a hero, Fallon, to do battle for you. Let me be that hero now."

"But I didn't know I would love you," she cried. "That it would hurt so much. This isn't what I—I expected. Ciaran, I don't want a hero anymore—some fairy tale made of mist and magic. I want you. Your arms around me late at night, your laughter in my ear when I awaken in the morning. I want forever. A lifetime—"

Could she possibly know how desperately he wanted the same things? To love her, to free her from grief, from sorrow, from the make-believe world where she'd sought refuge. To listen as she cradled his children before the peat fire and spun out the glorious tales of Cuchulain and Deirdre of the Sorrows. To create a life together, and never be alone.

There were no words of comfort he could offer, no way to salve the pain. He could only stroke her tear-damp face, will her to feel how much he loved her—a love as eternal as her castle in the mist, as honorable as the hero she'd dreamed in her heart, as beautiful as the land that had molded her into a woman of compassion and courage.

"It would have been beautiful, Fallon," he whispered, his voice ragged. "A forever to love you. But sometimes the tale ends before we wish it to. Remember how you told me the story of Deirdre and Naosi?"

She nodded. "I—I thought it was beautiful . . . until now. Love hurts too much. I wish I'd never let myself . . ." She broke off with a choked sob. "No, I could never wish that. I just never knew the truth—why Deirdre couldn't go on without him."

He smiled at her, a smile filled with pain and love, aching at the thought of Fallon's loss, her grief, the knowledge that she would have to face it alone, in the bed they had shared. "You won't die as Deirdre did, of a broken heart. You're strong, Fallon. As strong as the cliffs by our castle. This place has made you that way—poured everything brave and beautiful, generous and fairy-kissed into your hands. You'll hold your head high, lady. Proud. Sorrow won't break you. And you'll live a long life, a full one."

"What life? How can I do it without you?"

"I know you don't think so now, but in time Misthaven will heal you. That, and the knowledge that whatever happens in the future, we both found what we were searching for at your castle by the sea. You found a way to trust again, and discovered the love of your brother. You stepped through the gateway of your legends into the world of the living. And I—I had the privilege of loving you, if only for a little while. I had no life, no memory before you found me, Fallon, healed me. I consider it an honor to lay that life down to save everything you love."

"But I love you most of all."

"You taught me that no one who ever really loves this place ever leaves it entirely, no matter where they go—to the New World or to the life hereafter. They leave a piece of themselves behind." Ciaran stroked her cheek. "Don't you know I'll be with you every time you feel the kiss of the mist on your face?"

She clutched him tight, as if she were trying to meld them into one being, one soul. Didn't she know her love already had? When she pulled away, she looked stronger somehow, more beautiful than ever. He had never loved her more.

"I'll find some way to save you, Ciaran. I—"

Dark dread spilled through Ciaran, terror for her. Was there anything that would stop this valiant woman from attempting to snatch him from the claws of death? Anything that would make her cautious? Protect her?

He groped for something, anything that might give her pause. Suddenly an idea came to him, infinitely sweet and precious and—most astonishing of all—possible. The thought awed him, filled him with hope.

"You can't risk yourself, love. What if . . ." His hand slid ever so gently to her belly. Was it possible it felt fuller? Or was it only that he wished it were so? "There's a chance, just a chance, I've left a part of myself with you. A child made of our love."

A faint spark of joy, hope flickered in Fallon's eyes. "It's too . . . too soon to tell—" She stopped. Her lips trembled. "You're using it against me, to tie my hands. To stop me—"

"I'd like to believe that you carry my child. It might be true, Fallon. It might. Everything about our love has been so magical. From the very first—"

"Magic." Her voice was sorrowful. She drew away from him, a broken laugh stealing from her lips. "I–I brought you something. I'm not certain why. I just wanted . . . wanted you to have it." She slipped one hand beneath her skirts, drew out a soft bundle.

He ran his fingertips over the stitches she'd set into the shirt with such love. "It's beautiful. I'll wear it—" he couldn't finish. Was it cowardice in him—the comfort he took in the fact that he could wear this gift when he strode out of this cell to meet his death? All he knew is that it would help give him the courage he needed to leave his lady behind.

"There is something else," she said, a flush darkening her cheeks. Within the billows of the shirt he found another object wrapped up in a lace-edged handkerchief. Hard, heavy, it lay in his palm.

Ciaran folded back the bit of linen, and what he saw there made his throat constrict. Cabochon jewels glinted red on ancient, mellow gold. "The cloak brooch of Ciaran of the Mist," he whispered. "No, Fallon. I can't take this from you. What if Redmayne gets his hands on it?"

He tried to force it back into her hands, but she thrust them behind her back and shook her head.

"At first, I'd hoped the enchantment would protect you somehow, that you'd—I don't know—vanish in a puff of mist before they could kill you. I've discovered there is another reason I brought it instead. This belonged to a hero, lost centuries ago. Now it belongs to the bravest man I know."

The door opened, and the young soldier cleared his throat. "You'll have to leave now, madam."

Ciaran caught her in his arms one last time, the edges of gold cutting into his hand. "You can't leave Ciaran's cloak brooch with me, Fallon. The legend—you're supposed to keep it, pass it down through the generations."

She gazed up at him, a lifetime of fairy tales in her eyes, the magic of myths and legends softening her lips. Yet he knew that at long last, Mary Fallon realized they were make-believe. His lady had stepped forever into the real world. The certainty filled him with stark regret.

"Then you'll have to find a way to live, won't you?" she said. "Bring it back to me."

She pressed a parting kiss on his lips, then turned and left the cell. Ciaran stood there, clutching the ancient talisman, foreboding gnawing his nerves. Both she and Hugh would fight with all their might to save him. Put themselves at risk. There was only one thing to do. The sooner this was over the better. He hid the brooch in the billowy folds of his shirt, then went to the door.

"You!" He called out, hammering at the thick wooden panel. "Guard!"

The youth opened the door.

"Tell the captain I wish to see him. There is something of importance I need to ask him."

"Aye. I'll tell 'im." The guard shut and locked the door again, returning with Redmayne in an astonishingly short time.

The captain's eyes betrayed the slightest hint of curiosity, amusement, until his gaze flicked to the lace-edged handkerchief Ciaran still held in his hand. Something shifted, ever so slightly, in the captain's look, his voice a little softer. "There is something you needed to ask me about, MacDonough?"

Ciaran's mouth set, grim. "How soon can you manage to arrange a hanging?"

"You are so eager to die?" Redmayne's brow raised a fraction. "I confess, I am astonished. I think few men would be hasty to embrace the grave if Mary Fallon Delaney ever gazed up at them with such adoration."

The words chilled Ciaran. Was it possible Redmayne had feelings for Fallon? Wanted her? That once Ciaran was hanged, he'd . . .

No. Hugh would keep Fallon safe. She was in far greater danger of putting herself in some sort of peril in an effort to save Ciaran's life. The only way Ciaran could end that danger was to die.

"My wife has suffered enough because of me," Ciaran said. "I want an end to this, Redmayne."

Was there a flash of something almost human in Redmayne's countenance? Understanding? Strange. Whatever it was, Ciaran found it far more unsettling than his animosity or his scheming.

"An end to this," Redmayne echoed. "Yes. It is time. We should be able to have this settled by morning if my superior, General Scargill, arrives by then. He was most insistent that he be in on the kill."

"How long will it take for him to get here once he scents blood?"

"I've already sent word to the general that Silver Hand has been captured. He should be here before noon. The instant he reaches Glenceo, I promise you this, MacDonough." Redmayne crossed his arms over his uniformed chest. "I'll do everything in my power to hasten the day we make Mary Fallon a widow."

CHAPTER

19

꩜

The night keened beyond the glass panes, as if the salt sea wind were already mourning the death of a hero, a loss the mist shrouded land had suffered countless times before. Blood had watered the heather. Grief had fallen free as summer rain, countless women surrendering their courageous lovers to eternal sleep.

The sounds and the stories had been Fallon's lullaby since she was a child, but tonight the sorrowing all but drove Fallon wild. For now, it was her beloved who would die. The man who had awakened her heart, healed the raw, lonely places in her soul. Ciaran.

It was as if, even now, separated by rolling hills, velvety green glens, and thick iron bars, she could feel every precious beat of his heart, his tenuous hold on the world of the living. A fragile thread Redmayne was eager to sever as soon as possible.

It felt so strange, this panic that tightened inside her with each tick of the clock, each subtle movement of the moon across the sky beyond the windowpane.

She'd lived all her life in a land where time seemed to stand still, where the past was more real than the present, and the future as unreachable as the fairy kingdom of Tir na nOg. But suddenly, time was galloping past with the reckless speed of a Celtic charioteer's horses, careening toward disaster.

While, most infuriating of all, Hugh sat at his desk, almost terrifyingly still, as quiet in his desperation as Fallon was restless in hers.

"There has to be something we can do to save him," Fallon insisted, pausing in her frantic pacing long enough to cast Hugh a pleading glare.

"You're Silver Hand. How did you manage to make so many narrow escapes? You must have been bold, dashing—"

Hugh winced and drove his fingers through his hair. "Fallon, there was nothing dashing about it! I'm still the same man I always was! I was scared out of my wits most of the time, and spent the rest concocting damned careful plans, considering alternatives, weighing consequences. It took me months to plot out every move Silver Hand made."

"But time is the one thing we don't have! You're the one who sent Padraic to the garrison. You heard what he found out. The soldiers are claiming Redmayne intends to hang Ciaran tomorrow!"

"I know."

Frustration raged through her. "God in heaven, this is impossible!"

"If the old commander, Will Scargill, were still in charge, I might be able to bribe the guards, break Ciaran out that way. But the troops are more afraid of Redmayne than the devil, and no amount of coin would make them risk betraying him. If there were more time, I could infiltrate the place, send some of my men in as servants, or laborers or some such, manage to slide into the garrison that way."

She wanted to throw something, hit someone. She wanted to break into sobs, but she didn't dare. If she started to cry she might never stop, and her tears wouldn't save Ciaran's life. "This is insane, babbling on about things we bloody well *know* can't work!"

A flush darkened Hugh's cheekbones, his voice strained, level. "Sometimes it helps to just fling out ideas. Something might pop into your head unexpectedly."

"Of all the stupid, brainless, futile things I've ever heard!" She was hurting Hugh, but she was too desperate to care. "We don't have time to waste dithering that way! Matters are hopeless enough as they are! If Silver Hand himself rode into Redmayne's office and shot the buttons off his uniform, I'm not certain the English cur would let Ciaran go."

The words were scarce out of Fallon's mouth before she wheeled toward Hugh, a single idea making her hands tremble, her heart lurch with hope. "That's it! That would prove Ciaran isn't Silver Hand!"

"Fallon—"

"Don't you see? Someone could dress up in Silver Hand's disguise and—"

"Silver Hand didn't wear any bloody disguise!"

"No mask or cloak?"

"Emblazoned with the smuggler's coat of arms to announce his presence to half the county? No."

"What kind of an outlaw were you, for pity's sake?"

"A damned poor one, by your standards, I'm sure!" A muscle twitched in Hugh's jaw, hurt tempered with infuriating patience darkening his eyes. It was an expression she'd seen far too often before. One that spoke of his sorrow at failing her.

"I'm sorry to disappoint you again, but blast it, Fallon, all I wanted was to sell the wool from my sheep, put clothes on my tenant's backs! I wasn't intrested in being written about like Sixteen String Jack or Rob Roy. My best disguise was just being myself. Who would ever suspect me? No one ever saw Silver Hand."

"No one saw you? Then no one would know . . ." Fallon grasped his arm. "How would the English know you didn't wear some sort of disguise?"

Hugh's brow furrowed. "What the—"

"They wouldn't know, Hugh! If we threw together some sort of—of makeshift costume, put it on and rode, they would think it was Silver Hand." A smile broke over her face. "After all, what kind of smuggler king would run about without hiding his identity?"

"A very inept one," Hugh said, but she could see the spark of hope in his eyes. "But where would we get such a disguise? There isn't time—"

"I could fling it together before morning—one of papa's old cloaks, that old silver gauze mask I used to play highwayman in. And a letter—you know, one like the sheriff of Nottingham posted in the Robin Hood legends—'To whom it may concern: No innocent man shall hang in my place.'"

"And this costumed Silver Hand would what? Saunter into Redmayne's office, deliver the missive, then saunter back out?"

"Of course not! We'd have to find another way! But, Hugh, at least it's something. It just might work."

Hugh looked at her, grim. "As long as the rider doesn't get caught by Redmayne's soldiers. The place is crawling with them."

"It's a chance we'll have to take," Fallon said.

"But we vowed not to endanger Misthaven. Promised Ciaran. The tenants—"

"That is why we'll have to be incredibly careful. But we can do this, Hugh. I'm certain of it." Her voice cracked, her fingers trembled. "Hugh, I can't lose him."

Hugh stood, gathering her in his arms. "I know, little one. We'll make this work somehow. Together."

She hugged him fiercely, taking comfort in his steadiness, his loyalty. Hugh was as solid and unchanging as the cliffs near Caislean ag Dahmsa Ceo. Why had she never known, all those lonely years before? She drew strength from him, gave him hope in return.

After a moment, she straightened. Sucking in a deep breath, she squared her shoulders. "There's only one question left to settle."

"What's that?"

Fallon raised her eyes to her brother's troubled face. "Which one of us puts on the cape and mask and rides as Silver Hand?"

The billows of the shirt Fallon had stitched should have offered comfort, but the folds she'd labored on so lovingly brought Ciaran no peace. He paced his cell, half wishing Redmayne would let the vindictive sergeant return for another inquisition. It would have been far less torturous than being imprisoned, alone with his thoughts. Every minute Hugh or Fallon might be concocting some mad scheme to free him. Every hour so much teetered in the balance. Dawn seemed a thousand years away.

What had Redmayne claimed? That all could be ended come morning? Even now, the sun was almost at its crest. It must be nearing noon, and still no word. Nothing except the foreboding knotting his gut, the dread that with each tick of the clock, disaster might be careening closer.

It was treacherous ground he and Fallon and Hugh were treading on, until his trial and the inevitable execution. Redmayne claimed he would be satisfied with the death of Silver Hand. But who could guess what was going on beneath the Englishman's inscrutable mask, what he might be plotting? He was a brilliant strategist with a blazing intellect and an innate ruthlessness no one could mistake. He might be waiting for the exact moment to spring some kind of trap.

And this General Scargill—he might be so hungry for blood he'd not be satisfied with one corpse dangling from the gibbet. And if he were eager for a bloodletting, who better to feed that sort of appetite than the woman who had done all in her power to protect the man condemned as Silver Hand?

Ciaran could stand before Scargill and swear by every god who had ever ruled over Ireland that Fallon knew nothing of his role as the smuggler, but if Redmayne and Scargill chose not to believe him, how could anyone ever prove that she was innocent?

He stalked to the barred window and stared out at the impossibly green hills bathed in buttery rays of sun. Death would be a relief. A blessing. He vowed he'd embrace it gladly for his lady. And yet, some part of him wanted to cling to life with all the primal strength in his body. A man who had had nothing, suddenly with so much to lose.

He took Fallon's handkerchief from his pocket and

unwrapped the cloak pin she'd believed so firmly had been fashioned for the fairy king. It had been her greatest treasure since her mother had died. Yet, could his lady know that what he found even more precious was the bit of linen she'd wrapped the brooch in?

He held the soft square of cloth to his face, the scent of her, ever so faint, still clung to its folds, and he knew that it would be in his hand when he mounted the scaffold to meet his death.

Soon, he pleaded with the fates. Let it be soon. Before Fallon had time to get into trouble. Before Hugh had too much time to think. Before both these valiant spirits he'd come to love hurled themselves into danger in his name. And they would, if given half a chance.

His hands tightened on the brooch. Blast, why didn't Redmayne send for him? Get this debacle over with, once and for all?

It was as if some unseen force answered his plea. The sudden scraping of the bolt being flung back made him hasten to tuck away the precious gifts Fallon had given him. He turned to face the door.

Ciaran's eyes widened in surprise. What the blazes?

Redmayne himself stood there, his lean, aristocratic features oddly strained. His eyes that seemed able to strike dread into anyone who saw them glittered, piercing. "The general has arrived. He's waiting in my office."

"At last. Good." Ciaran stiffened, relief warring in him with despair. His judge and executioner awaited. It was time to make an end. "We can finish this, once and for all."

"It's not quite that simple." Redmayne grimaced. "I don't know why I am surprised. Nothing ever is in this infernal land."

Trepidation thrummed through Ciaran, suspicion overpowering his sense of relief. By all appearances Redmayne had come to fetch him to meet with the general, but why? He had countless underlings to tend to such menial tasks. Something was wrong. "What the blazes do you mean things aren't that simple?"

"Just that I was forced to leave the general in my office with a bottle of my best brandy until I could get some rather, er, unforeseen difficulties untangled. It seems you are not the only Silver Hand in Glenceo."

"Not the only—what the blazes?" Ciaran's throat went dry.

"The fates have delivered a second Silver Hand into our custody."

"A second?" Ciaran demanded. "Who?" But there could only be one person brave enough, foolhardy enough to take such a risk. Hugh—it had to be Hugh—captured in some mad attempt to free him. Ciaran closed his eyes, panic racing through his veins. No! He'd find some way to get Hugh out of this, Ciaran vowed to himself. There still had to be time.

"It's some sort of hoax, some sort of . . . of prank," Ciaran reasoned desperately. "*I* am Silver Hand! I confessed! Why else would I put a noose around my neck?"

"Why indeed?" Redmayne asked softly.

"Question this imposter and you'll see the truth!"

"Unfortunately, I am having a bit of difficulty interrogating this prisoner at present."

"Your sergeant misplace his cat-o'-nine-tails?"

Something unreadable flashed into Redmayne's eyes. "Even such crude methods would have little effect in this case."

"Why?"

Redmayne's gaze seemed to bore to Ciaran's very soul. "Because the man is dead."

Sick horror welled up in Ciaran, his hands knotting into fists. "Who—who is it?"

"I don't know yet. Some Irish peasants brought him in a cart. I thought you should be present for the unveiling. After all, it is your life that hangs in the balance. Come with me."

Ciaran followed Redmayne down the corridor, up the stairs, grief, fury already pulsing inside him. Damn Hugh! He'd begged the man to leave things as they were, not to endanger his own life and the lives of everyone who depended on him. But the honorable fool hadn't listened! And now, the instant the mask was pulled from his face, Fallon would lose everything she owned, everyone she loved. The tenants who had trusted in Delaney protection for generations would be cast into the hands of another landlord, one who might well be brutal and cruel, or, if they were lucky, only benignly neglectful. Fury surged through him at the incredible waste of it.

He stepped into the courtyard, blinking fiercely against the bright light, or was it the sting of something akin to tears? A ragged group of people clustered around a crude cart, the one-eared donkey in its traces restive, scenting death.

Ciaran caught a glimpse of blue, saw a familiar face among them. Maeve McGinty, wearing the cloak he had given her the night Fallon had found him by the castle. She leaned on the arm of the most beautiful young woman Ciaran had ever seen—a maid with hair like moonshine and eyes wise and knowing, a babe cradled against her breast. A tall, handsome man held the donkey's rope halter, and from the glance that passed between him and the young woman, there could be no doubt he was her husband.

"Ye might want t' be hurryin', yer worship," Maeve said, without giving Ciaran so much as a glance. "Goin' t' me wee grandbaby's namin' ceremony, we were, an' there's a grand celebration waitin' fer us."

"You'll get there soon enough," Redmayne said. "Where did you find this man?"

"Washed up wi' the tide, 'e did. Heard ye kept another man prisoner in 'is place, an' there was t' be a hangin' an' all. Even our wee Eve's celebration couldn't keep us from bringin' th' villain here. How would it look t' yer fine general, ye hangin' the wrong man?"

"That remains to be seen. MacDonough has confessed."

Ciaran stalked to the side of the cart, peered over the rough wood edge. There lay a figure swathed from head to toe in a length of sailcloth. Unable to endure another moment of wondering, he grasped the cloth, ripped it back from the corpse's head. His stomach plunged. The features were obscured by a water-sodden mask of shimmery silver—the mask he'd discovered in the priest hole the first night he'd come to Misthaven. A piece of the fantasy world Fallon had created as a lonely, motherless child.

Heartsick, he drew the mask off the corpse's face. The world tilted on its axis, and he clutched the side of the cart to keep his knees from buckling as he stared into the face of the one they'd claimed was Glenceo's smuggler king.

"Butler!" Ciaran cried, stunned. "Phineas Butler!"

Even Redmayne couldn't pare away the shock from his voice. "Impossible!"

The thunder of hoofbeats neared, but Ciaran barely heard them as both he and Redmayne stared at the corpse before them. But in an instant, a flurry of skirts and thick flame-bright hair rushed to his side. Fallon's hands clutched his rigid arm.

"We came the instant we heard!" she gasped. "My God, Ciaran, you're free!"

"Fallon, don't—" Her words were too beautiful, the possibility too precious. The fear this chance would be snatched away was far too great for Ciaran to feel anything but stunned. He scarcely dared believe it.

But Fallon had already wheeled away to confront Redmayne. "It's obvious you've made a terrible mistake. Free my husband at once."

Ciaran's heart squeezed. She looked so regal, her chin tipped up, her eyes sparkling with defiance, as if she were some Celtic queen of old and no one would dare refuse her command. Yet there was desperation, too, half hidden in the ripe curve of her mouth. Desperation born of love. The knowledge humbled him, and the thought of the pain his lady would suffer if he died terrified him.

"You heard my sister, Redmayne," Hugh said, striding forward. "Release this man at once." Ciaran raised his gaze to the man he'd thought dead, scarcely able to believe—believe what? That sober, responsible Hugh Delaney could be neck-deep in such a crazed plot? Who could have concocted such a mad charade? It seemed even beyond the powers of Fallon's wild imagination.

But would anyone be demented enough to believe that Phineas Butler, that sniveling, whining, cowardly little bully of a man was really the smuggler Silver Hand? Not even an inmate in a mad house could be so crazed.

Redmayne crossed his arms over the breadth of his chest, one brow arching. "How convenient to have Silver Hand delivered mere hours before your husband was to die, madam. It seems a miracle, almost beyond belief, does it not? Of course, Butler here can scarce defend himself, so I've no evidence save a corpse and a somewhat sodden mask that might have been stitched by any woman in three counties." His eyes narrowed on Fallon. "Even you, I would imagine."

Ciaran hazarded a glance at his wife. The tiniest flush darkened her cheekbones. She might as well have flown a banner of guilt.

Ciaran couldn't breathe, his chest was so tight with fear for her. Blood and thunder, did the woman have any idea what kind of penalty she would suffer if Redmayne was able to prove she'd staged this scene? Blast, she'd promised she wouldn't endanger herself or Hugh. He'd believed her love for Misthaven would keep her safe, that Redmayne would see him hanged before she could get into trouble. He should have known better. The instant the woman had left his cell, Ciaran should have found a way to hang himself!

"Don't let your imagination run wild, Redmayne," Ciaran snarled. "My wife had nothing to do with—"

"Captain Redmayne, what is the meaning of this?" The clipped, military voice sounded behind them. Every face in the group turned to where a stocky, florid-faced man with iron gray hair was striding down the stairs, his uniform proclaiming his rank. Scargill. It had to be the general who had come to see Silver Hand die. Now the officer's hawklike eyes surveyed the scene before him with rank impatience.

Despite the sense of peril, Ciaran took fearsome pleasure in the dark flush that spread across Redmayne's cheekbones.

"General Scargill, sir—" the captain began.

"General, there has been a terrible mistake!" Fallon broke in, trying to hasten to the man's side, but Maeve darted in front of her, the old woman astonishingly spry.

Maeve fluttered over to Scargill, laying one hand on the general's sleeve. "'Tis just a wee problem we're havin' here, but now you've come, I can take care of it in a twinklin'." She winked at the officer. "We've a bit o' misunderstandin', that's what we have here, general darlin'. Yer good captain, here, he—"

The general stared, transfixed, at the old woman, then snatched his arm away as if he'd been struck by lightning, his militant features stunned. Doubtless, he couldn't believe a lowly Irish peasant woman had dared to crease his uniform. "My captain can speak for himself!"

Only the slight restless twitching of one of Redmayne's hands betrayed the captain's unease. "General Scargill, sir, I fear there has been some sort of misunderstanding. A ridiculous ruse played upon us. These people are claiming this is the body of Silver Hand." He gestured toward the cart. "But I knew this man—one Phineas Butler. He was a pitiful coward, afraid of his own shadow. If he is Silver Hand, sir, I will gladly swallow every medal that's been pinned on my chest."

Scargill scowled. "You couldn't possibly have made a mistake, Captain?"

"It's simple to make a mistake when one is working such—such long hours as the captain has," Fallon exclaimed, and Ciaran stared at her in shock as she rose to Redmayne's defense. "From the instant Captain Redmayne arrived here, he's been scrambling to bring Silver Hand to justice! Why, he's barely slept, scarcely eaten. It's little wonder he became confused."

"My dear lady," Redmayne began coldly.

But Fallon was a picture of innocence. "You needn't be humble, Captain. Everyone in Glenceo knows how much you've wanted this matter closed. I'm certain the west of Ireland is not the place an ambitious officer like yourself wishes to spend any length of time."

"Are you so eager to leave Ireland, Captain? Eager

enough to be slipshod in your work?" the general demanded.

Redmayne's mouth hardened, and Ciaran was stunned to glimpse something like outrage, almost wounded pride in the officer's face. "I do my duty, sir. Follow my orders to the letter. In all my years in the army, I've never left a post until the job I was sent to do was finished—to the best of my ability. I swear on my honor that this man, Ciaran MacDonough, is the criminal we've sought. He is the smuggler. I would stake my life on it."

"Then why is there another body lying here?" the general demanded.

"That is what I was attempting to find out when you joined us. This is some sort of trick."

The mere idea flooded the general's face with furious color. "Someone has arranged this charade? Do you mean to tell me that these . . . *people*"—the general cast a scathing glance at Maeve and her little family—"dared to mock the king's soldiers by producing a false brigand? Do they have any idea what they will suffer for such insolence?"

Fear for Maeve and her kin shot through Ciaran. "They said they found Butler by the side of the road," he reasoned desperately. "How could they know he was an imposter?"

The general rounded on Ciaran, jowls wobbling with the outrage that had doubtless struck terror into countless raw recruits. But before Scargill could lambaste Ciaran for his impertinence, the general froze, glaring at Ciaran, as if seeing him for the very first time. The man's eyes all but tumbled out of his head. When the officer spoke, his voice was low, dangerous. *"This* is the man you are so certain is an accursed Irish smuggler, Redmayne?" he demanded.

The captain stiffened. "I caught him in the smuggler's lair, there with the cargo. He confessed."

"My husband has been confused lately," Fallon leaped forward, her face achingly earnest. "He only went into the labyrinth because he thought perhaps one of the smuggler's men might recognize him. You see, I found him wandering near the castle. He didn't know who he was. He'd taken a blow to the head, and I–I found him, took care of him. No one in Glenceo had ever seen him before."

"That would have been difficult, considering that the man had been at sea for the last twenty years," the general grated.

"Twenty years?" Fallon echoed.

"His ship went down six months ago. He was the only man who escaped alive."

"You know who I am?" Ciaran could scarce breathe.

"I met you a month ago. You'd just come ashore in Dublin. You were having trouble with the horse you'd hired. Seems you'd forgotten how to ride after so long at sea."

"But I . . . I don't remember—"

"I hadn't talked to you five minutes before I realized you were Gordon Butler's son. Your father was a schoolmate of mine."

"Butler?" He heard Fallon's stunned gasp, felt her grasp his numb fingers.

"At first I thought you were the younger son, Phineas, I think his name was. A worthless whelp, by all accounts. One Gordon risked everything for. When I realized you were James, the elder son—I could scarce believe my eyes. It only proves that sometimes justice triumphs in spite of all odds."

"This is impossible," Ciaran said.

Scargill's eyes narrowed. "You really don't remember, do you?"

"Nothing," Ciaran rasped. "If you could—could tell me anything that might make it clearer."

"I know more than most men. You see, I was with Gordon during a wild holiday in Kerry when he met your mother. Your parents never should have wed. The match was doomed from the start. Gordon was handsome as the devil, but brutish when he'd had too much to drink. Your mother, so sheltered and gentle, her nose always poked in books. The marriage was annulled within three months. Gordon claimed it had never been consummated. They parted ways. He had no idea he'd concieved a son until eight years later."

Ciaran remembered the fierce lines of his father's face the day he'd dragged him from his mother's arms.

"Then my father wanted me?"

"Wanted you? Wanted to make you disappear, more like. He'd remarried soon after the annullment, had a second son he adored. When he discovered your mother's secret, he realized that you were the legal heir to all he possessed."

Ciaran struggled to grasp the general's words, the tale that meshed with what little he remembered of his past. But he *had* come back, hadn't he? When he was newly grown into a man, he'd returned to find his mother dead. And afterward, what had happened? Heartsick, had he returned to the only life he could remember? At sea? And what had he left behind? His mother's grave and a father and brother who hated him.

"Phineas . . . Phineas Butler—" he tried to put it in words, failed.

"He is—*was*—your half brother," Scargill insisted.

Then why had he been so certain he'd always been alone? Ciaran wondered. Why couldn't he remember?

"Ciaran, is it possible . . ." Fallon stammered. "Your name—your real name . . . your past—"

"No! This can't be!" If Scargill had announced Ciaran was the son of the Celtic sea god Redmayne couldn't have looked more stunned. "Sir, you have to be mistaken!"

The general bristled. "I most assuredly am not."

"General, sir, you're claiming this man is *English?*" Redmayne choked out in disbelief. *English.* The word struck Ciaran like a lance. English—Mary Fallon's enemy by blood. He stiffened, his worst fears coming true. Scargill must be mistaken. He winced as he felt Fallon's hand fall away from his.

"Do you dare to doubt my word, captain?" Scargill scowled.

"No! Of course not, sir, but—"

"Mr. Butler and I exchanged bits of knowledge about ancient weaponry. It seems he had quite a collection he'd gathered from some castle ruin before his father stole him away."

Ciaran reeled, remembering the only possession he'd had when Fallon found him—the ancient dagger. From the first it had puzzled him, a mystery he couldn't solve. Was it possible Scargill was right? That it had belonged to him even as a boy? Yet, if it *was* true, hadn't he been everything Fallon hated? He glanced at her, saw her face, white, strained, every bit as shocked as he was. He wanted to touch her. Couldn't.

"Release Mr. Butler at once," the general ordered, "and offer him a gentleman's apology, Captain Redmayne. Sixteen years ago, James Butler was known as one of the bravest men in the king's navy, blooded in countless battles. You should thank God these people delivered the real Silver Hand into your custody before this innocent man died in his place."

Redmayne's gaze flashed from Scargill to Fallon, Hugh to Maeve McGinty and back to Ciaran as if they were the teeth of a trap snapping shut around his neck.

"Do it at once, Captain!" Scargill snapped.

Redmayne sketched them a stiff bow. "I regret not having been more . . . thorough . . . in my investigation." Ciaran's jaw clenched. He was certain the captain did regret it—that he'd not built up unshakable evidence, so that Ciaran would hang.

Fallon struggled to smile at the general. "Thank you so much for saving my husband's life. I am most grateful."

"You mean to tell me that this man married you, and he didn't even know his name?" The general turned to Ciaran, his features taut with distaste. "Tawdry business, this marriage—and to an Irishwoman no less." He suppressed a shudder. "Never approved of such hasty alliances. Always regret them in the end. Perhaps you can have it annulled." Scargill brightened at his own suggestion.

Ciaran started to protest, to dismiss the notion, then stopped. He tensed, uncertainty spilling through him. Perhaps *he* didn't wish to annul their union, but Fallon *had* married him, not knowing who he was. She'd married a man with no name, a man she'd believed to be an ancient Celtic hero. Yet to marry an Englishman—an enemy, one of the heedless gentry she had loathed. He winced at the memory of her hand, so warm, so filled with love, suddenly falling away, her face so white, so strained.

The general's voice broke through his tangled thoughts. "Now, I've spent a long night's journey anticipating the hanging of the man who killed my nephew. Since I've been cheated of that pleasure, I intend to console myself with more of that brandy you offered me, Captain."

For an instant, Redmayne looked as if he wanted to argue again, but after a moment he only nodded. "Of course, sir. My cellar is at your disposal."

The general turned on the heel of his polished boot, and stalked back into the building. Redmayne stared after him long minutes, then, suddenly, Ciaran was stunned to see a slow smile curve the captain's lips. "It seems you are free, MacDonough—or should I say Butler? I don't know how, but you've won our little game. Not only your life, but you've won a good deal more."

Hugh Delaney laid a hand on Ciaran's arm. "Phineas Butler's estates. With his death, they are rightfully yours."

"Quite an impressive victory. One that includes a particularly fine castle ruin," Redmayne said. "And a wife." His gaze flicked to Fallon, and for a heartbeat something raw glinted in his eyes.

"You wanted her." Ciaran drew her tighter into the protective circle of his arm. "After I died."

Redmayne straightened his cuff. "You needn't look so surly, man. I was hardly going to drag the woman off and ravish her. You, above anyone, know I abhor crude methods. And nothing is more unrefined than taking a woman by force."

Faint amusement played about the corners of the Englishman's mouth. "Do you really think she would have me, even if she'd never met you? A woman like her?

Not if I were the last man in Ireland." It was a mockery, a jest. Ciaran might have dismissed it as such if Redmayne's shoulders hadn't sagged just a trifle.

"Go, Butler," the captain ordered. "Take your wife and go. You're free."

The concept was still too incredible to grasp as he faced this man who had been his nemesis, this brilliant, ruthless opponent no one could hope to defeat. A man so single-minded, so fiercely determined, he seemed invincible. Yet now, Redmayne seemed to be surrendering, letting go of the enmity, as if it had no more substance than ashes carried in the wind.

"Why?" Ciaran knew he was a fool to ask it. Somehow, he couldn't stop himself. "We both know Phineas Butler was no Silver Hand. Why are you doing this for us? Or are you merely waiting for another time to strike again?"

"No. You are quite safe." The hard line of Redmayne's mouth softened, something flickering in the captain's inscrutable eyes. A strange sensation swept through Ciaran, as if for the first time the dreaded captain had allowed him a glimpse, just a glimpse of the man behind the smooth marble mask. "Perhaps I've grown bored with this whole business." Redmayne gave a dismissive wave of his hand.

Fallon spoke softly. "Or maybe, just maybe, the magic of the castle touched you, too?"

The slightest flush darkened Redmayne's cheekbones, his eyes hooded. "Don't be absurd. The notion is laughable. Come, madam, surely your Irish castle wouldn't spare any magic on the English soldier who attempted to destroy it?"

But he didn't wait for Fallon's response. Instead, he turned and signaled to the soldiers nearby. "Take Silver Hand to the stable until the general decides what to do with the body. And give these people a moment alone. It isn't every day a man is given a second chance at life, MacDonough. I've never envied any man before, but I almost believe I could learn to envy you."

The soldiers hastened to do his bidding, and Redmayne turned away. Ciaran slipped one arm about

Fallon as they watched the officer mount the stairs, his back ramrod straight, his austere features still hinting at ruthlessness. And yet, an aura of something painfully solitary clung to him, something Ciaran knew both he and his lady understood far too well.

A hush fell over the little cluster of people gathered outside the garrison. Within moments, they were alone.

Ciaran turned to Fallon, still reeling from all that had happened, feeling as if ghostly hands had drawn the noose away from his neck. A life he'd surrendered for her already in his heart, returned to him, brighter and more precious than before.

"Fallon, I still don't believe this—it's too incredible. I'm free. Free."

She held his hand, tight, so tight, as if she were trying to feel the very beating of his heart, and he felt the dampness of her tears against his chest.

"Lady," he breathed against her meadow-scented hair, "however did you manage this?"

"Hugh was going to ride in as Silver Hand. Don't be angry. We had to try it. We were on our way here, yet so afraid something might go wrong, when we saw something wash up on the shore. You know Hugh. Even though he was coming to rescue you, he couldn't just turn away from anyone who might need his help. When we got there, it was too late. We found Butler, dead. Maeve and her family happened on us moments later."

Maeve McGinty edged over, her eyes, lost in pockets of delightful wrinkles, sparkling. " 'Twas the most obligin' thing Phineas Butler ever did, drownin' an' depositin' himself on that beach. Though he couldn't have been in the water very long. Most unforgivin', the sea can be, when she gives up her dead."

"Fallon was the one who came up with the plan to dress him as Silver Hand," Hugh said, pride shining in his eyes.

"So she did, clever child," Maeve pinched Fallon's cheek. "An' me an' me family, we were jest too happy t' help."

"When I think what might have happened if you hadn't found Butler . . ." Ciaran couldn't suppress a shudder. "If Hugh had been foolish enough to come, they'd have shot him."

"More than likely, I fear," Maeve put in. "Our Mr. Delaney is a good man, me darlin', an' a wise one most o' the time, but he's weighted down wi' honor somethin' terrible. Only one man I ever knew was more so." She patted Ciaran on the cheek. "An' as fer the general rememberin' ye—why, 'twas a fine piece o' luck, don't ye think? Hard t' believe, if I say so meself."

He should have been relieved, Ciaran knew. Grateful. Without the general's announcement, would he be free right now? And yet, he couldn't help but feel unsettled, as if the revelation chafed him.

"I just wish . . ." Ciaran frowned, searching for some way to explain. "I should feel something, shouldn't I? Some stirring of recognition? I was in Butler's house, but I felt nothing, no link with it at all, nor with the man himself. And when Scargill said my real name I felt nothing. It's as if—as if it doesn't fit me." Or was it that he wouldn't allow it to fit? Recoiled from owning anything that might drive a wedge between him and Fallon?

"Don't let it trouble ye, me fine darlin'." Maeve's wise eyes seemed to understand not only what he'd said, but what he'd left unsaid. "A mere name could never change the man that ye are. Ye'll get used t' it in time, an' the crofters, they'll bless ye for it. Ye're a man o' means, now. Landlord t' plenty who need ye."

Fallon brightened, and she clutched his hand. "We'll be able to help them, Ciaran. Build them new cottages! Make certain they're never hungry, never cold."

"And you, Fallon, you can feed their spirits, their imaginations, spin out the stories they cherish. Stories like Ciaran of the Mist." He reached into his pocket, withdrew the brooch, wrapped in delicate linen.

"I'll do my best by the people on my lands. See them safe. I swear it, by the stones of Caislean ag Dahmsa Ceo, and by the brooch of the fairy king."

Hugh nodded, too moved for words, a wise ally Ciaran knew he'd need in the days to come. Fallon's face shone with joy. But it was Maeve who held his gaze, her lips smiling.

"Maeve, I—"

"Ye needn't say a word t' Maeve McGinty, lad. I know ye better than ye know yerself." She stroked the cloak he had given her on that rain-slick road what seemed an eternity ago.

Ciaran stared into Maeve's ageless eyes, so wise, so merry, so filled with courage and beauty—the face of an aged Celtic goddess despite her ragged clothes. He'd never know what moved him, only that a tribute was due to this woman with inner strength that reminded him of his Fallon, a woman who would never surrender to death the way his own mother had, betraying the boy he had been. Slowly, he dropped to one knee before her, took up her withered hand and brushed it with a kiss.

"What is it ye're doin' that for?" the old woman asked, a lovely blush staining her cheeks.

"To thank you. You were the first to give me a glimpse of myself, the first to—"

"Caught more than a glimpse o' ye, too, in the process, me boy." Her eyes twinkled with tender amusement. "Take yer love back t' the castle, back t' the cliffs. Ye've won yer freedom now, an' yer lady. No hero, be he flesh an' blood or woven of legends a thousand years old can ask fer more."

Had he won his lady? Fallon had claimed she loved him, risked her life to save him. Yet, had he lost some precious part of her heart when Scargill had helped him to find himself? A part he would never be able to win again. Because of who he was. Who she was. The possibility was far more terrifying than the prospect of hanging could ever be.

He had to know for certain.

Ciaran held out his hand, closed Fallon's in his own, then led her to where Cuchulain was waiting. He mounted the horse, then gathered Fallon up before him, holding her in his arms.

They left the garrison behind, with its iron-barred cell and uniformed soldiers.

He carried away something as well—the tiniest seed of doubt.

CHAPTER

20

Something was wrong. Fallon could feel it, sense it, with each ripple of Ciaran's muscles against her as he guided the horse across the fields.

A sea of green enveloped them, embraced them, the salt-scented breeze offering benediction. Cherry blossoms waved on their tangled branches, their loosened petals floating on the wind to spangle her hair and the folds of her gown.

Life—it had been offered to this man anew. A name—his own. A home—rich enough to care for a wife, for children, as he'd told her he longed to do so long ago. And yet, lines of unease carved deep into the planes of his face, his eyes hooded, uncertain, dark with some hidden unease.

Scargill had flung open the door to Ciaran's past, given him a place to begin to put his life together again. Why did some part of Fallon want to slam that door shut, to keep things as they were—Ciaran, her husband, her love, conjured as if by magic out of the Castle of the Dancing Mist?

Because she was afraid all this news would change things between them, might make him regret—what?

Having married a wild Irish girl who believed in fairy kings? A woman who had spent a lifetime hating what he was—English.

Fallon winced. Wasn't that exactly what she'd scorned the English for? Their loathing of people just because they were Irish? She'd never thought that such prejudice was a knife that could cut both ways.

She closed her eyes, hardly noticing where Ciaran took her, misery a hot knot in her chest. She wanted to smooth away the tightness about his mouth, wanted him to kiss and laugh, wanted to feed him ripe, crimson cherries and pretend to enchant him the way the fairies had enchanted Ciaran of the Mist.

Yet when she opened her eyes again, she saw something that made her heart squeeze. The castle. He was taking her to the castle on the sea cliffs, where bard songs still echoed pure and the wind was sweet. To the place where magic began. Was it possible there was enough enchantment left to wash away the doubts clouding his eyes, the uncertainty that tugged at her like an importunate child, asking a thousand questions?

Towers of stone still soared skyward, garlands of rose-tinted mist draped the gray stone, arched windows in broken walls shaped the light, while intrepid wildflowers nestled into any small pocket of earth, blooming between the cracks in the stone.

Her place. This had been her castle of dreams from the time she could remember. The place where she had spun such wondrous dreams.

Ciaran dismounted, then reached up to help Fallon down. He peered into that lovely face, feeling suddenly, achingly uncertain.

"Ciaran," she began, then gave a strained laugh. "I–I mean, James. I should grow used to calling you that, shouldn't I?"

"I suppose." He looked so bleak she couldn't bear it. "But—"

"What is it? What is wrong? Something is. I can tell." She was babbling. But she was afraid. Suddenly so afraid. To lose him to death would have been unthinkable. But to lose even some tiny part of his heart while he lived would be more torturous than she could endure. "Please, tell me what you're thinking."

He paced to the nearest stone wall, pressed his palm against it. "I'm an intruder here now. Not part of the magic anymore."

"You can't know—"

"No, Fallon. Let me say this. If I am a Butler, I'm part of a family who has let their people suffer for generations. Abandoned them to hunger, to cold, let them die hopeless." The words were laced with despair, far deeper than when he'd faced hanging.

"You were a child when your father stole you away—" she began, wanting desperately to comfort him, but he reached up, laid his fingertips on her lips. His eyes burned with pain and hope, sadness and love, the expression of a man suddenly, terribly lost.

"You wed a stranger, a man with no name," he insisted. "A man you thought was a hero born in the legends you love. Now they say that I'm English. James Butler. I don't even know what kind of man he was, what kind of man *I* am."

"But I do know," she said fiercely. "A name can never change who you are. What you are. A man who would give his cloak to shield an old woman from the rain. A hero who would sacrifice his life for those weaker, more helpless than he. Whatever blood flows through your veins, this much I can tell you. You have an Irish heart."

A soft groan tore from his throat. "Ah, Fallon, I love you so much. But you vowed you'd die before you wed an Englishman. That it would make you a traitor to the people you loved. If you have any doubts now, any fears—lady, I will set you free."

"Is that . . . is that why . . . why you looked as if you were hurting? Did you think for even a moment . . ."

"You were so still, so pale, when Scargill identified me, I thought perhaps you might have regrets. That was always my greatest fear—that if I ever discovered who I was, it might somehow hurt you, disappoint you. That was the one thing I could never bear. You believed in me so fiercely I wanted to be a hero in your eyes. Now, this changes things."

"No." She curved her hand along the hard line of his jaw, her thumb stroking his lower lip. "I love you, no matter what the world calls you. I want you in my arms, in my bed. Forever to laugh with you, love you."

Her voice broke, tears burning her eyes. "All my life, I believed that happy endings were for other people. I would always be alone. I was brave enough to dream of castles and heroes bewitched by enchanted cherries. But I didn't have the courage to dream about someone who would love me forever, someone who would never leave me."

"If you want me, Fallon, love me, then no power on earth could take me from you."

"I want you more than dreams or magic or bardsong. I love you more than the mist or the sea or the castle."

His eyes glistened overbright. "The first time you brought me here, took me down into the souterrains, I felt something . . . something I can't explain. That no one ever leaves this land completely. That no matter where else on earth they wander, they return—to the hills and the sea, the cliffs and the castle. If I had died—"

"Don't even say it!" Tears broke free, trailed down her cheeks. "If I'd lost you—"

"You never could. I'd wait for you here. And when you closed your eyes in eternal sleep, I'd carry you in my arms to whatever comes after."

He smiled, believing in Fallon's dreams down to his very soul. "And when our babes are born, we'll bring them here."

"And we'll tell them about a lonely girl who came here, searching for a legend. What she found was so much better."

"What was that, *mo chroi?*" Ciaran whispered, drawing her into his arms, pressing a kiss to her temple.

"She found you." Fallon raised her gaze to his, her eyes filled with tears. "That is when she discovered what the real magic was, the magic she'd been seeking forever. Love. You'll always be my very own Ciaran of the Mist."

"And you the valiant maiden who set me free from the fairies' spell."

Her lips, flavored of springtime and sea breezes and enchantment as old as time, found Ciaran's in a kiss that promised the kind of love bards would sing of for a thousand years. Heart filled with joy, with love, with hope, Ciaran took his lady up into the castle tower to fulfill every vow they'd made to each other the day they had wed, and other covenants, more ancient still: to worship her with his body, to cherish her bright spirit, to drink of her dreams.

And the mist shimmered around them in a veil of rose and gold, silver and blue, weaving its ageless magic as if the fairies themselves were offering their blessing from the land where legends were born.

EPILOGUE

Maeve McGinty perched on the castle wall and popped a cherry into her mouth, her eyes twinkling as she peered at the figures below—two long-legged boys of nine and eight running and leaping with their handsome father, hurling sticks slicing the air.

Saffron-colored *leine* billowed about them, caught at the waist with thick leather belts as if they'd just stepped through the mists from the time of Cuchulain and Deirdre of the Sorrows.

"They are beautiful, are they not? And strong. So much like their father when he was young." Maeve smiled at the man beside her, a delighted laugh rippling from a throat smooth and fresh as new cream, cascades of sun-gold hair floating about her supple form.

"It's most unbecoming for a king to pout, my love, just because you've lost a champion. After ten years, one would think you'd get over your disappointment. After all, hurling is just a game."

"A game?" Jarlath folded his arms across his chest, his heartbreakingly handsome face crumpling in a scowl. "Humphf! Just like a woman to spout such nonsense! 'Tis a tragedy I'm watchin' here. The finest man ever to raise a hurley, he was. An' he could've remained so forever if he'd stayed in Tir na nOg. Now, look at him. 'Tis a trifle gray at the temples he's growin'. An' he's a wee bit slower, I'll be bound."

"Only because he keeps rememberin' last night, when he brought our Fallon here for their lovin'. He can't keep his eyes off *her.*" Maeve cast an affectionate glance to where Fallon sat beneath a tree, attempting to dissuade a most determined toddler from eating the strings of an exquisite harp—Fiachra's, resurrected from the depths of the labyrinth, the most coveted prize to be awarded to the finest harper, entrusted to his keeping for the year to come.

"Sure, an' even you can't begrudge them such happiness," Maeve said. "The good they've done—well, it pure makes my heart ache. When they surprised Siobhan Moynihan by bringin' back her lost Michael, 'twas the most touchin' thing ever I saw. And Ailis MacGrath an' her babe—the way they've cared for them—"

"I couldn't be carin' less about the doin's o' mortals."

"Even when they keep the old magic alive?" Maeve smiled, tender. "Look about ye, ye great fool! This promises to be the most glorious festival ever. Every child who can lisp, memorizing the old epic poems to recite, Tom Dunne collectin' every musician in the county t' play in the bard contest. Rememberin'—all of them rememberin' where they came from—the glory of it, the pride in it. The past. They'll keep the magic alive here, when the rest o' the world stops believin'.*"

"Ye expect me t' believe that people will stop trustin' what's in front o' their very noses?"

"You don't seem to see what's in front o' yours," Maeve pointed to the family framed by billows of green hill. "Look at them, Jarlath. Her face pure glows with love for him."

"Love! Bah! I offered him immortality. He could have stayed, forever young, forever beautiful if not for your meddling."

Maeve's face softened, and she looked down tenderly at Fallon. "I had little enough to do with it. She was the one who broke the enchantment by winning his love. A love so strong not even fairy magic could hold him."

"I almost had him back, the night he sent that coward, Butler, runnin'. Got him up t' the castle, but then . . . then *she* made love t' him there, tightened *her* hold, instead o' lettin' him walk through the mist door, the way he was supposed to. But at least he would have suffered the way he deserved at that Redmayne's hands, if it weren't for ye, goin' in an' snippin' out the tangles— bewitchin' that general, givin' him a name, a whole bloody past to cling to."

"The real James Butler won't be needing it anymore. He'll be spendin' forever in the mermen's Soul Cages beneath the sea with the rest of his crew. Besides, don't be blaming me for all this. Our Ciaran would never have lost his memory in the first place if you hadn't whapped him in the head with your own hurling stick."

"He was leavin' in the middle of a match, an' Liam of the Green's men all but grovelin' for mercy! I had t' try t' stop 'im! Did it the only way I could think of in the heat o' the moment."

"Ye knockin' him in the head an' the rest o' your fool team clutchin' at his clothes till he tore free—aye, *that* was childish behavior, Jarlath, an' ye ten thousand years old."

He shot her a blistering glare. "What kind o' man runs off in the middle of a match, anyway, an' his king needin' his services?"

"Ciaran's loyalty never belonged to us, nor to Tir na nOg. Always, it was pledged to the people here. When Fallon called him, no force in the land of mortals or the land of the enchanted ones could keep him from fulfilling his vow." Maeve pinched her husband on his stubborn chin. "Come, Jarlath, you'd stolen nine hundred years away from our Ciaran. Ye could at least let him go with good grace. 'Tis the fair thing to do."

"Fair? Pah! You are even thinking like a mortal! That is what comes of all this nonsense—our own daughter runnin' off with one, then my champion. An' you wanderin' about entertainin' yerself with 'em like they was a little girl's poppet—what in the name o' Cuchulain is that?"

Maeve turned to see another figure burst from the woods. A wild tangle of auburn hair flew about Fiona Delaney Butler's winsome face. Her skirts, embroidered with gold-thread interlacing, were tucked scandalously into her sash, displaying scraped knees. Without pausing a heartbeat, the six-year-old girl snatched up a hurley abandoned in the heather just as Ciaran whacked a ball with bone-shattering force.

Both boys dove for it, but it whistled past their outflung sticks with enough speed to carry it half-way to Derry, and the girl suddenly leaped into the air.

Jarlath gasped in amazement as she slammed her stick into the ball, driving it past the makeshift goal. A howl of outrage erupted from her brothers, young Hugh flinging down a hurley in a fit of temper.

"Make her stop, Da! She promised she wouldn't!"

"Only because you paid her two shillings," eight-year-old Connor said with a smirk.

"They were mine to do what I wanted with!" The boy cuffed his tattling brother with one grubby fist. "Uncle Hugh gave 'em to me! Girls aren't supposed to play hurley anyway!"

Ciaran laughed. "Especially when they're better at it than their older brothers, eh, Connor? You needn't be shamed that your sister plays hurley better than any boy in three counties. Celtic women have never been the sort who sat sipping tea and sniffing smelling salts. In ancient times, they were warriors as mighty and powerful as the men. In fact, they were the ones who trained the young men in fighting."

He went to his daughter, tossing her up into the air. "Where have you been wandering, treasure mine? Off battling dragons?"

"I've been searching an' searching, Da, for the door to where the fairies live so when Mama gives me the pretty brooch to keep I'll be able to find it." She cast her brothers the haughty smirk that had gained her more than one black eye. "Ciaran of the Mist b'longs to me now."

Her father chuckled. "Is that so?"

"Mama told me all 'bout the magic, an' how I get to call 'im back if things get dreadful. But I don't think I want to call him back. I think I'll go find him instead."

"You're daft!" Hugh groused.

"Maybe. But someday, I'll be the best hurler in all Ireland. So fine that the fairy king himself will carry me away, an' I'll beat Ciaran of the Mist himself."

Ciaran turned to his wife with a grin. "What do you say, Fallon-my-heart? Shall we surrender her to the magic?"

Fallon scooped up the baby, and came toward them, her face shining. "Someday, the magic will find her. It found me."

Ciaran leaned down and kissed his wife, his face glowing with love, with happiness, with dreams more beautiful than any legend could be.

Maeve sighed. "'Tis a happy ending they've found, isn't it, my love? How can you have any regrets when you see—" Maeve caught a glimpse of her husband and stopped. A crease appeared between her winged brows. "I mislike the look in yer eyes, ye rogue. What are ye thinking?"

"Just wonderin' . . ."

"Wonderin' what?"

Jarlath's eyes sparkled with ages-old mischief. "Do ye think that wee Fiona likes cherries?"

Kimberly Cates

"A truly gifted storyteller. Reading a novel
by Kimberly Cates is sheer heaven."
—Kathe Robin, *Romantic Times*

Crown of Dreams 79601-1/$5.99
To Catch a Flame 68494-9/$5.99
Only Forever 74083-0/$5.99
The Raider's Bride 75508-0/$5.99
The Raider's Daughter 75509-9/$5.50
Restless is the Wind 63395-3/$5.99
Stealing Heaven 89745-4/$5.99
Gather the Stars 89746-2/$5.99
Angel's Fall 56872-8/$5.99
Morning Song 56873-6/$5.99
Magic 01494-3/$6.50

Simon & Schuster Mail Order
200 Old Tappan Rd., Old Tappan, N.J. 07675
Please send me the books I have checked above. I am enclosing $_____ (please add
$0.75 to cover the postage and handling for each order. Please add appropriate sales
tax). Send check or money order—no cash or C.O.D.'s please. Allow up to six weeks
for delivery. For purchase over $10.00 you may use VISA: card number, expiration
date and customer signature must be included.

POCKET
BOOKS

Name _____

Address _____

City _____ State/Zip _____

VISA Card # _____ Exp.Date _____

Signature _____ 945-05

POCKET BOOKS
PROUDLY PRESENTS

BRIAR ROSE

KIMBERLY CATES

Coming Soon
from Pocket Books

Turn the page for a preview of
Briar Rose. . . .

The pistol ball seared a lightning-hot bolt through flesh, the bitter tang of gunpowder burning in the air, but Captain Lionel Redmayne scarcely felt it. Death—every reluctant soldier's lover—was coming to claim him at last on this barren, deserted stretch of Irish road.

Redmayne leveled his own pistol at shadowy attackers who melted into clumps of heather, behind outcroppings of rock, seemingly from the mist itself. Three of them. Maybe four. Scenting his blood.

He could almost taste their victory. He'd have to make this shot count. It might be his last. Anyone familiar with a pistol knew as well as he did that it would take precious seconds for him to reload, seconds in which they could close in for the kill. And in the twenty minutes he'd managed to keep them at bay, these men had shown themselves practiced in every method of dealing death.

It was a miracle he'd held them off this long. If he could fight them blade to blade, he might stand a chance. But they had no interest in a fair fight when they'd ambushed him here. They didn't want a battle. They wanted a corpse. His.

He objected, of course. Not out of any grand passion for life. He'd been barely six years old when he'd realized that dying was easy. It was living that was far harder. In his years in the army he had stared into the face of his own death so many times he'd come to dismiss it as a fleeting nuisance, like the buzzing of a bee too close to his ear. He just figured this would be a damned embarrassing way to die.

The infamous, terrifyingly omniscient Captain Lionel Redmayne cut down on a deserted stretch of Irish road because he'd been fool enough to travel without a cadre of guards in a land that would sooner have tea with the devil than the English army. Not to mention, he'd been too distracted by thoughts that tugged at him, troubled him, like importunate children no matter how resolutely he'd tried to shove them away.

He fired at a blur of movement, heard a cry of pain. At least he'd have company on his way to hell, he thought with some satisfaction, fighting to reload his pistol.

Who the devil were they? he mused, struggling to jam another pistol ball down the barrel of his weapon. A man liked to know who was shooting at him.

Who hated him enough to hunt him down? A grim smile twisted his lips. It would be far easier to sort out who *didn't*. Less capable officers he'd tramped over on his way to promotion, common folk caught in a vise between their well-being and his duty. Those who feared him, hated him, or saw him as an impediment standing in their way.

Yes, plenty wanted him dead—but few would take

the perilous step from desiring it to making it a reality.

Only one thing was certain: Once this fight was over, there would be no one to mourn him. Lionel Redmayne would slip beneath the silvery surface of life, leaving not so much as a ripple of grief or loss in any other living soul.

It hadn't mattered a damn to him in fifteen years of campaigning. Why did the thought suddenly leave something hollow, aching in the pit of his stomach?

It was this infernal land, where passions lay so thick that one sucked them in with every breath. It was the memory of one moonlit night, flame-red hair tumbled about a woman's flushed face as she danced for another man, love hot in her eyes. A pulsing ember of life so vivid that for the first time in his life he couldn't crush it, even in the name of duty. Mary Fallon Delaney had made a glaring mockery of everything he'd believed about himself. Something that made him question . . .

Another shot rang out, and he felt it tear through his thigh. His eyes swept the area, suddenly glimpsing a ring of ancient stones, half-toppled. If he could reach it, he might be able to . . . to what? Escape was impossible, but the stones might provide enough shelter to let him take yet another assasin with him when he died. That would be reward enough.

Redmayne grimaced, scrambled upward, his thigh burning, his head swimming with bitter irony. He'd come to Ireland determined to destroy relics of the past like this one—tear them down and fling them into the sea. That way everyone could forget . . . the absurd kiss of magic, the tales of long-faded glory, the past that was of no use to them. They would accept the future that was inevitable. He'd been so certain he'd understood the people of this place. He hadn't expected to be sucked in to their special brand of madness.

His elbow jarred into a stone, pain jolting through him. He gritted his teeth, pushing harder with his good leg, one hand clamped tight over the wound in his other. He heard a shout, glimpsed the pale flash of a man's face. Near. Too near.

They were closing in on him.

The stone ring swirled around him—dark, cool, unearthly—as he dragged himself into a crook between two stones. As if there were any place dark enough to conceal him!

Black haze tugged at him, drawing him deeper into cold waters, still waters. He heard vague shouts of confusion, but it didn't matter anymore. They would find him. And when they did . . . death.

Redmayne winced at the twisting pain somewhere deep inside him where no bullet could touch. No one would come from heaven to take his hand on this barren hill.

Redmayne closed his eyes, fighting back a wave of quiet despair, waiting for the end. He was tired, so tired. His very body seemed to be fading away a piece at a time. Soon there would be nothing left. But then, had he ever really been anything . . . any*one* at all?

Redemption—the word flashed through the red haze of his pain and shimmered there, but he turned his face away. He'd be wiser to put his faith in fairies and magic, in destiny and fate, than to ever believe in forgiveness for a man like him.

"To the devil, then," he muttered in a rasping breath, reaching into the swirl of mist. "Take me, if you dare."

* * *

The fairies were whispering, the faintest of warnings that tingled along Rhiannon Fitzgerald's freckle-spattered cheeks and settled deep into her bones. She braced herself against the rocking of her rainbow-hued gypsy caravan and gripped the reins more tightly. Eyes the warm green-gold of a forest primeval searched wild, rocky hills swept clean of afternoon's mist, the standing stones with their well-kept secrets just visible above the green of the next rise.

"Don't let your imagination run wild, Rhiannon," she chided herself, dashing a wayward lock of cinnamon hair from her cheek. "There's nothing amiss. You're only reacting to this place. Echoes of old pain, old sorrows. They grow louder when you're alone." The thought should have offered more comfort.

After all, her reasoning might be true enough. From the dawning of her first memory, Rhiannon had felt as if an invisible ribbon stitched into her breast bound her to the heartbeat buried deep in these timeless hills, a link carrying piercing sweetness, sorrowful yearning, a joy and a curse. Stark awareness of things seen and unseen beyond the drab veil of most people's reality—ghost-shadows of ages long vanished, silent cries of wounded woodland creatures, the fragrant magic of healing herbs white witches had gathered when the earth was new, and the irresistible pull of tides called destiny.

It was the gift of the fairy-born, her da had told anyone who would listen. Her mother's parting boon before she'd returned to the magical kingdom of Tir na Nog, leaving her mortal lover and her child behind.

There were times Rhiannon wished most fervently her mother had seen fit to leave something a little less troublesome—a pretty locket, perhaps, or a letter Rhiannon could read, precious words that might bring to life the woman she'd never known.

"The least she could have done was leave instructions how to turn this . . . this 'gift' *off* once in a while so I can have some peace," Rhiannon complained to the soft-eyed vixen peering between the slats of an overturned basket beside her. But her vague attempt at humor fell flat. The unsettled feelings only intensified as she peered into that pointed little face, so wise yet vulnerable beneath wisps of russet fur.

"Perhaps I'm just feeling strange because of you, *mo chroi,*" she said, her throat tightening. A sense of pride and impending loss tugged at her as she shifted both reins to one hand and eased her finger into the basket to stroke a silky ear. "Your foot is all mended now. It's time to set you free."

Free. Far from the foxhounds that had nearly killed her, or from their rich masters, chasing after her in a mad rush of wind and scarlet coats and blooded horses, delighting in the chase.

She gazed at the rocky, wild terrain about her, deserted, too distant from any of the great houses that would host such sports to be a danger. Not even the most intrepid foxhunter would dare traverse such rugged land. Out here, the little vixen would have a fighting chance to survive.

So just let her go here, now, and turn around, a voice inside Rhiannon whispered. *Don't venture deeper into whatever disturbance is troubling you. What possible difference could a few more miles make?* All the difference in the world. She could always feel when the place was right to release her creatures, sense it, a tingling in her chest. She'd been so certain the standing stones here above Ballyaroon would be perfect, felt herself drawn toward them. Was she listening to warning whispers now or had she merely discovered the handiest way to postpone releasing her little charge for as long as she could? The creature nibbled gently on her finger.

Rhiannon blinked back tears. Yes, that had to be what was troubling her. From the time she'd carried her first wounded bird home to be mended, she'd both loved and hated the day she released them back to the wild. But it had been different back at Primrose Cottage. Papa had been there, to drive her out in his gig to the small parkland surrounding the modest estate. Her cousins had scampered about, Orla's eyes round with wonder and excitement, as she and Triona pilfered the picnic that cook had prepared. Warm gingerbread and sour lemonade to take away the bite of sadness Rhiannon felt when she let the creature go.

Now there was only the wide, empty sky, the whickering of Socrates, the dray horse; the bumbling of Milton, the foxhound, as he ran into anything in his path; and the self-satisfied purring of Captain Blood, the one-eyed feline with a pirate's heart. The family that had delighted in those soft summer skies was gone.

No, that wasn't true, Rhiannon thought. She could still feel their presence in the mist. Hear the echo of their laughter in the wind. Sometimes it was almost as if they touched her. Papa stolen by the hungry waves of the sea, Mama, that beautiful, misty face who lived only in her imagination. But she could call back so many precious memories, finger them like polished stones. And she could visit Triona and her new husband, John, whenever the silence got too loud or the road too solitary. Her mouth curved, a little wistful at the memory of Triona's pleas that she stay on at the MacKenna farm forever, the worry in her cousin's eyes warming Rhiannon's heart. *You shouldn't be alone out there with Uncle Kevin gone. Something could happen. You could get hurt, grow sick, and no one might know until it was too late. And there are men—desperate men who might . . .*

You know I don't have to be afraid, Triona, Rhiannon had replied. *The fairies look after their own.*

Triona's brow had crinkled, troubled. *It's a lovely story, being fairy-born, Rhiannon, but . . . but you can't still believe it's true.*

Taken by a mischievous streak, she'd peered at her cousin with wide-eyed innocence, protesting that she accepted her father's tale as gospel. And yet, long ago, she'd realized that, pretty as the tale was, it was also the perfect way to ease the pain for a little girl whose mama had abandoned her and never looked back. And it had softened the pain, at least a little, with glittering, magical possibilities.

She had brushed aside Triona's concerns, but held fast to the precious gift of love that lit her hazel eyes. And she tried so hard never to forget how very lucky she was.

Besides, Triona couldn't understand that she was never *really* alone. She smiled, stroking the fox's ear one last time. "One thing I can be certain of, little one. Your basket will be filled before I know it. It won't be long before the fates will put another wounded creature in my path."

She turned her attention back to her driving with wry humor, uncertain where she'd find herself. Socrates was given to taking shameless advantage of his mistress's lack of concentration, veering off course to munch any patch of likely-looking clover.

She peered up in surprise at the towering fingers of the standing stones, closer now. So close she could see the ancient symbols carved into their surfaces, hear the echoes of bardsongs still tangled about them.

She'd always felt fascination when stumbling across the fairy forts and dolmens, the standing stones and crumbling castle ruins that dotted the land. But this time there was something different in the haunting melody of the wind, something more urgent.

She tried to grasp it, hoped to unravel its meaning, but suddenly Socrates dug his hooves into the turf, balking so abruptly he nearly overset Rhiannon. She clutched at the overturned basket, just managing to keep it from flying off the seat, the vixen darting about in alarm as pans hanging from the ceiling inside the caravan crashed down in a resounding cacophony of clangs.

"What in the name of heaven?" Rhiannon choked out, trying to calm the horse as he tossed his head, attempting to shy sideways. The unease she'd done her best to explain away flooded back, more insistent than ever.

"Whist, now, Socrates, whist," she murmured in the special voice that had soothed countless wild things. The beast pricked his ears toward it, stood still, but she could see the fine tremor skating beneath his disreputable gray hide.

Carefully, she got down out of the cart and tied him to a low-hanging branch. The last thing she wanted was to have to go chasing after him. She doubted he could rouse enough energy to run very far, but there was no point in taking chances. She grabbed another basket dangling from the cart-side. If there *was* something wounded taking shelter hereabouts, she didn't want to give it a chance to slip away. And she wouldn't do it any good if she scooped it up with her bare hands and got the blessed daylights chewed out of herself. But even such reasoning didn't ease the tremor in her stomach. She'd made this journey countless times. Why did this time feel so different?

Rhiannon moved toward the ring of stones, her bare feet soft and soundless as the vixen's paws, her gaze searching every clump of gorse or heather, every shadowed nook, looking for the tiniest glimpse of fur or shine of a wary eye.

But there was nothing, no velvet-eared rabbit, no broken-winged hawk or lame fawn. Then why did she feel so . . . so odd? Her arm ached. Her left leg threatened to crumple beneath her. And her chest—a cord seemed to be tightening about it until it was hard to breathe, her heart pounding so loud it seemed the birds overhead must hear it.

She frowned, listening for the slightest stirring that might betray a hiding place. Perhaps if she climbed to a higher vantage point, she might be able to see better. That overturned slab near the largest crossbar of stone looked like a promising spot.

She moved toward it, knee deep in a tangle of gypsy roses the glorious mauve of a sunset. But she scented something there far different from the sweet flower fragrance or the meadow-winds. The metallic tang of fresh-spilt blood. Burned sulphur . . . gunpowder. And pain—blinding red.

Caution vanished in its wake. She scrambled toward the stones, certain that something injured lay near. Had some hunter found this place? Had his prey eluded him, dragged itself away somewhere, wounded? Wild creatures had a gift for hiding themselves, quietly bleeding to death where nothing or no one could find them. The thought of any living thing suffering alone, possibly dying without so much as a comforting touch to soothe it, ripped at Rhiannon's heart more than she could bear.

She hadn't spoken the plea since she'd been a girl, full of rich imaginings, still believing everything her papa had told her. But the aura of pain was so strong, the desperation so fierce, the hopelessness so deep, she couldn't help but use it.

Help me, Mama, she whispered to the wind. *Help me find—* The words died on her lips. She slammed to a halt, a cry tearing from her throat as her foot nearly tramped on a man's bloodstained hand.

She blinked fiercely, still scarcely believing her eyes.

Why in God's name hadn't she seen him from a mile down the road? His red coat gleamed like a fresh wound in the hill. The merest glimpse of the uniform sent spikes of unease shooting through her.

An officer. English. Up here, in these wild lands alone. What could he possibly be doing here? She caught her lip between her teeth, hesitating, wary.

An English soldier could be far more dangerous than a pain-maddened wolf, and more unpredictable. For an instant, just an instant, she wished she could turn, run back to her cart. No one need know she ever found the officer. For all she knew, he deserved the bullets that had wounded him. And yet . . . even as the thought formed, she shook herself fiercely.

He was hurt—be he human or beast, English or Irish, that was all that mattered.

Fighting to steady herself, she dropped to her knees beside him, pressing her fingertips to the pulsepoint of his throat. The faint thrum of heartbeat against her skin jolted through her with the unearthly sizzle of lightning splitting a druid tree. It breached something deep inside Rhiannon, left her shaken.

In that instant, his features seared themselves into her consciousness. Silvery-blonde hair tangled about a face no one could look upon and forget. Papa had told her once of a prince so beautiful no one could ever tire of looking upon him. They'd buried him in a magical coffin of glass when he'd died. She'd always thought the tale absurd until now.

Power emanated from every line and curve even in unconsciousness, strength and intelligence in the broad brow, ruthlessness and arrogance in the angle of prominent cheekbones. Yet there was just a hint of softness about his parted lips, so subtle few would be able to discern it.

This was absurd! she raged at herself. She had to tend his wounds, see how he'd been injured. Just because he was alive at this moment didn't mean he would remain so while she stood here, gaping at him like a dolt.

Scrambling to gather her wits, she searched for the wounds—a torn sleeve, bloodied. Another ragged, glistening tear in his left thigh. From the amount of blood, it was obviously the worst. Cursing herself for her ridiculous hesitation, she ripped off a strip of her petticoat, wrestled with the dead weight of his injured leg as she tried to tie it above the wound to stop the bleeding. Then, fishing in the pouch she always kept tied at her waist, she took out her papa's penknife and worked to cut the fabric away from the wound.

The slightest groan squeezed from between the man's white lips, and he shifted, trying to get away from the pain. If he awakened, the process of baring his wounds would be all the more painful. He might hurt himself, or fight her—and he had the look of a man who could overpower her in a heartbeat, wounded or whole.

Voice unsteady, Rhiannon began to sing, low, soft, the soothing song she'd always used to quiet her animal patients. The song Papa had insisted Mama brought from the land of the fairies. Whether it was just another of his stories, Rhiannon was never certain. But the haunting melody did seem to hold its own brand of enchantment. One of the soldier's hands knotted in Rhiannon's skirts, as if to assure himself he wasn't alone. Then he quieted, allowing her to bind the nasty gash in his arm.

She glanced back at the smear of color that was the gypsy cart, uncertain. God above, what was she going to do? She'd stopped the worst of the bleeding, but she could hardly treat his wounds here. What if the men who had done this to him returned to make certain he was dead? She'd have no way to fend them off.

What if you discover he deserved the bullets that had felled him? a voice whispered in her head. "That's absurd," she said aloud. "I'd be able to *feel* it." Truth was, she *should* be able to sense his goodness or wickedness. From the time she was a babe, she'd had that gift. She should be able to probe into the essence of his soul with just a touch. But it was as if this place, with its ancient voices, were hazing this man in its mist. Or was it this place at all? Was it the man himself who was so resolutely closed to her, closed to anything or anyone that might breach his defenses? Whatever kind of man he was, she couldn't leave him to suffer.

No one deserved this kind of agony. The only thing to do was to patch him together to the best of her ability.

Climbing to her feet, she stumbled toward the cart, determined to drag Socrates as close as possible. Praying she could manage to get the officer inside it.

She had to lift him into the wagon, and then . . . then hasten as far away from this place as she could. Somewhere not even the fairies could find them.

Look for
BRIAR ROSE
Wherever Paperback Books
Are Sold
Coming Soon from Pocket Books